CANNIBAL KINGDOM

A Novel

JOHN L. CAMPBELL

This book is an original publication of Wild Highlander Press

Printed in the United States

Cover design by Allen Lawlor

Titles by John L. Campbell

CANNIBAL KINGDOM

OMEGA DAYS

SHIP OF THE DEAD

DRIFTERS

CROSSBONES

THE FERAL ROAD

RED CIRCUS

IN THE FALLING LIGHT

THE MANGROVES

Writing as Atticus Wulf

A CRUEL AND BITTER NOTHING

A JUDGE FROM SALEM

To Linda,
the source of my twenty year love affair.

ORIGIN

-1-

The South Pacific – 566 AD

The king stood in the center of the smoking village, looking at the dead, and at the destruction the enemy had visited upon his people. The heavy jungle air smelled of fire, blood and burnt flesh, and birds concealed in the high trees called out in raucous voices in anticipation of the banquet to come.

None had been spared. The enemy had slaughtered every last soul, leaving them for the scavengers. *No,* he corrected himself, *not all.* Before burning the village, the enemy would have taken a number of slaves, people who would live a brief life of severe labor and torment before ending up on the enemy's feasting tables. Of course the king and his own people partook of human flesh as well, but only during high ceremonies, and that made it different. The enemy was truly barbaric; human meat was a regular part of their diet.

Kopi, king of the *Galuh* people, walked slowly toward the message left for him by the enemy, his warriors moving with him and watching the jungle nervously. At thirty, Kopi was in his prime, tall for his people, naked except for a simple loincloth, the better to display his bronzed and muscled body, covered in sacred tattoos and ritual scarring. In one hand was a heavy spear with intricate carvings running the length of the shaft, the weapon of the *Galuh* kings since time forgotten. A heavy, fearsome thing, it felt ineffective in his grip, for it had not been able to prevent the destruction that lay all around him.

The king stopped before a post that had been driven into the ground, and he waved a hand at the black cloud of flies that rose briefly from the thing that was tied there, only to settle back again. The smell was nearly overpowering in the jungle heat. It had been a man, the village elder, now completely peeled of his skin and left for the carpet of flies crawling over the red meat. The chest had been opened and the heart removed. By now it would have been placed in a trophy basket to grace the hall of the enemy king, resting amid similar baskets.

The remains and their disrespectful treatment had been left as an insult, a show of contempt for the *Galuh* people. Kopi would have done the same, *had* done the same with smaller, neighboring tribes, and he had his own collection of trophy baskets around his throne back in *Pakung,* the royal village. But these were *his* people, and the insult was unbearable, made more so by the fact that this was the third of his villages destroyed in such a manner, as well as the third elder left by the conquerors as a grisly demonstration of their might.

Kopi's people would soon come to believe (if they didn't think it already) that he was weak, unable to protect them, and the spirits of the kings that had gone before him cried their outrage. Kopi trembled with his own fury. This could not stand.

But the enemy was so strong. The *Sunda* people in the west, with their grand temple city and their seemingly endless army of warriors, had been consuming the villages of the *Galuh* people for more than a year now, feeding their king's insatiable appetite for power. The regular destruction of villages like this made the *Sunda* message clear; "Do not oppose us, surrender your king for execution and submit to our rule." Kopi knew that many tribes had done just that, and with every such capitulation the *Sunda* Kingdom grew in strength and reach.

King Kopi glanced at his men. How much more of this would it take before his loyal warriors, fearing for their own families, turned on him and delivered him to the enemy? The *Galuh* had tried to fight against the *Sunda,* but his tribe was so small, and the enemy so numerous. He needed help, the kind of strength that only the gods could provide.

And he knew where to find it.

Kopi gestured to one of his warriors, a fifteen-year-old boy, the fastest runner among them. "Return to *Pakung,"* he told the boy. "Summon the priests and have them ready for my return."

The boy nodded and raced into the jungle.

Kopi took a last look at his shattered village and clenched his fists. No, this would not stand.

The priests waited quietly before Kopi, who was seated on the throne of his fathers and flanked by his two biggest and most fearsome-looking warriors. At the front of the cluster of priests stood an old man with a shaved head, his scalp dyed red, with a trio of crimson, wooden beads piercing his bottom lip. The high holy man of the *Galuh* scowled deeply as his king spoke.

"Tapak, God of Darkness and Light," said Kopi.

"Lord of the dead," the priests chanted in unison. "Father of the living."

"From his lofty temple he watches over his beloved people." Kopi gestured at the mountain that overshadowed the village resting at its base, dark green with foliage and its higher elevations obscured by clouds.

"His reign is eternal," chanted the priests.

Kopi nodded. "Since the beginning of my father's people, we have given *Tapak* our respect and obedience. We honor his image, offer our prayers and sacrifices in his name. Now his beloved children are in peril, and we call upon his strength." Kopi pointed to the high holy man. "You will climb the mountain and enter *Tapak's* temple. You will summon our dark god and extract the power we need to defeat our enemies. And you will agree to any sacrifice he requires."

The gathering of priests paled and glanced at one another. The old man's eyes narrowed and he shook his head slowly. "One does not make demands of the gods, great king. Their powers are not meant for mortal men, *Tapak's* least of all."

"And that is why it is necessary, Wise One. Our enemy is powerful, and only a dark gift from *Tapak* will defeat them. You will bring me that gift."

The old man shook his head again. "With the greatest respect, I serve the gods. This should not be done. *Will* not be done."

"You serve me first, old man."

The holy man crossed his arms and stared. "My king is mad. I will not tempt the God of Darkness and Light with such insolence."

Kopi leaned forward in his throne and looked at the holy man for a moment, and then the hint of a smile touched his lips. "Seize him."

The warriors flanking the throne moved at once, gripping the old man by the arms and forcing him to his knees as he cried out. Kopi looked at the other assembled priests. "Do you think me mad as well?"

One of them stepped forward. "I will go, great king."

Kopi eyed the priest, a young man eager for advancement. "Are you capable of such a thing?"

The young priest nodded nervously. "I know the path to the temple, great king. I know the summoning words and can perform the ritual. I will return with *Tapak's* dark gift."

Kopi motioned the boy forward and rested a palm on his shaven head. "May the God of Darkness and Light bless and protect you. Return to me with the power I seek," Kopi said, gesturing at the kneeling old man, "and you shall take his place among our people."

The boy bowed deeply and ran from the throne room.

"You will destroy us all," the old man said, looking up at his king.

"And you," Kopi said, "will be the first to feed *Tapak's* glory."

Three days had passed since the boy left for the mountain, and as promised, he had returned with a dark gift from the God of Darkness and Light, what he declared to be *Tapak's Tears.* The entire royal village was gathered at its center now, but the boy remained alone off to one side, his bare head now dyed red, identifying him as the new high holy man of the *Galuh* people. To Kopi the boy looked distracted, troubled, and that was not a surprise. The summoning of a god was no light matter, and whatever he had seen on that mountain must have been terrifying. Clearly it had left him disturbed.

Then again, Kopi thought, perhaps the Temple of *Tapak* had been a disappointment, the reality of it unable to measure up to generations of mystery and lore. To Kopi's knowledge, no one had actually seen this temple before the boy's journey, no other priest and certainly no mortal king. Who knew what actually dwelled on that mountain? Kopi didn't want to know, and in truth did not care. He held in his hands the power of the gods – his new high priest assured it – and very soon Kopi would be victorious over his enemies.

At the center of the villagers, in a space cleared for them, stood ten of his people; nine who had volunteered for the honor of a journey about to begin, and Kopi's former high priest, the old man with three red beads piercing his bottom lip. Each of these chosen people had their hands bound before them, and ropes around their necks stringing them together in a chain. The old man was first in line, and it was he whom the king approached first, carrying a simple gourd.

"The *Tears of Tapak!*" Kopi cried, holding the gourd aloft.

The entire village murmured the dark god's name in unison.

"You see?" Kopi said to the old man. "You will obey me after all." The king nodded, and a warrior jerked the old man's head back, forcing his mouth open. Kopi tipped the gourd and poured a measure of clear liquid down his throat. The former high priest choked, then swallowed.

When he could speak once again, the old priest said, "I will see you again."

"Not in this life." Then the king moved down the line, offering the gourd to the other nine, bound villagers. Each drank willingly. A pair of warriors drank as well. They were tasked with making the four day journey to deliver the chain of villagers to the *Sunda* king, an offering of slaves and a sign of submission. The two men knew they would be killed and devoured, of course, but like the villagers they had asked for the honor. The end of their mortal lives meant nothing to them. They would make the ultimate personal sacrifice for their great king, delivering a mighty weapon into the midst of their enemies. Surely glory awaited in the next world.

"May *Tapak* guide and protect you," the king said to them.

Within two weeks his scouts would report that the royal city of the *Sunda* king was populated by a scattering of corpses rotting in the jungle heat, but was otherwise deserted. The *Galuh* were victorious.

King Kopi ran through the jungle, wounded and alone, limping from a savage tear in his right thigh. His people had been slaughtered, his family ripped apart right before his eyes, and now monsters stalked the royal village. The screams of his dying warriors echoed through the trees, and all Kopi could do was run, run with no idea of where he was going.

How had it come to this? Why was *Tapak* angered?

The screaming cut off abruptly, and then the jungle was silent except for the king's heavy breathing as he stumbled through the undergrowth. Bleeding and leaving red on every leaf he brushed past, Kopi leaned on his family spear as if it were a crutch.

And then there was another sound, the laughter of the dead floating through the trees. It seemed to come from all directions, and Kopi froze, the spear trembling in his hands. A figure leaped to a mossy, fallen trunk before him, an old man with three red beads through his lower lip, his head no longer red with dye but with smears of fresh blood.

The man's eyes were like silver discs, no longer mortal.

King Kopi let out a war cry and lunged, plunging the spear into his former high priest's belly. What came out of the wound was a corrupted mass of red and gray, sticky fluid. The priest made a thick, chuckling sound, then tore the spear from his body and out of the king's hands, flinging it away. Kopi stumbled backward with his hands raised, as more figures appeared within the trees around him, each of them bloody and grotesque.

The old man snarled and leaped from the fallen log, and the last thing the king saw was teeth and silver eyes.

A week later, a massive earthquake sent a tsunami throughout the South Pacific that would claim the lives of ten thousand of the world's coastal-dwelling population. The violent tremors themselves effectively sealed the cave the *Galuh* people called *Tapak's* temple, high on its mountain.

For centuries the land would remain quiet and unexplored. Rumors of war and plague made trade attempts unrealistic, and even the Spanish and Portuguese stayed away. The indigenous people of the region considered it an accursed place, a land of the dead, and dared not go there. It was this very isolation that kept *Tapak's* dark gift contained, sparing the world from an extinction-level event.

More than fifteen hundred years after a king attempted to harness the powers of a dark god, another earthquake would unseal the cave. By that time the world was a very different place, and *Java,* the largest island of what became Indonesia, was no longer isolated.

EXPOSURE

-2-

DEVIL DOG

The Royal Marriott – October 18

With a soft groan, Garrison Fox leaned back into the couch, swirling the ice in his gin and tonic. The expansive hotel suite screamed opulence, right at the edge of being overdone. Despite the direction his life had taken him, the man didn't think he'd ever get used to the constant luxury, hoped not, for his had been a life based on achieving the goal, not the trappings that often went with success.

At forty-nine, Garrison was fit (he ran almost every day) and had rough good looks; striking blue eyes, lean features and a strong jaw. He still had a full head of dark hair, and could have grown it into a real mane if he'd wanted, but that would fit neither the position nor the man. His wife and those close to him considered it a constant battle preventing him from reducing it to the razor-close, high-and-tight he had worn for so many years. He'd grudgingly compromised with a short but professional, corporate-style cut.

"I think it went well," Garrison said to the man seated on the opposite couch, a coffee table between them.

Thomas Barrow sat in a rumpled gray suit and sipped at a bottled water, looking over his glasses. He needed a shave, as he always seemed to. Barrow was one of those men who needed the razor twice a day in order not to look scruffy, and as a result, certain people referred to him as *Werewolf.* He not only didn't mind, but found it amusing.

"I suppose," said Barrow. "The press ate it up, but you're already taking heat from the talking heads. They're moaning about how the timing of the trip was ill-advised so close to the general. The senator is claiming it was your way of running away from him."

Garrison made a face. "When are they not moaning? And who does the senator think he's fooling? I've got him by twenty points."

Barrow shrugged. "That's television. Hannity said it was 'a demonstration of true leadership, putting the country first.'"

A chuckle and a sip of gin. "Sean's a good guy, but he'd be complimentary of Jack the Ripper if he was running against a Democrat."

Barrow smiled and shook his head at his friend of more than twenty years.

"Do you think the Prime Minister was sincere?" Garrison asked.

The other man thought for a moment. "A cautious yes. I'm just not sure how much change he'll be able to affect. He's up against a strong opposition."

"He's a forward thinker."

"And a Muslim," said Barrow. "Hard to know where his loyalties lie."

Fox nodded. They had been through all this before, of course, had gamed out how the conversation and proposal would go, whether the Prime Minister would be receptive and if so, whether he was even capable of following through. So many questions and variables, all leading to an uncertain outcome.

Garrison had made this trip – arriving early this morning, in fact – in response to the recent bombing in New Orleans, a tragedy that had claimed the lives of twenty-two Americans and foreign tourists. It had been carried out by a home-grown American, a young man who had fallen under the influence of extremists and been trained at a terrorist camp right here in this heavily Islamic nation. Saddened and angry over the attack, instead of directing his fury militarily Fox had chosen to use the incident as an attempt to bridge the differences between their two countries. It was a move that hurt him with his base on the right, but Fox insisted on meeting the Prime Minister here in the hotel for a private dinner and talks. The other head of state had left the meeting with the promise to do more to fight terrorism here in his home, starting with the use of his military to uncover and wipe out their training camps. Garrison wanted to believe him, did believe in the man's desire to make change, but like his Chief of Staff he had his doubts. A progressive leader in such a faith-based country was something of a blue-eyed-wonder in this part of the world, and killing terrorists was only a small piece of what had to be done. Culture change was the greater challenge, combating generational hatred, and as Barrow had said, the Prime Minister was up against fierce opposition.

Garrison rubbed the bridge of his nose. He wasn't averse to flexing military muscle or even ordering strikes, his record proved that, but he believed in diplomacy first before ordering young men and women into harm's way. "I still think the trip was the right thing to do," he said.

"So do I," said Barrow, then tapped a folder on the coffee table. "The Ohio numbers are seeing it a little differently. We can talk about it on the plane."

"How long do we have?"

The other man checked his watch. "We're wheels-up in about ninety minutes."

Garrison smiled. "Good, there's time for a call."

His Chief of Staff left the room briefly to talk to an aide, and a few minutes later he returned with a young man holding out a cell phone. "Dark Horse is on the line, Mr. President."

An eleven hour time difference separated Garrison from Devon Fox, the fifteen-year-old, only son of the President, code-named *Dark Horse* by the Secret Service. While it was 9:30 PM in Garrison's part of the world, it was already 8:30 AM tomorrow at the Harrison School, the preparatory academy in Vermont where Devon spent his academic year. Try as he might to coordinate his calls with his son's schedule and his own hectic life of responsibility and changing time zones – especially now with the campaign at top speed and less than three weeks to go until the general elections – calls between father and son were often difficult to arrange, and Garrison had frequently misread the time and awoken his boy. Devon was good-natured about it and said he understood, but Garrison still felt guilty. The duties of a President were rarely conducive to a stable family life, and he frequently chastised himself for not being a better father, not only to Devon but to his older sister Kylie.

"What's on the agenda?" Garrison asked, smiling for what felt like the first time today. On the other couch, Thomas Barrow busied himself with reading poll results and waved without looking up. "Thomas says hi," the President told his son.

"Not a bad day," said Devon. "I have to turn in an American History paper, there's a quiz in Latin and I have practice before the match. Kinda a normal day."

Garrison could almost hear the boy shrug, and his smile broadened. His son's "normal" day would be exhausting to a great many adults, but the boy shouldered the load without complaint. Academically the kid was a powerhouse, each of his classes advanced placement, and he maintained a grade point average high enough to keep him on the Dean's list every semester. But he was no mere bookworm. The *practic*e he referred-to was the school's basketball team – he was a starter despite his age – and the *match* was an intra-academy competition where Devon was one of five representing the Harrison School's chess team. The boy was rapidly becoming a master, and was absolutely surgical with his knights. Garrison couldn't be prouder.

"The week after next I have an event in Ohio. I'm going to see if your mom and sister can make it, and I'd like you to be there. Not to do press, just to see you." Garrison had been compelled to put his family in front of the cameras during campaigns, just like anyone running for office, but he was very protective of his children and did it only when absolutely necessary. Once the election was won, he wouldn't do it again. This was not one of those times. He just missed his son.

There was hesitation in Devon's voice. "By then you'll be doing what, three states a day?"

"More like five or six."

Another pause, and when Devon spoke his father could hear how uncomfortable the boy was. "I want to see you too Dad, but wouldn't it be better after the election? Your schedule is packed. Besides, I have papers I need to work on, and I think I have another competition around then. I just…"

"Say no more, buddy," Garrison said. "I get it. And school's way more important." He heard a grateful sigh his son tried unsuccessfully to conceal. God, sometimes he really hated this job. "No worries. The holidays are coming up fast. We'll get to spend plenty of time together." Garrison set down his drink and wished for a Tums.

They talked a bit longer about school, sports and girls. Did he have a girlfriend? Not really. Nothing serious, anyway, and since he was at an all-boys academy, there weren't that many opportunities to interact with the opposite sex. Not that he and his friends didn't make the attempt every chance they got. Then the boy had to go.

"Love you, Dev," said Garrison.

"You too, Dad."

As the leader of the free world disconnected, feeling like a greater parental failure than he had before starting the call, his Chief of Staff hung up his own cell phone. "We're going to walk the lobby for the cameras," Barrow said, "then it's straight to Air Force One."

Garrison nodded. "Let's go home, Tommy."

Near the door to the suite, a Secret Service agent spoke into his cuff mike. "Devil Dog is coming down."

-3-

SOO YIM

Jakarta – October 18

They were opposites; one a long-legged Swede with blue eyes and hair so blonde it was nearly white, the other small and compact, dark-haired and dark-eyed, a South Korean girl with perfect skin and dazzling white teeth. Both were young and strikingly attractive, though it was the blonde – so tall and exotic in this land of small, dark people – who drew the most attention.

At two hundred fifty eight million, Indonesia was the fourth most populous country in the world, and half that population lived on the main island of Java, most of them here in the capital city. The frenetic swarm of life in Jakarta flowed steadily around the sidewalk café where the two women sat dressed in breezy clothing and shielded by a table umbrella from an early morning sun. It promised to be another withering, humid day.

"I swear, if I have to see one more temple or market I'm going to scream," said Soo Yim, watching an endless stream of bicycles churn past on the street. Small cars and trucks competed with the two-wheelers, close to each other and driving too fast. The air was filled with honking horns, the barking of dogs, calling vendors, a traffic cop's whistle and the incessant clamor of someone banging on a metal pot. The smells were even more varied; a blend of strange foods being cooked and engine exhaust.

"I know," said Alexa. "They're all starting to look the same."

The two women were flight attendants for Pacific Trans Air. Young and single, they caught the extended, international runs, and their travels had taken them to many of the world's most exotic locations. They'd long ago lost track of the places they'd visited and the sights they'd seen; museums and castles, ancient ruins and cultural celebrations, historical sites and temples, oh so many temples. Both had become jaded, and although the nightclubs were fun in many parts of the world, even these were losing their allure.

Soo Yim watched as a truck driver screamed for a bicyclist to get out of the way. The bicycle had a big basket strapped to its tail, and the enormous goose being carried within honked its annoyance back at the driver.

"So what do you want to do?" Alexa asked. They were on a layover, due to fly to Paris but not until tomorrow. They had the day to kill.

"I don't know," the South Korean said, shrugging. "I want to do something different. A real adventure."

Bhandri moved up and down the sidewalk, shaking a cardboard sign and chewing the inside of one cheek. His eyes darted across the crowds, searching for foreigners. He was short and leathery, dressed in cut-offs and a khaki shirt, sandals and a straw hat. Though only forty, a hard life in the Indonesian sun had caused him to look twenty years older. Nicotine stains had turned his teeth and fingers yellow.

His nephew Faisal was back at the Jeep, the fourteen-year-old making sure it wasn't stolen from its spot by the curb. *The Jeep.* It belonged to his cousin, and although he was allowed to use it on occasion, today he'd taken it without permission. His eyes swept the busy street, locked on a police car, and watched it glide past. His cousin wouldn't report it stolen, would he? Bhandri was more than willing to cut him in on a portion of the day's profits. *If* he saw any profits, that was.

It had been five days since he'd made any money at all. Not afraid to work, he often sought employment as a day laborer assembling toys in a plant outside the city or toiling in the sun at the tea fields. When those jobs were unavailable, he tried to pick small, usable goods from apartment building Dumpsters, cleaning them and offering them for sale at one of Jakarta's markets. Often, at least when he was allowed to use the Jeep, he ran unlicensed tours for foreign tourists, as he was trying to do now. Work of any kind was scarce, and Bhandri hadn't eaten in three days.

"I want to do something different," he heard someone say in English. "A real adventure." Bhandri's head snapped in that direction, and he spotted the two young women drinking bottled water at an umbrella table. He moved to them quickly, keeping to his side of the low, wrought-iron fence separating the sidewalk from the café, looking around for hotel security that, if they found him harassing guests, would drag him into an alley and beat him with bamboo canes. He didn't see the telltale blue blazers and radio earpieces anywhere, so he moved in, wiggling the cardboard sign that read, TOURS.

His native tongue was Bhasa, but he understood English well enough to get through a conversation. "I have adventure," he said, smiling and shaking his sign. "Sacred place."

Soo Yim eyed the little Indonesian. "I've seen plenty of sacred places. No thanks."

Bhandri's grin widened. "Special place. Forgotten. No one go there. Very ancient."

Alexa looked at the little man and curled her lip. To her friend she said, "He looks sketchy. Tell him to go away."

"No one goes there?" Soo Yim asked, leaning a bit forward in her chair. Bhandri knew he'd hooked her.

"Yes, yes! Hidden place in *Puncak* Mountains, two hours away. *Tempat Berbicara Mati.* You hear the dead speak there."

Soo Yim started nodding, but Alexa gripped her friend's hand. "You are not going out into the jungle with this guy. He'll chop your head off and leave you by the road."

"That's why you're going with me," said Soo Yim, smiling. "And the boys too." She quickly negotiated the price of a day trip with Bhandri, then led her friend into the hotel to get ready, and to tell their pilot and co-pilot that they were all going on an adventure.

Bhandri sprinted back down the sidewalk to get the Jeep.

The Jeep was an older Willys, a version extended to seat six, its tan paint losing the fight against darker splotches of rust. The engine knocked when it was idling, but at traveling speed it ran well enough. A canvas canopy patched with duct tape shielded its occupants from the intense morning sun.

Expansive green tea plantations stretched away on both sides of the highway as Bhandri drove them toward the dark green *Puncak* Mountains, the upper elevations still heavy with morning mist despite the sun. The women who had chartered the excursion chatted in back, riding with his nephew and one of the airline pilots. The other pilot rode in the front seat beside Bhandri, snapping pictures with his phone. All four foreigners wore wide-brimmed hats, linen shirts and pants and sunglasses. They all smelled of sunscreen, something Bhandri had never once applied to his skin.

Not quite two hours outside of Jakarta, Bhandri took them off the highway and into the jungle spreading outward from the base of the *Puncaks,* making his way down muddy, rutted roads that narrowed and worsened as the Jeep climbed higher. He was still worried about taking it without permission, but more worried about how he would explain a broken axle to his cousin, wincing every time the vehicle bounced madly through a crater made by the rain or jounced over a fallen log. Even more than this, Bhandri was terrified that the foreigners would see through his fraud.

He knew nothing about where they were going, and his "historical" tales about their destination – told during the drive from Jakarta – were complete fabrications. He had only been to this place once before, finding it accidentally one day while scouring the jungle for primitive artifacts he could sell to tourists, climbing the mountain in the hope of finding a place unexplored by other scavengers like himself. And indeed, he had found it.

The place frightened him, and the crude illustrations on the walls (who knew how old they were, but they were clearly ancient) had given him nightmares. It was those drawings that gave him the idea to call the place *Tempat Berbicara Mati,* 'the Place where the Dead Speak.' Like his stories of ancient tribes and rituals, the name was a fabrication as well. Bhandri had always been too preoccupied with survival to learn much about his country's history.

They are foreigners. They won't know the difference.

In the back, the women were talking animatedly, especially the Korean girl, calling out bird sightings or marveling over the thickening jungle. The road grew increasingly overgrown, and Bhandri focused on his driving, searching for the marker he had left beside the road so that he might find the place again. Had the rains washed it away? Had the jungle grown over it? The little Indonesian sensed that he was close – had to be, for the men were growing impatient – and strained to spot his marker among the trees to the right.

There it was; a pair of branches lashed to a trunk in an *X,* a small animal skull shoved down onto one of the uprights. He'd used the skull thinking it would add a macabre touch, and it had worked; the women pointed and whispered excitedly. He stopped the Jeep and shut off the knocking engine.

"We are here," Bhandri said, turning in his seat and smiling at his guests. "We walk now."

Faisal shouldered a backpack holding bottles of water, and Bhandri took a machete and a flashlight from the Jeep, leading them up the jungled mountainside, away from the rut that could no longer even be called a road. The airline crew followed, the girls talking incessantly. The small Indonesian spoke to his charter about snakes and trees, made up stories about how the ancient tribal people had lived at the base of this mountain, anything he could think of as he picked his way upward through heavy foliage, chopping at vines and brush.

They climbed for an hour, stopping frequently so the foreigners could rest, until Bhandri came to a halt beside a large, mossy rock with the image of a stern face carved into its surface.

"This is King *Anjasmara,"* he lied, running his hand over the image. "He ruled these lands a thousand years ago, and was much loved." Bhandri had taken the name from the host of a popular Indonesian game show on television. "King *Anjasmara* named this a holy place to honor the dead."

The women touched the mossy face. The pilot took another picture with his phone.

The little tour guide looked up at a rock ledge another fifteen feet above, swallowed hard and led them up to it. A narrow cave opening was set in a rock face just behind the ledge, and Bhandri snapped on his flashlight, forcing a smile. "Must be quiet now. You hear the dead speak."

The Korean girl hopped with excitement and squeezed one of the pilot's arms. The tall blonde simply looked at the guide with vague disgust.

He led them inside, panning the flashlight around a small cavern with high walls and a crack in the floor at the back. It was significantly cooler in here, quiet except for a constant, muted whispering.

"I hear them!" Soo Yim gasped. "I hear the dead speaking!"

Bhandri smiled, ignoring the skeptical looks of the men and the rolling eyes of the blonde. It was the Korean girl who'd paid for the charter, and as long as she was happy, that was what mattered to Bhandri.

"It's water you're hearing," said the blonde, pointing toward the back of the cave.

Bhandri moved between the tall girl and the Korean, looking at her and pointing upward, raising the beam of his flashlight and revealing the horrors depicted on the walls.

"Oh my God," whispered the blonde, putting a hand to her mouth.

"Fuck…" the pilot with the phone said, then switched on his flash and took a picture.

Soo Yim stared at the cave drawings, drinking it in. Their guide had been right; it was like nothing she had ever seen in her many travels. Blood and horror, she thought. Both featured prominently in the ancient depictions. There were images of skulls piled high, people quite clearly feeding upon one another, even on children, and images of blank-eyed tribal people tearing others apart. Over it all, arms outstretched, was a massive, silver-eyed entity that could only be a god, grinning with a mouth full of sharpened teeth. The scenes made her skin crawl, but she shivered with delight. *This* was an adventure.

"Come, come," said Bhandri, waving them toward the crack at the back of the cave. The sound of water running deep in the crack no longer sounded like whispering. It was more of a babble now. "This was holy water to *Anjasmara's* people," he said, expanding the lie. From his nephew's backpack he produced a dented tin mug tied to a long length of twine, and lowered it into the crack. He'd come up with this idea only this morning, thinking it would add to the experience. "The ancients drank from here so they could hear their ancestors speak, and to honor the gods." Bhandri pulled the twine back up (hoping it had reached the water he heard far below) and gripped the dented cup, now half-filled with clear liquid.

"No way," said Alexa.

Both pilots shook their heads, but one snapped a picture of Bhandri holding the cup.

Soo Yim stepped forward, holding out her hands.

"Don't," said Alexa, grabbing her friend's elbow. "Do you want dysentery?"

The Korean girl pulled away and took the cup. "It's a natural spring, that's all. How do you think people here get their water?"

"From bottles, if they're smart," said Alexa. "Like you're not being."

Soo Yim ignored her friend. "Don't want to insult the gods. And life is meant to be lived." She took a long drink. It was cold and tasted of minerals.

Bhandri smiled. He did not drink, but it didn't matter.

What would come to be known as *Trident* raced through Soo Yim's body. The simple act of bringing it up from the deep, cavern pool (not a spring as the young Korean woman believed, and the whispering they heard was not a breeze through a cave) carried it up through a natural pressure seal of cold air that existed far below and had kept it contained for centuries. Now everyone in the cave was exposed, whether they had taken a drink or not.

When they headed out for the journey back down the mountain, Bhandri left the cup and twine on the floor near the crack. He told himself he might bring more tourists here another time, but in truth he simply didn't want to touch the cup anymore. As appealing as the idea was – having his own, private tourist destination – he didn't think he'd be back, and was happy to put the cave behind him.

On their way back to Jakarta, Bhandri stopped for gas. He, Soo Yim, his nephew and the others passed Trident on to everyone at the station. When he dropped them off at the Royal Marriott, the little Indonesian waved and drove away with a smile and a pocket full of cash. He and Faisal would now carry Trident into one of the world's most populated cities.

Soo Yim got the chance to add yet another experience to her collection; the American President had been staying in the hotel, and the girl was thrilled to see him being escorted through the lobby to his motorcade, his Secret Service detail holding people back. The President was a friendly man, however, just as she'd seen on television, and when Soo Yim pushed against one of the agents and thrust out a hand, the man shook it briefly, smiled at her and moved on.

Happy and tired, the young woman headed for her room, infecting staff and guests along the way, she and her flight crew spreading Trident throughout the entire hotel before leaving in the morning. Tomorrow they would fly to Paris, beginning a journey that would bring Tapak's dark gift to the world.

Aboard Air Force One, President Fox and his entire entourage were bringing it to America.

INCUBATION

-4-

SOO YIM

Paris – October 26

The whirring of treadmill belts and the thump of athletic shoes was almost enough to drown out the wall-mounted TVs. Floor-to-ceiling windows looked down from the third level of the busy Paris health club onto a crowded city street.

"Where are we going tonight?" Soo Yim said, loud enough to be heard over the noise. She was in black Spandex and a bright pink, nylon tank top.

On the treadmill beside her, the tall blonde shrugged. "I'm bored with all of them," Alexa said.

Soo Yim smiled. Whether Alexa was bored or not, she was confident her friend would make the rounds with her at the city's most popular night spots. The Swede's looks made her an automatic to bypass the lines and get right in, and Soo Yim – pretty in her own right – would follow in her wake. Both loved to dance, loved the clubs, and Alexa especially enjoyed all the attention she got from the men.

"I'll pick the spot," the Korean girl said, and her friend shrugged again. Several minutes later, Soo Yim stopped the treadmill and stepped off, wiping the sweat from her face and neck and hanging the towel over the handrail.

Trident made the transition at once. Not that it had to; Soo Yim's sweat, touch and breath had already covered the machine with infected particles. In fact, all two hundred-plus visitors and staff in the Paris health club had been infected within twenty minutes of the two girls' arrival. Twenty of them had already picked it up from other locations, and the club was well on its way to being contaminated even before the two flight attendants got here.

Fluid transfer.

Contact transfer.

Airborne.

Like the young woman who had unleashed it, Trident was a traveler.

Eight days had passed since *Tapak's* dark gift came up from that Indonesian well and hit the air. The girl hadn't even needed to drink it; she, her crew and their two guides had been infected before they left the cave. Their journey back to the city, the hotel stay, and Bhandri's trip home had started the infection of both Jakarta and, through a simple handshake, the United States as well.

Every single person touched by Trident immediately passed it on, spreading it rapidly, and leaving the organism on everything; doorknobs and drinking fountains, restrooms and light switches, ATM machines and bus benches. The silent little plague molecules transferred by the slightest touch and drifted through the air. Goods on grocery store shelves and shopping cart handles, TV remotes and elevator buttons, bar surfaces, glasses, magazines in waiting rooms and escalator handles, mail and money and karaoke machines… It got into the water supply. It got into air conditioning and ventilation systems. Every sneeze, cough and handshake, every hug and kiss and lover's embrace, and every conversation. Trident traveled.

By the time all of Indonesia was infected, Soo Yim and her crew – along with a spread of millions of others – had moved on to bring the plague to the world.

In these eight days, the South Korean flight attendant had visited six major European and four major Asian cities, spent time in hotels and restaurants, ridden trains and taxis and subways, shopped in dozens of stores, seen a movie, gone to two yoga classes and infected nearly a dozen international airports, their travelers and employees, and every aircraft she came in contact with.

With every transmission, Trident extended its reach. Those carriers went to banks and schools, trade shows and concerts, sporting events and church. No place was spared; it lingered on playgrounds and swing-sets, bottles and blocks at daycares, found its way into theme parks and hospital operating rooms.

Soo Yim might have been the index patient, or *patient zero*, but she was now just one more carrier among billions.

After two days in Paris, where she and Alexa had been attending an annual flight attendants conference with more than ten thousand in attendance, it was almost time to get back in the air. Paris was great, but the girls were eager to get back to work. Tomorrow morning they were headed to New York, a city they both loved and one that offered some of the best night life in the world.

Trident was already there, of course. By now, the two young women were contributing little to the rapid and constant international spread of an infection that would – once it revealed itself – bring the world to its knees.

The clock was ticking, and would soon expire.

The girls showered, dressed and headed out, hailing a cab. The young Frenchman driving had just started his shift in a cab that had been unused for two weeks, parked at the back of a garage, and he had been home for more than a week, sick with the flu. Neither he nor his taxi had been infected. Soo Yim and Alexa quickly rectified that.

Eight days from initial exposure, and Trident remained dormant and benign.

But not unnoticed.

-5-

DEVIL DOG

The White House – October 26

After a morning run on the treadmill followed by a shower, Garrison now walked the colonnade from the residence to the Oval Office, a Secret Service agent trailing behind and looking out over the Rose Garden. The President looked too, not for anything dangerous as his agent was doing, but at the foliage of the grounds dressed in its autumn colors. It was 5:35 AM and he breathed deeply of the October air, enjoying the cooler temperatures that had finally come to Washington after a prolonged Indian Sumer.

Enjoy it while you can. He would be back in the sky in a matter of hours, heading out on a two day blitz of the south, southwest, California and ending in Ohio. Less than two weeks until the election, and he had some damage control ahead of him. Visiting Indonesia on a mission of diplomacy instead of sending in SEALs to wipe out terrorist camps had cost him with the Republican base.

As he approached the French doors with their vaguely out-of-focus, bulletproof glass, the two Marines in dress blue uniforms posted there stiffened and saluted crisply, one of them smoothly opening the door on the right.

"Good morning, Marines," Garrison said as he entered.

"Good morning, sir," they replied in unison.

The United States Marines serving at the White House and on Marine One had been standing just a bit taller for the last four years. For the first time in American history, they had one of their own in the Oval Office.

His senior secretary came through a side door just as he entered, placing a legal-sized folder on his desk. "Good morning, Mr. President."

"Thank you, Grace," he said, tapping the folder as he passed but leaving it there, heading for a side table where coffee waited. "How packed am I this morning?"

"You're wheels-up at eight o'clock, sir. You're busy until then." The older woman checked her watch. "You have fifteen minutes before the show starts."

Garrison smiled. No one knew about the show better than Grace. He was surprised she didn't call it the circus. She'd been with him through his entire term when he'd been a senator, and now here during his first term as President. He knew he would be lost without her. He thanked her as she left.

He liked these quiet times before the starter's pistol went off and the workday began, a day that could easily (and often did) run seventeen to twenty hours long. These precious morning minutes gave him a chance to reflect, to think about what he wanted to accomplish – not just for the day but as President of the United States - before becoming a slave to his schedule.

That was just what awaited him inside the folder his secretary had deposited on his desk, and he opened it to find seven pages stapled together; the day's agenda. As he scanned the pages, a man in his thirties with a dark suit and military haircut entered from a side door, a similar folder tucked under one arm.

"Good morning, Mr. President." The younger man placed a paper cup on the desk containing two white and yellow pills, then went to the side table for a glass of water. "You forgot these upstairs, sir."

"Right," said Garrison, washing them down with coffee and waving off the water. "Thanks, Danny."

The younger man nodded and looked over his own copy of the President's itinerary, retreating to an adjacent room to give his boss a last few minutes of peace. He was Garrison's personal assistant, or body man, someone who handled the hundreds of under-the-radar needs of a busy professional, from ensuring his bags were packed and aboard Air Force One to arranging meals (or gently scolding when the President skipped them.) Unofficially nicknamed the *Chief of Stuff,* the body man was a powerful, though often overlooked individual in the White House. Along with the actual Chief of Staff (the hammer in any administration) he controlled the President's schedule.

Danny was also a former combat Marine, a sergeant who had served under Garrison's command in Afghanistan.

During his third tour (and Garrison's second) the two men had found themselves alive and alone after their column had been attacked, the only survivors from their Humvee. While a firefight raged up and down the line with the rest of the column, Garrison and Danny had run into automatic weapons and mortar fire, making three trips to drag critically wounded Marines out of danger and behind the safety of a burning armored vehicle. Both had been hit by small arms fire but kept going, and all five Marines lived. Both men had received the Navy Cross for their actions.

Garrison had long ago decided that the younger Marine would have a job in the administration as long as he held the White House.

The forty-nine-year-old Virginia native leaned back in the high leather chair behind the Resolute Desk, a gift from Queen Victoria to President Hayes in 1880, and constructed from the timbers of a British Arctic exploration ship. He noted that today's schedule had him going until 1:00 AM, another twenty hour day and almost all of it campaign-related. It was the part of this job he cared-for the least, and one which – for the past year – had seemed to eclipse the actual duties of the presidency. "Didn't care-for" was putting it mildly. He did the dance, but he despised campaigning.

It hadn't always been like this. Garrison Fox was no career politician, and *campaign* used to have a different meaning for him.

At twenty-two he graduated third in his class at Annapolis, receiving a degree in poly-sci and a commission as a second lieutenant of infantry in the United States Marine Corps. In 1991 he found himself with the first allied infantry force to enter Kuwait during Desert Storm. Garrison's unit cleared mine fields and harassed the retreating Iraqis, and the young officer managed to bring all his men home alive.

The next year, a newly promoted captain, Garrison and his company launched an amphibious assault from the USS Tripoli into Mogadishu, Somalia. Captain Fox's Marines along with the rest of his battalion captured the city's port and secured the airfield. Two of his men were wounded, and a bullet had passed so close to his face that he swore he could feel the heat on his cheek, but again, everyone came home alive.

Garrison drained his coffee and poured a second cup, staring out the windows behind his desk and watching the light come up.

The Marines turned into a career, and eleven years later in 2003 Garrison was a lieutenant colonel in his second tour in Afghanistan, his fourth combat deployment and a war very different from those he had fought before. This enemy wasn't in retreat, or some poorly trained militia working for a local warlord. Here the opposition was fearless and highly motivated, and Marines under Garrison's command lost their lives. He felt every death. He was wounded in his first tour when a sniper's bullet hit the meat of his shoulder and nicked the bone (he still felt the ache on chilly mornings) but he'd been luckier than many. Now the recipient of a Purple Heart, he was back in the field the following year, when he and Danny would throw themselves into harm's way to save their fellow leathernecks. After that it was back to Washington as a full-bird colonel and well on his way to earning his star, an officer being groomed by the Pentagon.

But Garrison Fox, as much as he loved the Corps, had had enough. He wanted to do more for his country. At thirty-eight he resigned his commission to run for Virginia's open seat in the U.S. Senate, a contest he won in a landslide.

He was popular, a tireless advocate for national security, a strong economy and debt reduction. A decorated war hero, he was a man loved by the military and law enforcement, whose good looks and charm also gave him high marks among female voters (something that both pleased and embarrassed him.) He had no skeletons or scandals, and was vocal about the things in which he believed; honor, integrity, family, service to others, duty to country. His wife told him he had been born in the wrong century, though she was fiercely proud of her man. Garrison couldn't have seen the world in any other way.

After a single term in the Senate, at age forty-five Garrison Fox ran-for and was elected President of the United States.

He drank his coffee as staff members entered the office and gave him quiet good-mornings.

It had been quite a journey. Along the way he had married his college love, now First Lady Patricia Rand-Fox (a woman who still made his heart beat faster when she entered a room) and fathered two amazing kids.

A man could do worse, he thought, smiling out the windows at the morning sun.

Six o'clock chimed softly on the clock over the fireplace, and Garrison greeted his visitors; Thomas Darrow his Chief of Staff, a naval officer who would present his daily national security briefing, and the White House press secretary. Another Naval officer, this one a lieutenant commander with medical insignia on his uniform, entered carrying a small black satchel. He stood quietly against a wall.

Garrison nodded to this last arrival, then looked at the others in turn. "Is the world on fire, or can we push back fifteen minutes?"

The Chief of Staff looked at the NSA briefer, who nodded and said, "Things are pretty quiet out there, Mr. President. Nothing that requires immediate action." The man let out a small giggle.

The President raised an eyebrow, and Thomas Barrow looked over the top of his glasses, glowering at the briefer, who had suddenly turned bright red. The man looked down and shook his head, uttering a soft apology.

Garrison looked at him for a moment, then at Barrow. "Give me fifteen." He motioned to the medical officer to accompany him into an adjacent room, the President's private office. Behind him, Tommy pulled the NSA briefer into the hall for a withering tongue lashing. While the doctor removed a blood pressure cuff and stethoscope from his bag, Garrison sat on the edge of a desk and picked up a phone. He was immediately connected with his personal secretary.

"Grace, can you put me through to Dr. Rusk?" A few minutes later, while his blood pressure was being taken, Garrison was on the line with *Sec HHS,* his Secretary of Health and Human Services.

-6-

LABCOAT

Atlanta - October 26

Moira Rusk walked the carpeted hallway, tapping and sliding a finger across the electronic tablet in her hands, engrossed in what she was doing and unaware of the people who sidestepped her, or the young man who nearly slammed into her with a cardboard tray of full coffee cups. Dressed in a gray business suit and low heels, she was a woman in her late fifties, tall and slender, with collar-length hair that was more white than silver. She pushed her glasses higher onto the bridge of her nose and tapped the tablet again, almost running into a woman with an armload of files.

She chewed her top lip, a habit that revealed itself only when she was nervous, a state she didn't often experience. Moira was an extremely intelligent, highly educated woman who didn't scare easily and who had seen many of the horrors life had to offer. She wondered if she was seeing one now.

Tap, tap...slide...tap.

In her entire professional career she had never been so frustrated. The damned thing just wasn't acting properly, and she didn't mean the tablet. The goddamn thing on screen...although she'd seen nothing like it – *not true, it was* like *something else, but only a little* – had to follow the basic rules, and it wasn't. Moira didn't like the unexplained. Unlike most physicians, who took that as a challenge, it was the one thing that truly frightened her.

Her cell phone began ringing with *Every Breath you Take,* by The Police, specifically the verse with, *"I'll be watching you."* Virologist humor.

"This is Moira Rusk," she answered, still looking at the tablet as she walked.

"Madam Secretary, this is the White House calling. I have the President on the line."

"Just a moment," she said. At least the White House secretary didn't call her *Labcoat,* her Secret Service code name. She moved into the next open office door she saw. A young woman sat at a computer, and Moira caught her name off the plastic photo ID card clipped to her jacket. "Miss Roberts, will you find Dr. Fisher and have her meet me in conference room three in about half an hour?" The woman nodded and disappeared, and Moira shut the door, taking her seat. She knew there wouldn't be a problem with her commandeering the office. Not only was she a U.S. Cabinet

Secretary, she was one of the top physicians in the country, and that practically made her royalty in this place.

"Go ahead," she said into the cell phone.

"Moira, it's Garrison Fox."

"Good morning, Mr. President. Are you in the air or on the ground?"

"Still earthbound."

"And have you seen Lieutenant Commander Wheeler this morning?"

The President chuckled. "As a matter of fact he's with me right now. You do enjoy mothering me, don't you?"

Moira didn't smile. She was looking at the image on her tablet, biting her top lip. She swept it away and tapped, bringing up some information.

"So where are we on this thing?" Garrison asked.

"Let's talk about you first," she said. "The good news is that your body has almost completely killed off Trident. Per yesterday's blood test, there's only a trace of it left, and I expect your immune system will have finished it off by the end of the day."

Trident wasn't her term. A doctor in Indonesia, the first to spot it and call it out, had named it for the unique, three-pronged construction of the organism, a pitchfork shape that otherwise chillingly resembled Ebola.

"What about my family?"

"The same," she said. Along with the President, the First Family (as well as many others) was having their blood monitored daily. "The First Lady and both your children are nearly free of it, just like you." She heard a small, expelled breath on the other end of the phone. She was relieved too, but the irritating thing was that she couldn't say what she was relieved *about.*

Trident had shown up worldwide, acting like a virus.

And it was absolutely without symptoms.

"Unfortunately," she continued, "it doesn't appear as if the antivirals you've been taking as a precaution are what's killing it off. I'd like you to complete the regimen just to be safe, but that's not our solution."

"Why do you say that?"

"Because we're administering antivirals across a wide range of patients, and they're having no effect. We are seeing cases identical to yours – the body attacking and killing it – but that is happening only about ten to twenty percent of the time. In all the others, it's as if the body doesn't even recognize that Trident is present."

"And it's still benign?" the President asked.

"So far. People all around the world have died, of course, and die every minute, but for all the normal reasons. We've seen no connection to Trident." It had been eight days since the organism, something previously unknown to science, had shown up in routine blood testing in Indonesia. In that intervening time, at had been reported globally and was now everywhere. Internationally, physicians had identified how it spread (through almost every conceivable form of transmission) and that it was a hearty little bastard. Some viruses were tough, but this thing was ferocious. It could live in sunlight, cold, rain, surfaces exposed to the elements, and *God* could it travel! The medical community was *calling* it a virus, but no one was really sure.

"How are you doing?" the President asked.

Moira leaned back in the chair. "Fine. Never been healthier. Yet it's not only filling my bloodstream, it's spread to every tissue and organ. Not a single effect. Not for me or anyone else, here or in the world."

The President was quiet for a moment, and Moira thought about how surreal it was that almost everyone here at CDC, the Center for Disease Control, was infected with an aggressively moving, highly contagious organism that didn't cause so much as a sniffle. Its lack of symptoms was perhaps the worst part.

"You've been talking to Bob Chase about the NRP," he said. It wasn't a question.

"Daily," Moira replied. Bob Chase was the Secretary of Homeland Security. In every conversation their one and only topic had been the *National Response Plan,* also known as the *National Response to Pandemic.*

"What do the two of you think?"

Moira chewed her lip. She knew Homeland Security would have been briefing the President, but she also knew that her Commander-in-Chief wanted a doctor's opinion.

"Executing the truly dramatic aspects of the NRP is a big step, Mr. President," she said. "Without any signs that Trident is malignant, I can't advise that course of action." God, she hated sounding like a politician instead of a healer. "It's killing me to say that," she added.

"Because you're afraid that it's dormant," Garrison said, "a sleeping monster that could wake up at any time."

Moira nodded at her cell phone, reminded yet again of how very smart the man was. "I don't have any evidence of that, Mr. President. We need more information, but yes, that's exactly what I'm thinking."

"Okay. You keep at it, and I want you and Homeland to have a no bullshit talk about the NRP. It would cause a shit-storm, that's for sure, but maybe cleaning up after that would be preferable to…" he trailed off.

"I will," Moira said. "And I want you to inform Lieutenant Commander Wheeler immediately if you feel *anything* other than normal, including fatigue."

Garrison laughed. "Moira, I've been fatigued for four years."

"And I know you're hearing me, Garrison."

"Still mothering. Yes, ma'am, I know how to follow orders. Got to run."

The President clicked off, and Moira once again used her tablet to call up the magnified image of Trident. As always she marveled at how it resembled Ebola in both texture and structure, but then deviated with those three little prongs.

"Trident…you better not turn out to be a damned *pitchfork,* she whispered, then left for her meeting with Dr. Fisher.

If not for the blue and white sign out front, most people would think the CDC nothing more than another office building complex, dominated by a pair of high, rectangular towers. In many ways it was, but there were secure areas within that housed the most deadly organisms known to man.

The conference room on the eighth floor of the east tower was small and unremarkable; eggshell-colored walls, beige carpeting and a table ringed with simple swivel chairs. A flush-mounted computer terminal set in the table and a seventy-two-inch wall-mounted flat screen were the only other features.

Two women sat in here, Moira with her tablet and an attractive but weary-looking woman in her early forties with dark smudges around her eyes. She wore a white doctor's coat and was seated in front of the terminal.

If there were three top talents for virology in the world, two of them were sitting here, Dr. Fisher being the highest ranked in Moira Rusk's opinion. The younger woman could easily have been appointed Secretary of Health and Human services, but Moira had more natural political savvy. The Surgeon General had announced his attention to retire at the end of the year however, and Karen Fisher was on the short list to replace him. She would have Moira's enthusiastic endorsement. The two women had been friends for many years.

Moira was drinking tea from a paper cup, and she blew on it. "Thanks for taking the time, Karen. The boss is getting edgy about this."

"I'll bet. What does Homeland Security say?"

"Bob's reluctant to pull the trigger, as you can imagine," Moira said. "It's understandable, and I can't say I disagree. Not yet. But Jesus, this thing…"

Dr. Fisher nodded. "I'll show you the Power Point so you can walk him through it with what we have so far. I dumbed it down."

Moira smiled her appreciation. Bob Chase, the Secretary of Homeland Security, was an intelligent man, but no one other than a physician or researcher in this field wanted to stare at screen after screen of enzyme and protein tables. It had to make sense so he could present to the chief executive, even though Moira knew Fox wouldn't sign off unless she said go.

Dr. Fisher brought up an image of the world's geography, with a small red pulse centered on Indonesia. "First appearance was on October eighteenth at the Pondak Indah Hospital in Jakarta. A bus driver came in with breathing problems. Standard blood testing revealed that he had pneumonia, but it also showed Trident running like a madman through his bloodstream. The lung issue turned out to be unrelated, but a sample was sent to Dr. Wulandari because the internist had never seen anything like it."

The image of a middle-aged Indonesian man in glasses came on screen. Wulandari was the third in Moira's "top-three" ranking. Probably more like second.

"Wulandari named it Trident because of its structure. Due to its sudden appearance, behavior and uniqueness, he called us."

"The bus driver isn't the index patient, though," said Moira.

The other woman shook her head. "Not a chance."

They both knew that the odds of the original exposure subject walking into a doctor's office, in a city of millions and without symptoms, were tantamount to the same Powerball number coming up three times in a row. "It's a good indicator that it's Indonesia, though," said Fisher. "Specifically Jakarta. Dr. Wulandari reported that the patient hadn't traveled, and wasn't in contact with any foreigners, just locals on his bus route. And unless or until Trident starts showing effects, patient zero will remain a phantom."

The younger doctor advanced the screen image. "By the time Wulandari's samples arrived on the nineteenth, Trident was already showing up in the States, and being reported in other countries all over the world."

"Air travel," said Moira.

"Yes. The best friend a virus ever had."

"And no reports of malignancy from overseas?"

"Not one," said Fisher. "It's only been found during routine testing. Now people are looking for it, of course, but no malignancy whatsoever. It sure doesn't behave like something with good intentions, though."

The older woman chewed her lip. Without causing so much as a rash, the bizarre little organism was already causing global hysteria. The word was out, and the media was stoking the flames of fear. News programs interviewed supposed medical experts who touted theories about its nature and potential. Some claimed it was a new strain of Ebola, others that it was a sister to the Zika Virus. Moira had given two press conferences already, assuring the nation that it was the CDC's priority, and repeating that there was no new information, no indicators of malignancy, and so no need to panic. Her statements hadn't slowed the media one bit. They knew when they had latched onto something juicy. There was talk of plague and an extinction-level super flu, others who debated that it was simply a natural event, a part of human evolution with potentially beneficial healing properties.

The internet and social media was even worse. Tales caught on about accidentally released government germs, the beginning of a biblical Armageddon (especially since there hadn't been a single documented occurrence of Trident showing up in animals, only humans,) biological warfare launched by the Chinese and even alien testing. Everyone had an opinion. Moira Rusk tried to contain the speculation, but an absence of hard information was merely fuel for panic and wild theories.

Another graph came up on screen. "As we've discussed before," said Fisher, "so far about ten percent of the population appears to have a natural immunity, for lack of a better word. Their bodies see Trident as hostile, and immediately destroy it. Early indicators are that this immunity extends along genetic lines, and we're seeing Trident being extinguished within entire families."

Moira nodded. That could explain why the entire first family was successfully fighting it off. She made a mental note to order testing among the President's relatives. Then she frowned. The genetic theory would explain the children and one parent, but there would be no biological link to the other spouse, and yet both President and Mrs. Fox were demonstrating this immunity. Might they *both* be part of that ten percent immunity pool? What were the odds of that?

About one in ten. Not so long odds.

Fisher continued. "This immunity percentage appears consistent around the world, with no variables due to ethnicity, gender, age or health condition. In another ten percent, Trident struggles and appears to be slow to spread and quickly weakening." The screen jumped to a close-up of the organism, a sample from one of the patients she'd just mentioned. It appeared withered and deformed. "There's no indication that this second group is actively fighting it off, but it still appears to be dying. My guess is that, for whatever reason, this group represents an unsuitable host for Trident. They're just lucky. No one has done the genetic work yet to find out why."

"And the other eighty percent?" Moira asked.

"It's alive and well," said Fisher, "continuing to spread throughout the body; first in the bloodstream and eventually taking up residence in organs and tissue. Our Indonesian bus driver, and many like him, seems to be the farthest along in the spread. Everyone else is – and I hate to use this word, Moira – *infected* to varying degrees. It's given us a picture of the day-by-day growth over the past eight days."

A new image came up, this of several Trident organisms slowly moving across the screen. One by one they seemed to bulge for a moment, and then a new, identical organism emerged from the original.

"It's replicating," said Fisher. "Not feeding on cells, simply duplicating itself."

In less than a minute, one of the originals bulged and gave birth again.

"Using those infected the longest as a baseline, we can determine an individual's length of exposure. We're also able to estimate, at its current speed of growth, that Trident will have completely spread through a patient in nine or ten days."

"And then what happens?" Moira murmured. It wasn't a question directed at her friend. She watched the strange images, chewing her lip while the tea went cold in front of her.

"A side note to this," said Fisher, "and I don't know right now if or how this information will be useful, is that Trident is vulnerable to intense heat. It kills the organism."

"Maybe that's good news."

The younger woman shook her head. "The kind of heat I'm talking about also kills the host. House and car fires, where the body is charred, a power plant worker in Japan who caught a fatal dose of radiation…autopsies showed that Trident was exterminated in those cases. In almost every other kind of death, the organism not only remains alive after the host is deceased, it continues to replicate and spread, even as the body decomposes."

"Like bacteria consuming a corpse," said Moira.

Fisher shrugged. "Sort of. But bacteria feed. Trident isn't eating anything. It just carries on as the body breaks down. Not even formaldehyde can flush it out. Nothing can, so far."

Moira drummed her fingernails on the conference table and scowled at the screen. "Next steps?"

Fisher quickly ran through a few more slides of information that contained her summary and shut down. "The labs downstairs are working on it twenty-four-seven, the same overseas, and I'm in regular contact with our colleagues at USAMRIID and around the world. We have a good number of voluntary test subjects here at the facility, a representation of every length of contagion, and we're tracking its progress constantly. We're also thinking that the immune and resistant twenty percent will be our source for an eventual cure or inoculation, but it's very early."

"Not much information," said Moira. It wasn't intended as a rebuke, and Fisher didn't take it that way.

"I agree," said the younger woman. "Certainly not enough to make an informed decision about initiating the NRP." She sighed and rubbed her eyes. "You'll know more when we do. Are you heading back to Washington?"

"No, I'm staying right here."

A tired smile. "We can sure use the help."

"Good briefing, Karen, thank you." She gestured at the darkened flat screen. "Send me your presentation?" Dr. Fisher said that she would, and Moira returned to the office the CDC had loaned her for the duration of her stay. Her thoughts were filled with the image of an alien, three-pronged organism that offered more questions than answers.

-7-

FEATHER MOUNTAIN

Western Pennsylvania – October 26

The temperature inside the small wooden building hovered at just under ninety degrees, a pair of open windows doing little to mitigate the late October heat. Several flies buzzed through the heavy air, but the men sitting in here on folding metal chairs did not wave at them or wipe at the sweat on their foreheads and necks. It would be undisciplined. Instead they listened to the man giving the briefing, someone whose bored voice was as irritating as the droning of the flies.

Donny Knapp, twenty-two-years-old and only two months past his commissioning as a second lieutenant in the United States Army, was the most junior man in the room. The razor-close haircut made the sides of his head look white, and his face was as smooth as if he'd just shaved (although that had been hours ago); a baby face, some said. Lean and in the best physical condition of his life, he was just under six feet and observed the world around him with dark, intelligent eyes.

The three other second lieutenants (butter bars) that made up the platoon leaders in his company were seated in a row to his right. His company XO, who was a first lieutenant, and the captain who was his company commander sat to his left. The briefer, an Army captain wearing a military police armband, sat facing the group with one arm leaning on a nearby desk, delivering a rehearsed and often-given speech. *Phoning it in,* Donny thought.

"...two days of small unit exercises. The Miles gear you and your men will wear will track and transmit performance data, which you, and your battalion CO back home, will be able to review at the end of each exercise."

Donny saw the briefer looking at his captain and another man beside him, a soldier not part of Donny's company. Also wearing captain's bars, this man was a Green Beret out of Fort Bragg. He was relaxed, the heat seeming not to bother him in the least, and his face wore an expression of easy confidence. The name patch over his chest pocket read, *Stavros.*

"Three of my sergeants," the briefer continued, "will serve as referees during the exercises, and will have final say in all rulings. The Miles gear should resolve any questions, however."

Miles gear was an electronic combat simulation system, a harness and helmet band of sensors that picked up signals from lasers mounted to rifle barrels. Blank ammunition was used to provide realism, and the laser fired with every round. When the sensors everyone would be wearing detected a "hit," the Miles gear gave off a loud electronic shrieking that could only be silenced by a plastic key attached to the laser. Removing the key also deactivated the rifle's ability to score hits, eliminating cheating. Older systems were simpler, didn't transmit digital information, and allowed a soldier to turn off his alarms, "resurrecting" himself so he could get back in the fight. Not anymore. A hit now ensured that the soldier was either "dead" or "wounded," and out of action regardless. The data it transmitted – rounds fired, range, effectiveness of fire, position at time of "death" or type of casualty – allowed evaluation of combat performance, similar to the way football teams reviewed films of games in order to identify mistakes and make improvements. Donny had used the Miles gear during ROTC and officer's basic training.

"Captain Dunham's company will be the blue team," said the briefer. "Captain Stavros and his men will be the red team."

Awesome, Donny groaned inwardly. *Green Berets as the opposing force. We're gonna get creamed.*

The briefer buzzed on, but Donny barely heard him. One of the flies had taken an interest in the sweat on his right ear, landing, crawling, flying off and landing again. He ached to swat at it, to rub the sweat away, but he couldn't. The crawling sensation was maddening, but as the junior man he refused to be the first to break his military bearing and reinforce with the others that he was just another rookie.

"Captain Dunham," the briefer said in his slow, bored tone, "Captain Stavros has relinquished his deployment responsibilities, and they now transfer to you." The MP officer handed a manila, clasp envelope to Donny's CO, who immediately passed it to his executive officer. "If the balloon goes up," said the briefer, "your protocols, rules of engagement, radio frequencies and key cards for the armory are inside. Do you acknowledge receiving your orders?"

"Acknowledged," said Dunham.

Donny looked at the superior officers. What the hell were they talking about? The term *balloon goes up* was a military euphemism for war. Feather Mountain was a back-water training facility in Western Pennsylvania, about as far from a war zone as you could get. *Rules of engagement? Armory key? And what* deployment responsibilities *were being passed from the Green Beret to his CO?* Dunham didn't look confused – maybe he'd been here before – and if Donny's fellow platoon leaders weren't making sense of this, they were smart enough not to reveal it with their expressions, unlike Donny who realized he was staring like a moron. Had he missed some meeting? He panicked for a moment, certain he hadn't but wondering how he could be the only person in the room who didn't seem to know what was going on. The young officer decided he would remain quiet and discretely ask one of his fellow junior officers later.

The briefer checked his watch. "It's sixteen-thirty hours. The first exercise will be a night maneuver commencing at twenty-one-hundred hours." The MP stood. "Captain Dunham, that should give your officers plenty of time to orientate (Donny *hated* when people mangled that word! *Orient* you ignorant ass!) themselves to the facility. The mess opens at seventeen-hundred."

The Green Beret smiled and shook Dunham's hand, telling him he would see him later, the briefer already exiting the room through a rear door without another word. Donny thought he heard the man yawn.

The younger officers looked to their CO as the executive officer handed out photocopies that showed an overhead diagram of the base and identified all the buildings. "Make sure your platoons are settled into their quarters and get them fed," the man said. "Company meeting in the officer's barracks in one hour."

They were dismissed, and Donny Knapp filed out into the October afternoon, finally able to swat at the persistent fly that had followed him outdoors.

He missed.

Donny's platoon sergeant was waiting for him outside a long, one-story wooden structure painted white and roofed with black, asphalt shingles. A Cold War-era barracks identical to the surrounding buildings, the many windows running down both sides were open to air it out. Identical buildings mirrored it on each side and across the road. It had been closed up and unoccupied since the last Army unit rotated through here, and it still carried the funk of fifty men quartering here in the late fall heat.

The sergeant saluted his officer, not a particularly crisp move. "The men are squared away, sir," he said. "Just waiting to go to chow." Two dozen of Donny's men were lounging outside the barracks, sitting on picnic tables or leaning against the walls. The young lieutenant felt their eyes on him.

"Thank you, Sergeant. The mess opens in about twenty minutes. You can take them over whenever you're ready."

Donny looked over at a cluster of his men, all looking at him and talking too softly to be heard. One of them laughed at something.

The platoon sergeant didn't notice, or at least pretended he hadn't. His face and gaze was neutral, but Donny could guess what he was thinking, had felt it from him and the other men since he took command of the platoon a month ago. The sergeant had *been there,* as had almost half the men under Donny's command. Donny had not. They were combat veterans of Afghanistan, and he was a wet-behind-the-ears butter bar who existed in a constant state of confusion and cluelessness. The disparity in their experience was obvious in the casual, confident way they chatted and walked, the ease with which they went about their assignments, a sharp contrast to Donny's general awkwardness every time he was around them.

Pay attention and listen. Learn from your NCOs. But remember that you're still the boss, and don't let them forget that. This had been the repeated counsel of his senior officers throughout ROTC, as well as Captain Dunham's advice when he first arrived at the company. But the platoon sergeant standing before him had given no indication that he desired to be Donny's teacher, and the young lieutenant was unsure of the right way to ask. There had been no outright disrespect; more like a quiet disregard.

Donny cleared his throat. "The first exercise is tonight. The captain will brief me at seventeen-thirty, and we'll have a platoon meeting with the NCOs at eighteen-thirty."

The sergeant nodded.

"Any issues?" Donny asked. He didn't expect any. If there was a problem within the platoon, the *sergeant's* platoon, the man would deal with it without involving his lieutenant.

"Just a question, sir." The sergeant produced a photocopy of the base identical to the one Donny had been given. "I was wondering if you knew why they flew us into Akron and trucked us in for hours, instead of landing us right here?"

Donny blinked and shook his head.

The sergeant pointed at the diagram. "The airfield, sir. Look at the size of it. The thing is long enough to handle a C5 Galaxy, much less the C130 we came in on."

Donny looked at the diagram, seeing an airstrip that seemed ridiculously long for such a tiny, out-of-the-way base. He shook his head again. "I don't."

"Yes, sir." The sergeant folded up the paper and tucked it into a pocket. "Will there be anything else?"

Donny dismissed the sergeant, who began gathering the men to walk them over to the mess hall. He said something to a corporal, who rolled his eyes. As the platoon shuffled off, Donny went in the other direction to search for the officer's quarters, trying to make sense of his own map.

Feather Mountain, the towering, pine-studded granite peak for which the base was named, dominated the skyline to the north. The land occupied by the base was a hundred square miles of fenced forest, sloping down from the base of the peak in a steep, rocky jumble of mixed terrain. The pine forest was thick and filled with shadow, a place where elite, combat-hardened Green Berets would soon be hunting him and his men in three days of exercises; war games that Donny was certain would emphasize his utter lack of experience as an infantry officer.

He knew little about the place. It had apparently been a nuclear missile silo of some sort once upon a time, but the ICBMs had been removed at the end of the Cold War, the base being repurposed. Now it was an infantry training site with a new company rotating in every two weeks. Captain Dunham's Alpha Company, part of the 3rd Infantry Division based at Fort Stewart, Georgia, had flown into a field in Akron, Ohio this morning to begin their two week training cycle, bringing their gear with them. It struck Donny as odd that a single company would be shaved off from his battalion to fly up here and train on its own. But then so many things about the Army didn't make sense, as the newly commissioned officer was quickly learning.

Donny got turned around and ended up at the motor pool, where a smirking enlisted man redirected him toward the officer's barracks. The young lieutenant tried to conceal his embarrassment. Tonight's exercise would no doubt provide more than enough of that.

"What were you *thinking,* Knapp? *Were* you thinking?"

Donny stood at attention in the common room of the officer's barracks, bare bulbs casting the Spartan space in a harsh white, an oscillating fan humming in a corner. It was 3:00 AM, and the rest of the company officers had already showered and headed off to bed. Alpha Company's executive officer stood before him, fists planted on his hips. "You *did* learn how to use a compass during training, didn't you?" the man demanded.

Donny swallowed. "Yes, sir. No excuse."

"Well, that's not good enough," the man said. "I'd like an answer as to why you got fifty percent of your men killed in the first thirty minutes of the engagement, compromised our right flank and allowed the company CP to be overrun." The man stared at him. "Well?"

Donny tried to meet his gaze. His first official exercise as Third Platoon's leader had been a disaster, worse than he'd feared. Misreading his map and directions, Donny had led his platoon right into an ambush, and the Green Berets opposing him had raced through his position and hit the company command post, scoring a quick victory.

He struggled for words, but the first lieutenant cut him off.

"You don't have an answer because you're dead, isn't that right?"

Donny nodded. He had been the first casualty. Peeking around a tree to assess the terrain ahead of him, seeing the forest in bright green through his night vision goggles, he had failed to notice the man only thirty yards away. There had been a flash and the crack of a rifle, and suddenly his Miles gear was giving off a high-pitched electronic shriek. A headshot. A moment later the opposing force concealed in the trees ahead of him opened up and neutralized half of his platoon, the forest echoing with the hollow ripple of blanks and the screaming of sensors up and down the line.

And there had been the laughter, his men falling down *dead* and howling at their sudden demise.

"My sergeant-"

"Don't blame this on your platoon sergeant, Knapp. You're the commanding officer and you own it. You're also expected to be able to read a map. Third Platoon was more than a mile away from where it should have been."

Donny swallowed again. His platoon sergeant had his own compass, and hadn't said a word as his officer led them off course.

"Captain Dunham is pissed beyond words," said the XO. Then he pointed at Donny's chest. "You *will* come up with a better line of bullshit explaining this clusterfuck performance when you explain it to him at oh-six-hundred. You're dismissed."

Donny headed down the hallway toward the showers. He'd get about two hours of rack time before he'd have to be up again to face another beating, but he knew he wouldn't be able to sleep.

Maybe the Army had been a bad choice.

-8-

DARK HORSE

Vermont – October 26

Devon Fox awoke at 5:00AM and dressed quietly so as not to disturb his roommate, using only the glow of a digital alarm clock to find his clothes and running shoes. It was still full dark outside. Tall (with a ways to go yet) and with a head of thick, dark hair, blessed with good looks like his father, he was already starting to appear as the man he would become, and girls were starting to notice.

"What's wrong with you?" said a sleep-muffled voice from the bed on the other side of the room. "Normal people are sleeping."

"Which explains why you're awake. Want to come with me?" Devon asked.

A snort and the sound of a pillow being punched. "Not a chance. I only run when someone's chasing me."

Devon sat on the bed and tied his shoes. "Keep stuffing pizza in your hole like you did last night and soon you won't even be able to do that."

Another snort. "Pizza is the cornerstone of the food pyramid."

Devon smiled in the darkness. Sean Peters had been his roommate for only a couple of months, a boy his age who was new to the Harrison School, but they had quickly become close friends. Sean didn't seem to care about Devon's status or all the oddities that went with it. He treated Devon like any other kid, and that made him pretty cool.

"See you in class," Devon said, heading for the door.

"Say hi to Captain America."

Devon nodded and slipped into the hallway. Captain America was already waiting for him. "Good morning," said the man standing outside the door. He was dressed in a gray track suit and running shoes, and wore a fanny pack on one hip. This accessory would have made anyone else an instant geek, but on Captain America it was something else entirely. Everyone knew what was in that pack, although no one – not even Devon – had actually seen it.

"Hey Marcus," he replied, bumping fists with the man. "Five miles okay with you?"

"I don't know. I might need to stop and take breaks."

Devon smiled and shook his head as the two of them headed down the stairs from the third floor dorm room and out to the commons. At thirty, Special Agent Marcus Handelman was about as fit as a man could be, tall and muscular with a shaved head and tightly groomed goatee. When he wore his dark suit, reflective sunglasses and earpiece he was a terrifying sight, an image he no doubt cultivated for the intimidation benefits. He'd been in Navy Special Operations before joining the Secret Service, and Devon knew that a five mile run around the Vermont campus would barely cause the man to break a sweat. In fact it was Handelman who often pushed Devon when the boy started to fatigue, coaxing another mile out of him. The primary agent on Devon's Protective Detail for the last three years, the two of them enjoyed a friendly and casual relationship. Devon knew that such a relationship did *not* exist between his sister and her own detail agents.

"How about route three?" he offered. "We haven't done that one in a while." The agent was very persistent about not allowing Devon to fall into predictable patterns when he was out.

"Sounds good."

"Dark Horse is on the commons," Handelman said into his wrist mic. "Five miles, route three."

Devon took a few minutes to stretch on the steps outside his building, one of several four-story, Ivy-League-looking structures surrounding a park-like green space, the administration building anchoring the commons to the far left, and classroom buildings extending to the right. Gaslight-style streetlamps lined the many sidewalks, pushing back the early morning darkness. Although lights glowed in windows here and there, the two of them were the only ones out at this hour. The rest of the prep school was still asleep.

They moved at a steady pace, the agent running easily beside his young charge, head turning constantly and eyes roving, doing what he called *bird-watching.* As the son of the President, Devon Fox had the unique opportunity to see

Secret Service operations behind the scenes, something few people ever experienced and the details of which Devon was forbidden to discuss. In addition to witnessing their many procedures and protective arrangements, Devon had the inside track on their language, specifically their colorful dictionary of code words and phrases. Handelman had told him that other than principals (those they protected) and other agents and law enforcement, there were only two kinds of people; *Crows* and *Parrots.* Crows were terrorists or assassins. Parrots were those with unknown intentions, and that meant everyone else. An agent's life, Handelman had explained, consisted primarily of bird-watching.

"Rounding Elmore Hall," the agent told his radio. A moment later they turned left, keeping to the street instead of the sidewalk, an ivy-covered building where Devon had a couple of classes on their left. Parked in the fire lane before the building was a black Chevy Suburban with the engine running. A man seated on the passenger side threw a wave that Handelman returned.

Although the temperature would rise steadily throughout the day, right now their breath steamed in the chilly, late October morning air as the sky began to slowly lighten above a line of trees dressed in red and orange leaves. Devon felt himself loosening up as they neared the end of their first mile, his lungs drawing easily and the first warmth of a pleasant burn appearing in his legs. He picked up the pace, and Handelman stayed with him.

"You still want to be a jarhead?" Handelman asked as they passed a shrub-ringed statue of one of the school's founders. He always engaged in conversation when they were out in the morning, insisting that it was good for the breathing. He said it was the reason military units sang cadence when they ran, not simply for the fun of obscene rhyming.

"I'm going to be a Marine like my dad," Devon said. "Not infantry, though. I'm going to be in intelligence."

The Secret Service agent seemed to think about this for a moment. "You've got the brains for it. I've seen your grades."

"Really?"

A grin. "I peeked. You need to work on the math, though."

Devon made a face. He *crushed* math. At fifteen he was already in college-level classes. When he looked at the agent, the man was grinning. "You like breaking my balls, don't you?"

A shocked gasp. "Language, Mr. Fox."

Now it was Devon's turn to grin.

"I guess you're smart enough. But do you have the killer instinct?"

"Not all Marines are trained killers," the boy said.

Handelman laughed. "Oh, yes they are. Just ask one, he'll tell you. Even the cooks and the clerks. Trained killers, every one of them. The question is, are you tough enough to be a Marine?"

They ran across another street and onto a path that would take them in a wide loop past the sports fields and eventually back to the dorms. "If I'm too much of a wimp," he said, "I'll just join the Navy like you."

Handelman let out a deep laugh. "You already sound like a jarhead."

They ran the next mile in silence, until Devon spoke again. The playfulness was gone from his voice. "This Trident thing…does it make you nervous?" In his heart he doubted *anything* made the big man nervous.

"I worry about the things I can see and touch," the agent replied.

"But it's in you, right?"

"Yep, just like everyone else. Does it make *you* nervous?"

Devon shook his head. "I saw the doctor yesterday." Then he frowned at his own stupidity. Of course Handelman knew that. He'd been at the appointment with Devon, checking the office before allowing the boy inside. What he didn't know was that Handelman had taken a long look at his medical record as part of his mission to identify any threats to life or health. Not entirely ethical or part of Secret Service policy, it was something many agents did quietly with those for whom they were responsible. "The doctor told me my body has almost killed it off," Devon said. Handelman knew this too. "What about you?"

"The Service has us checked regularly. Mine is dying off too, but at a slower rate."

"How about the other guys? The rest of the detail, I mean."

"Crossing Bingham Road," Handelman told his wrist mic, then to Devon said, "Most of them still have it, but it's not hurting anyone. Nothing for you to worry about."

They crossed at an intersection and moved onto a sidewalk on the other side to avoid some parked cars. The brick building they were now passing had a few more lights on than they'd seen before. People were waking up.

"What does your biology professor say about it?" Handelman asked.

Devon shrugged as he ran. "He told us there's not enough information to make an informed decision, but that it's definitely something new. He says it's probably a result of pollution and mishandling of the environment." He looked over at the agent's face, but the man's expression didn't change. Agents discussing politics where protectees could hear them was forbidden by the Service, but it happened, and Devon knew the men on his Detail (and, he suspected, most of law enforcement and the military) leaned to the right and weren't big believers in the often-liberal views his professors espoused. His biology teacher in particular was not a strong supporter of Garrison Fox. The President spoke more often about a robust economy and a strong national defense than he did about global warming. Devon still wasn't sure where he landed on any of these issues himself, but he believed in his dad, and that was good enough for now.

"The doctors will figure it out," Handelman said, trying to end the discussion.

The young man was quiet for a while as they ran. Despite his bodyguard's casual dismissal, Devon *was* worried. The news was reporting that everyone had it. Sure, some were fighting it off, as was the case with his family and, apparently, Marcus Handelman. Trident seemed harmless, but if that were true, why would his body be killing it?

His forehead still wrinkled with a frown, Devon said, "Let's pick it up," and ran faster.

Handelman stayed right beside him.

The dining hall was packed for the noon meal, two hundred young men between the ages of thirteen and eighteen, all dressed in khakis, dark blue blazers and striped ties talking at once, making the high-ceilinged hall buzz. Devon was eating with Sean and a few other boys his age at a table near one of the fire exits (an insistence of the Secret Service so that he could be quickly removed if need be) with Handelman standing against a wall fifteen feet away, watching as always. While Devon had showered and gotten dressed for the day's classes, Handelman had changed back into his dark suit.

"The boss is stopping by today," he'd explained on the way to the dining hall. Normally, within the Secret Service the Boss referred to POTUS, but in this case it was Handelman's immediate boss, a supervisory agent named O'Brien. "Be sure to tell him I'm the greatest."

"I'll tell him you couldn't take out a Cub Scout with a limp."

"Outstanding."

Between bites of hamburger, Devon and Sean talked about the last season of Game of Thrones, something they secretly streamed on their laptops (the school would never allow a program with so much sex and nudity to be shown in the rec room) and it was precisely those two elements that captured their fascination. Along with the storyline, of course.

"Cersei is the hottest one," Sean said.

Devon made a face. "Dude, she's like, your mom's age."

The other boy grinned. "She's a cougar."

"Sansa Stark is the hot one," said Devon. "I wish she'd do a nude scene. I love redheads."

Neither boy had any experience with the opposite sex, other than a little kissing with some of the girl's from St. Jerome's, the neighboring, all-girl Catholic prep school. The occasional dance or sporting event brought boys and girls together, but nothing *real* had ever happened, especially with watchful nuns lurking about. Sean called them *The Penguins.*

Devon noticed that a boy seated just down from Sean, a kid of about thirteen whose name he couldn't remember, wasn't eating but instead sat and stared at Marcus Handelman. It was something Devon had become accustomed-to. Most of the kids at the school were past being impressed or curious about Devon's Protective Detail, but for the newer students, like this one, they were as exotic as zoo animals. Many tried to strike up conversations, and the agents were polite but brief, not permitting their attention to be drawn away from their assignment.

Devon gave Sean a little nod, then spoke to the staring boy. "He kills on command, you know."

The younger boy looked at Devon. "Bullshit," he said, but his eyes told a different story.

"Oh, yeah. Last year some kid cut in front of me at lunch. I just looked at Handelman and he dragged the kid outside, beat the shit out of him."

The other boys at the table all nodded, straight-faced as the thirteen-year-old looked back at the agent and paled.

"You don't fuck with Captain America," Sean whispered, glancing around to make sure no adults had heard his profanity.

"He's bad-ass," said another boy, jumping on board. "A few weeks ago some terrorists tried to snatch Devon outside the library. Handelman shot four of them right in the head."

"He did not," said the younger boy.

"I heard it was five," said another.

The thirteen-year-old looked at each of them in turn, eyes narrowed.

"They don't like us to talk about it," whispered Sean. Across from him Devon rolled his eyes. His friends would overplay it like they always did, and the gag would come to a swift end. It did just that when a fourth boy announced that the Secret Service agent had shot down a helicopter over the Lacrosse field with a rocket launcher. No one could hold it in after that, and the table exploded with laughter. The boy's face reddened.

Devon laughed, but winked at the younger kid. "He's a normal guy, and he's cool. I'll introduce you later. You'll like him."

"Ah, Dev," moaned Sean, "why'd you let him off the hook like that? He was buying it."

Devon threw a French fry at his friend. "A rocket launcher? Really?" He stood. "I've gotta get to class."

Agent Handelman left when he did, suppressing a smile. He'd heard it all, of course.

In the dining hall behind them, Trident lived on every table, every tray and plastic cup, in the kitchens and in the food. It drifted through the air, virulent and unseen. Within the bodies of the students and staff in the dining room, it advanced at different rates, silent and relentless, a threat that not even Captain America could protect them from.

-9-

DESIGN

Dallas, Texas – October 27

The media referred to her as “The Softer Side of Fox” because of her many humanitarian efforts and wildly popular housing programs for the poor, but the word *soft* had rarely been an accurate descriptor of her life or personality. Before becoming First Lady, Patricia Rand-Fox had been a Marine’s wife, a senator’s wife and a successful architect, this last the source of her Secret Service code name. A smart, confident woman, she was also the mother of two, a job that was often as challenging as any faced by a Marine.

A graduate of UVA, at forty-nine Patricia was a bit of a maverick among First Ladies; beautiful and gracious, photogenic and well spoken, the perfect hostess, but also extremely savvy about political matters and unafraid of expressing her opinions, even if at times they didn't mesh perfectly with her husband's. The American people loved her, and both her marriage and the presidency was a true partnership.

Like a Marine, she now found herself deployed in terrain that was potentially hostile, a minefield where a misstep could lead to disaster. She had just finished a forty-five minute address to *NOW,* the National Organization for Women, an event hosted by the University of Texas at Dallas, with more than three thousand in attendance. They had come to the Q&A portion, and a woman in her thirties wearing glasses had just approached the microphone.

"Mrs. Fox," the woman said, "you gave a good speech, but I'd like to know why your husband hasn't focused more on women's issues. Surely they're more important than the expense to commission yet another aircraft carrier."

The cameras focused on Patricia's face to capture her reaction. She gave a confident smile.

"Let me first say that, like my husband, I believe in both a strong national defense and a strong economy. The expense and launch of the *USS Dragoon* achieved both those goals, providing jobs during the construction and providing a state-of-the-art cornerstone for our nation's military.

"Concerning women's programs, the President is as committed as I am. If you will recall, just six months ago he called upon Congress to double federal spending for rape education and crisis centers, and last year he sponsored legislation to make rape a federal offense with lengthy, mandatory sentencing. I'm sure you remember the Palmer Bill."

"But neither of those passed," said the woman.

Talk to your congressman about that, Patricia thought but didn't say. Instead she gave the woman a smile and said, "My husband is working hard with Congress to bring everyone together on this, to achieve true bipartisanship. Yes, the bills were defeated, but the fight isn't over yet."

Another woman took the microphone. "Can you tell us why he is still on the fence about abortion?"

Here was the real landmine, one of the most heatedly debated topics in the political landscape, something that fired volatile passions on both sides of the issue. She'd been waiting for it, and knew that this group wouldn't be satisfied with her answer. Neither would the Republican base.

"My husband believes in life," she said. "We have two children that he loves very much, and we're both proud of the young people they've become. Neither of us could imagine life without them. He also believes in a woman's right to make decisions about her own body. But regardless of his personal opinions, the President believes, as he has said all along, that this is a state's rights issue, and something that the federal government should leave to the individual legislatures."

Although there were more questions and some scattered shouts from the crowd, that was all they were getting. Patricia moved past the topic and quickly wrapped up by thanking the National Organization for Women and the University for having her here today, and asked those gathered here to return her husband to the White House for another four years. Despite the sensitive subject and the non-answer she had given, Patricia received a standing ovation and waved as she left the stage.

"It went better than I expected," said the young woman, a sharp political operator with a law degree from Yale. The First Lady considered her indispensable, which was why she'd picked her for her Chief of Staff.

"Thanks, Maria," Patricia said. They were in the limo heading to the private airfield where a jet would take them to Boston. "But after all the applause, they're still going to vote for a democrat."

Maria nodded, her boss's leather-bound agenda resting on one knee. "It's a hard sell, and your husband's opponent is intensely vocal about being pro-choice."

Patricia looked out the window as her own small motorcade moved through Dallas, realizing that in these circumstances and in this place it was almost impossible not to replay the events of 1963. She forced the morbid thoughts aside.

Part of her wished Garrison would take a firm, official stand on abortion, one way or the other, but what she'd said about him was true. He felt both ways, and didn't think the federal government should even be involved. It wasn't a strong position politically, but it was what her husband believed and she respected him for it.

"What time do we land in Boston?"

The younger woman didn't need the itinerary to answer. "We're wheels-down at six-thirty. Dinner with Kylie at eight. You're staying at the Westin, downtown."

"And in the morning?"

"An hour with the Massachusetts governor over breakfast, then you and Kylie are in the air and headed for Ohio. You'll arrive in Cleveland just as the rally is ending so you'll miss it, but that was what you and the President wanted."

Patricia nodded absently. It was a trip that promised to be stressful. It wasn't that Kylie Fox, her twenty-two-year-old daughter and firstborn didn't love her family and want to see her father, but the girl *hated* being the child of a U.S. President, and strained at the restrictive yoke that went with it. She would resent being pulled away from her post-graduate life at Harvard, even if only for a weekend, to be "Part of the circus" as she put it. The fact that Garrison would keep her away from the cameras wouldn't matter.

"Any change with Devon?" Maria asked.

"No, he's still not coming. Too much going on at school." *And wouldn't* that *start an argument.* She could hear it already. *Why do* I *have to go and Devon doesn't?* Patricia sighed. Daughters.

The First Lady looked at her young Chief of Staff, at the dark circles appearing around her eyes. "You're not getting much rest," she said.

Maria smiled. "I'm fine, ma'am. Nothing a couple of gallons of Starbucks won't fix."

"Did you see the doctor?" Caroline had insisted that everyone on her staff see a physician regularly to keep track of what appeared to be, for lack of a better word, an unidentified virus. She knew the Secret Service was doing the same. Unlike Patricia, whose body had effectively killed off the intruder in short order, her Chief of Staff and everyone in her entourage was carrying an expanding strain of Trident, alive and thriving in their bodies.

"Yes, ma'am," said Maria. "No symptoms, no change." The younger woman let out a little giggle, then opened her eyes wide in surprise and covered her mouth. "I'm so sorry,

Mrs. Fox. I don't know where that came from." She started to turn red. "I don't…"

Patricia looked at the girl. "You're exhausted. As soon as we get to the hotel you go straight to bed. I don't want to see you until we're on the plane tomorrow. Understand?" She squeezed the young woman's knee.

"Yes, ma'am."

-10-

DEVIL DOG

Airborne – October 27

Angel cruised at 35,000 feet, the massive blue and white aircraft heading east with Oklahoma passing far below. The sun was setting behind Air Force One, painting the sea of clouds in shades of amber and coral. Lifting off from Travis Air Force Base in California only hours ago, the plane was on the final leg of what had been a four-state tour beginning at five o'clock this morning, with Ohio still ahead, the final stop of the day.

In his airborne office, Garrison Fox smiled and accepted a cup of coffee from a uniformed steward, rubbing his eyes.

The day had been exhausting, like every day since he could remember, a non-stop blur of travel, speech-making, handshakes and polling reports. There was yet another event ahead tonight, a dinner with the Ohio Prosecutors Organization where Garrison would drive home his message of being tough on crime.

He knew he should be napping in the bedroom at the nose of the aircraft, but Ohio was a critical state in the election, a swing state and still up for grabs. He needed to go over his speech to the prosecutors, making changes where necessary. His speech writers would quickly make the adjustments, but Garrison was also not averse to going off-script and speaking on the fly, something that drove the writers mad. He didn't care. He was the one who would be held accountable for every word he spoke, not them.

Seated on a couch on the other side of the desk was Thomas Barrow, looking rumpled and in need of a shave as usual, along with the press secretary and his National Security Advisor James Blaine. A communications officer stepped into the room to announce that both Labcoat and Cement Mixer were online, just as a pair of faces appeared in split-screen on a large, wall-mounted LCD TV. This video conference was another reason Garrison wouldn't be napping before landing in Ohio.

Moira Rusk's image was on the right, the Secretary of Health and Human Services conferencing in from the CDC, and Bob Chase from Homeland Security was on the left, a balding man in his late fifties, currently seated at a table in *Cement Mixer,* the White House Situation Room. Bob looked fresh, but Moira's face showed her fatigue.

"Good evening, Mr. President," both said.

"Thanks for calling in," Garrison said, tilting back in the high leather chair and sipping his coffee. "Where are we?"

Bob Chase started. “Moira sent me her briefing video. You’ve seen it too. She’s updated me on the latest information.”

The President gestured to the physician.

Without preamble Moira said, “The virus continues to embed itself in organs and tissue, and so far has not given any indication that it is malignant. In the advanced cases – those people who have had it the longest, since it presented nine days ago – we are seeing a filmy sac developing around the heart, brain and base of the spinal cord. This has only been discovered during autopsies of patients who died of unrelated issues.”

“A sac?” Garrison said, leaning forward.

“Yes, sir,” she said. “The substance is made up of proteins with the Trident organism attached to them. The sac is not showing up in day-eight patients or earlier, but appears to develop in a matter of hours on day nine.” She frowned. “And like everything else, these sacs appear benign, not interfering with bodily functions or overall health. Patients with these sacs are just as healthy as those without.”

“How much of the population now has these sacs, Moira?”

“About twenty percent, as near as we can tell, Mr. President, and that number will triple by tomorrow. Trident itself remains highly virulent, and appears to have infected all but the world’s most remote populations, as near as we can tell.”

“And we still don’t know what it is or where it came from.” It wasn’t a question.

“Our best guess is a point of origin somewhere in Southeast Asia,” said Moira, “based on the pace at which it spreads through the body, but an exact origin remains unconfirmed. Jakarta, is most likely.”

Garrison shuddered. He'd only recently been there, shaking hands. He rubbed his palms on his trousers without realizing it.

"Patient Zero is a unicorn at this point," Moira said. "As to what it is, it spreads like and has characteristics similar to Ebola, but even those descriptors are thin. It's something new. We have no idea what it will do."

"If anything," added Bob Chase.

Now it was Garrison's turn to frown. That a foreign organism had so aggressively expanded throughout the global population in such a short time was unsettling. The fact that it hadn't revealed itself to be harmful was of little comfort. And now there was the added mystery of filmy sacs forming around the body's most critical organs. Garrison was no virologist, but he understood logic. Organisms didn't spread and then develop into new structures without a reason or goal, and that was the most chilling aspect of all. What was Trident's objective?

"What do the numbers look like?" he asked.

The Sec HHS chewed at her top lip. "It's holding steady at earlier estimates. Ten percent of people, like you, kill it off immediately. We're confident that this is a genetic defense, and that is the angle for our inoculation work. Another ten percent, also genetically based, take a little longer to fight it off, but Trident is weakening in those people. The remaining eighty percent are hosting the organism." She went on to explain how Trident was completely drug-resistant, its response to intense heat, and how it continued to thrive even after a host was deceased.

Garrison drummed his fingers distractedly on the desk. "Recommendations?"

Again, the Secretary of Homeland Security deferred to the medical professional. Moira looked at the President through the video link and said, "I'm recommending full implementation of the National Response Plan."

The President leaned back, even though he'd sensed it coming. The implications to the country if the full NRP were implemented were more than serious, potentially devastating. They went beyond anything the U.S. had ever faced from natural disaster, and in fact the only thing *more* serious would be if the nation went to war with another superpower.

Medical experts in the United States defined a pandemic as, *An epidemic of infectious disease that has spread through human populations across a large region, continents or even worldwide.* Trident fit that description, except for the disease part. Not technically, that was, because a disease was a disorder with specific symptoms, but it was right on the cusp of the definition. The NRP was a three-part national security strategy, much of which was continuously in effect. It was the third step that they were really discussing.

The Director of Homeland Security was responsible for running the National Response Plan, but it was the Secretary of Health and Human Services who coordinated medically and advised. Other agencies would provide plans and help with decision-making, with the entire process chaired by the White House. In the end, the final green light had to be given by the President.

The model for the NRP was based upon influenza outbreaks, with classical disease attack rates at around thirty percent, forty percent among school-age children. In such an outbreak, those most at risk for fatality were infants, pregnant women, the elderly and those with chronic medical conditions. With a typical influenza strain, those infected would, on average, infect ten other people. The epidemic would last between six and eight weeks in affected communities.

Some strains were more deadly, such as the outbreak of Spanish Flu (now called H1N1) in 1918 that claimed around a hundred million lives, five percent of the world's population at the time. The NRP assumed worst case scenarios like that.

The three-part strategy consisted first of *Preparedness and Communication*; creating a national stockpile of anti-viral drugs, between twenty and seventy-five million doses. Pre-positioning of medical and non-medical supplies (to provide pop-up field hospitals) was also part of the first step, as well as maintaining public confidence. This last usually came down to education and media spots to assure the American people that their government had a plan and would move quickly to protect them.

At the moment there was equipment stored across the country, and the anti-viral stockpile was in place and being distributed, for what little good it was doing. Public confidence in the government's ability to deal with a massive crisis was something else entirely, support that had been waning year after year as Americans became increasingly jaded and skeptical. The FEMA response to Katrina hadn't helped matters, and continued to be the event people pointed to when discussing government incompetence in the face of disaster.

The second part of the plan was *Bio-surveillance and Detection,* elements also already in place. Commonly referred-to as *hospital surveillance,* this part of the program was a cooperative effort not only domestically but abroad, where physicians worldwide constantly engaged in screening, monitoring and sharing information. In a "normal" pandemic, this advance warning would help slow the spread of disease to the United States. It was this screening and communication that had identified Trident in the first place. Had there been a vaccination against the organism, its implementation would have fallen under this part of the plan.

Garrison's coffee was now getting cold on his desk. "Did I hear you correctly, Moira?"

"Yes you did, Mr. President."

Bob Chase jumped in. "With all due respect to Dr. Rusk, I can't support this course of action at this time, Mr. President. Trident hasn't *done* anything."

"I'm convinced it will," Moira said. "It's acting viral in every way, it's highly contagious and aggressive, and it *has* done something. It has infected almost every living soul on the planet – and continues to grow even in the deceased – and now we have these sac-like growths in critical areas."

"Which you can't say pose a threat," said the Homeland director. "Despite how it acts, you can't tell us it's medically harmful."

"Bob," said Moira, "you don't have to be a doctor to know that the train heading toward you will be destructive to your body if you're still standing on the tracks when it gets there." She sighed. "I've been a physician for a long time. I recognize a killer when I see one, no matter how it's masquerading."

"It hasn't *killed* anyone," said Bob Chase.

The President held up his hand to stop the back-and-forth. His advisors were intelligent, well-intentioned professionals, but they were human. What Moira was saying had them scared, and it wasn't simply the idea of unknown disease effects or global pandemic that was putting them on edge. Implementing phase three of the NRP was frightening all on its own.

Response and Containment. This phase went into action once the genie was out of the bottle. It was designed to mitigate disease, suffering and death, maintain a functional health care system infrastructure and ensure that critical services could be provided to the public; essential commodities such as gas, food, medical assistance and chlorine water purification. It would also serve to sustain the country's power infrastructure and lessen the financial impact of a widespread outbreak.

It sounded orderly and comprehensive on paper. In reality it was merely a lesser chaos.

The opening moves were benign; public notices to drive frequent hand-washing, encouraging social distancing and providing both surgical masks and Latex gloves to the population. Then the U.S. would inform all foreign governments that it was executing the NRP in order to ensure societal continuity and national defense.

The United States would move to DEFCON 3.

After that, it got really messy. The President would order price-freezing and close the stock market indefinitely. He would order a stop to all domestic and international travel, call up and federalize all National Guard units, declare a state of martial law and close the borders. Those citizens determined to be sick would be isolated, and those not yet sick would be quarantined.

Garrison looked out the window as the last hint of the sun was replaced by a rapidly deepening night. He knew the plan. Every President did.

Widespread contagion and a fully implemented NRP would lead to school closures, workforce shortages, a breakdown in public order and civil disobedience. Illness within their own ranks coupled with enforcing travel restrictions and dealing with civil unrest would strain local law enforcement agencies to the breaking point, and putting troops in the streets was bound to result in tragedies all over the country, no matter how disciplined the unit. The economy would take a nose dive, and there would be a national panic. And that was all just here at home.

The global economy would take a hit, probably a crippling one, given the complex and interconnected nature of international trade. America's rivals might take advantage of the situation to expand into contested areas (like the South China Sea or the Middle East) and enemies might see the moment of weakness as the perfect opportunity to strike at the hated western devil.

If only the NRP could be implemented in selective bits and pieces. Garrison knew it was a naïve and juvenile thought. For the plan to work, to stop a pandemic before it could do too much damage, there could be no half measures. You had to be all-in.

"Mr. President," Moira said from the screen, "I fully understand the impact of my recommendation. I don't make it lightly, and I wouldn't make it at all if I didn't believe that Trident is a nightmare, the proportions of which we have never seen." The doctor surprised even herself at the dramatic delivery. She was a controlled, thoughtful scientist not given to emotional commentary. She didn't correct herself, however.

"And I say it's still too early, Mr. President," said Bob Chase.

If there had been even a single case of symptoms, Garrison thought, just one indication that Trident was hostile, he would pull the trigger on the NRP without a second thought. He trusted Moira Rusk, and her analogy of a train coming down the tracks had resonated with him. But could he throw his country into turmoil over a theory, no matter how sound the reasoning? And with that same logic, what disaster might be approaching – a potentially avoidable one – if he did nothing? His number one priority as President of the United States, despite what anyone else might think, was protecting her citizens. Did he do that by executing a plan designed to prevent widespread disease and death? Or did he better protect them by not turning their world upside-down with a devastating series of events to defend against something that might not even come to pass? *Better safe than sorry* applied in both cases.

"Tell me what you're doing about this, Moira."

"Mr. President, this is the only thing CDC is working on right now. We're in constant contact with researchers and physicians around the globe, sharing information. Here in Atlanta we have more than a hundred voluntary test subjects being monitored twenty-four-seven. It's the same around the country.

The President's frown deepened and he was silent for a long moment. "I can't approve it, not without more evidence of a threat. Find it for me, Moira. I want updates from you every six hours, regardless of the time, and sooner if anything breaks."

"Yes, Mr. President."

Garrison pointed at his Chief of Staff, seated on a sofa. "Set up a conference in thirty minutes, Tommy. I want the Joint Chiefs, Sec Def, Sec State and FEMA on the call." He looked at his Homeland Security director's image. "Bob, we're going to prep with the assumption that Dr. Rusk and her team is going to confirm her theory. If that happens I want to move fast and put phase three into action immediately. You'll need to be on that call as well."

"Yes, Mr. President," said Bob Chase, and the signal to CDC and the Situation Room cut off.

Garrison looked at Tommy Barrow and his National Security Advisor. "God help us if she's right."

The leak came not from anyone on the video conference, not from the Situation Room or Air Force One. It was the IT tech at CDC who had set up the supposedly secure call for Dr. Rusk. He had stayed on the line, eavesdropping. He supposed he was breaking one federal law or another by doing it, but how often did a person get to actually hear a private conversation with the President of the United States?

What he heard, however, rattled him so badly that as soon as the conference was over he started making calls.

Within hours the media was spinning. Talking heads told the world that *sources* were claiming that medical experts close to the President believed Trident was dangerous, and were being ignored. They spoke of discord within the White House and Garrison Fox's refusal to implement national strategies that would protect the American public. Some accused the President of playing politics, trying to conceal the risk and failing to act so as not to disrupt the final weeks of a re-election campaign. The most frightening aspects of the NRP were put up on screen in bullet points, driving the fear factor in order to ensure viewers and listeners stay tuned. Congress responded by demanding answers, and Garrison's democratic opponent immediately began holding press conferences to hammer at the idea that the country needed a leader who was not self-serving and would put *their* best interests first.

None of it would matter in the end. Trident was less than twenty-four hours away from revealing its true nature to the world.

OUTBREAK

-11-

SOO YIM

Over the Pacific – October 28

Trans Pacific Air flight two-seven-two Heavy flew at five hundred forty mph, 39,000 feet above the South Pacific headed for Hawaii, with Sydney, Australia two hours behind it. The passengers had settled in for the long flight and were quiet, awaiting the first round of beverage service. In the galley up front between First Class and the cockpit, a male flight attendant was filling carafes with coffee.

Soo Yim should have been helping him, but instead she sat on the jump seat near the aircraft's main door, rubbing her arms. She'd been having the chills for almost an hour now, and a headache was throbbing at the base of her skull. She was miserable and knew she was getting sick. The last time had been eight months ago, a bronchial infection that kept her out of work for five days and used up a large portion of her paid sick time. Illness was an occupational hazard for flight attendants, stuck in a sealed tube for hours with so many people, exposed to every cough and sneeze, every surface they touched. Only a rare few could work in the airline industry and not get sick at least once a year. And Soo Yim hated being sick. She sat and stared at the fiberglass divider between her and First Class.

The male attendant looked over at the young South Korean, feeling sorry for her. "I'll take this one," he said, arranging coffee cups on a tray.

The woman said nothing.

"Soo? Did you hear me?"

Again no response.

He reached out and touched her lightly on the shoulder. She flinched and her head snapped over. Her mouth was open just a little, showing her teeth, and her eyes were glassy.

"Do you want me to tell the captain you're not feeling well?" the man asked.

The girl stared at him. She'd heard only a couple of words, couldn't remember her co-worker's name. It was so hard to focus.

The man said nothing more and moved into the First Class cabin with his coffee. Soo Yim kept staring at the place where he had been standing. Sweat was beading on her forehead, and her petite frame was shuddering. The headache had grown, and now she was uncertain of where she was. Her thoughts were scattered and random, unable to lock onto any one thing.

She didn't notice when her bladder released, was barely aware of the hot urine running down her legs, unable to register the sudden, sharp tang of ammonia. Her mouth dropped open and a thin line of grayish drool spilled onto the front of her uniform.

Soo Yim giggled, still staring, and her hands started clenching and unclenching reflexively.

There was a sharp *click* behind and to her left as the cockpit door opened and the navigator stepped out to use the restroom.

Something *clicked* within Soo Yim as well, and in that instant she ceased being the young woman who loved travel and nightlife. No longer worried about getting sick, incapable of feeling the chills or headache, what she felt now was a sudden *rage*.

Soo Yim came off the jump seat with a snarl and slammed into the navigator, clawing and biting at his face, the force of her attack driving him back into the cockpit. They landed on the deck between the pilot and co-pilot. The navigator, bigger and stronger than the petite flight attendant, tried to fight her off as the other two men looked over their shoulders, shouting in alarm.

Fury overcame size. Soo Yim got in past the flailing arms and drove the manicured nails of her thumbs into the navigator's eyes. Blood and screaming erupted in the cockpit, and she silenced some of the latter by ripping out the man's throat with her teeth. A red jet shot grisly patterns across the white bulkheads and instrument panels.

The captain shouted a curse and unsnapped his harness, scrambling out of his seat as the co-pilot took hold of the yoke and brought the aircraft out of auto-pilot and into manual flight control. Soo Yim saw the man getting up and leaped off the dying navigator, launching herself at this new movement. The pilot was unprepared for the violence of her attack and was thrown backward as she slammed into him, suddenly defensive, trying to deflect bloody fingernails and push back at snapping teeth. Their two bodies crashed into the yoke and instrument panels on his side of the aircraft. On the right, the co-pilot was fighting against the abrupt jerk in the dual control yokes, hauling back against their weight in a fight to regain pitch and angle as the massive aircraft banked sharply right.

Soo Yim killed the pilot the same way she had the navigator, gouging out his eyes and biting deeply into the jugular.

Screaming now, still buckled in his seat, the co-pilot was easy prey as a girl wearing a bloody mask turned on him with a growl.

Back in the aircraft, one First Class passenger was ripping into his wife seated beside him, and in Coach, four others were savaging their fellow air travelers. The 747 filled with panicked screams.

Trans Pacific Air flight two-seven-two Heavy tipped to starboard, nosed over and went into a three minute dive toward its impact with the Pacific Ocean.

The killing went on for the full three minutes.

-12-

SIERRA-3

Cleveland, Ohio – October 28

Two days. Not so long ago it had been six months, then one month, then a week. Soon it would be hours. The countdown was making David King anxious. *Retirement.* It had come at last, and although he'd been planning it for years and was certain he'd made the right decision to put in his papers, the thought of leaving this life had him nervous in ways he hadn't anticipated. It had become such a part of him, *all* of him according to his late wife. What came next? How would he handle not being a part of this anymore? It was a question faced by everyone in the law enforcement community, no matter how much they talked about looking forward to getting out.

No, he knew the answer. Almost three decades of giving his all to his country – the danger, grueling travel, an absence of children and in the end, an unhappy marriage – was finally over. Now just shy of his forty-ninth birthday, ahead of David lay a life of quiet, a pace that would be decided by him, not the national climate. Kayaking and fishing and a house in Alaska that was completely paid-for, thanks to the bitter blessing of a lawsuit settlement.

Quiet. Outdoor activities and life on his own terms. *Yeah, right.*

Dressed in the black tactical gear of the Secret Service's uniformed division, wearing a black ball cap with the letters *ERT* (Emergency Response Team) sewn in yellow stitching on the front, David stood at a concrete parapet atop an eight-story office building overlooking Key Plaza in downtown Cleveland. A *Sierra Team* leader, the call-sign for Secret Service counter-sniper teams, he scanned the scene below with a pair of binoculars. At forty-eight he was still in excellent shape, the first traces of gray only now showing up at the temples of his close haircut. Working in sun and all sorts of elements had weathered his skin, adding to the crinkles at the corners of his eyes.

It was approaching ten o'clock, and POTUS was scheduled to arrive within the hour. David lowered the binoculars, smiling briefly at the clear sky and pleasant weather.

Positioned around the plaza were five Sierra teams, or two-man shooter positions. Each had a high-powered rifle with an enormous scope, its front end supported on a snap-out bipod. One of the two men (the shooter) would keep an eye pressed to the rubberized end of the rifle optics while his partner (the spotter) swept the part of the plaza that was their responsibility with a small, telescopic sight of his own. The shooter teams commanded the high ground, positioned on rooftops in a rough square that covered every angle of the plaza, alternating between watching the crowd and sweeping across windows, looking for threats. The advance teams had already cleared and continued to check these buildings, but they couldn't find everything. Someone might slip through. David King had shoot authority for all the Sierra teams, and if a window opened or a hostile showed themselves anywhere in the plaza, he would give the order to engage without hesitation.

In twenty years of federal law enforcement service David had been required to use his own weapon during three actual combat engagements in the field, killing four men and one woman, though he hadn't fired a single shot in anger during his time with the Secret Service. He'd been FBI for ten years before transferring over, and during that time spent most of his service in the bureau's elite *HRT,* the Hostage Rescue Team, SWAT-trained muscle for the FBI. The last decade with the Secret Service had been more varied. He'd run counterfeiting investigations, stood a post on a Vice President's Protective Detail, done four years with CAT, been a firearms instructor and eventually rose to supervisor in the uniformed division's Emergency Response Teams. A shooter once more. He never seemed to stray far from the rifle.

Three bank robbers. One domestic terrorist in an Amtrak station wearing an explosive vest. One crazy – the woman – in a Kansas City Social Security Office who had murdered a police officer and taken hostages. David didn't regret taking any of those shots (the woman up close and with a pistol), but he neither liked nor disliked combat. It had always just been *the job,* and he slept fine.

Except for the nightmares, a fairly recent development, and they were exclusively about Emily.

He keyed the radio handset clipped to the left shoulder of his combat vest, still watching the crowd below.

"Sierra-Three to all positions," David said. "Sitrep."

"Sierra-One clear," came a response.

"Sierra-Two clear," said another.

Four and five reported the same, but there was no response from Sierra-Six. They were on the same roof as him, and it was a short walk around the rooftop elevator and mechanical structure to reach them. Probably a bad radio.

He called in to *Shotgun,* the blacked-out motor home that was the Secret Service mobile command post, reporting that his positions were all clear, but number six was having comms issues and that he was checking on them now. As he crossed the roof, he looked down at a classic, layered defense.

The platform and podium where POTUS would appear was at the north end of the plaza. Members of the PPD, the Personal Protective Detail, were in position at the steel-barred barriers that ringed and put a twenty foot space between the platform and the crowd. More members of the PPD would surround the platform itself and remain close when the President took the stage. Out beyond the inner barrier, the Service's Uniformed Division in their white shirts maintained the perimeter. Access points to the plaza – streets, walkways and building entrances – were closed off and guarded, with strategic choke points put in place for crowd control. The two main access points for the public, at the far end away from the platform on the east and west, were also controlled by the uniforms (with ERT backup close by) who would screen for known faces and operate both the metal and chemical detectors. A pair of agents with radiation detectors concealed in backpacks constantly circled and moved through the plaza.

Parked on a sidewalk not far from the podium was a black Chevy Suburban with what appeared to be a curious-looking sunroof. This was CAT, the Counter Assault Team and the "Bad Boys" of the Secret Service, one of two such SUVs. The other would be mixed into the motorcade.

David smiled every time he saw the vehicle. He'd been one of them for four years.

Here in Cleveland, the CAT vehicle carried five highly trained combat operators, all dressed and armed for fast, tactical combat. In the event of a coordinated attack on POTUS, a single word from the team leader ("Left, Rear, Right") would instantly put the team into action and give them a direction. Their job was simple; engage and lay down a devastating amount of fire so that the Personal Protective Detail could evacuate the President. They were there to buy time for the PPD and put a serious hurt on anyone foolish enough to come at the Commander-in-Chief. Since their inception, CAT had never needed to engage in that manner in the field (the operators simply called it *"deploying."* There had been some close calls during overseas visits, though, with both POTUS in Korea and the VP in the Philippines.

Additional layers of security included local law enforcement, K-9 units and David's Sierra Teams, with the nearest U.S. military units on alert. The Secret Service's intelligence division had conducted threat evaluations and was tracking everyone who was known to harbor or was even suspected of hostile intent (an imperfect chess game where a great deal of coffee and Tums was consumed.)

Advance teams with their own K-9's had swept the area days in advance. There were escape routes and evacuation contingencies, safe houses and shelter points, medical units close at hand and hospitals on standby for a worst-case scenario. While the President was in the open, the armed and armored motorcade would be waiting nearby, surrounding the *Beast,* the chief executive's tank-like limousine. Air Force One, a back-up jet and both Marine helicopters would be waiting to whisk the President away in the event of an evacuation, and a Black Hawk filled with ERT operators would be floating overhead, just out of view but ready to roar in and lay down fire.

No man in history was ever better protected than the current President of the United States. And yet everyone in the Secret Service existed in a mild but constant state of anxiety and fear. It kept them sharp, and a touch of paranoia was not only a part of the job, but an essential element to successfully carrying out the protective assignment.

Cleveland crowds were filling the plaza below, their excited conversations drifting up to the Sierra Teams as a low buzz. David checked his watch. Forty minutes to arrival. He pushed thoughts of the two days until retirement and a dead wife out of his head. He was still operational and needed to focus on the job, starting with his out-of-contact sniper team just around the corner ahead.

-13-

DEVIL DOG

Cleveland, Ohio – October 28

INBOUND

The twelve vehicles of *Bamboo* rolled through Cleveland at thirty mph along an approach route that had been cleared of traffic, with squad cars and yellow barricades blocking every side street. Crowds lined the sidewalks, waving and cheering, people turning out to catch the rare sight of a presidential motorcade, hoping for a glimpse of the man himself.

A police escort of two squad cars and a pair of motorcycle cops led the procession, followed by a Lincoln

Towncar full of Secret Service agents. Next came *Stagecoach,* the armored Cadillac limousine, lovingly known as the *Beast,* in which the President rode. An identical back-up limo followed, with a suburban carrying the second half of the CAT team close behind. This vehicle's rear hatch was open, and a counter-assault agent with a fully automatic rifle poked his weapon out through the opening as he watched behind the SUV. This was the muscle car of the motorcade. *Halfback* was next, another Suburban full of agents, and finishing off the column was an ambulance followed by another pair of Cleveland Police units.

"Nice turnout," said Thomas Barrow, looking out the window at the excited crowds. He rapped his knuckles against the armored glass. "Vote Republican."

Seated across from him, Garrison looked up from his speech, now covered in hand-written notes. It had been decided that he would not lower a window in order for the people to get a look at him. Cleveland wasn't necessarily considered a hostile city, but the supervisory agent of his detail had advised the President that there was a credible threat related to a local mosque with some extremist views. He told his boss not to worry, but also suggested that it was better to remain out of sight until they reached the venue. "Use the odds and let the bad guys try to guess which car you're in," had been his counsel. Garrison listened.

Along the sidewalks the President could see more than a few surgical masks, people not waiting for an executive order to take precautions. There was also more than the usual amount of protest signs, one depicting a grinning cartoon President Fox stabbing an outline of America with a trident.

Garrison was tired, but his Chief of Staff looked exhausted, his complexion pale with dark circles under his eyes. "When did you last sleep, Tommy?"

"I caught a nap on the plane."

The President tapped his friend's leg with the tip of a polished shoe. "You're full of shit. I didn't nap, and you were with me the whole time. You look like hell."

"Thank you, Mr. President. I'll catch up on my sleep after the election."

"When, in four more years?"

"Sounds about right. Although I'll be able to sleep a lot sooner if we don't win Ohio."

Garrison snorted. The media was tearing him up over this leak, and a White House press statement to allay the public's fears hadn't done much good. As early as seven o'clock this morning he'd been getting calls from "concerned" congressmen, the friendly ones full of advice and offering to consult, the opposition respectfully but pointedly demanding action, also wanting to be consulted. The talking heads on television were less charitable; many spouted acidic rhetoric and others were openly sarcastic and hostile. Even after four years as the chief executive, Garrison had yet to develop the thick skin professional politicians used to deflect these kinds of personal attacks. But then he'd never considered himself one of those. At his core he was just a former Marine who thought he could help the country he loved. He hadn't expected to gain the presidency, but now that he was here he was determined to be effective. Playing politics didn't enter into his decision not to move forward with the NRP. He had the welfare of the American people in mind, and remained convinced that the third phase of the plan would lead to panic and economic collapse and was the worst of two bad choices. Although Dr.

Rusk's fears were disconcerting (and he was quietly certain that she would find something) as of the briefing two hours ago there was still nothing new from the CDC.

"We're coming in, Mr. President," said a voice over the intercom, the speaker a front seat figure on the other side of the armored divider.

Bamboo slowed as the vehicles filed up a side street and into Key Plaza. They stopped, and once his Detail determined the area was clear, Garrison got out and was escorted to a ready area in the lobby of a building behind the stage. Thomas Barrow moved off to talk to someone, and an aide fussed over Garrison's suit and hair before Danny, his body man, ran her off. "You look fine, sir," he said, straightening the knot in the tie. "Squared away as always."

"Thank you, Sergeant," Garrison said, giving the younger man a wink.

Another staffer approached to tell him that in a few minutes he would meet Cleveland's mayor and the governor of Ohio. The two men, both endorsing his candidacy, would make brief remarks to the crowd before introducing him.

Then it would be show time.

KEY PLAZA

He was a computer salesman, part of his company's international division, and he found it ironic that both he and the President had been in Jakarta at the same time. He hadn't seen Fox when he was there, of course, but now the President had come to his home town. He was excited and had taken an early lunch in order to come to the rally. He wasn't particularly political, didn't care much about the issues (as long as his taxes didn't go up) but how often did a person get to actually see a President of the United States other than on television?

But now he was feeling like hell, sweating on a mild October day, a headache at the back of his skull and working its way forward. He couldn't stop swallowing, his mouth seeming to fill with saliva as soon as he cleared it. *Shit. I picked up a bug overseas.* He'd be forced to take days off, might miss his trip to Hong Kong. He'd have to see his doctor, but was having trouble remembering the man's name or even how to make an appointment.

As the mayor and governor wrapped up their remarks and the President took the stage to a swell of cheers and applause, the salesman blinked, his vision growing blurry. *He was certain he'd come here to see someone...who was it?*

What was happening to the salesman was being repeated around him in the crowd, others who had reached the end of Trident's incubation.

Just as Soo Yim had done over the Pacific.

THE STAGE

Agent Sheffield stood behind and to the left of the President as he spoke, dressed in a dark suit and wearing sunglasses, just like the other men on the detail. He wasn't feeling well, but that was no surprise. The members of the PPD, also known as the *working shift,* kept the same hours and pace as POTUS (and then some) and the constant travel and preparation was bound to take a toll. He'd just have to muscle up and get through it. There was no other acceptable option.

His attention was currently focused on Brown and Atwell, the two agents positioned in front of the podium at the base of the stage, facing the crowd. Atwell was alternatively wiping his forehead and rubbing the back of his neck, and Brown was fidgeting, shifting from foot to foot. It was out of character for the two men, agents who were among the most disciplined Sheffield had ever known. At these events they were always menacing slabs of rock, their only movements the slow, constant swivel of their heads as they scanned for danger.

Sheffield blinked. *What had he been thinking about? And what was that irritating droning noise? Someone talking, or a small, private plane diving toward the plaza?* Even this thought didn't make him look up or alert in any way.

His eyes began to tear as his vision blurred.

THE PODIUM

"We have work to do," President Fox said into the microphone, his voice booming across the plaza. "We have to focus on our problems here at home while still maintaining a strong presence around the world."

Cheering greeted the statement.

"And we're doing it. The new jobs package, increasing veteran's benefits, providing for families and schools, pushing for greater research to make us less dependent upon foreign oil." Another pause for the cheering. "We've begun trade reform, reaffirmed our commitment to overseas allies through training and equipment, increased our naval presence around the Horn of Africa to combat piracy. We're on our way, but more must be done."

The crowd roared, and Garrison gave them a genuine smile, pleased by the response. Maybe they *could* win Ohio. He was about to move into the portion of his speech that was specifically directed at the state's steel industry, to give assurances that the federal government would be on their side when it came to unfair trade arrangements with the Chinese. As he waited for the last wave of applause to subside, he noticed the two agents below him in the front, Atwell and Brown. Brown was slowly drifting off-post to the right, and Atwell was walking straight toward the waist-high metal barricade that held the crowd back, picking up speed.

He hesitated, distracted. *Are they seeing a threat? What-?*

Atwell reached the barrier, now almost running, and grabbed a middle-aged woman waving a small flag. He sank his teeth into her shoulder, then used her body as leverage to pull himself over and into the crowd, bearing the woman to the ground.

Screaming erupted and people tried to scatter in the densely packed gathering. To the right, Agent Brown was crossing the barrier as well, attacking a man wearing a baseball cap. More screams split the air, coming from different points within the plaza – lots of points – and suddenly the entire mass seemed to be moving.

"Crash! Crash!" someone yelled to his right, and a second later Garrison was hit from that side with a near-tackle, his body thrown left as big arms swept him into a hug. It was LaBeau, a massive black man with a shaved head, the biggest agent on his detail bearing him toward the stairs on stage left. Sheffield, the other agent who should have joined the tackle at the cry of *Crash,* instead bared his teeth and grabbed onto LaBeau's arm as he passed, letting out a snarl. He bit at the big man's coat sleeve and tried to drag him down, but LaBeau threw an elbow, smashing Sheffield's nose and breaking him loose, not slowing as he lifted the President and launched down the stairs.

All around them, Secret Service agents were pinning screaming people to the ground, savaging them with hands and teeth, oblivious to the evacuation. Garrison's legs tried to keep up, but Agent LaBeau was a juggernaut, almost completely carrying him and accelerating. Gunfire cracked from somewhere behind them and then again to their left, and everywhere people were running, running.

A close shriek made Garrison look to the right, and he saw his Chief of Staff backed against a large window, flailing his arms as a presidential staffer and another agent clawed and bit and tore open his neck. Thomas Barrow's eyes widened in surprise as a scarlet jet of arterial blood shot across the glass behind him.

"Tommy," Garrison gasped.

The *Beast* was ahead of them, its rear door open and an agent standing nearby, his firearm out but dangling at the end of a limp arm as the man stumbled against the side of the limousine, holding his head with his other hand. More gunfire as the screaming climbed in octaves. LaBeau drove him toward the limo's rear door.

They were hit again from the side, someone in a suit who growled and snapped and clawed at them both. A groping finger went into Garrison's eye and he cried out. It was Danny the body man, Garrison's former Marine, now glassy-eyed with grayish drool spilling from his lips. Danny bit LaBeau in the ear, teeth crunching on cartilage and the plastic of a radio earpiece. The big agent didn't scream, only twisted the President away from the attack and tried to move forward, the weight of a second man now slowing him.

Another hit, this one from behind, Agent Sheffield who had caught up to them from the stage. The impact and mass of four struggling men took them all to the ground, and Garrison grunted and lost his breath as he hit with the other three on top of him. Out of the corner of his eye he saw Sheffield take a bite out of LaBeau's cheek, then his neck, and the big black agent let out an enraged roar. LaBeau twisted again, this time the pistol coming out of his holster, and he rammed the muzzle under Danny's chin and blew out the top of his head. The body man crumpled, falling away. The big agent heaved upward, rotating his body yet again while still holding onto the President, firing twice at point-blank range into Sheffield's chest. As the dead man slipped off to the side, LaBeau was on his feet once more, hauling Garrison up and moving him toward the open limo door.

The agent who had stumbled away along the Cadillac snapped his head around, his pistol clattering forgotten to the pavement, and rushed them with a mad howl. With one arm wrapped around the Commander-in-Chief, LaBeau shot him three times in the chest. Then he was shoving Garrison inside, scrambling in after him and slamming the heavy door, locking it.

"Drive!" LaBeau bellowed, his voice carrying through the closed divider, and the agent behind the wheel hit the gas. The grille threw a pair of running bodies aside as the heavy Cadillac accelerated and swung left toward the side street that would take them out of the plaza. LaBeau pushed Garrison to the floor as he spoke rapidly into his wrist mic, ignoring both a cheek and an ear that hung in bloody flaps, crimson spreading across his white shirt from the neck wound.

The black Suburban of the CAT team shot in front of the *Beast,* moving left to right with agents sticking automatic weapons out its windows and a circular roof hatch split down the window springing up and back in two half-moons. A pintle-mounted mini-gun slid up and out with an agent in black tactical gear standing behind it. Then they were out of sight, and a second later there was the deadly *whirr* and stutter of the mini-gun going into action.

The *Beast's* grille thumped again – something wet sprayed across the windshield – as it rocketed out of Key Plaza and into the streets of Cleveland.

THE BEAST

With only a few exceptions, Agent LaBeau among them, every member of Garrison Fox's Personal Protective Detail, advance teams, support teams and civilian and military entourage contracted Trident in Indonesia on day-one, when Soo Yim drank of Tapak's dark gift and began quickly passing it along. LaBeau had missed the trip, staying behind to attend his mother's funeral in Memphis. He hadn't picked up Trident until day-three of the spread, so his incubation was running behind the others. And just like they had been (until now) he was asymptomatic.

That changed with the very first bite, the one from Danny that had left his ear a bloody ribbon. Danny's now-active Trident organism transmitted instantly with the bite, awakening a dormant virus three days early.

Even as they were leaving the plaza, LaBeau started to shake from the chills, and a headache erupted at the base of his skull and quickly rushed over the top and into his eyes.

SHOTGUN

Special Agent Sanders, the coordinator and supervisor for all Secret Service operations at the Cleveland event, stood in the front of the USSS Mobile Command Center, a black motor home with tinted glass that sat parked at the rear of the plaza. Two other agents were in here with him, frantically working communications consoles. An agent on the speaker's platform had called *crash,* and what should have been a swift, well-orchestrated response to an *AOP* – Attack on Principle – was instead degenerating into chaos.

According to what Sanders was hearing on the radio as well as what he'd seen with his own eyes, CAT was deploying into the crowd, its mini-gun chopping down what had to be hostiles in order to provide cover for the *Beast.* The President was reported to be aboard with his driver and a wounded agent, heading for exit route number two and the secure area at Cleveland Hopkins International Airport where *Angel* was waiting. Marine One had gone airborne for a pick-up, and the Black Hawk carrying the Secret Service ERT was overhead, tracking the fleeing limo. Radio traffic clogged the airwaves, and the supervisory agent's two communications men were trying to keep up with it all.

But the wheels were coming off.

The only agent from the President's Personal Protective Detail he could contact was LaBeau, racing away in *Stagecoach* with POTUS. None of the other agents were responding.

After a violent burst of emergency calls from units stationed around the perimeter and the report of "engaging" from a single Sierra team, there had been nothing. There was also no response from any of the agents positioned out at Air Force One, and similar silence from the crews of the aircraft itself, as well as its sister plane. Other than the chatter coming from the two responding helicopters and the *Beast*, the only USSS voice out there came from a lone agent positioned somewhere between the plaza and the airport, shouting into his radio that the extraction route was compromised and for the *Beast* to switch to an alternate. His voice was cut short by a scream before he could identify *which* route was compromised.

Sanders tried to get him back, but it was the agent's final transmission.

"Cement Mixer is on," one of the communications men announced. The supervisory agent was about to move to the console when he noticed two things outside the big front window of the motor home that froze him in his tracks. The first was that the nearby press corps bus was being overrun by frenzied, bloody figures. News anchors and White House correspondents were caught against the metal sides and torn apart as raving figures scrambled up through the open door, pursuing their prey inside. Sanders saw the bus shaking, and bloody hands streaking the windows from inside.

More startling than that, not twenty feet from the mobile command post, he saw a Navy officer shuffling across the lawn of the plaza, moving aimlessly, a steel briefcase handcuffed to one wrist. It dangled on its chain, twisting and bumping against his leg.

"Shit! Fumble, fumble!" Sanders grabbed one of his comms men by the shoulder and pointed at the Navy officer. "Go get the football!"

Without hesitation the agent bolted out of his seat and shot out the side door. Sanders watched him make the short run across the grass, then turned back to the console where the Director of Homeland Security's face filled one of the screens.

"We're *black,* Mr. Secretary," Sanders said. "POTUS is in our control but is not secure. Comms are failing and his Detail is unresponsive, assumed fully compromised. *Angel* is not responding. We're working on an air evac with Marine One."

In the White House Situation Room, Bob Chase looked grim. "I'm initiating *Bank Vault."*

Immediately the supervisory agent pointed to his remaining comms man and directed him to put it out. A moment later the agent was calling to all USSS units, *"Bank Vault, Bank Vault."*

On screen, Chase shook his head. "Things are coming apart here, too. There's gunfire in the White House, and we're locked down. No one is responding at Service headquarters, and we can't…"

He never finished the sentence. Special Agent Sanders saw a Marine in his dress blues appear behind the Homeland Security Director, eyes glassy, mouth hung open and drooling. The Marine pulled Bob Chase from his chair before Sanders could even shout a warning, then killed the Cabinet Secretary with his hands and teeth.

Sanders recoiled from the screen, failing to notice that his remaining comms man was leaning his head against the console, sweating and shuddering, staring at nothing. The roar of the CAT's mini-gun made him dart to the front window again, and although from this angle he couldn't see the counter assault team or what they were firing at, he did see the agent he'd sent outside.

The man was flat on his back in the grass, the Navy officer straddling him and ripping the man's insides out through a horrible stomach wound, cramming them into his mouth. The steel case containing the nuclear launch unit, the *Football,* still dangled from its handcuff.

"Mother of God…" said Sanders, reaching for his sidearm.

He never made it. The giggling communications agent behind him saw to that.

SIERRA-3

David King rounded the corner of the rooftop structure, expecting to see his two-man shooter position in place, the men kneeling behind a rifle propped on the concrete parapet and a spotting scope. The rifle was there, but the shooter was standing upright next to it, arms limp at his sides as he stared down at the plaza. The spotter was twenty feet away, sitting with his legs splayed, gripping the sides of his head and drooling between his knees.

David stopped cold.

The shooter made a grunting sound and moved forward, going right off the roof, knocking his rifle over the side as he went.

"No!" David shouted, running to where the man had been. Then someone shouted, *"Crash! Crash!"* over the secure radio channel, and below him thousands of people were instantly in motion. From his high vantage point he had a wide view of the entire plaza, and his first impression was that of a stampeding herd on the African savannah. Barriers were tipped over, people began screaming as bodies crushed against each other, trampling the slow to react. Over the radio, one of his positions called, "Engaging," even as he swung his binoculars toward the presidential podium.

The crack of gunfire came from half a dozen locations below, and he grabbed his radio handset. "All positions, this is Sierra-3, you are green to engage." He didn't know where the attack was coming from, but it was underway and he wasn't going to make his teams wait for individual permission to fire. They had eyes on the scene, and would know what to do. One of them already had.

None of his positions acknowledged the order however, and other than a single sniper calling engaging followed by the boom of a sniper rifle, there was nothing more.

He couldn't even start to process what had happened with the two men at Sierra-Six, one still sitting in a drooling daze on the roof and the other now broken down on the sidewalk in front of the building. David snapped up his binoculars and looked to the podium. There he saw an agent he knew, LaBeau, shoving POTUS into the rear of the *Beast,* a trail of fallen bodies behind him. The CAT vehicle crossed the limo's path, and an agent already in the roof turret, swinging up the 7.62mm mini-gun (a modern day version of the Gatling gun that could fire between two and six thousand rounds per minute) opened up on a crowd of civilians rushing toward the stage. He swung his weapon left to right with devastating effect. David could see clouds of pink mist as high velocity, heavy caliber slugs shredded human bodies.

The presidential limousine made a turn and accelerated out of sight, chased by a single Cleveland Police car with its lights and sirens going. David radioed to the mobile command post that POTUS was away, CAT was deploying and that he had zero comms with his Sierra teams. There was no response. Even as he was calling *Shotgun,* Special

Agent Sanders was being devoured inside the motor home by one of his own men.

David cursed. He had no rifle! There was nothing he could do from up here with only his sidearm except watch events unfold and make radio transmissions that no one was answering. Below him the chaos escalated as many in the crowd began turning on their fellow spectators, ripping and biting, chasing down those who tried to get away. Sirens howled, gunfire popped from all directions and thousands of terrified people fled in waves to escape the madness that had erupted in Key Plaza. Maimed and twisted bodies littered the lawns and sidewalks in their wake.

The sniper team leader saw the counter assault vehicle slow and drift to a stop against the rim of a small fountain. The driver's door swung open and a SWAT-clad figure stumbled out, holding his head in both hands and staggering away. In the turret, the agent who had been firing the mini-gun suddenly vanished into the hatch, as suddenly as if he'd been snatched down a rabbit hole.

Over the secure radio channel Agent LaBeau's vaguely slurred voice said, "*Stagecoach* is diverting to route three. We are fully defensive and heading to *Angel,* but *Angel* gives no response. All agents, collapse onto the airfield." The transmission was followed by the man's deep voice letting out a short giggle.

David King acknowledged and ran for the rooftop door, pulling his pistol. What he had already seen reminded him that everyone was now a potential hostile, even other agents. He elbowed through the door and launched down the stairs.

He did not see what happened in the plaza. Among all those fallen bodies, those who had been wounded by their fellow man but not killed outright began rising to their feet. They moved off in every direction, slowly at first, eyes cloudy and grayish drool slipping past their lips, then moving faster.

They joined in the killing at once.

-14-

DANCER and DESIGN

Twenty thousand feet – October 28

Patricia Fox sat in the rear of the large, private jet facing her daughter in the seat across from her. The First Lady was dressed in a smart, red suit, a classy-looking middle-aged woman with shoulder-length chestnut hair and good skin. Considered lovely by any standards, she knew she could not begin to match her daughter's beauty. At twenty-two, Kylie Fox could easily have been a highly successful, professional fashion model. The Secret Service had given her the codename *Dancer* because she had been a cheerleader at UVA, and had the physique to prove it (and the brains to contradict the stereotype.) Not only did she have an enviable figure and her mother's perfect skin, she also had the most captivating blue eyes her mother had ever seen, and that was an objective observation, not simply because she was her daughter. Kylie's hair was the same color as her mother's, thick and glossy, hanging about her shoulders in natural curls. She wore designer boots and jeans, a top cut a little too low (in her mother's opinion, certainly her father's) and a short, brown leather jacket.

Attitude influences beauty, though, her mother thought. *Not so pretty at the moment.*

Kylie's arms were crossed and she was glaring at Patricia. "You heard me. I said bullshit."

Patricia sighed. "What part's bullshit? That you're being made to go to Ohio, or what your father and I think about Trey?" That was the nickname Terrence Weaver used, Kylie's boyfriend. Patricia even disliked using his name.

"Both," said Kylie. "I'm not part of all this." She waved a hand, indicating the plane full of staffers and Secret Service agents. "Daddy doesn't need to parade me around to win this election."

"Whether you like it or not, you're part of this family. And besides, you know it's not like that. You're not doing any press. He just wants to see you."

"Yeah, right. And the photo op with his smiling, perfect family will just *accidentally* happen. I've been through this before. And why isn't Devon coming?"

"Your brother has been to the last two of your father's events. You took a pass both times. Now it's your turn, and your dad misses you." Patricia resisted the urge to cross her arms to match her daughter's defiance.

"You don't have any idea how busy I am," said Kylie. "It's grad school, and it's Harvard. The pace is faster. I don't have time for this."

Patricia did appreciate how packed Kylie's schedule was, and that Harvard was a high-pressure, unforgiving environment. But they were a family first, and in this bizarre world of the presidency she was doing everything she could to maintain at least a measure of normalcy. Seeing his daughter was important to Garrison, who suffered from the same parental guilt as his wife. He adored the girl, who, despite all he said and did, couldn't seem to grasp how much he loved her, the pride he felt for his first-born. Frankly, Patricia was surprised she'd gotten the girl onto the plane.

"It's just for the day. We'll have dinner with him in Cleveland, and you can fly back to Boston tomorrow. Or even late tonight if you like."

Kylie looked away, glowering out the window.

"I think you need to be a little more understanding," said Patricia.

Kylie's head snapped back, and she turned that glower on her mother. "Like you and daddy are about Trey?"

Patricia wanted to snap back that Kylie was acting like a spoiled child, a petulant teenager who wasn't getting her way and so lashed out at everyone around her, no matter who she hurt. She didn't, was able to control her temper – barely – and resisted an immediate comeback. Still her brow creased as she frowned. Terrence Weaver had been seeing their daughter for only a couple of months now, but already he'd had a serious (and in Patricia's opinion negative) effect on her. Patricia doubted it was love, didn't know if it was the sex but was almost certain that the relationship was some childish *screw-you* to get back at her parents in retaliation for whatever millennial angst they had inflicted on the poor child. It made her ill, and it frustrated her that this young woman, a *grown* woman, was behaving like an obnoxious thirteen-year-old. Kylie was too old, and too smart for this nonsense. Although Kylie had never concealed the fact that she was resentful and unhappy about how her father's role had impacted her life, she'd always been either calmly articulate about her objections or simply quiet and distant, throwing herself into her studies and doing her best to ignore the many restrictions circumstances placed upon her. This regression in maturity was a new development. Patricia didn't wonder at its source.

Also a grad student, Trey was an angry young man who was vocal about his opinions and politics and completely at odds with everything for which her husband stood. Not just vocal; toxic. Trey used words like *fascist, tyrant* and *warmonger, right-wing elitist* and *racist,* all the trendy, inflammatory favorites the Left liked when referring to the opposing party. He was also a blogger, spewing his radical views to anyone who would read them and – also in Patricia's opinion – using his relationship with the First Daughter as legitimacy in promoting his agenda.

The Secret Service was digging into his background and monitoring him closely. Patricia had no objections.

"Your father and I respect your choices, Kylie. We know you're an adult. But we also want you to make up your own mind about things, not simply parrot what someone else is saying."

Kylie smirked. "Do you know how hypocritical that sounded? Especially in this family? Besides, it comes down to the fact that Trey doesn't like daddy's politics, and that makes him unacceptable to you both."

"He doesn't treat you well," Patricia said. "He's all about himself, and he talks *at* you, not to you. I've seen it. That's what's unacceptable."

"You don't know anything about us."

Patricia tried not to roll her eyes. It was like the trite script to a melodramatic teenager movie. And in fact Patricia knew Trey quite well, or at least his type. Terrence Weaver wanted everyone to agree with his rage so he would feel validated. Every conversation was shouted and bitter, and anyone who didn't share his righteous indignation was either a sympathizer with the opposition or one of its crafters. There was no attempt to see another point of view. She believed in his right to an opinion, to give voice to unpopular ideas – that was America, and she supported that right as strongly as her husband – but she was still a mother and a person. The first and only time Patricia Fox had met the boy, Trey had offered his condolences that she was married to a man who intentionally hurt minorities and the poor. She'd wanted to slap him at the time, and remembered the smug look on his face. Her own expression must not have been well-concealed, because he followed up with, "What, are you going to pull a Clinton and make me disappear?"

Patricia had steamed, an ugly part of her thinking that Trey was probably lucky he *wasn't* speaking this way to Bill or Hillary.

"And I do make my own decisions," Kylie was saying. "You've just never given him a chance."

"Never? He's only been around for a few weeks."

Again Kylie looked away. "You don't know," she said to the window.

The First Lady crossed her legs and now her arms as well. Her daughter hadn't used the word *bitch,* but she'd have no trouble with it when she was out of her mother's presence. Patricia couldn't argue. It was the word she wanted to use as well.

In the cockpit of the First Lady's jet, both the pilot and co-pilot were having trouble focusing. During the forty-five minutes since lifting off from Boston, both had developed headaches and chills, and now their faces glistened with sweat.

"I feel like shit," said the co-pilot, looking over. He was pale with darkening circles around his eyes.

The pilot nodded. "Me, too." An Air Force lieutenant colonel, he was the regular pilot for FLOTUS, the First Lady of the United States, and the responsibility of safely transporting her, or any member of the First Family, was something he took seriously. Protocol demanded that if either pilot (especially both) were feeling unwell, the aircraft was to land immediately.

But the pilot was having trouble remembering *any* procedures, and the multitude of controls, switches and gauges were starting to lose their significance.

He strained against the disconnected feeling, bearing down in an attempt to think straight. It helped a little. "I'm declaring an emergency," he told his co-pilot. "I'll call it in, you let the Detail know and then get back here."

The co-pilot sat there blinking, palming away sweat and shuddering. After a moment he rose with a dull expression and headed for the cockpit door.

Special Agent Alexander, a woman with eleven years in the Secret Service and the senior agent in the First Lady's Detail, pressed a finger against her earpiece and asked for the radio transmission to be repeated. She would have paled, but she already was, her body shaking with chills and a headache pounding behind her eyes and at the back of her skull.

"Copy that," she said when the information came again, then switched to the Detail frequency so all the agents aboard, Design and Dancer's both, would hear her. "Alexander. We have an AOP on Devil Dog, and we're initiating *Bank Vault.*" Then she rose from her seat and headed back to the First Lady and her daughter, supporting herself with seat backs as she went, not due to any movement from the plane but because of how she was feeling; dizzy, weak, disoriented and sick to her stomach. The First Lady looked up when the female agent stopped at her seat.

"Mrs. Fox," the agent said softly, "there's been an attack on POTUS in Cleveland. He's being…evacuated now. The White House…has ordered that… we initiate *Bank Vault.*"

Patricia Fox had heard the term before, vaguely remembered it from a briefing, but at the moment it meant nothing. Only her husband mattered. Her complexion suddenly matched her bodyguard's pallor. "Is he alive? Has he been wounded?"

Agent Alexander just stared at her. Past her. Through her.

"Alexander!" Patricia said sharply. "Is he hurt?"

The other woman shook her head slowly. "We…don't know… We're going to be…diverting." Her eyes swam out of focus, and she shook her head again, blinking, wiping at the sweat beading on her forehead. Alexander moved back up the aisle. She should be talking to headquarters for instructions. She should have been able to remember all their alternate landing locations along their route across Massachusetts, New York State and Pennsylvania. She should be talking to the agents on Design and Dancer's Details.

None of that was happening, because she was suddenly struggling to remember where she was. And none of the other agents on board were asking questions or even responding to the fact that she had announced an AOP. They were all either staring at nothing or holding their heads in their hands.

The cockpit door opened, the co-pilot standing in the doorway, blinking. Then he snarled and rushed Agent Alexander with his fingers hooked into claws, just as the aircraft banked hard to the right, throwing everyone against their seatbelts and the starboard bulkhead.

D*on't crash, don't crash...* The pilot repeated the words in his head like a mantra, squinting and forcing himself to pay attention to yoke and rudder, altitude and airspeed. He gripped the yoke so hard his knuckles cracked, while his body shook violently with the chills and sweat streamed down his neck, into his collar. His vision blurred in and out. *Don't crash, please, God, don't crash...*

Somewhere within cloudy thoughts that wanted to fog over completely, he knew he was supposed to be using the radio. Had he done so already? What was it he needed to say? He couldn't remember, only knew that he needed to put this plane on the ground. Hanging onto bits of lucid thought that were tattering by the moment – a battle he knew he was about to lose, and wouldn't that be a relief? – he continued his steep descent. *Cut airspeed. Decrease altitude. Landing gear down.* His right hand worked the controls by muscle memory alone, and there followed a loud bump and a hydraulic whine from below.

Screaming and savage growls came from the main cabin beyond the open cockpit door, the terrified cries of penned animals during a thunderstorm. The noises had no meaning for the pilot, who leaned forward in his seat, still squinting. A body thudded to the floor in the doorway. The pilot didn't notice.

The Gulfstream's wings dipped left and then right, the aircraft drifting side to side as the green and brown earth reached up for it.

The pilot began making a high, keening sound as he fought for control, not only of the jet but of his own body and awareness. He cut back on the throttle, barely noticing the ripping sound of treetops scraping the lowered wheels and white belly of the screaming plane as it came in too fast. A large green square appeared beyond the windshield.

Field. Too short. Trees.

He cut speed further, leveling the wings, feeling the bottom drop away from him as gravity took hold of an aircraft no longer moving fast enough to maintain flight. Then like the flick of a switch, the only things the pilot understood were the needs to kill and feed.

First Lady Patricia Fox had a bloody nose and was trying to tuck herself into a protective ball on the carpeted floor between the seats. There were splashes of red everywhere, bodies thrashing in the tight cabin and ungodly screams and snarls making her ears hurt. She was sure she heard her Chief of Staff Maria screaming, thought she heard Kylie doing the same, but didn't know where they were. All she did know was that she was about to die.

An agent from her own Detail was on her, clawing and snapping his teeth. His eyes were glazed and distant, seeing not his protective charge, only prey.

Patricia felt the plane shudder, the nauseating way it sagged left and right, heard the engines screaming outside and the sickening plunge of what could only be a freefall. She uncoiled from her ball and tried to fight off the agent, knowing a crash was coming at any second. Impact and fire. She knew she'd never feel it, not because it would be so sudden but because she would be torn apart before it happened. The agent was bigger and stronger, and now he had her by the shoulders, pulling her toward him even as his drooling, snapping mouth rushed in.

She let out a scream as she tried to push him away, her hands trying unsuccessfully to force his bulk away, and then one hand slipped off his chest and went into his jacket. Patricia felt that hand now touching the grip of a holstered pistol, and her eyes widened.

Being a Marine family, there had always been guns in the house, and Garrison Fox had insisted they all learn to shoot, both handguns and rifles. Even at an early age both kids had been taught gun safety, care and cleaning and proper shooting stances. Before their busy lives and the turmoil of Garrison's first term as President made getting together so difficult, they had often gone to the range as a family.

In all her plunking at paper targets, Patricia Fox had never expected to turn her skills on another human being. Although she was a fair marksman, at this range she didn't need to be. Just as her attacker's teeth came in at her face, close enough for her to smell his sour breath, she ripped the handgun from its holster, rammed the muzzle against the madman's chest and pulled the trigger three times in quick succession.

The agent's heart exploded out his back in pieces.

And the Gulfstream went down.

-15-

DARK HORSE

The Harrison School, Vermont – October 28

He's going to use his bishop, Devon thought. *Threaten my queen. He doesn't see it coming.* He looked at the chessboard, one of ten lined up in a row in the event hall. Groups of teachers, parents and students both from here and the competing Winston Scott Academy stood back and watched quietly as pairs of boys in their school uniforms faced off across ten small tables.

Devon, playing black, stared at the pieces, seeing how it would all unfold. Normally he thought seven moves ahead, but at this point he only needed to think about four. Checkmate and victory was that close.

You're not paying attention to the knights. Too focused on your own attack. Too aggressive. You're not protecting the flanks. The kid could have his queen, and Devon had moved her intentionally to be attractive bait. It was his knights that would prove to be the kid's downfall.

"Devon Fox employs his knights with surgical precision," the school newspaper recently said in an article that Devon was certain had been read by only a handful of geeks like himself. This talent was the source of his Secret Service code name. His chess coach, however, frequently warned him that he was overly dependent upon his knights, making his strength also his weakness. He didn't care. Not today, anyway. It was good enough to finish off this kid.

Devon looked up at his opponent, a pale, narrow Asian boy with an intense expression. He'd been introduced at the start of the match – he'd seen the kid at other events but had never played him – but already he'd forgotten his name. The boy was sweating and squinting at the board, looked as if he hadn't slept. He was trembling, too.

Got you scared, don't I? You should have gotten more rest last night. In contrast, Devon was fresh and feeling good. This win would move him to the semi-finals.

The Asian kid's hand hovered for a moment, then he moved his bishop into a position where he would, without fail, capture Devon's queen on the next move.

Devon concealed a grin, and immediately moved one of his knights. "Check." It was over at this point. The kid would be forced to move his king – knights couldn't be blocked by an interposing piece – and then Devon would bring in his second knight in the final move for checkmate.

The kid really began to tremble now, his entire body shuddering like a disaster survivor pulled from icy water, and he closed his eyes as sweat ran down his temples and along the bridge of his nose to bead at the tip. A shaky hand reached out, poised over his king.

Tip it over, Devon thought. *It's all you can do.*

Then the hand jerked, sweeping half the pieces off the board to clatter across the floor. Devon looked up sharply. *Jesus, a temper tantrum won't-*

The Asian kid's eyes were locked on him, glossy and dark. His lips peeled back to reveal small, white teeth, and the rumble of a growl came from somewhere deep in his chest.

What the...?

The kid launched across the chessboard, reaching as he let out an unhuman cry. Devon shoved away from the table so violently that his chair tipped and suddenly he was on his back, hitting so hard that his head bounced off the floor with a numbing thud. Snarling, the kid scrambled over the table and was on him at once. Devon kicked at the boy's chest, trying to keep him away as he crab-crawled backward, his vision blurring from the impact, feeling like he was moving in slow motion. Somewhere in the hall a woman screamed, then a man.

The Asian kid got a grip on Devon's school tie and pulled himself forward, tangled for an instant in the legs of the overturned chair. The other hand swiped at Devon's face, trying to claw with fingernails. A thin, gray drool spilled from the boy's lips. Devon tried to kick at the boy's face, actually landed a blow with the heel of his dress shoe, right in the nose, but his attacker didn't seem to feel it. Now lots of people were screaming, and within it was growling that wasn't coming from the Asian boy.

There was a sharp, metallic *SNAP*.

Agent Handelman was there standing over them, his collapsible steel ASP baton now fully extended and raised. With a brutal, downward swing he cracked Devon's opponent across the base of the skull, rocking the head forward.

The kid kept coming, eyes locked on his prey, teeth snapping.

CRACK! CRACK! Two more blows, the second one accompanied by the sickening sound of bone fracturing. Then blood was flowing down the Asian boy's neck and he was sagging, eyelids fluttering and still feebly pawing at Devon. The Secret Service agent kicked the kid hard, knocking him off Devon and onto the floor, and then a strong hand was gripping the collar of Devon's jacket and hauling him to his feet, pulling him close.

Handelman dropped the ASP and shouted into his wrist mic. "AOP Dark Horse!" Then to Devon, "Stay close to me!" He pulled his sidearm and with one hand still clamped on Devon's collar, started running through a room full of brawling people, the air pierced by snarls and death screams.

The fifteen-year-old stayed close as ordered. He didn't have a choice. His bodyguard had shifted his grip from the jacket collar to Devon's neck – an almost painful hold – in order to control and steer the boy. All around them, everyone seemed to be moving, and Handelman used his own body as both a shield and a ram to charge through the chaos. Devon caught glimpses of horror; a girl in a plaid skirt and knee-high socks was savaging a teacher against a wall; two kids from his school were biting and tearing at a knot of parents trying to get out a fire exit; kids and adults alike were crying, wailing, even standing still and covering their eyes as teeth ripped into flesh and bodies fell.

Handelman dodged around an overturned table, shouldered a stumbling teacher aside and headed for a pair of large walnut doors that stood open and led into the rest of the event building. They were almost there when a shape appeared in the doorway, a slender figure in a Harrison School uniform, a boy with his mouth and hands wet with fresh blood. He sprinted toward them with glassy eyes, letting out a long wail through bared teeth, his hands coming up.

Devon recognized him. It was the thirteen-year-old from the dining hall, the gullible one who thought the Secret Service agent was Devon's personal killer.

Handelman confirmed it when he shot the boy twice in the chest, knocking him down and racing through the doors with Devon before the body even hit the floor.

The agent released his grip on his protectee in order to shift gun hands and use his wrist mic, the two of them running down a hallway now. "Shade One to Shade Mobile, AOP. Repeat, AOP. Extracting to location two." Doors flashed by on both sides, some of them open with screaming, fighting people beyond; professors and children suddenly thrust into life or death, hand-to-hand combat. Ahead was a pair of glass doors with sunlight streaming through them. They would lead to a parking lot, and emergency extraction point two for this building. The black Suburban carrying the Detail's two backup agents would be racing for that point after Handelman's broadcast, and would then whisk their principle to safety. The call of an AOP – Attack On Principle – would trigger the immediate notification of local police, the nearest Secret Service field office as well as HQ in Washington, and within minutes there would be both military and federal law enforcement helicopters in the air.

The glass doors were streaked by a sliding, bloody hand print, and the motionless body of a boy lay crumpled at their base. Handelman covered the body with his pistol and steered Devon around it and out the doors into the sunlight. Then he swept the parking lot, eyes and pistol muzzle moving together.

It was quiet. Nothing moved.

"They're not here," Devon said, looking through the lot for a black Suburban and seeing only parked cars. His heart was pounding, and he felt the urge to just start running.

"They're coming," said Handelman. He moved them to the right, behind the shelter of an ancient walnut tree growing close to the building. A teenager's long scream drifted across the parking lot from somewhere to the distant left, followed by what might have been the sound of breaking glass. "Shade Mobile, Shade One is at the extraction point. Where are you?" He began frowning.

Devon looked at him. "What's going on? Why aren't they here?"

"Shade Mobile, respond." The frown deepened.

"They're not coming, are they?" Devon said, his pulse quickening further.

"Nope," Handelman said, looking around. "Come on, and pick your feet up." On the run, he led them to the right down the sidewalk in front of the event hall, passing in and out of the shade thrown by more, sprawling walnut trees. Devon didn't need the agent's grip on his jacket collar; he had no trouble keeping up, and no desire to do otherwise. There was no time to think about what was happening, other than the fact that people were suddenly attacking and killing each other without warning. The only certainty was that he had to do exactly what Handelman said, and not trip and fall as they ran.

They reached the corner of the event hall, a point where two tree-lined streets intersected in front of stately brick buildings with many windows. Somewhere to their rear a girl began shrieking – *one of the girls come to watch a brother or classmate at the tournament?* – her voice high and wavering and then abruptly cut off. Down to the right, about two hundred feet away, they saw a pair of boys in school uniforms running across the street, a pair of teachers and another student in pursuit.

Handelman tugged on his collar and they ran at an angle across the intersection, away from the hunters. The agent kept an eye on them over his shoulder until they were out of sight. He nodded at the building in front of them. "That's Darby Hall, right?"

"Yes," Devon said as they reached the sidewalk. "It's the science building." He pulled against Handelman as the agent headed for the entrance. "Wait, it's Saturday, it's going to be locked."

"Then we won't use the front doors." He turned them left, and as they sped down the sidewalk they heard distant, frightened cries of boys from somewhere behind them. The hunters had caught up to their prey.

They ducked around the corner of Darby Hall and stopped in the shadows at the side of the building, pressing themselves against the brick. Handelman swept his pistol in every direction, looking for movement. When he saw none, he looked at the boy and squeezed his shoulder. "You okay?"

Devon nodded. "I'm good. Are you okay?"

Handelman grinned at his protectee's question. "Thanks for asking. I'm good, too." The man tried another transmission to Shade Mobile, but once again his backup didn't respond. "We need a phone," he said.

"Don't you have a cell?"

"Against regulations when we're on post. Potential distraction."

"They don't want you playing video games while you're working, huh?"

Handelman shook his head. "I'm more of a Netflix guy. Do you have your cell?"

"It's in my room." The Harrison School had very strict policies about when and where students could use or even carry their cell phones.

"Shame on us both for following the rules," Handelman said. He looked up at the building. "We're going to break in, find a land-line."

Despite what was happening and the horrors he'd seen, Devon couldn't hold back his grin. They were going to break into a school building, and the Secret Service said it was okay. He couldn't possibly get in trouble for it.

Handelman took them down the side of the building, eyes roaming over the nearby parking lot and glancing regularly behind them. The place was dead, no sign of movement. Even though it was Saturday and many of the students as well as most of the faculty would be off-campus, it shouldn't be *this* empty. There should have been some activity.

Devon wasn't sure if the silence and absence of life was a good sign for them or not. His protector was thinking the same thing.

"Hey," Devon said, putting a hand on Handelman's arm, "instead of breaking in, couldn't we just jump someone and take their phone? Everyone has one."

Handelman raised an eyebrow. "*Jump* someone? When did you start living the thug life, Dev?"

Devon blushed, but the agent gave his shoulder another squeeze. "I thought about doing that too. But cell phones all lock up automatically and we wouldn't have the code if we just took it from someone."

The boy felt a little better. "Borrow one, maybe?"

Handelman looked around again, lowering his voice. "I want to stay away from people right now. People who aren't like us."

"Secret Service and cops?"

"Kind of."

"You mean people who aren't crazy, goddamn freaks," Devon said. "I saw what they were doing."

"That's absolutely right, Dev. And we have no way of knowing when a person who looks normal is going to turn into one of those things." His eyes were still roaming. He tried to call the mobile back-up again but there was only dead air.

"It's the virus, isn't it?" Devon asked, his voice almost a whisper.

"That's a good bet. We can talk later once we're inside. Stay quiet and keep close, okay?"

Devon nodded that he would.

After checking the park-like area behind Darby Hall, a place of tall trees, sidewalks and benches, as well as a small parking area where a campus maintenance pickup truck was parked near some Dumpsters, they headed out. Both ran in a crouch the way people did in combat, Handelman out of training and experience, Devon Fox out of instinct. They hurried like a pair of rats keeping close to a wall, their senses bristling as they searched for hostile movement and sound. But to them, at this point *hostile* seemed the new normal.

There were plenty of windows in the building, but even at the ground floor they were too high even for Handelman, as tall as he was. He kept them moving, and soon came to a fire exit. On this side it was a smooth slab of painted steel, without a handle or a window to break, and thus of no use to them.

A distant scream floated through the air, a man or a woman, and as if a warning of things to come, it made Handelman move faster.

Just beyond the fire door, however, they found what they needed; a dark green metal, industrial air conditioner unit with a fan set in the top protected by a grille. It was partially concealed within a row of hedges growing against the side of the building. A ground floor window was set in the bricks directly above it. The Secret Service agent took another look around the area, then scrambled up onto the unit, cupping his hands against the glass and peering inside.

"Stay back," he ordered Devon, then cocked back an elbow and smashed the window. Handelman used the barrel of his pistol to clear away blades of glass still hanging in the frame, then shrugged out of his suit jacket and draped it over the sill. "Come on up," he told the boy. "Be careful not to cut yourself climbing through. I'm right behind you."

Devon did as he was told. He avoided the broken glass and a moment later the agent was inside with him. Handelman tried unsuccessfully to shake his jacket free of glass fragments, gave up and tossed it over a nearby chair. Devon saw that the shoulder holster stretched across the man's back had a pair of handcuffs clipped beneath one arm, and on the other side hung twin leather cases holding spare pistol magazines. The armpits of Handelman's white dress shirt were ringed with sweat.

They were inside a classroom with two dozen chairs pulled up in pairs to twelve, black-surfaced tables, all facing a lectern with a large dry-erase board mounted to the wall behind it. Colorful posters around the room depicted human anatomy in various forms, and in the corner stood a complete human skeleton with every bone numbered in white digits. Some joker had knotted the striped blue and gray tie of the school uniform around the skeleton's neck. It might even have been the teacher who did it, Devon thought. Some of them were pretty cool.

"This isn't one of your classrooms," Handelman said in a soft voice.

Devon wasn't sure why he was whispering. The noise from the breaking window probably could have been heard throughout the building. Still, he matched the man's tone. "No, I don't take anatomy until next year."

"There's no phone in here. Where do the science professors keep their offices?"

"Second floor," said the boy, "like in the other buildings. Hey, I thought you had all these floorplans memorized."

Handelman snorted. "It's a big campus. Give me a break, will you?"

They slipped out of the classroom, pausing to listen in the hallway, then moved toward a flight of stairs. The building was silent except for their footsteps. Upstairs they found a door with a brass plate set in its face reading, *Prof. A. Martin.*

It was locked.

Handelman threw his shoulder and his weight into it, splintering the frame near the knob. The crash echoed throughout the halls. Inside, the agent closed the door as best he could and moved to a desk that sat amid towering clutter; books, charts, wooden file cabinets piled with files and more books.

"Stay behind me," Handelman said, "and stay away from the window." Then he punched an unlit line on the desk phone and dialed the number for the tiny field office in Burlington.

No answer. Only a recorded message.

He dialed 9-1-1. Again an automated voice, this one asking him to please hold the line.

Handelman punched in the number for USSS Headquarters in Washington, and made the connection on the first ring. A communications duty officer asked him for his name, federal law enforcement ID number, social security number and assignment code word. The agent provided the information, then finished with, "I'm the primary for Dark Horse. I have an attack on principle."

The duty officer peppered him with questions, which he answered. "My back-up team is not responding. Neither is local law enforcement, and I can't reach the field office. I have engaged hostiles. The principle is currently secure, but I can't say for how long." He gave his location and a summary of the situation.

The duty officer read back the information, then there was a long pause. "There's been an AOP on Devil Dog," he said. "And we've lost contact with Design and Dancer. We are at condition Black, agent."

"Copy," said Handelman, his voice tight.

"I'm dispatching assets to your location," the duty officer said. "Stay close to your phone if you can. We'll contact you with more info."

"I can't be sure we'll be here," Handelman said. "I may have to go mobile."

"Understood, agent. We're on our way."

"What now?" Devon asked once his bodyguard hung up the phone.

Handelman looked out the window for a moment, then took up a position near the door. “Now we wait for the good guys.”

-16-

DEVIL DOG

Cleveland, Ohio - October 28

The heavy, supercharged Cadillac limousine tore through the streets of Cleveland, streets that had previously been cleared and closed off to all traffic but the presidential motorcade, but were now avenues of chaos, destruction and slaughter. The driver, trained in tactical driving by the CIA and in protective measures by the Secret Service (though if it ever came to the point where he would have to engage targets, then things would have gone very wrong – as they seemed to be now) slewed the big car left and right, accelerating and braking, rubbing fenders and door panels against vehicles stopped at angles in the street, even clipping a fire hydrant that left a four-foot gash in the limo's armored side.

A powerful engine thrummed beneath the hood, the touch of the gas pedal making the *Beast* leap forward like a race horse at the gate.

A wrecked squad car went by on the left.

A police motorcycle pinned beneath an overturned auto parts truck flashed by on the right.

People ran in the street, and other people – with their arms outstretched – ran after them. Several went to the pavement, their pursuers atop them and instantly ripping and feeding. The limo driver tried to avoid a middle-aged man chasing a screaming woman, but the man had no concern for the racing vehicle and ran right in front of it, despite the driver's swerve. The body hit with a sickening crunch and was thrown sideways, sparing the fleeing woman from his reaching arms.

It didn't matter. Out the side window the driver saw the woman run straight into a trio of people that killed her almost instantly.

The Cleveland PD squad car that had followed them out of the plaza was keeping up, staying close with its lights and sirens blasting. It tried twice to move into the lead position, the cop probably thinking he could clear the way, but the limo's driver wouldn't permit it. After what he had seen, he'd decided that he wasn't slowing down for anything or anyone – not even terrified pedestrians – and besides, the streets were getting too crowded for even one vehicle, much less another attempting to pass.

The dash-mounted radio crackled with a few panicked voices, not nearly as many as there had been only ten minutes ago, and nowhere near as many as there *should* have been. He needed both hands for the wheel, but a voice-activated mic clipped to the driver's lapel caught his transmission to the secure field where Air Force One was waiting.

"Angel One, this is *Stagecoach.* We're on extraction-two, inbound to your location, ten minutes out."

There was static, what might have been a voice, but no intelligible response.

The driver repeated his message, dodging a man in a dark suit (*was that agent Rickover?*) stumbling into the street, holding his head in his hands. In his side-view mirror the driver saw that the police car behind him did *not* manage to dodge, and took Rickover out at the waist with its front bumper, hurling him like a ragdoll across the street and painting the hood of the squad car red. The police unit swayed, fell back and almost lost it before the cop recovered and rejoined the pursuit.

Another call to Air Force One yielded nothing, so the driver radioed for *Gulfstream,* the identical back-up aircraft that traveled with her sister VC-25. No response there, either.

"Shotgun," the driver called, reaching out to the USSS mobile command center back at the plaza, *"Stagecoach* requesting immediate assistance, condition critical." Up ahead he saw an ambulance and two police cars blocking an intersection, a group of what had to be twenty civilians battling with the first-responders. The cops fired into the crowd, and the medics tried to scramble up onto the roof of their vehicle. All were pulled down.

The way ahead was blocked, no chance to get through.

"All posts," the driver broadcast, "extraction-two is compromised. Redirecting to extraction-three." He cut the wheel hard left just as he reached the emergency vehicles and the homicidal mob, tires screeching and the heavy car leaning into its suspension as it raced up a side street.

He hit the gas.

The chills and a painful headache hit him back.

Garrison simply couldn't lie on the floor between the seats anymore, and Agent LaBeau was in no condition to tell him otherwise. The President braced himself against the sudden maneuvers of the car and levered into the seat that faced backward, LaBeau in front of him. The agent was bleeding badly from numerous bite wounds, and now his bald, black head was beaded with sweat, his eyes taking on a hazy look.

Going into shock. The President squeezed the big man's knee. "Hang in there, LaBeau. We're almost out of here." He keyed the intercom so he could speak directly to the driver. "How far are we from Air Force One?"

"About five minutes, sir," came the tense reply.

Garrison left him alone to concentrate on his driving. Over LaBeau's shoulder, out the small tinted window at the rear of the limo, he could see the Cleveland police car weaving as it tried to keep up. The horrors the driver was seeing coming at them appeared to Garrison in reverse, retreating behind the limousine. New horrors followed the previous; people killing one another in the street, fleeing people falling to the pavement to be torn apart and…eaten.

Impossible. Something from a movie.

But he was seeing it.

Biological attack? Chemical warfare? Doctor Rusk's fears about Trident come to pass? He thought about his family. Were they safe? He had personally met with each member of their Secret Service Details, and the organization's Director had assured him that every man and woman in those teams would, without hesitation, lay down their lives to protect the President's family.

But what if their Details are like mine? Suddenly gone mad and turned dangerous? Images of Tommy Barrow being devoured by a bodyguard flashed before him, of his supervisory agent and body man turning into savages. White House insiders, attacking without reason or warning. His family was surrounded by them. How could they possibly be safe?

He wanted to use the intercom again, have the driver contact someone and get some information about his family, but he resisted. The man could not afford to be distracted, and if he was a really good agent – as the President knew he was – he would politely but firmly tell his Commander-in-Chief to shut up and let him drive.

Plague. Bio-war. Garrison knew he should be thinking about the country and its three hundred million citizens, but right now he was simply a husband and father, and all he could see were the faces of his wife and children.

Out the back window again, in the air above and behind the chasing police car, he saw the Secret Service's Black Hawk swing in to line up with their street, closing rapidly.

Someone's still on the job.

And then Marine One, the blue and white Sikorsky SH-3 Sea King helicopter, appeared in the frame, coming in from the left in a crazy, nearly horizontal high-speed bank. It slammed into the Black Hawk, and suddenly there was an airborne bloom of red and white fire so intense it hurt the eyes. Then debris was falling, trailing black smoke.

"Oh, God," Garrison whispered.

A moment later the squad car swerved and jumped a curb, slamming into a store front and flipping onto its side.

"LaBeau..." the President started, looking over at the last member of his protective detail, but then stopped when he saw him. The man was slumped forward, hands dangling between his knees but one still gripping his pistol. His head was down, chin bouncing off his chest, and stringers of both blood and grayish drool were dripping to the carpet between his shoes. The President grabbed the agent's arm and shook it, bracing himself with his other hand as the limo went through a tight turn. "Labeau," he said. "Labeau!"

The agent looked up at him slowly, circles like smudges of black ink ringing his glassy eyes, not bothering to wipe at his chin. "Mr...President..." he said thickly.

Garrison didn't know what to do for him.

LaBeau shook his head, then keyed the intercom. "Driver...stop."

The limo kept going. "Are you nuts?" came the reply.

The big agent bellowed, loud enough that he probably could have been heard through the bulletproof divider without the intercom. "I said *stop right now!*"

The *Beast* braked hard, shimmied and came to a halt in the street.

"I'm...compromised," LaBeau said into the intercom, then opened the rear door. He set his pistol on the leather seat beside him. "Lock it...behind me..." Then he got out, slamming it closed even as Garrison shouted his name. The President saw him stumble away a few feet, holding his head, and then the big man stiffened, turned and threw himself against the side of the limousine, clawing, bared teeth scraping the window glass.

Garrison jerked back, and the driver hit the accelerator, leaving Agent LaBeau behind. The last Garrison saw of him, the man was stumbling after the limo down the center of the street, reaching out as if he could catch and stop the fleeing vehicle.

A shiver ran through the President, and he switched to the seat LaBeau had recently occupied, picking up the Sig-Sauer nine-millimeter the agent had left behind. A quick check showed him that about two-thirds of a fifteen-round magazine was left, with one round in the chamber.

He shoved the magazine back in and hung on as the *Beast* raced through Cleveland.

They were on the final stretch, out of the city itself and on the access road that would take them to the private part of the airport where Air Force One and her back-up twin were parked within a secure perimeter. There was silence now on the radio, no one responding to the driver's repeated calls for assistance.

The road curved, leading to a gatehouse with a high, chain-link fence stretching away into the distance on either side, high weeds blowing in a breeze along its length. Beyond was a flat expanse of concrete, where the two magnificent blue and white birds – each with *UNITED STATES of AMERICA* emblazoned down their lengths – were parked some distance from one another.

The driver's vision blurred. His body shook with chills and the pounding of a headache felt like it would drive his eyeballs right out of his skull. He squinted and forced himself to concentrate, gripping the wheel tighter.

A camouflage-painted Humvee with a uniformed gunner standing behind the turret-mounted machine gun shot toward the gate from the other side, and for a moment the limo driver thought it might stop, blocking the road to intercept them. It should have. It didn't. The Humvee blew by on the limo's left, passing them and driving at high speed back down the access road toward Cleveland.

The driver caught a glimpse of the gunner's dazed expression, of spent brass shell casings covering the vehicle's hood and rattling off onto the road. *Why were they leaving? They had to have been put on alert, couldn't have not recognized the car.*

The striped bar that would deny traffic entry was in the raised position and the small gatehouse was unattended, so the driver shot right through, aiming for the big white aircraft in the distance on the left. There were a few black vehicles parked around the two planes, and he noticed dark lumps scattered across the concrete near them. His vision swam in and out, making it hard to focus, hard to think.

Bodies. Those are dead bodies.

Empty shell casings from a thirty-caliber machine gun – like the one mounted in the Humvee – glittered on the pavement in the morning sun. Not everyone was down, he saw, his vision cloudy as if he had opened his eyes underwater in a heavily chlorinated swimming pool. There were people in dark suits, Air Force uniforms and civilian dress moving around the two aircraft, and a few coming down the stairway pulled up to the door of Air Force One.

All of them swung in the limo's direction at the same moment, and started moving in that direction.

I made it. He's safe.

It was the driver's last conscious thought, and like a switch being thrown, his body jerked, his right leg reflexively stiffening, jamming the accelerator to the floor. He took his hands of the wheel and twisted in his seat, clawing at the smoked glass partition that separated the driver from the passenger compartment.

Food back there.

Kill it.

The *Beast* sagged to the left, the steering wheel turning on its own, and began a high-speed curve to the right across the field of concrete.

Garrison Fox felt the vehicle shift, the sickening sway and speed of a car out of control, and he gripped the door handle, bracing his feet against the other seat. Part of the driver's face appeared beyond the partition, a slavering, snarling thing twisted into a mask of rage. He clawed the glass, but couldn't attack it completely; his seatbelt restricted his movement. He also was no longer driving.

He can open the partition with a button, Garrison thought, and started to raise the pistol. *If he comes through, I'll have to-*

There was impact, a flash of white and Garrison was flung across the passenger compartment.

Then only darkness.

-17-

SIERRA-3

Cleveland, Ohio – October 28

David King, Secret Service shooter, widower and only days from retirement, burst through the fire door at the bottom of the stairs and into a marble-floored hallway. Daylight flooded in through high windows from the lobby to his right, and he moved in that direction on the run, his nine-millimeter in one hand. As it was Saturday, the office building atop which he and his Sierra team had taken up position was empty, and his rubber-soled combat boots made a thudding, squeaking sound on the polished floor as he ran to the light. He passed banks of elevators on his left and right, then moved into an airy, three-story lobby with a glass wall facing Key Plaza.

He could see people running in every direction outside, heard the muffled and distant pop of gunfire. Single doors flanked a trio of large, revolving doors in the center of the glass wall on the other side of a circular reception desk, and he curved around to the left to reach them-

-and saw the dead security guard on the floor, his chest cavity open and exposed.

Saw the pool of blood, reflective on the marble.

Saw the young man rising from where he'd been crouched over the body, now up and moving toward David. He was a well-groomed twenty-something in skinny jeans and loafers, a light blue button-down shirt with a big red, white and blue *RE-ELECT FOX* pin on the pocket. One of those enthusiastic young campaign volunteers who tirelessly went door-to-door promoting a candidate. Only this young man's shirt was spattered red, and blood smeared his hands and face.

David slid to a halt on the marble and his pistol came up. A double-tap, deafening in the quiet lobby, but the volunteer was fast, coming up under his extended arm and moving inside, one bullet tearing through a shoulder – he didn't even flinch – the other missing completely and punching a hole in the glass wall, creating a dizzying spider-web of cracks. The kid hit him hard, a full tackle, and they crashed to the floor, the campaign worker snarling and raking his fingers down David's black nylon combat vest. The Secret Service man shoved back with his other forearm, trying to keep those snapping teeth away from his face.

The kid grabbed the arm with both hands and sank his teeth into the wrist.

David howled in pain, then rammed the muzzle of the nine-millimeter into one of the kid's eyes and blew skull, scalp and brains across the polished marble floor.

Shrugging out from under the body, David looked at his wrist; it was bleeding from where the teeth had broken the skin. He cursed, wanted to kick a boot into that dead and frozen expression of rage on the kid's face, but figured the bullet had been retaliation enough. He ran for the doors, finding one of the singles unlocked, and headed out into Key Plaza.

The last transmission he'd heard from *Stagecoach* had been a plea for all agents to converge on the airfield where the President's planes waited.

"Sierra-Three to *Stagecoach,* what's your location?" he called into his handset. There was no reply to that call, or the next two he made. He knew where the airfield was, though, and had reviewed the main and alternate extraction routes. Now he just needed to get there.

A quick look at the carnage on Key Plaza told him there was nothing else he could do here.

David sprinted across the grass in the general direction of the stage and *Bamboo*, the presidential motorcade that had gone nowhere and remained parked where it had been when the *Beast* roared out of the plaza. There were agents moving around over there, but after what he'd seen from the rooftop he could no longer consider them friendlies.

He needed a vehicle, and he'd have to fight too hard to get one from the motorcade. Instead he veered left and put on speed, passing fallen bodies that were clearly dead and others with terrible wounds that were nonetheless climbing to their feet. A pair of civilians ran toward him across the grass to his left, and a bloody Cleveland cop came in fast from the right. All three were savaged and bitten, grayish drool slinging back from gaping mouths as they ran. All three would reach him at about the same moment.

David King stopped, assumed a shooting stance and fired twice to the left. The two running civilians crumpled. He pivoted right and fired, catching the cop in the chest. The man staggered but kept coming.

Bulletproof vest. Stupid.

He raised his aim and fired twice more, one round hitting the cop in the throat and putting him down.

Then he was sprinting again, his objective sitting where it had come to rest against the trunk of a tree. The black Suburban with the turret-mounted mini-gun sticking out through the roof – the CAT vehicle – sat with all four doors and its rear hatch open, engine idling. As he reached it, he first found a mauled and dead CAT operator lying on the rear seat beneath the open turret, so savaged that it was difficult to determine his race, or even that he'd been human. David grimaced and grabbed the corpse by its boots, pulling it out of the blood-slicked interior and out onto the grass. There wasn't time for it, and it made no practical sense, but he was moving out of a primal instinct to distance himself from a corpse. Then he ran a lap around the vehicle to slam all its doors.

Another CAT operator was waiting for him when he rounded the hood to reach the driver's door, the team commander, an agent with whom David had been friends for many years. The man was bloody, his eyes glazed and not processing as they once had, and there was something dark and wet in his right hand, something with a bite taken out of it.

Is that a liver?

The team commander opened his mouth and a stream of dark blood and drool spilled down his chin. He let out a throaty chuckle and attacked.

David was better prepared than he'd been when the campaign worker jumped him; with one hand he seized the team commander's combat vest and used the man's own momentum to bounce his face off the side of the big SUV, kicking out one knee and sending him face-first into the grass. He planted a boot in the middle of the man's back and shot him once in the head. There was an explosion of blood, gray matter and what looked like a burst of sticky gelatin. David blinked at it for a moment. He'd seen head shots before; nothing like *that* was supposed to come out.

He felt like being sick, choked it back.

Then he was in the driver's seat and backing away from the tree. Dropping it into drive, he hauled a sharp U-turn and accelerated, gouging the lawn and kicking up turf, heading for the street where the President's limousine had made its exit.

David keyed the mic to the dashboard radio. "All agents, Sierra-3 is mobile in CAT, heading for *Angel.*" Static answered him. Hundreds of agents and law enforcement officers were on-scene to provide a secure perimeter and safe evacuation routes, and *none* of them were on the air? Not good.

The heavily armed Suburban roared as he punched out of the plaza and raced after *Stagecoach.*

-18-

FEATHER MOUNTAIN

Western Pennsylvania – October 28

Second Lieutenant Donny Knapp stood just inside the tree-line breathing hard, drawing in the scents of mountain air and blood. He trembled, looking down at the dead man crumpled in the pine needles at his feet, at a green camouflage uniform that was dark and wet.

At only twenty-two, Donny Knapp had now taken a human life, and not even during war, which would have been expected of a soldier. The combat knife with which he'd done it felt heavy in his hand. A rank pin with three stripes and one rocker was attached to the Velcro chest strip sealing the dead man's body armor. His platoon sergeant.

Does the Army still hang you for murdering your own men?

You bet your ass they do. Especially when you waste an officer.

Donny looked over at the *second* crumpled figure, another body in bloody camo. His company executive officer, the one who had chewed him out that first night.

Twenty-five to life for the sergeant, maybe, but they definitely give you the rope for killing a first lieutenant. No question.

The three young soldiers standing nearby just stared at him wide-eyed.

Donny's body shook and he wanted to cry, wanted to fling the bloody combat knife into the forest, but he did neither.

It had all happened so goddamn fast.

It was their third day of field exercises – OPFOR had kicked their ass in every engagement – and the Green Berets who made up the opposing force were about to rotate home to Fort Bragg. Time for one more humiliation, though.

And here they came, rushing through the trees at his position, howling and raving like mad Celts. Donny stared at them. What the hell kind of assault was this? Until now the Green Berets had been stealthy, setting off devastating ambushes and aggressively maneuvering into the flanks and rear. Their fire had been swift and brutal, filling the forest with the screeching of combat-simulation MILES gear-registering hits. Donny had yet to "survive" a single engagement.

And now they were attacking head-on, screaming and running through the trees, not firing or even carrying their weapons.

A final insult, Donny thought, his anger rising. *We're not even worth treating like trained soldiers.* He clenched his teeth. "Open fire!" he shouted, and all along the line the men of his platoon, concealed in underbrush and in dips in the forest floor, opened up with their rifles, the woods suddenly alive with the rattle and pop of blank cartridges. The MILES gear worn by the attacking Green Berets squealed and chirped at once, dozens of units going off, a complete slaughter. Donny grinned his satisfaction, squeezing off shots of his own. *Screw these Special Forces guys!*

The Green Berets kept running, kept howling.

No, no they're supposed to stop when their gear goes off! Where's the ref-

The attackers slammed into Donny's platoon, the Green Berets tackling men who were kneeling to shoot and dropping on those who were prone, scrambling on hands and knees to get at men hidden in the brush. Then the screaming started, louder than the electronic shriek of the activated combat simulators.

Donny saw his men fighting back, throwing punches and grappling and kicking. Their attackers seemed to feel none of it, coming right back to seize hold of their fellow soldiers, gouging and biting and ripping. Young men shrieked in panic and terror, but the Green Berets weren't among them; they only screamed in fury.

The young lieutenant's jaw worked silently for a moment, and then he screamed, "Radio!" He had to call this in, had to-

His RTO, a private-first-class named Fernandez, was fifteen feet to Donny's left and trying to crawl away as two Green Berets clung to him, one holding onto his backpack radio and using it to climb the boy's back, the other with his arms locked around Fernandez's legs. This one bit deeply into the boy's thigh, and the one on his back sank his teeth into the PFC's neck.

The boy was babbling, "Jesus save me Jesus Jesus *JESUS!"*

Donny moved then, reversing his impotent rifle with its blank ammunition so that he could use the stock as a club, leaping toward his overwhelmed radioman. Before he got there he was knocked flat by a tackle from the left, a camouflaged figure slamming into him and taking him to the ground. Donny sensed it more than felt it, the thrashing limbs and grabbing hands, teeth slashing at him as a head whipped from side to side, hot breath and something wet in his face. He tried to curl into a ball, to wrap his arms around his head, and realized in a distant part of his brain that *he* was screaming.

There was a tremendous *crack,* and the body atop him went limp. A hand grabbed the shoulder of his combat harness, pulling hard, and the voice of his platoon sergeant came through gritted teeth. "Get your ass *up!"*

Donny did, scrambled to stand, looked around. A Green Beret with a crushed skull was at his feet, and the platoon sergeant was gripping an assault rifle with a now-shattered plastic stock. The screech of activated MILES gear reverberated through the trees all around them, competing with the screams of dying men. Bodies lay still on the forest floor.

The young lieutenant looked at the carnage, then at his platoon sergeant who was sweating profusely and had raccoon shading around his eyes. "What…what…?"

The sergeant gave the boy lieutenant a hard shake. "We fucking *retreat,* Lieutenant, that's what-what!" He looked around and shouted, "First Platoon, fall back to the rally point!" Then he gave Donny another shove and the young man was running, running, dodging through the trees, remembering to head downhill but little else. He caught glimpses of men from his company running with him, weaving in and out of the pines, most missing their helmets and none carrying their rifles anymore. And when he dared to look back, he saw other soldiers chasing after *them,* only these men wore bloody face paint and made gurgling, chuckling noises as they pursued, arms outstretched.

The hunters caught up to the fleeing men, and one by one they tumbled into the pine needles with a raving figure thrashing atop them. Soon it was only Donny and a couple others, sprinting down the hillside, leaping over fallen logs and trying not to run into a tree. Some of his senses returned, and Donny shouted, "To the right, the right!" remembering where the rally point was. The soldiers running with him followed. Donny couldn't tell if their pursuers did, too. He no longer dared to look back.

They reached the tree-line, stopping and breathing hard with their hands on their knees, fearfully watching the forest for what might come rushing out of the pines.

Nothing came at them.

He looked to his left and right to see that only three men had made it out with him, all younger than he, all privates or PFCs whose names he didn't know. They were pale, shaking, staring at him, and threw quick looks between the forest and their platoon leader.

They want me to explain what's happening. They want me to give an order.

What the fuck do I *know about any of this?*

The soldiers picked up on his indecision, and looked at each other instead of their leader. "He's had it," one of them said, nodding toward Donny.

"Fuckin' officers," another murmured.

"We are so fucked," said the third, edging away from the trees. "We need to get the fuck out of here."

Donny shook his head. "Stand where you are."

"Fuck you," the third soldier said, his voice cracking. His name patch read *AKINS.* "You're not doing shit!"

Donny couldn't believe how fast discipline had simply fragmented. He straightened and glared at the boy. *He's scared, and he's right. You're not doing shit. Why shouldn't he be this way? 'No bad troops, only bad leaders.' Remember hearing that?*

Akins looked at the other private and the PFC. "Come on, let's get out of here." He started down the hill, and the other two made to follow him.

"I said stand-" Donny started, and then he saw his platoon sergeant running toward him from within the trees, followed by the company XO. Donny sighed his relief and started to smile, but then he saw the glazed eyes, the bloody faces and hands, the gnashing teeth. He heard the horrible sounds that were part growl, part throaty chuckle. Then they were on him, and without conscious thought Donny went for the knife strapped upside-down on his combat harness.

The three soldiers stood and stared at their bloodied platoon leader, a man who had just taken out two experienced combat veterans with a knife. He'd first dropped their platoon sergeant by ramming the blade up through the neck's soft spot beneath the jaw, driving the razored steel into the brain, then repeated the move with the XO even as the sergeant was falling. The XO had first managed to claw a line down their officer's face and had bitten deep into Knapp's shoulder, but the young lieutenant hadn't seemed to notice then or now.

Donny looked down at the dead staff sergeant. He'd only been working with the man for a short while, didn't really know him at all. Their first meeting had been the day the sergeant returned from leave in the Philippines, only a week or so ago. The gossip was that he had a wife (or something close to it) and kids living in Subic Bay, all off the Army's books. The NCO had shown off the souvenir he'd brought back from the Philippines, the tattoo of a blue and green Chinese dragon twining about his right forearm from his elbow to just below his wrist, so new it was still raw and pink at the edges.

He'd slid the sleeve down and stood as soon as his new officer opened the door, appraising Donny with a cool eye and quickly appearing to dismiss him. Every conversation between them since and right up to the moment he'd saved Donny's life in the forest - a gift Donny had repaid by running eight inches of steel into the man's brain – had been clipped and impersonal. Donny had hoped they could be friends. That wasn't going to happen now.

Unknown to Donny Knapp, the platoon sergeant brought more back from the Philippines than just a new tattoo. He'd picked up Trident there, in the food and water and air, on every surface he'd touched and in every sexual encounter (he had kids in Subic Bay, ones he didn't know, but the wife was nothing more than a rumor) and Trident had even hitched a ride in the ink of his new dragon.

The sergeant passed it to everyone he came in contact with during his trip back, and delivered it to his company. Many of them had already been infected from other sources.

The Green Berets had caught it even earlier.

All Donny knew now was that he'd killed a man who had saved him, as well as a senior officer, and whether or not it had been self-defense didn't make much difference.

Donny looked at his men, waiting for curses, accusations, desertion.

"What are your orders, sir?" the PFC asked. Akins and the other boy just nodded.

The lieutenant blinked. *What* were *his orders? What now? What the hell had happened to transform these Green Berets – as well as men from his own unit – into homicidal madmen?*

"We can't stay here," he said at last. "We're going to have to sweep these woods, look for survivors and find a radio. We have to call this in. But we're not going back in *there,*" he pointed into the shadowy pines, "until we're properly equipped." He had only a vague idea about what that meant, but it absolutely involved live ammunition instead of blanks.

"I'll make the run for the base HQ, sir," said one of the privates, not Akins, a kid named Jones.

Donny shook his head. "Negative. We'll head for HQ, but we'll do it together. The MPs guarding the base will have weapons and live rounds. We'll hook up with them." He looked at the young soldiers and hefted the knife in his hand. "Until we get something better, be ready with this."

All three pulled their combat knives. None looked more confident because of it.

The scream of turbines and thump of rotor blades exploded across the trees over their heads, and an Army

Black Hawk roared in, banking and flying downhill. The soldiers turned to watch it, and Donny took in the scene below, finally realizing where they were. He'd lost his plastic-coated tactical map somewhere in the forest, probably during the initial attack, but he dug into a cargo pocket and pulled out the folded, photocopy diagram of the base he'd been given that first afternoon of orientation.

Downhill from them about three hundred yards was the overly long runway he'd seen in the diagram and wanted to ask about, a great concrete strip amid a cleared section of forest. A cinderblock building had been built at the edge, sitting upon a square of close-cropped grass, a cluster of antennae poking out of its roof. A pair of Humvees was parked beside the building. From there a road led away and climbed the hill Donny and his men were standing on, passing just twenty yards to their left. According to the diagram, that road eventually led back to the core of the small base, where all the barracks, admin and support buildings were located.

As they watched, the big chopper flared and did a fast landing on the airstrip near the cinderblock building. The moment it touched down, a dozen figures in uniform poured out the side doors, troops with packs and weapons and what looked like small suitcases, running for the Humvees. Another figure emerged from the building, spoke briefly with one of them, then went back inside. In moments both vehicles were filled and rolling, racing up the road toward Donny's position. Behind them, the helicopter had already lifted off and was banking away, disappearing over the tree tops.

"I thought that was our evac," moaned Private Akins.

"We're not going anywhere," Donny said without looking at him. He started jogging toward the road, waving his arms at the approaching Humvees. His men followed without being told.

The lead vehicle's braked squealed as it came to a halt. It had to; Donny was standing in the middle of the road. The side door opened and a uniformed, older man with a silver crewcut stepped out, pointing his sidearm at Donny's face. Several more men emerged, these with M4 rifles all trained on the man in the road.

"Identify," the older man growled.

Donny saw his collar, saw the three stars of a lieutenant General, the name ROWE over one pocket. He snapped to attention, dropping the knife and saluting. "Second Lieutenant Donald Knapp, First Platoon, Bravo Company-"

The general waved a hand at the rest of it, not lowering his pistol. "Come toward me. Tell your men to get in the road." Donny did as ordered, as the general looked them over. He finally holstered his pistol. "Are you the outgoing unit, or the incoming?"

Donny processed for a moment, then understood. "Incoming, sir. Replacing a Green Beret company. We were wrapping up our final exercise when-"

"When everything went bugshit crazy," the general said, cutting him off.

Donny nodded, then gave him a *brief* (you were always brief when talking to generals – not that shavetails like him got many opportunities to talk to senior commanders) explanation about what had happened in the forest. He swallowed hard and ended his story by confessing to the murders of a superior officer and an enlisted man, waiting for the general's sidearm to reappear as he was taken into custody for capital offenses.

The pistol didn't come out, and the older man's expression didn't change, not at the junior officer's wild tale of maniacs or his murder confession.

"There might be survivors out there," Rowe said, "but I wouldn't count on it."

"We were going to go search for them, sir," said Donny.

"The hell you are, Lieutenant. Did the sirens go off?"

The younger officer shook his head. "We didn't hear any sirens." The three men with him shook their heads as well.

The general muttered something to himself. Then aloud said, "Means the MP detail has probably had it, too. God knows what's waiting inside the mountain."

Donny didn't know what he meant.

The general walked over and clapped a hand on Donny's shoulder, his face grim. "Son, this makes you and your squad our perimeter security. Follow the emergency protocol and hang tough. There are probably no friendlies out there, so no hesitating. Your mission is to keep that field secure for inbound aircraft." He pointed back down the hill at the airstrip. "Secure at all costs." He climbed back into the Humvee. "Don't let me down." Then both vehicles were driving past, leaving Donny and his men in a dust cloud as they climbed and then disappeared over the top of the hill.

Perimeter security?

Hold the airfield?

What *emergency protocol?*

Squad? There were only four of them for Chrissake!

"What was he talking about, Lieutenant?" one of his men asked. It was Vaughn, the PFC.

Donny didn't answer, but held up a hand, needing to think. Holding the airfield and providing perimeter security were duties he could understand, no matter how unlikely it was that they could be accomplished by four unarmed men. But emergency protocols? What was…?

The briefing. The MP captain who had briefed them the afternoon of their arrival, in that sweltering, fly-infested hut. He had used those words – *emergency protocols* – and handed an envelope to his CO…who handed it to the XO. The briefer said he was to carry it with him at all times in case the 'balloon went up.'

Siren or no siren, that's exactly what happened, Donny thought. The brutal attack in the forest, the dying screams of his men, the crunch of a combat knife punching into skulls…anxious, three-star generals didn't just drop out of the sky to wave pistols and bark nonsensical orders.

We're at war.

Or at least something approximating it. The emergency protocol would be orders for an *in-the-event-of* situation. The XO had those orders, and he was right there in the trees where Donny had left him. Ignoring his men's shouted questions, he grabbed his combat knife and sprinted back up the hill, stopping at the edge of the pines.

It was dark in there, and getting darker as the sun fled the sky. A breeze whispered through the trees, and it was followed by a distant giggling from deep within the shadows. The giggle was repeated off to the right, then echoed several time to the left. Donny peered into the darkness but saw nothing moving.

Are they watching me?

He gritted his teeth and ran the few yards to his executive officer's body, rolling it onto its back and tearing open the body armor's Velcro seal. He reached in, feeling around blindly because he wasn't about to take his eyes off the trees.

Another giggle, a throaty sound that seemed to hang in the pines.

Movement in the shadows, more than one figure.

His fingertips grazed something rigid that gave him a paper cut, and he grabbed, pulling out the folded manila envelope. *RED PROTOCOL – FEATHER MOUNTAIN* was stamped on it in red ink, and was the only marking. He tore it open, finding several laminated pages and a red plastic key card on a chain.

The giggling came again, and this time there was no mistaking the silhouette of a man slipping from behind one tree and disappearing behind another, moving closer. Donny slipped the chain and card around his neck, shoving the big envelope into a cargo pocket. He hurried back to his men.

"What are your orders, sir?" his PFC repeated.

Donny pointed up the hill. "That way, back to the base." He looked at the sky. The sun was below the trees now, setting early in late October and even earlier in the mountains. Gathering clouds that promised rain drained the light even further. He didn't want to think about how bad things would get once night fell.

"Aren't we supposed to hold the airfield, sir?" asked Jones.

"Do you want to try to do that with a knife, Private?" When the man shook his head, Donny said, "Then follow me." The four soldiers ran up the dirt road in the direction the Humvees had gone, while night stole into the mountains.

-19-

LABCOAT

Atlanta, Georgia – October 28

CDC Atlanta was in protective lockdown, its doors sealed against the outside world. It didn't make a difference. The infected were already inside, searching the halls and offices and labs, searching for prey.

That's what we are to them, Dr. Moira Rusk thought. *A food source.*

The research – the *live* research, conducted simply by witnessing what they did – supported the idea.

"Are we secure?" Moira asked, emerging from a small office where she'd just had a hurried phone conversation with a Deputy Joint Chief of Staff, a two-star Air Force general at the Pentagon. He was the highest ranking official she could reach, since no one at Homeland Security – the agency that would make the official call – was answering. Neither were a lot of people. What Moira had said to the two-star had been good enough for him, and he'd immediately made the call to initiate *Bank Vault,* not knowing that the late Bob Chase of Homeland Security had already given that order to the Secret Service.

"We're locked up tight," answered Dr. Karen Fisher, standing in the aisle that ran down the center of a cluster of work cubicles, the offices at this end of a lengthy suite of labs and test subject wards. The woman looked haggard, as if she might drop at any moment, dark smudges completely encircling her eyes and her face drawn with deep lines. She was holding a cup of coffee in a hand that trembled slightly, and there was a dried blood splatter across the front of her white lab coat.

Moira touched her friend's arm as she went past, moving to a door with a thick glass window that looked out at and opened onto a common hallway here on the third floor. The glass was streaked with a red smear that ended in a bloody palm print, but the thing that had made it was nowhere in sight. Moira looked as far left and right as the window would allow, just to make sure.

She turned back to face her fellow physician. "Karen, did you check every door? Personally?"

Dr. Fisher nodded. "No one is getting in here."

No one? Moira thought. No *thing* was more like it. And it wasn't really true anyway. They were already in here, just a few doors away.

"And we have a complete headcount?"

Fisher rubbed her eyes. "Nine lab staff, you and me, one duty nurse. Ten subjects. Every interior door from end-to-end is punch code secured. The exterior doors from the office (she nodded at the one where Moira was standing) and the ward are now key card only, and only from the inside. You and I have the only cards. We've followed the lockdown protocol."

Moira took Karen's arm. "I'm sorry. I know you know what you're doing. I'm just-"

"I get it," said Fisher. "No worries."

"Plenty of worries.

The younger woman just nodded, then sat down in a swivel chair in the nearest cubicle. "What did Washington say?"

Moira found a chair of her own. She spoke in a soft voice so that none of the other staff would hear, although it wasn't necessary; there was a pressurized, steel and reinforced glass door between them and the doctors' conversation. "It was a brief call. I did a lot of the talking, trying to convince a general to initiate part three of the NRP and get *Bank Vault* rolling. He didn't need much convincing."

"A little late for the NRP," Fisher said without a tone of recrimination. She knew how hard Moira had tried to convince the White House to put it in place.

"From a preventative perspective maybe," said Moira, "but I won't give up hope on the medical aspect, and both the military and economic features just make sense." She sighed. She was exhausted too, and the adrenalin that had so recently hit her during the *incident* had quickly depleted, leaving her feeling worn and weary. "They've lost the President," Moira said. "Somewhere in Cleveland. The rest of the First Family, too. Bob Chase from Homeland Security is missing, along with most of the Cabinet members, the Supreme Court justices, the Joint Chiefs and lots of senators and congressmen. The general I spoke with said he thought the Vice President and the Speaker were secure, but he couldn't confirm."

Dr. Fisher could only stare and shake her head.

"Even more are missing, or at least they can't be located or reached. Everything is falling apart."

"The military?"

"All he said was that they were 'responding to the crisis as best they could.'"

"That sounds like a bullshit answer," said Karen.

"Agreed, but there was no point pushing it."

"We've been monitoring the internet and watching the news," said Fisher. "There's a TV in one of the cubicles. It's chaos out there. What we saw in here multiplied by hundreds of thousands. Millions, even."

Moira took a long look at the tired doctor. "What day are you, Karen?"

The response was immediate. "*I-Plus-Nine,* but closer to ten than nine."

The older woman paled.

"You're *I-Plus-Seven,*" Karen said. "You've got a few more days to figure this out."

The *I-Plus* language Fisher was using was simply a measurement. It stood for how long a person had been infected with Trident in terms of days, determined by research into the infection's growth rate through the body, which had thus far been consistent in every study worldwide. How much the infection had spread through the body was now giving an extremely accurate (to within hours, at least) picture of when a person had contracted Trident, and thus how long they'd had it. And now they all knew what happened around *I-Plus-Ten.*

A monster was born.

Fisher saw her friend's look and gave her a thin smile. "Don't worry, I'll excuse myself before I turn into a threat."

Moira flashed anger. "You're not going anywhere! And I'm not worried. I don't want to talk about it." It wasn't the response of a professional researcher and virologist, someone who searched tirelessly for knowledge and solutions. They were the words of someone terrified of losing a beloved friend.

She moved back to the subject of the call. It was safer. "The Pentagon said that they have a federal judge with them, and they're initiating executive succession procedures, trying to assemble everyone who is in line for command. They're sending some people to come get me and take me back to Washington, just in case."

"Damn," said Fisher. "The Secretary of Health and Human Services is what, twelfth down the list?"

"Something like that. I've never done the math. It was always a ridiculous idea to think that things would ever be bad enough for me to be sworn in as President."

"Until now. But instead of sending people to collect you, why aren't they putting everything into finding the real President?"

"I asked the general that very question," said Moira. "He said they were using every available resource to find him, then something about those resources rapidly dwindling, and finished with a policy quote about maintaining a working government." The older woman shook her head. "Anyway, I have my doubts about any rescue team." She tried to smile but it failed. "If they're unable to locate and evacuate the most protected man in the world, do you really think they're going to be able to make it to Atlanta and get me back there?"

"Sure," said Karen. "They know exactly where you are."

"Doesn't matter," Moira said. "I'm not leaving you here to deal with this alone."

"Now *that* is a bullshit answer," Fisher said. "I'm not much of a flag-waver, you know that, but Jesus…we're talking about the country here. And you knew the score when you accepted the Cabinet appointment. If they make it here, you're going." She gave the older woman her sternest doctor's glare, then tilted her head toward the pressurized inner door. "What are you going to tell them? About what the Pentagon said and everything else?"

"As little as I have to," said Moira. "Nothing about the President or succession or all the deaths."

"Moira, they're seeing it for themselves on the TV and the internet."

"Well, it's not going to come from me. We're in lockdown, the research is our only priority, and I want everyone working. Turn off the TV and online news. Keep them busy. That will keep them calm."

Fisher nodded her agreement.

"The body is autopsy, right?" She knew it was – she and Karen Fisher had wheeled it in there on a gurney themselves, a long lump covered in a bloody sheet. As they had moved through the lab, a middle-aged woman named Annabelle had burst into tears and looked away from the sight.

Moira stood. "Let's go take a look at it."

The autopsy room could be accessed through a door from the main lab on one side, and another door on the opposite side that led to the patient ward. The room was cool, with white walls, steel and hard lights making it colder still. Dr. Rusk pulled the sheet off the body on the table in the center, revealing a young man in his late twenties wearing Dockers, a button-down shirt and a white lab coat. His complexion was the ashy, paper color of the recently dead, and his lab coat was soaked red. A fragment of glass jutted out of his neck, right where his carotid artery was.

Terry Butters, one of Fisher's research techs, had been dead now for a little over twenty minutes. Moira used surgical scissors to cut away his clothing, pitching it into a damp pile in the corner of the room. Mr. Butters had been *I-Plus-Ten.*

Both doctors snapped on Latex gloves and switched on a bank of high-intensity lights directly over the table. Moira wasn't ready to conduct an autopsy just yet, but that would come soon enough. For now, she wanted to make some initial observations.

"How long was he symptomatic before it happened?" Moira asked. She'd been in the patient ward at the time, and had missed the event.

"I'd say less than an hour," Fisher replied, lifting the young man's eyelids one at a time, turning the head from side to side and inspecting the pale gray lines that marked the skin, crawling upward from his neck to curl around his jaw. Marbling, it was called. "He complained of a headache, was perspiring and had visible tremors, complained of chills. He sat down for a while, and gave him a quick examination. When I spoke with him he appeared mildly disoriented. That increased right before the attack. His blood pressure and respiration was slightly elevated, but no indication of fever."

Chills and sweating, but no fever, Moira thought. "Anxiety or signs of aggression?"

"He was passive," Fisher said, opening the man's mouth and peering inside with a pen light. "Some reflexive motor activity, repeated clenching and unclenching of the hands. He didn't seem to be aware of it. I thought it might be anxiety-based."

"Lungs?"

"Sounded clear."

"What about the eyes?" Moira asked. They looked at the corpse. Terry Butters was staring unseeing up at the ceiling, his blue eyes clouded over as if by cataracts and containing a silvery sheen. Far from normal for this type of death as well as the short length of time since he'd expired.

"They'd become glassy just before it happened," Dr. Fisher said, "but nothing like this."

Rusk chewed her lower lip. "Did you notice any external triggers?"

"Nothing I could see." Fisher explained that she had just stepped away from him, and a few seconds later Terry Butters had snapped. He'd come off his chair with an animal growl, snapping his teeth and lunging for one of his fellow researchers, the woman named Annabelle, grabbing her by the shoulders and lunging in to bite. The woman had been saved by a freak chance and her own reflexes. She'd been running blood work at the centrifuge and happened to be holding a long, glass vial of O-negative from one of the patients in the ward. As Terry Butters came at her, she'd reacted instinctively and lashed out with the hand holding the vial. Whether because of her terrified grip or simply the way it struck him, the vial had splintered, driving a three-inch shard of glass right into his neck, completely severing his carotid artery.

Terry Butters fought on despite the mortal wound, even as she tried to push him away and other researchers attempted to pull him off the screaming woman, but the damage made him bleed out fast and he'd quickly weakened, then collapsed. No one had moved to apply pressure to the wound, which might have saved him. After what he'd just done, no one *wanted* to save him. Covered in both the tech's and a patient's blood, having just killed her co-worker, Annabelle became hysterical and Fisher was forced to inject her with a sedative to get her to stop shrieking.

At almost the same moment, CDC went into lockdown as incidents like this were repeated throughout the building.

Moira began to mentally organize the stages.

Phase-One: Asymptomatic infection for approximately nine to ten days.

Phase-Two: Chills, perspiring, headache, disorientation. Duration approximately one hour, perhaps less.

Phase-Three: Violent, physical aggression, loss of reasoning and comprehension. Predatory, stalking behavior. Cannibalism.

Much of this last evaluation came not from what had happened with Terry Butters, but from what they'd seen on TV and the internet, as well as the violence that had – and still was – taken place right here at the CDC. Like the "flick of a switch" Karen Fisher had described, Phase-Two victims presenting symptoms moved to savage Phase-Threes without warning, and it had been demonstrated again and again that once they did, they immediately began to pursue, kill and consume human prey.

Viral cannibalism?

Moira shook her head. Inexplicable.

Phase-Three duration...unknown.

Would there be a Phase-Four? She couldn't imagine what that might look like, but considering the bizarre things she'd seen and encountered thus far, she knew that she had to keep an open mind. At this point another evolution was more than possible, even likely.

"Something turns them on," Moira Rusk said. "We have to find out what it is, and find a way to turn it off."

Dr. Fisher nodded, but she wore a resigned expression. Any such cure would come too late for her. She was *I-Plus-Nine,* and if their calculations were correct, less than twenty-four hours away from devolving into what the young man on the table had become.

Moira switched off the overhead lights, throwing the sheet-covered body back into shadow. "Get them back to work," she said, then told her colleague what she wanted done. "I'll be in the ward," she finished.

"We'll have to decide what to do with Annabelle," Fisher said quietly.

"That will be on me. It won't be your burden."

Dr. Fisher gave her a thin smile. "Right."

There was nothing more to say, and they went their separate ways.

Karen Fisher moved slowly through the lab with a single sheet of computer print-out, a pad of yellow Post-its and a Sharpie marker, carrying out the assignment Dr. Rusk had given her. Everyone at CDC had been tested, of course, and Fisher's print-out reported the most updated information on Trident's progression through every staff member here.

One by one she approached a lab worker, referred to the print-out and wrote on a Post-it. Then she peeled it off and stuck it to each person's laminated CDC ID clipped to their white coats.

I+7

I+5

I+8

They all knew what it meant. Each worker reacted with different emotion when the note was applied, from relief that they still had several days to go, to tears, grim resignation or even anger at the inevitability, regardless of their number. Karen had applied her own note first so they could all see it.

She came to Annabelle last, the woman who had been attacked by the late Terry Butters. An Atlanta native, the woman had been a Miss Georgia in her youth, and even at fifty-five retained much of her good looks, taking care of herself as the years had marched on. Rather than pursue a career in modeling or even film, she'd been drawn to science and made it her life. That and her children, and now young grandchildren, whom she spoke about with adoration, always ready to show off the latest photo on her cell phone. She was a kind, soft Southern lady, and her lower lip trembled as Dr. Fisher approached.

The sticky note went on.

I+10.

A soft Southern lady who was about to turn into a monster. She began to cry again, and all Karen Fisher could do was hold her.

Moira stood in the patient ward, a long, sterile, hospital-like room where subjects filled the ten beds lined up along one wall. Every patient had been put in chest, arm and leg restraints, "for everyone's safety" they'd been told. An RN in green scrubs, the ward nurse, sat before a computer terminal at the far end, monitoring their vitals. The physician walked slowly past a desk covered in files and an open laptop, the screen turned away from the patients. The volume was turned down. It was streaming an online news channel, and violent, horrific images flashed constantly across the screen.

The door to the lab was behind her, the second entrance to autopsy on her left. Down by the nurse was a door that led to a pharmacy and supply room for patient needs, a second that accessed a tiny restroom and another that opened into a larger storeroom filled with unused lab equipment and refrigerators filled with samples. A quick glance at the patients showed that nine appeared to be resting comfortably, but one, ironically the tenth in line, was sweating and wincing as if in pain, eyes open and distant.

Phase-Two, Moira thought.

She didn't go to him, though. Instead she moved to an oversized, pressure-sealed door on the right, wide enough to permit a gurney and handlers to pass through. The card scanner set in the wall beside it displayed a red light to show that it was locked, but Moira tugged at the handle anyway to be sure. She looked out the small, reinforced-glass window set at eye level. The hallway outside was bare and unremarkable, except for the hand of course.

It was sticking out of a white lab coat cuff, limp and turned upward, just barely visible at the far left. A splotch of red stained the cuff. The rest of the arm and attached body (she *assumed* it was attached but didn't know for sure) was out of sight. A presumably dead CDC employee left to lie unattended in the hallway, which spoke to the grim reality of what was going on inside the secured building.

For a while there had been PA announcements to inform everyone of the lockdown and order them to seek secure shelter. The announcements stopped after a short while. Moira had a few brief phone conversations with other physicians, similarly locked down in other offices and labs, but for the last hour no one was picking up the phone. CDC administrators couldn't be reached, and there was no sign of facility security. Her driver, a bodyguard provided by the State Department because of her status as a Cabinet Secretary, didn't pick up. She'd reached that two-star at the Pentagon, but when she'd tried to call back there was no answer. Calls to Washington just rang and rang, except for a single call to the White House where she'd been put on hold for ten minutes before the line disconnected. Moira had even called the President's confidential line, the cell phone carried by his body man. It went to voice mail.

Phase-Threes were loose in the building, roaming the halls in search of victims, while people tried to hide behind locked doors. Moira knew that it was only a matter of time (and had likely already happened) before Phase-Threes started appearing among the people who thought they were safe *behind* those locked doors.

As would no doubt happen right here within Moira's group if preventative steps weren't taken.

She looked at the dead hand in the hallway again and thought about the information Dr. Wulandari had sent her from Indonesia shortly after the incident with Terry Butters, the results of an autopsy conducted on a Phase-Three subject. Trident appeared to be *hatching,* the odd, fork-shaped particles all at once birthing some new, unknown organism. The original pitchfork structure became a useless husk and disintegrated, as the new organism (Trident 2.0? she thought) began its own, rapid multiplying, taking root in organs and tissue, concentrating heavily around the brain, heart and spinal cord and forming those protective, mucous sacs.

Was the original pitchfork structure simply a vehicle to move Trident 2.0 through the body? This new organism was spreading quickly, attaching itself to every bit of tissue, organ and muscle. *Was it feeding off them?* That would make it parasitic. She couldn't guess at its purpose, other than the intent of all parasitic organisms; to feed and survive. There was no doubt that she would find the same thing when she cut open Terry Butters. Her scientific mind and human instinct also told her to stop deluding herself; there would absolutely be a Phase-Four, and it would likely be more terrifying than anything that had come before.

Moira Rusk looked at the dead hand one more time, rubbed the bridge of her nose in an attempt to chase away the fatigue starting to creep over her, and walked toward the row of patients. Time to get back to work.

-20-

DEVIL DOG

Cleveland Hopkins International Airport – October 28

Death wasn't so bad, Garrison thought. Except for the headache, and the pain low on the left side of his chest. He heard drums, a rapid, unceasing thumping. Drums? Weren't they supposed to be angelic trumpets?

Depends on where you arrive. It was a sobering thought.

Death was a dark place, as he'd expected it would be, at least at first. He peered into the gloom. Not really black, more of a charcoal gray. Where was the light? There was supposed to be a magnificent, welcoming light.

Depends on where you arrive, his mind repeated.

There might have been light somewhere to the left, out of the corner of his eye. If not light, at least a brighter gray than the rest. He tried to go to it, feeling resistance that made it difficult to move. He hissed at what felt an awful lot like cracked ribs. He'd had one of those at Quantico many years before, and knew what it felt like.

What was holding him back, he wondered? Was it the weight of his sins, preventing him from reaching the light, pulling him back to that other place? Garrison feared Hell, as his upbringing had taught him to, but not to the point where he'd become obsessed with the fear as some people did. Perhaps that was because of his belief that God was a simple, merciful force, and Heaven wasn't achieved through unswerving service to any particular religious organization, but by being a good and decent man. He thought he was both those things.

So what were these sins that were weighty enough to hold him back? Some bad behavior as a kid, certainly, but nothing hateful or harmful, more along the lines of mischief and rule-breaking. He'd never stolen anything, and was honest even when telling the truth worked against him, a trait that had made political life and especially the presidency more difficult than it was for many who had gone before him. He'd never cheated in school or dishonored himself as a U.S. Marine.

A shy academic (a super-nerd, he'd often told him son) his first sexual encounter hadn't been until college, and it was with Patricia Rand, the woman he would eventually marry. He'd only ever been with her, and it not only satisfied him but was a source of personal pride. He loved her fiercely. She and the Marine Corps cured him of his shyness, but he'd remained an academic, and – in his mind –

a bit socially awkward. Not something to earn a ticket to Hell.

Was it because he'd fallen short on being a good father? Especially the last few years? He loved his kids so hard that sometimes it ached, but between the demands of military command and an increasingly complex political climb he hadn't been as involved in their lives as he should have been. Was that it?

Garrison tried to turn toward the light once more and hissed again, the resistance still there. The drumbeat went on. Was it truly drums, or the pounding of his own head?

He had killed his fellow man. That must be it, something unforgivable. But that wasn't quite right. He'd been taught about forgiveness. The lives he had taken, in war as a Marine, had been to save his own life as well as others. He'd ordered it done as President, again in military operations, and that had also been necessary to save the lives of innocents. Never hateful. He had never hated his enemies, even thought they had given plenty of reason for him to do so. He'd always had the best of intentions.

The road to Hell is paved with good intentions. Who had said that? He'd also read somewhere that *the road to Hell is paved with adverbs,* and who had said *that?* This was some pretty fuzzy thinking for a dead man, he decided. And how had he ended up dead anyway? Were you supposed to feel cracked ribs and headaches when you were dead?

What happened?

He remembered that LaBeau was sick… *Who was LaBeau?* …and the man got out of the car… *What car?* …and then…nothing…

It was so hard to focus, as if his brain was a swimmer doing laps in a pool full of oatmeal.

Oatmeal. Mom used to make it on cold mornings before school. Maple and brown sugar is my favorite.

Oh, this was ridiculous! He fought against the pressure holding him back, really put some muscle into it, ignoring the rib that was starting to sing a heated opera. He pushed toward the gray light, saw it brighten, but not as much as he'd hoped. It was still muted somehow. He kept going.

Heaven or Hell? Come on, Heaven!

With a groan and a final push he forced himself past the weight of sin – discovering what turned out to be a pair of deployed airbags pinning him to the seat – and emerged to find that he was facing a square of tinted glass smeared with blood. On the other side, hammering its fists against the window in an attempt to get inside and collect Garrison's soul, was a red-faced devil. It bit at the glass with broken teeth, glaring at him with hungry, soulless eyes.

Not Heaven.

The motorcade's primary and alternate routes might have been cleared initially, but that was no longer the case. Barricades had been pushed aside, police cars that were once parked in blocking positions had been shoved out of the way by bumpers. As the people of Cleveland realized that their city had suddenly become a killing ground, they piled into vehicles and flooded the streets in an attempt to reach safety. Most didn't know where that was, exactly, just someplace other than here.

Order disintegrated, and now cars were filling every lane in both directions, causing gridlock. Traffic accidents created additional blockages, and fires were beginning to spark up in places. There were no firemen to put them out, no police to clear the way for their trucks, only frightened people bumping their cars against each other in an attempt to force movement. Horns, shouted curses, fistfights between angry motorists, distant sirens and more than a few gunshots.

Within it all, the infected hunted the living, each bite swelling their ranks as Phase Threes triggered the Trident organisms in those not yet come fully to term, quickly sending them into an active state. Birthing killers.

In the CAT vehicle, David King hit the siren and the red and blue lights concealed behind the Suburban's grille, trying to bully his way through the congestion. It did little good. He was moving at a crawl through a river of cars stopped at every angle, most attempting to change lanes in an effort to get a few feet farther ahead. And although the lights and sirens of law enforcement weren't making anyone get out of his way, they *were* attracting attention. Running civilians converged on his vehicle, leaving cars and sidewalks to get to him. To them, the vehicle represented safety, the authorities who would *make everything alright.*

They tugged at the locked door handles, rapped on the tinted windows, cried and pleaded to be let in. David wanted to save them, but there were too many; they would swamp the Suburban like an overloaded lifeboat. And as much as his heart ached to see their helplessness and fear, the part of him that shouted the word *duty* – a principal that had been a driving factor all his adult life – reminded him that his first and only priority was ensuring the safety of the President of the United States.

He kept the doors locked, continued to nudge through traffic and tried not to look at the faces. When the cries and rapping on glass turned to angry shouts and beating fists, when people tried to climb the Suburban to reach the roof, one young man scrambling onto the hood and raising a brick to smash against the windshield, David reacted. He buzzed down the driver's window, stuck his gun out and fired three quick shots in the air.

They scattered, the young man dropping the brick and sliding off.

David hit the gas, ramming a minivan out of the way and driving up onto a sidewalk, taking out a U.S. mailbox and clipping a sapling growing from a large planter. More people leaped out of the way of the charging SUV, but not all.

Several drooling civilians with outstretched arms and bared teeth ran straight at the truck and died beneath the bumper and tires. David winced at the thump and crunch but kept going, wishing the siren would drown out the horrors all around him.

At the next corner he hauled the big vehicle left, accelerating up a cross street that the fleeing vehicles had not yet decided to try, empty except for an abandoned police unit and a couple of cars racing in the other direction toward the traffic jam. David keyed the radio handset and started calling again; the USSS mobile command center called *Shotgun,* Air Force One, the *Beast.* No response from any of them, and the airwaves were almost silent now except for the occasional frantic voice within the static, voices that didn't answer when he tried to contact them.

He slowed at an intersection, weaving around a car accident and more running figures, then shot across. He had to get out of this city. Each passing minute brought him closer to the point where the streets would be so gridlocked that any hope of escape would be lost. He'd already seen enough to know that he didn't want to be in downtown Cleveland when that happened.

He switched frequencies, hoping that the satellite link would make the connection, and called Secret Service headquarters in Washington.

Because of Fate's sense of humor, he got through at once.

David wanted to shout, "Where the hell have you guys been?" Instead he gave his ID number, his duty assignment and a quick brief of the situation. "I'm enroute to Hopkins International," he concluded, "the last known destination for POTUS."

"Confirm, Sierra-Three," said the communications officer. "Be advised that per its GPS, *Stagecoach* is stationary out on the flight line of Hopkins. Unknown if Devil Dog is aboard *Angel*, but *Angel* is also stationary."

Not good, David thought, slowing again and forcing his way through a gap between a pair of cars, scraping metal. He didn't look at the faces in those cars, either. The President's limo was at the airport, but Air Force One was still on the ground. By now he should have been aboard with the pilot putting the big plane in the air, standing it on its tail as he rocketed for altitude, dropping a string of anti-missile flares in his wake as the protocol demanded.

The communications officer returned. "Sierra-Three, be advised that *Bank Vault* has been initiated. There is a team in the air and inbound to Devil Dog for extraction, two Blackhawks and one gunship. ETA ten minutes. If you're there when they arrive we can get you out, too."

And if not, you're on your own, the voice didn't have to add.

"Copy that," David said, "I'm en-route."

The Suburban took a hard right, squealing its tires, David alternating between the brakes and accelerator as he wove through vehicles along Rocky River Road, rubbing cars with a screech of metal and moving far out onto the shoulder when he had to. There were running figures here too, and his meager consolation was that only the savage, drooling ones crunched under the Suburban. Black smoke from unseen fires temporarily blotted out the sun. Bloody figures chased after the fleeing, often pinning them against cars and walls and taking them apart in a frenzy of hands and teeth.

He forced his way across Brookpark Road, aiming for the on-ramp to the Berea Freeway, but angled right at the last second, speeding toward the airport's outer fence and a closed gate blocking a frontage road. The briefing for all agents told him *that* would take him to where the President's plane sat isolated from the rest of the airport. He hit the gate at speed, blowing it aside, then nearly had a head-on collision with a military Hummer with gunner standing in the turret racing *out* of the airport.

You're going the wrong way, asshole!

In the distance, David could see the two, enormous white birds. He pushed the accelerator to the floor.

The *Beast,* heavy with armor, rocked from side to side as dozens of bodies shoved against it, hands clawing at metal and glass. In the rear passenger compartment Garrison Fox rubbed his eyes, his thoughts beginning to clear. *Crash. Airbag deployment. Not moving.* Up front, the driver had somehow slipped his seatbelt and was now attacking the bulletproof screen, smearing the glass with drool. Beyond him, through a badly fractured windshield, Garrison could see what had stopped the big Cadillac so abruptly. The car had plowed into one of the airport's runway vehicles, a pickup with a set of aircraft stairs mounted in the rear. The truck was caved-in on one side, mated with the now-wrinkled hood of the limousine from which steam was escaping.

Not going anywhere.

Bloody, snarling faces pressed against the windows on both sides, fists beating against the glass and tugging at door handles. Despite their contorted and horrific expressions, Garrison recognized many of them; a couple of staffers, the co-pilot and a flight steward from Air Force One, several Secret Service agents. Others he didn't know. Between their bodies he caught a glimpse of more bloody figures running across the tarmac toward the limousine.

He ejected the magazine of LaBeau's Sig-Saur, thumbing off the rounds into his other palm so he could get a count, then feeding them back in before reloading. Nine bullets, plus one in the chamber. A dozen people outside and more on the way, people who only hours ago were professionals dedicated to the service and protection of the President. Hostiles now, all of them.

If he tried to get out of the car, they would take him down in an instant. Ten bullets wouldn't stop that. He could stay here and treat the presidential limo like a bunker, as he'd been taught to do by the Secret Service should the worst come to pass. He doubted they could get in, but how long could he survive in here? How long before a rescue? Was a rescue coming?

There was no radio back here, and his private cell phone was in Danny's coat pocket back at Key Plaza. He picked up the secure, satellite phone that rested in a cradle between the rear seats, a phone that could connect him with anyone, anywhere in the world. Right now he only wanted to talk to Patricia, to hear her voice and have her assure him she was okay.

The phone produced nothing more than a dull, electronic buzz.

The limo kept rocking.

Garrison found it difficult to take his eyes off the ghastly faces pressed against the side windows. The beating fists of the infected were an unending drumroll.

Infected. That's the right word. It's Trident, no doubt about it. I ignored the warnings and now the bill has come due. If he'd acted sooner, when Moira Rusk had advised him to do so, could he have saved lives? Probably. Maybe. He suspected he wouldn't live long enough to bear the guilt resulting from his choice.

Over the pounding came a new noise, and he looked up at the roof of the car. The heavy beat of approaching rotor blades. Garrison let out a selfish and very human breath of relief.

Then the sound of the thumping rotors changed, a change in pitch combined with the high shriek of a straining turbine engine. Through a side window, between the bodies, Garrison saw a Black Hawk touch down a hundred feet away from the limo. Through the open side door of the helicopter he could see figures in black thrashing against each other inside, as one man in body armor and a helmet, a stubby machine gun hung across his chest on a strap, fell from the opening, found his feet and staggered away. The man was clutching his throat as a jet of red shot between his fingers. Then he fell to his face.

The long scream of a turbine grew closer, rising in volume to the point he winced and covered his ears. The blur of another Black Hawk, shrieking, dropping, slamming into the one that had just landed.

A half-second crunch of steel.

The *crump* of an explosion.

Then the world outside the limo's window turned red as a pressure wave hit the *Beast,* rocking it harder than the infected ever had and flames washing over the car. Garrison was knocked to the floor between the seats as pieces of fast-moving metal slammed into the limousine's side, one of them tearing a six-inch gash through the roof. An intense heat followed through the hole.

Looking up, Garrison saw a Secret Service agent rising from where he'd been knocked down, returning to pound at the glass. His hair and suit were on fire, but still he gnashed his teeth.

Then there was a loud, metallic *clack* that came from both doors at the same time, and in the space of a second a string of thoughts went off in Garrison's brain.

Door locks just opened.

Wasn't me.

Driver has a lock control.

Still beating at the partition.

Hit the control with his foot.

The left rear door swung open and a gust of super-heated air and flames rushed in. With it came the burning Secret Service agent.

Garrison held up an arm to shield his face against the heat and fired LaBeau's Sig twice at close range, hitting the burning man twice in the face and throwing him back. Then he thrust an arm into the fire and grabbed at the door handle, felt the burning, hauled back.

Heavy! So heavy.

Even as he pulled at it he realized that in four years he had never once touched the doors. Agents had always been there to do that. It slammed with a deep thump, and he hit the door lock button to once again secure the passenger compartment.

Clack. The raging driver's foot unlocked the doors again, and before Garrison could hit the button, the door on the other side swung open. A man and a woman – it was hard to tell who they were since they were both on fire – tried to climb through the opening together and briefly became wedged shoulder-to-shoulder in a gruesome parody of a sitcom gag. A wave of heat rushed in behind them, stealing Garrison's breath, and he recoiled even as he opened fire, three quick shots, then a fourth when one didn't go down immediately. He kicked the corpses out of the doorway with one polished shoe, scorching the cuff of a pants leg, and pulled that door shut.

Even as he reached for the lock button the opposite door groaned open, letting in heat and fire. He twisted on the seat, bringing up the pistol to blast at yet another pair of figures trying to claw their way inside. Three more shots, the bodies fell away and then blackened fingers were gripping the metal frame, trying to pull it open further even as he fought against the weight and pressure and flames to keep it closed. The door behind him opened again and he held onto this one, pointing the pistol at the other opening and squeezing off a single round at a body bathed in fire before the pistol's slide locked back on an empty magazine. The air, now tainted with the chemical stink of burnt jet fuel, tore the oxygen from his lungs and made his eyes water so badly that he could see only a blur. The inside of his nose was scorched, and his face felt as if it would bake right off his skull.

His left coat sleeve was burning, but he couldn't let go of the door handle. If he did, they would get inside. If he didn't close that other, open door, he would burn to death, be overcome by smoke or become a quick meal for the infected that still stumbled beyond the leaping flames. The car was too wide for him to hold onto both doors at the same time.

Blackened hands gripped the edge of the open door. Garrison dropped the useless pistol and used both hands to haul the door away from those charred fingers.

David King gunned the CAT Suburban and shot through the unattended gate. Air Force One and her sister sat isolated out on the tarmac, but he accelerated to the right instead.

Toward the burning limousine.

The black marks of tires in a high speed right turn arced across the pavement in a wide crescent, ending at the blaze. The *Beast* had struck an airport vehicle – presumably what stopped its forward movement – and the nearby inferno of a pair of wrecked military helicopters had spread to blanket the President's car in curling orange and white flames. These two had to be part of the trio of rescue choppers HQ had told him were inbound. Far beyond the treetops of a wooded area to the south of the airport, he could see a pillar of dense black smoke climbing into a clear sky. The missing gunship, no longer inbound.

David had been close enough to the airfield to see the second Black Hawk diving in out of control, close enough to hear the long scream of its turbine, and for a moment he'd frozen behind the wheel, transported to another long scream from not so long ago. *A cruise ship. A vacation that was supposed to be a last attempt to make things right again. A long scream that changed his life forever.*

He was in the present now, though, and couldn't even take the time to wonder at the mathematics that would be required for Trident (*it had to be the virus, what else could all this be?*) to take out *all three* helicopters. Now there was only the *Beast*, and a man who – he hoped – was inside and alive.

Black paint was blistering off the limo's skin, but as he neared he saw it wasn't completely engulfed. The fire was worst on the left side, closest to the helicopter crash, and within those flames he could see immolated figures still flailing at the side of the car before succumbing and falling to the pavement. Not all of them, though. Several were still tugging at the door, even as they burned. There was also a crowd of figures moving around the trunk to reach the right side, where the fire was less intense. These people were burning too, but not as much as the others.

Another dozen or so were running across the tarmac from the direction of the planes.

David doubted they were friendlies, and wouldn't take chances.

He jammed the brakes and threw the big Chevy into park about twenty feet behind the President's car, then scrambled out of his seat and into the back.

He'd slapped out the flames on his coat sleeve, barely managing to hold the door handle against the pulling from outside. Flames licked through the narrow opening, and he turned his head away-

-to see several smoking, burning figures appear at the opposite, open door. He was unarmed now. There was no way to keep them from getting in. It was over.

And then he heard a high-pitched, metallic whine that seemed to spin up somewhere behind the limo, followed by a menacing chopping sound that he knew well from having heard it overseas. *Mini-gun.* Instinctively he hunched as a string of 7.62mm fire tore into the pavement outside, several thumps rattling across the armored limousine. He hung onto the door as the firing seemed to walk up and down both sides of the car, across the back and then off to the left.

Suddenly he lost his grip and went back on his ass between the seats as the opposing pressure from outside vanished, the door banging shut. Heat, smoke and something else was coming in through the other door. It was one of the female stewards from the presidential aircraft, an Air Force sergeant with her hair burned down to blackened stubble and the skin on her face bubbling and scorched. She glared at him with glassy eyes and let out a choking noise as she snapped her teeth.

Three short bursts of a smaller, automatic weapon – *BRRRAP, BRRRAP, BRRRAP* – stitched across the steward's torso, nearly cutting her in half before exploding her head in a grisly cloud. The body slithered out of the opening. Then there was the sound of running boots, and a man appeared in the car's doorway, backlit by flames. He was dressed in black tactical gear and carried a science fiction-looking sub-machinegun. His black ball cap bore the letters ERT in yellow stitching.

The man glanced around the interior for only a moment, then at Garrison. "US Secret Service, Mr. President."

It was all Garrison needed. He scrambled out of the car, and then the two men were sprinting across bullet-pocked pavement toward a black Chevy Suburban parked close by. He recognized it as the CAT vehicle from his motorcade (the smoking mini-gun poking out of a roof turret made it hard to confuse it with anything else) but didn't recognize the agent as part of the CAT team.

Garrison climbed into the front passenger seat, and through the windshield saw the many crumpled bodies ringing the burning limousine, lying where the mini-gun had cut them down. He glanced toward the distant aircraft and saw more of the fallen, only a couple up and moving. His rescuer jumped into the driver's seat.

"The plane…?" Garrison started, but stopped, quickly realizing that Air Force One was no longer an option.

The shooter dropped the Chevy into drive and cut the wheel as he accelerated into a tight U-turn. "Special Agent David King, Mr. President."

"Happy to meet you, David. Happier to be out of there."

"Yes, sir."

-21-

DANCER and DESIGN

Eastern United States – October 28

Kylie opened her eyes. One eye, at least. The other refused to obey and remained closed. Her head hurt, and so did her back. She closed her good eye. Didn't she have a research paper due? Was she late for class? No, it was Saturday, she was certain of that. Had she been working on it and fallen asleep? Her thinking was slow and muddled. She opened her eye again.

Shadows and purplish light. The smell of freshly turned earth, a dead leaf, fall smell and the reek of spilled gas. A blob in the gloom a few feet away resolved itself into the figure of a man, staring back at her. He was sitting, legs splayed out before him, back pressed against a curving white wall with a small, oval-shaped window above his head. He'd bitten off his own tongue, the ragged stump of it peeking out behind shattered teeth. One eye bulged, and his head on that side had been flattened. Kylie thought of a pumpkin left too long on the doorstep. Even in the shadows she could see that his jacket, tie and white shirt were soaked red.

She looked at him, oddly not repulsed by his damaged condition, certain she knew him from somewhere. *Horse? His name was Horse. No, Horsch. Secret Service agent in her Detail.*

Then it all rushed back at her. The screams, the fighting, a gunshot…the plane shaking, tipping and then…nothing. *We crashed. I'm still alive.* Then another thought, one which she spoke aloud. "Mom?"

Kylie's last lucid memory was of her mother being pinned between two rows of seats by an agent who was attacking her. There had been the *BOOM* of a pistol being fired twice, and the agent was thrown back. Where had Kylie been during that? She had a vague impression of someone dragging her out of her seat by the hair.

"Mom?" she repeated, rising painfully to a hands and knees position, wincing at a sharp stab in her lower back. Something came close to her face and she jerked away just in time to avoid being cut by the ragged, aluminum shard of a broken seat armrest, and then she saw that the executive jet had been torn in half. She was in the tail section. A lavender glow of twilight came through the opening, and thirty or so feet away she could see what had been the front of the aircraft, crumpled and almost unrecognizable. The place where the jet had been torn in half was a jagged circle, shards of metal bent down like teeth in a gaping mouth, wiring dangling in tangles of blue and red, some of it sparking.

She smelled the jet fuel, looking at the sparks. "Mom!" she shouted, moving in the direction she thought her mother had been, crawling over a motionless body.

"Over here, honey," called a voice, barely above a whisper. "Oh, God, Kylie…are you okay?"

Kylie moved toward the voice, finding her mother in the semi-darkness. She was on the floor and wedged between two seats that had broken loose from their mountings. The young woman pushed at them, straining when they didn't want to give, and finally moved them aside.

"Are you hurt?" Patricia asked, not moving despite the blockage being cleared.

"I'm fine," said Kylie, crawling close, trying to see her mom in the shadows. "Are you okay? Can you move?"

"I think so. My arm hurts."

Kylie could see that her mother's arm was bent behind her at an odd angle. Broken or just sprained?

"What happened?" Patricia Fox's voice was thick and fuzzy.

"The plane crashed."

"Where are…?"

Kylie shook her head. "I think everyone's dead. Mom, I smell fuel. We have to get out of here." She couldn't stop thinking about those sparking wires, imagined the air shimmering with vapors as it reached that exposed electricity and then *WHUMP.* Patricia nodded, tried to sit up and let out a cry.

The girl flinched away at the sound, then clenched her teeth and gripped her mother by the shoulders, pulling her into a sitting position, closing her eyes but not stopping when her mother screamed. Now partially upright, Patricia sat and breathed heavily, her eyes shut for a moment, then nodded silently. With her good hand she pulled the broken left arm (it was *absolutely* broken) around in front of her, screaming again, then cradled it in her lap. Her chin rested on her chest.

Kylie wanted to give her a few minutes to recover, but the fuel smell seemed stronger now. "We have to go."

Her mother bobbed her head, then let her daughter pull her to her feet, biting back another scream that ended up sounding like the whine of a wounded animal. Kylie supported her under the arms and moved them through the shattered fuselage toward the opening, picking her way over obstacles of twisted metal and sharp fiberglass, tilted seats and bodies. Dead people seemed to be everywhere, their broken shapes tangled with the wreckage, some badly maimed and others seemingly intact. These were most disturbing, for their eyes were open and appeared to look at her, as if they were about to speak. The young woman tried not to stare back.

"I shot a man," Patricia whispered as they moved.

"Good," said Kylie. "He was trying to kill you." She wished *she* had shot him, remembering the sight of a snarling agent trying to rip her mother apart. "Fuck him."

"Right. Fuck him." Then they both laughed weakly.

Kylie caught movement outside one of the cabin windows that remained intact. In the purple light of the descending evening she could see a person walking through the field into which the jet had crashed, headed this way.

"Help is coming, Mom. Keep moving."

Stooping and moving carefully through the open end of the broken aircraft, avoiding the teeth-like aluminum shards, the two women emerged into a corn field that had recently been harvested. Now it was littered with aircraft debris. She led them away from the wreckage and toward the remains of the forward section of the plane, where they would find the cockpit and main cabin door.

The person crossing the field began to run toward them.

"Help!" Kylie shouted to the figure. "We need help!" She kept them moving. What she wanted was in that front section of plane (unless it had been thrown clear and was now somewhere in the field.) She remembered seeing it when they boarded in Boston, a white box strapped to the bulkhead, a red cross on its hinged lid.

They reached the forward section and Kylie helped her mother sit down on the gouged earth, then stood and turned. The figure running toward them was thirty feet away now, a boy of about ten dressed in overalls and a simple, long-sleeve blue shirt. Seated squarely on his head was a black hat with a wide, flat brim. For an instant Kylie flashed on an old horror movie she'd watched in her early teens with her girlfriends at a sleepover; *Children of the Corn.* Then she thought, *no, he's Amish.* In the twilight she saw his shirt was ripped at one shoulder, the flesh beneath torn by a bloody bite that had stained the clothing around it.

The boy let out a throaty chuckle, hands curled into claws, and charged at Kylie.

Like the agents on the plane.

Fear and anger collided within her, and as the kid arrived she did not run, but planted her feet and punched him in the face, putting her shoulder and body weight into the blow. There was an explosive *crunch* of bone and the boy was knocked flat.

"Kylie, what did-?" her mother shouted

The boy snarled and got to his feet, his face now a bloody mask, nose flattened and both front teeth knocked out. That hit should have made him stay down! Kylie looked around quickly and spotted a piece of debris, a three-foot strut of heavy aluminum twisted at each end by the impact. She snatched it up. The kid lunged, catching hold of her short jacket and bit, teeth (minus his incisors) ripping into leather. Kylie screamed and pounded at his head, knocking the wide-brimmed Amish hat free. The boy ignored the blows, hands scrabbling at her as he let go of the jacket and moved to bite her hand.

It was the instant she needed, and Kaylie swung the aluminum strut like a baseball bat. There was a dull *crack* when she connected, just above the boy's left ear.

The Amish boy crumpled, landing on one side and quivering like a sleeping dog in the midst of a dream. His hands pawed at the earth, and one eye rolled up to glare at her. The boy snapped his teeth and let out another thick chuckle. Horrified, Kylie let out a cry and began hitting him in the head with the impromptu bat, striking again and again, heedless to what was spattering across her face and making gruesome, spotted patterns on her hands.

When the boy was no longer twitching, she let out a wail and stumbled away, holding onto her weapon even as the tears started to flow. "Mommy," she cried.

Ignoring her own pain, Patricia stood and went to her, pulling her close with one good arm. "Shhh, it's okay, honey. It's okay now. Shhh. It's the virus, baby," she said through her daughter's sobs, "you didn't have a choice. It has to be the virus."

They stayed like that for a while, then Kylie sniffed and wiped her face on a jacket sleeve, smearing blood across her skin. She nodded slowly. "I'm okay," she said, looking into her mother's eyes for signs of condemnation over having killed a child, seeing only her mom's concern. "I'm okay." She let out a rush of breath.

Patricia nodded back.

Kylie went into the wreckage of the front half of the plane a few minutes later. Patricia heard rummaging sounds, a cry of revulsion, and then her daughter returned no longer carrying the bloody strut, but an armload of first aid supplies. She dropped the items on the ground. "The pilots are dead," she said, looking away and blinking, reliving the scene in the cockpit. "I found a sling in the medical kit." She helped her mother put it on, and Patricia sighed relief as the pressure instantly came off the fracture. The rest of the supplies consisted of alcohol and peroxide pads, bandages and some individually wrapped pain relievers. The young woman stuffed it all in her jacket pockets. She kept a break-and-shake ice pack for her swollen eye. At least she could see out of it now, but not much. She thought she must look like a cage fighter who'd come out on the losing end of a match.

They looked around. The field was ringed with woods, a darkened farm house at one edge about a quarter mile away near a large barn. Nothing moved in the field or near the buildings.

"Someone will come for us," Patricia said. "The Secret Service tracks these planes, they'll know we went down. And I'm sure the agents on the plane called for help when…when things started to happen."

"I didn't hear anyone call for help," Kylie said. "One of them said *Bank Vault,* like a code word, but no one reacted to it."

Patricia frowned. *Bank Vault.* It was familiar, something from a briefing maybe? She wasn't making the connection. She and Garrison had had so many security briefings over the past four years. She was sure it would come to her when her head didn't feel like it was filed with damp mattress ticking.

Kylie looked at the sky. "It wasn't even sunset when we were in the air. We've been down for a while. Someone should have been here already." She huffed. "I don't even know what state we're in!"

Patricia looked at the unmoving Amish boy, then quickly looked away. "Pennsylvania, maybe? Ohio?"

Kylie started back toward the back half of the aircraft, from which they'd emerged. "A radio. All the agents had-"

The air was split by a half-second of high-pitched, otherworldly squeal, and then the world turned white as that section of aircraft (and the wings carrying the fuel) detonated. Both women were hurled to the ground, hair and eyebrows singed as a heat wave washed over them. A full minute later, Kylie regained her breath and managed to rise, gasping at the scorched-tasting air as she helped her mother to stand. Hitting the ground so hard hadn't done Patricia Fox's arm any good, and she hissed at a pain that the sling couldn't alleviate. Together they hobbled around to what remained of the nose of the executive jet, putting it between them and the fire.

"Someone will find us now," Patricia finally said.

"Yes," Kylie said, looking toward the darkened farmhouse. "Someone."

They stood there for a while as the color drained out of the sky, yielding to an indigo night. The blaze of burning jet fuel caused orange demons to dance across the field, and their shadowy cousins to caper among the nearby trees. There were no wails of sirens, no beat of helicopter rotors or probing searchlights, only the crackle of flames.

Kylie looked at her mother. "Daddy…?"

Patricia hugged her daughter one-armed. “He’s fine. You know how well protected he is.”

“Like we were?”

Patricia couldn’t respond to that, and when she didn’t, Kylie went once more into the shattered front fuselage. She emerged carrying a holstered pistol and a matching leather pouch holding two loaded magazines. “There was a dead agent near the cockpit. I couldn’t tell who it was…his face…” She coughed. “He doesn’t need this anymore and we do.” She clipped both the holster and magazine pouch to the waistband of her torn, designer jeans.

“My phone was back there,” said Patricia, looking at the blaze.

“Mine too,” Kylie said. “I thought of that, checked the bodies up front, but the agent didn’t have one and the two with the pilots were smashed. But we’ll find one.” The fire was exhausting the fuel and the flames were receding, allowing nightfall to reclaim the field. The darkness of the trees grew increasingly menacing.

They looked toward the distant farmhouse – as black and forbidding as the woods – and by unspoken agreement started walking across the field in the opposite direction.

-22-

DARK HORSE

The Harrison School, Vermont – October 29

Devon kept out of sight at the side of the window, looking down onto a green space of lawns and a few old oaks, a sidewalk crossing in front of the building where he and Captain America had taken shelter. The office of an unknown professor was dark around them, the only light a thin, grayish glow coming through the window. Outside, the lamp posts lining the sidewalk had come on automatically hours ago. A clock on the office wall ticked past midnight.

"Thought I told you to stay away from there." Marcus Handelman had pulled the professor's desk chair to an angle in front of the door, and sat with his pistol in hand. In the darkness, Devon could see little more than the white of his dress shirt, his back crossed with the black X of his shoulder holster.

Devon didn't move from the window, and didn't respond to the agent's warning. Instead he looked at the night – still and empty – and said, "No one's coming, are they?"

Handelman paused before answering. "We don't know that. They might just be delayed." Both their voices were just above a whisper.

"The phone hasn't rung," Devon said, "and no one answers when you called them back. No one answers *any* of your calls."

The agent said nothing. Devon was right. No one had shown up, not a car from Secret Service backup, not local law enforcement. His repeated phone calls to Washington had not reached a duty officer or anyone else. Only endless, unanswered ringing, occasionally punctuated by an answering machine. 911 was the same, as well as the other numbers he'd memorized; the Service field office in Burlington, the White House, the FBI office in Boston, his supervisor's cell phone. When he punched zero for directory assistance (something he couldn't remember doing since he was a kid) he got a recording telling him to try again later. There were other numbers he might have called – the Pentagon, DEA, the US Marshals, any federal law enforcement agency – but all those contacts were in his cell, and he didn't have it. The professor's office didn't have a hard-copy phone book. He wondered if they even made those anymore.

"Our safest bet is to hold position," Handelman said. "They know where we are, we need to be patient. Please move away from the window."

Devon didn't, and Handelman didn't fight him on it.

The fifteen-year-old watched a night breeze make the oaks sway gently, and the wall clock ticked to twelve-thirty before he spoke again. "You shot a kid," he said softly.

"Yes, I did."

"Are you okay about that?"

"Perfectly okay," came the reply.

The words made Devon turn. "You're lying."

Handelman said nothing.

"Have you ever had to do that before? Shoot someone, I mean?"

The agent hesitated as if unsure how to answer the question, then said, "When I was overseas with the teams, yes. Not during my time with the Service, though."

Devon looked back at the window, seeing his own, ghostly reflection in the glass.

"Are you okay with what I did?" Handelman asked.

The boy shrugged. "It wouldn't change things if I wasn't. I guess I get it. I didn't really know him. I'm not sure how I feel about it. I've never seen anything like that."

"I'm sorry you had to. I'm sorry I had to." The agent rose from his chair and walked to stand at the other side of the office window, looking not at the boy but outside. "It's okay to be upset about it. It was a terrible thing."

"I'm not upset."

Handelman shook his head. "Even tough guys get upset when they have to do something…like that. It doesn't mean you're weak. Just means you're human." The agent was quiet for a moment, then, "I'm not sorry for doing it, though. And it might not be the last time I have to before this is over." He caught the boy's eyes. "You understand that, right?"

Devon nodded. "It's your job." He expected a speech about duty and self-sacrifice. Instead Handelman said, "Right, it's my job, and if you get killed your dad will fire me. I need the healthcare benefits."

The boy laughed, though he didn't want to. "Ass. You work for the Secret Service, not the White House."

Handelman snorted. "*You're* an ass. Your Dad's the Man, the big boss. Don't fool yourself." Then he reached out and gripped Devon's shoulder. "I'm not going to let anything happen to you. Just stay close and listen, okay?"

"Okay." The mention of his father caused a frown line to crease Devon's forehead. "Do you think my dad's okay?"

"Are you kidding? Your father is the most heavily protected man on the planet. He only gets the best agents, not second-stringers like me who watch over pukes like you."

Devon smiled. Handelman had to be one of the very best, or his father would never have allowed him to watch over his son. "What about mom and Kylie?"

"Safe," Handelman said without hesitation. "Again, the best agents we have, I know them all. And as for your sister, can you think of anyone stupid enough to tangle with Kylie? Her Detail would end up saving the bad guy from her."

Devon shrugged, but smiled again. His mom's word for Kylie Fox was *feisty.* His dad used *piss and vinegar.* He'd heard that her detail had other colorful terms for her. He wanted to feel better, but the frown line remained in place. "Do you think-?"

Handelman cut him off by putting a finger to his lips, then pointing out the window and down. The boy saw them at once; a trio of figures moved slowly across the green space, disappearing for a moment as they passed behind trees, then coming into view again. One was a boy Devon's age, wearing the school uniform of khakis, dark blue jacket and striped tie. The other two were grown men, one older and wearing a tweed sport jacket, the other younger, a red-head with a buzz cut and a dark suit. A coiled radio earpiece dangled from a clip on one of his jacket lapels.

Devon recognized them; Handelman's supervisor, Special Agent O'Brien, the biology professor who didn't like his dad's politics…

And Devon's roommate Sean.

They were slightly hunched, heads swinging left and right as if searching for something. In the light of the lamp posts Devon could see that each was bloody, their clothing torn. He didn't like the way they moved. It looked unnatural for a reason he couldn't explain, or at least unnatural for people. And then the light touched their faces, making Devon recoil. Their eyes were like silver coins, vaguely luminescent and nowhere near human.

After he regained himself, Devon whispered, "They're different from the people earlier. They're not dazed or raging like the others were. They look…" he frowned, *"deliberate."*

Handelman nodded silently. He didn't like the way they moved either, and it was oddly familiar, something he'd seen before…a way *he* had moved on certain missions overseas. Stalking behavior. Killers looking for a target.

The trio approached the building and moved out of sight below the window. "It's about to get real, Devon," Handelman said, then pointed to a corner of the office. "Go crouch down over there." The agent's tone had changed from funny older brother to no-bullshit operator, and the fifteen-year-old obeyed at once. Handelman took position facing the door, arms extended, pistol gripped in both hands and pointed at the wood, right about where a chest would be if someone was standing on the other side.

Devon knelt beside an overflowing bookcase, staring at the outline of the door, feeling his heart accelerate. It was as if he could already hear the smashing wood, the roar of his protector's pistol and the howls of the silver-eyed trio as they rushed in, nothing but teeth and grabbing hands, and…

He swallowed hard. *Keep it under control.*

They waited, straining to listen. Only the tick of the wall clock.

And then there was a sound, a muffled laughter echoing down the hallway beyond the door. It sounded choked, not like a real laugh. Both of them tensed.

The phone on the professor's desk went off with a shrill and deafening urgency, making them jump. Devon lunged for it and snatched the receiver out of the cradle, knowing it was too late. In the silence of this night, that single ring would have traveled the entire building.

"Hello?" Devon said in a whisper, expecting to hear a man, the Secret Service duty officer calling back at last. Instead there was a pause, followed by a soft whimper and a girl's voice.

"H-hello? Is anyone there?"

"Who is this?" Devon asked.

"Sandra," said the girl, sniffling, her voice a quaver. "Sandra Block. I'm in the gymnasium. Where is everyone? Who are you? I saw…I saw… I was just pushing extensions and-" It all came out in a rush, a frightened girl talking too fast.

"I'm Devon," he said, cutting her off. "I can't talk too long."

Handelman glanced back and shot the boy an evil look, mouthing the words, *hang up.*

"I can't talk at all, Sandra. I'm sorry." He was about to hang up, but the girl's voice rose several octaves and she started to cry. "Please don't go! My parents are…my brother was at the chess match…someone was biting and…they're all like them now! I saw them! I ran and I've been hiding. There's people out there, but they're not people. Help me, I'm in the gym, *help me."*

Devon hadn't felt true heartache in his life until this moment, and he didn't know why he said what he said next. "We're coming, Sandra. Stay where you are and don't use the phone again. We're coming, we'll find you." He hung up before she could say anything else, then unplugged the phone in case she called back.

Standing only a few feet away, Agent Handelman shook his head slowly without looking at Devon.

There was nothing from the hallway for a while, and then the echo of more laughter, abrupt and barking. It was impossible to tell if the source of the noise was nearby or deeper in the building. Handelman was a statue, his service weapon aimed at the door.

The building went silent.

The wall clock ticked, reaching one in the morning.

Devon felt like the air and silence were smothering him, wanted to ask questions, wanted to move, anything to break this insane waiting. Why had he told the girl they would come for her? He only had a vague impression of a few girls among the spectators at the tournament, for he'd been fully concentrating on the matches. Had she been there when his opponent attacked, when people went crazy and turned on each other? She must have been. Handelman was pissed, he could tell. What had made him think that his bodyguard was going to take him wandering around school looking for some hiding girl? He shook his head, ashamed. He'd made a promise to her, and he didn't lie. If he and Marcus didn't find her, someone else – *something* else – would. He couldn't live with that. Handelman wouldn't like it, but if Devon went looking, he'd have to follow. That was that. The boy felt better at his decision, a strength that came with resolve.

"We're going to move," Handelman whispered, breaking the silence at last. "We're too closed in, and I need a better field of fire. You ready?"

Devon moved to stand next to his bodyguard.

"We'll go back to where we came in," the agent breathed. "Down the stairs, back into the classroom and out the open window. I'm going to find us a car. We're safer on the move."

The boy didn't argue, only nodded.

With the agent leading, they slipped out of the office and into the hall, the man's head and pistol tracking together. Then they scooted across the tiles to the stairs, moving on the balls of their feet, watching the shadows for movement. In the first floor hallway at the foot of the stairs, Handelman came to an abrupt stop.

There was blood on the floor, black and gleaming like spilled oil in the darkness, touched with red from the glow of a fire exit sign not far away. It was a trail leading into the open door of the classroom where they'd made entry…or coming *out* of it, Devon thought.

Handelman took a few steps toward the door, and then the throaty laughter came again, close this time, just up the hall ahead of them. It was followed at once by the sound of running feet and the rattle of bouncing keys. A shape came at them from the darkness, a custodian running with arms outstretched, his radiant eyes a pair of silver discs.

He snarled.

Handelman grabbed Devon by a shoulder and propelled him though the classroom door, then fired one-handed, three quick shots. In the doorway, not quite inside the room, Devon flinched at the blasts and raised an arm against the brilliant white muzzle flashes, blinded. Right before the painful whiteness exploded behind his closed lids, he saw the janitor stagger into a wall. Then all he had left was his hearing, and he could tell that the running feet and bouncing keys were coming at them again.

Handelman swore through gritted teeth, elevated and fired twice more. The back of the custodian's head burst from the double-tap, and he crashed to the floor.

Rubbing his eyes, Devon blinked some of his vision back. Handelman was pivoting, aiming back toward the stairs. Special Agent O'Brien was racing at him from that direction, snarling and reaching as the custodian had done, only a dozen feet away. The bodyguard fired, hit his supervisor in the heart, a kill shot, but the man's momentum carried him into his executioner and they both went down in a tangle. Handelman was scrambling at once, fighting free of a limp corpse, getting to one knee. Two more figures in the hall, backlit by the exit sign, little more than silhouettes; the biology professor and Sean. Devon's roommate let out a sickening giggle and they both charged.

Handelman dumped six rounds into the two of them, dropping both.

"My God," Devon whispered, holding onto the door frame and squinting, the white muzzle flashes still popping behind his eyes like camera strobes.

Handelman went to his boss and searched him quickly. Earpiece but no radio. No cell phone or car keys. *Shit!* He took the man's service weapon and spare magazines, then went to the dead custodian and relieved him of the set of keys clipped to his belt.

He grabbed Devon's collar. "Window. Move."

Outside, the breeze had rapidly cooled the October night, and Devon pulled his school blazer tight as they moved through the darkness at a trot. Overhead the northern sky blazed with cold stars. They reached Handelman's destination, the campus maintenance truck they'd seen before, found it locked, and the agent flipped through the custodian's keys until he found what he wanted.

Then they were in the cab, the engine running. A dashboard gauge revealed the fuel tank to be a little less than half full.

"The gymnasium is over-" Devon started.

"No. We're out of here."

The boy looked at his protector. "They'll kill her! I promised, we can't-"

"You shouldn't have, and it's not my problem. You are."

"Bullshit!" Devon grabbed the door handle. "I'm going."

A single palm slammed into Devon's chest with a force that nearly took his breath away, pinning him to the seat. He blinked, never having realized just how strong the man was.

"If you think I won't restrain you," Handelman said, his voice soft and conversational, but carrying a tone the boy had never heard before, "you're wrong. We're leaving. Don't touch that door again unless I tell you to."

The hand left his chest, and Devon didn't even look at him, just stared out the windshield. The maintenance truck moved into the night streets of the campus, the agent driving without headlights and taking a route he'd memorized.

As they left the Harrison School, Devon Fox turned and looked out the rear window, still not speaking. He'd just killed a girl with a broken promise.

-23-

FEATHER MOUNTAIN

Western Pennsylvania – October 28

The silos and underground support areas of Feather Mountain had been constructed in the early eighties, labyrinths blasted deep in the rock as part of the American build-up of strategic missile defense. Within a decade and a half the site was decommissioned, its ICBMs removed and the facility mothballed. Post-911 fears of terrorism brought the tomb-like mountain fortress back to life, with Army engineers expanding and rebuilding, transforming the site into a larger, more modernized facility designed not for launching missiles, but for survival. Although still capable of withstanding a nuclear blast (in theory), its new design made it resilient to a more likely, modern threat; chemical and biological terrorism.

The inside was maintained by a skeleton crew of fifteen man and women from the 114th Signal Battalion, who kept the site ready for a *just in case* scenario. A platoon of permanently assigned MPs took care of the small base outside – the buildings, airstrip and perimeter fence – and for both groups, it was one of the most boring assignments in the US Army. Since its repurposing, Feather Mountain had never gone live.

Until now.

General Joshua T. Rowe and his team reached the mountain's entrance, leaving the two Humvees they'd taken from the airfield parked nearby. Twelve uniformed men and women moved quickly toward a concrete and steel archway jutting from a sheer rock face, each loaded down with packs, laptop bags and personal small arms. With Rowe was his second-in-command, a major, two soldiers to provide security, a pair of communication techs and a pair of biohazard specialists, two IT techs, a combat medic and an Army surgeon. The general and his team had drilled in this exercise and knew their jobs, but now it was for real and their tension level was a tangible thing.

Inside the high archway, fluorescent bars chased away the coming night and illuminated a pair of heavy blast doors, one big enough to permit the passage of large vehicles, the other an oversized man-door off to the right. The major approached this one and entered a seven digit code into a panel, placed his eye near an optical scanner just above it, then touched a blue plastic key card to the proximity reader. A green light came on, and the pressurized door popped open with a hiss, swinging silently outward, revealing that it was thicker than a bank vault slab. Rowe led his team into a brightly lit corridor, and the door closed behind them as quietly as it had opened, making ears pop as it vacuum sealed once again.

"Proceed to decontamination," a voice said from an overhead speaker. Another door opened and the team moved into an airlock-style chamber sealed at both ends, everyone lining up in single file.

"Close your eyes," ordered the voice through another speaker, "and hold your breath until I tell you to release it. This will take about fifteen seconds." A moment later the room filled with white fog, which was sucked out through vents fifteen seconds later as promised. The next door opened, and the team entered the mountain complex.

"Good evening, sir," said an Army captain, saluting the general. "We received the alert that you were inbound. My group is bringing the facility fully online."

Rowe returned the salute. "Let's get moving, Captain."

The younger officer led them across a high, domed chamber nearly a hundred feet across, the floor and walls polished smooth but the vaulted ceiling raw, chopped granite. Light bars did what they could to reduce the gloom, but shadows still dominated. It was twenty degrees cooler in here than outside, the air heavy with the scent of minerals. Boot heels echoed as the team followed the captain toward one of four archways positioned around the circular chamber. To their left, lined up against one curving wall, were three Humvees covered with tarps. Overshadowing the utility vehicles was an eight-wheeled Stryker Dragoon, an armored assault vehicle that could also carry ground troops, armed with a remote-turret-operated Mk44 Bushmaster, a thirty-millimeter death dealer. It was flanked by twin .50 caliber heavy machineguns mounted in the turret, just in case the Bushmaster didn't provide enough lethality. Several bicycles leaned against the armored vehicle, the more obvious modes of transportation in what had to be an enormous space.

"Do we have comms?" Rowe asked the captain.

"The systems are all up, but we're not making contact everywhere. Many units are not responding."

The general already knew that fact from hours earlier, when he and his team had deployed from Maryland. Another reason why *Bank Vault* had been initiated.

The soldiers traveled down a long corridor, passing deeper into the mountain, trying to ignore the intangible sense of millions of tons of granite pressing down on them. Their guide seemed perfectly at ease.

In another chamber where five more, identical-looking passageways intersected, open-topped golf carts were parked against a wall and plugged into portable chargers. The captain removed a handful of blue, laminated cards from a plastic holder on one wall, passing them out. "If you're not here every day, it's easy to get turned around. These are diagrams of the facility so you don't get lost. These cards are not to be copied, and must be returned before you leave the mountain."

Rowe nodded. Although he had been here several times, about half his team had not, and so he let the man continue with his rehearsed briefing. Even the general had not been here in fourteen months, not since the last drill, and he found it ironic that his team had been scheduled for an annual Feather Mountain drill just two weeks from now.

Their guide gestured to a large, Plexiglas board mounted to a wall, a larger diagram of what was on the cards. "Most of the support areas are on this main level," the captain said. Enlisted and officer's quarters, mess hall, medical facilities with biohazard and quarantine sections. Sub-level one has the communications center, briefing rooms, executive housing and private mess. Sub-two houses our dry goods storage, supply stores and quartermaster. I recommend you stop down there to pick up some warm clothing if you didn't bring it. The mountain is a constant fifty-three degrees, and it stays pretty chilly. This much space is difficult to heat."

Those team members who had been here before nodded. They'd sworn that *next* time they would pack sweaters, but this deployment had come on too suddenly to grab anything more than the most critical gear.

The captain's hand moved to another section on the map board. "Sub-three is maintenance, the generator rooms, battery banks and fuel bunkers, as well as the armory. All the way down here," his hand moved to a long, blue rectangle near the bottom of the map, "is a one-point-five million gallon fresh water reservoir." He looked back at them. "Elevators and stairs connect all levels at different points. The mountain's ventilation system is equipped with a broad spectrum of filters to protect against known chemicals and airborne particles. You might have noticed the metallic taste and smell of the air. That's normal, but it takes some getting used-to."

"What's that section off to the left?" asked the major, Rowe's second-in-command.

"Those are the access tunnels, launch control center and missile silos. The elevators and stairs will take you down there too, but I don't recommend it. There's been only minor preventative maintenance there since the mountain was decommissioned as an ICBM site, and groundwater seepage has compromised some of the structural integrity. We also don't run power down there, other than the elevator, so it's pitch black. If you decide to visit, for whatever reason, you're required to have hardhats, flashlights and a qualified guide."

"No one's going sightseeing, Captain," Rowe growled.

"Yes sir. If anyone has any questions, please find me. You can drop your gear here and my people will take it to your quarters." The captain gestured. "Now let's get you to the comms room."

Minutes later Rowe and his team were humming down a wide tunnel in four white golf carts, the captain driving lead with the general and the rest of the group following. There were no windshields, and the already cool, coppery-smelling air came at them in a cold rush. The carts made little noise as they zipped along over polished cement, the electric whine of their motors swallowed in the vast space. One full mile into the mountain, the captain stopped his cart in yet another high, domed chamber with yet more tunnels exiting, and parked alongside several similar vehicles lined up and charging. He escorted his new arrivals to one of several freight-sized elevators, and soon they were all taking a thirty second ride down to sub-level one. There the captain led them across another wide intersection and through a door marked *COMMUNICATIONS.*

Within was a large, *Mission Control*-type room filled with tiers of consoles. They faced a wall of huge, flat screen monitors, about a third of them showing live video feeds. Others were black, showed static or held a test pattern. One of the screens to the right was a digital outline of North America, and nearby a similar diagram of the world. Colored dots with data beside them covered both of these boards. A pair of uniformed IT sergeants was working with laptops beside a far console, quiet and engaged in their work. They paid no attention to the general in the room.

The non-tech members of Rowe's team moved out of the way as the general took it all in, rubbing his hands briskly against the chill. He thought briefly of the scared, young second lieutenant he'd encountered outside, and the perimeter defense plan that had now apparently shit the bed. But that was the reality of live operations versus *THE PLAN.* It couldn't be helped. The kid would just have to make it work.

"Okay," said Rowe, moving into the room. "I want two people on the national board, one on international and one on satellite comms."

Team members moved to their stations, pulling on headsets.

"Find out why we're dark on those screens," he said, pointing, then turned to his XO. "Get me linked up with the Pentagon, the White House and Fort Meade in that order." Rowe stepped to a console and pulled on his own headset, looking up at a screen with a satellite image of several Red Chinese warships (the correct term was *People's Republic of China* or PROC, but they would always be *Reds* to him) moving through the Formosa Straits. Beside it was another screen with a high level view of New York City, chillingly familiar pillars of black smoke rising from Lower Manhattan.

"Let's see how bad it is," said the general.

It was every young infantry officer's fantasy; giving the command to "Fix bayonets." But he couldn't give that order. Their rifles were back on the forest floor where they'd been dropped when the Green Berets hit their lines like a howling, barbarian horde.

Donny Knapp glanced back at the three shadows hiding with him in the darkness next to a barracks wall. They shifted nervously.

"Private Akins," Donny whispered, "keep watch to our rear."

No acknowledgement, only silence. They were pissing him off. After their encounter with the general, who'd ordered them to hold the airfield, the three young soldiers had followed him back to Feather Mountain's small base readily enough. But as the sun went down and they'd caught glimpses of the horrors sneaking through the shadows of the base, the men had started to lose their nerve again, muttering about running away while they could and ignoring their officer when he spoke. Donny had given them a sharp reprimand, and they'd been quiet since, but that didn't mean they were in line.

Frightened. Probably because of what you did to their sergeant and executive officer. Donny knew that killing two of their leaders right in front of them – no matter how justified – hadn't helped with discipline.

He peeked back around the corner of the building, out into the asphalt-paved road that ran between the rows of barracks. Although the interiors of the single-story, white wooden structures were dark, some exterior floodlights were on at the corners, and a handful of tall streetlights had come on when night fell. All of them created circular pools of white, gray at the edges and making for a stark blackness beyond their glow.

There were monsters visible in the light.

Who knew how many were unseen in the darkness.

Right now there were four that Donny could see, a small gathering beneath a streetlight about twenty yards up the road to his right. All wore bloody uniforms; two men from his company, a Green Beret and a woman, probably part of the base support staff. They were slightly hunched over with their arms dangling, hands clenching and unclenching. Agitated by something, they shuffled constantly, turning in all directions. Donny could hear them making thick, mewling and chuckling noises.

Their eyes were the worst. Like bright, silver circles.

Dried blood smeared their faces and hands.

Not soldiers anymore. Monsters. They ate the flesh of those they killed. Donny had seen it on their way into the base, quietly detouring his men around scenes of growling soldiers crouched over their fallen brothers in arms. He'd wondered then, as now, if his little group represented the last living troops on base. Probably not, he decided, there were sure to be others out there, hiding.

Donny looked back and cupped a hand around the little flashlight he was holding, shining it onto the base diagram he'd set on the ground where he was crouched. If they were in the right place – and he was almost certain they were – then just beyond that knot of infected soldiers (that *had* to be what this was) there would be a side road that led to the armory and the supply building, both places he needed. But he had to get past the opposition first.

"Combat knives," he whispered. That got their attention. "We need to move. There's four of them, and if they don't go away in the next minute we'll have to take them. One each."

"Four what?" one of his soldiers asked. Donny thought it was Akins. "Four of our guys? You want us to knife them? No way!"

Donny stared at the shadows. "You all learned hand-to-hand techniques. Remember your training." It occurred to him that the average soldier received maybe one afternoon of hand-to-hand knife training in basic, and if they were lucky, another day of it in infantry school. Too bad, there was no other option.

"I'm not killing one of our guys," another whispered.

"They're not our guys anymore," Donny said, trying to keep his voice down. "They're killers now, and they'd kill you in a second. We need to go through them."

"Uh-uh," said PFC Vaughn. "Let's go around."

"Or we could just leave. I'm for running for the fence." Jones this time.

Donny pointed at them. "You men will keep quiet and follow my orders."

"Or what?" said Akins. "Are you going to Article-Fifteen us if we don't?

The lieutenant wanted to rage at them, wanted to threaten to have them shot. He took a second, then a deep breath and whispered, "If we don't get to the armory, none of you are going to live long enough to be brought up on charges." He gestured to the road. "*They* will see to that."

After a long moment he saw heads nodding in the darkness. He was past caring. Preparing to charge into even odds, knives against teeth, he gripped the handle of his combat knife and looked back around the corner of the barracks.

The pool of white cast by the streetlight was empty, the four figures now gone. That was even more unsettling.

"Follow me," Donny ordered, running into the street.

They did.

They were armed now, each of them carrying a loaded M4 assault rifle, except for PFC Vaughn who had a SAW, a Squad Automatic Weapon, the infantry light machine gun.

Donny also carried a nine-millimeter pistol, and all of them were loaded down with as many magazines and belts of ammo for the SAW as they could carry. Fragmentation grenades had been distributed among them as well.

The run to the armory, as tense as it had been, was without incident. They'd heard the echoing, non-laughter in the pine-scented night air, but no ghastly comrades had come at them out of the darkness. The red key card from the XO's envelope had gotten them inside, and while the men armed themselves, Donny had taken the time to scan the laminated documents that had come with the key card. He found it an enlightening read.

It was called a *Continuity Bunker,* and now things were making more sense to Second Lieutenant Donny Knapp.

The actual Feather *Mountain,* a former missile silo complex, had been transformed into a hardened shelter for the President of the United States, Cabinet members, Congress and senior government officers; a place of refuge in the event of war or national disaster, natural or otherwise. A place where a working government could be maintained. The documents stated that it was one of three spread across the country. The others (assumingly identical or nearly so) were located at Apache Flats, New Mexico and Mount Avalon in Washington State. Cheyenne Mountain in Colorado, mostly mothballed except for some communications people, was an alternate site.

Now the ridiculously long runway made sense as well. It was designed for Air Force One.

The reason for a constant training rotation of infantry units on the base fell into place as well. It meant that at any given time there would be from one to two companies of troops present, able to shift roles into that of a defensive force if *Bank Vault* – that was the activation code word he'd found in the orders – went live. This force was to be further supplemented by armor and mechanized infantry coming out of nearby Custer.

And where were those *guys,* Donny wondered?

His thoughts went back to the airfield. Were the President, Joint Chiefs and God knew who else inbound at this very moment?

“We need to hurry up,” he told his men, then moved them quickly across the street to the supply building. They seemed calmer now that they were armed; the terrors of the night weren’t as threatening when you were packing an assault rifle. For Donny, the darkness was no less forbidding than before. He feared the threats he couldn’t see more than those he could put a gun sight on.

The door to the supply building was locked, so they forced it. A scream from inside nearly triggered a burst of gunfire and ended a life, but Donny was able to yell “Hold fire!” before that happened. In the darkness they found a young, unarmed black woman in uniform, her hair pulled into a tight bun and holding only a flashlight that shook in her hands.

“C-corporal W-woods,” she said, saluting the lieutenant who’d just broken in. She explained that she’d been the only one here when everything started to happen, and had shut off the lights and locked the door. “I saw things out the windows, sir,” she said unsteadily, looking across the room as if some horrid thing might have its face pressed against the glass at this very moment. “Things…soldiers, killing each other.”

Donny nodded, looking her over. Compact, in good physical condition, shaken but not coming apart, and a corporal. He needed an NCO who outranked his borderline-mutinous troops. She would have to do. “Supply clerk?”

"Yes, sir."

"Well you're combat infantry now, Corporal." She didn't flinch, and he liked that. "We're going to need some gear."

Woods took them into the back of the building, a small warehouse filled with shelves holding everything from rain ponchos and night vision goggles to clean socks and skivvies. They geared up with packs and MREs, trauma kits, flashlights and spare canteens, then replaced whatever helmets, body armor and gloves that had been lost or discarded in the forest. Donny looked for a CNR (combat net radio), couldn't find one, and asked Woods about it. She said they had all been issued to the red and blue teams for their war games. *Of course,* he thought. Then it was back across the street – still no sign of hostiles – to get Cpl. Woods her own M4 and ammunition.

"We're heading back to the airfield," he told his squad as soon as they were ready. "Jones has the point. Watch your spacing and pick your feet up."

"Rules of engagement?" asked PFC Vaughn.

Donny snapped the charging handle on his M4. "If it's coming to kill you, kill it first."

-24-

DEVIL DOG

Ohio – October 29

The small hours of the morning, and a three-quarter October moon looked coldly down upon a world rapidly changing. Wind caused dead leaves to skitter across the pavement and swirl out into the night. The air had a fall smell. A dead smell.

Backed into one of several stalls in an open-faced garage behind a mom-and-pop gas station, the Secret Service CAT Suburban was just another shadow in the darkness. In the passenger seat, one of the two men had his eyes closed, head resting against the side window. The other was awake and watchful.

Agent David King sat behind the steering wheel, looking out at the night with a P90 SMG cradled in his lap. Nothing moved other than blowing leaves, and no headlights traveled the road on the other side of the little gas station. The Suburban's dashboard radio was turned off; David didn't want to drain the battery, and wouldn't run the engine for fear of the white plume the exhaust would make in the cold air, something to draw attention to a vehicle that wasn't supposed to be there.

He looked over at the man beside him, who was now wearing a blue, zip-up fleece instead of a suit jacket, and an Ohio State Buckeyes cap pulled down low over his eyes. With one exception, they hadn't stopped moving from Cleveland until this place. David's only concession had been to pull over behind an abandoned Range Rover – its doors were standing open and a bloody palm print smeared a side window – to do a quick search. He'd found a few bottles of water, along with the fleece and the cap, insisting the President put them on in order to blend in better.

David looked back out the windshield, grateful that the President was sleeping. It had been a long, stressful day, and he knew the man was exhausted not only by the ordeal at the plaza and the nightmare at the airport, but also from worry for his family and country, two things he was supposed to protect above all else. David was himself trying to process the horrors they'd seen. Being immersed in crisis and duty had kept it at bay, but now that it was quiet, the magnitude of it all was creeping in.

Getting out of the city…he was amazed they'd been able to do it. Cleveland Hopkins International Airport was on the west side of the sprawl, the opposite direction of where they needed to go. Under normal circumstances it would have been a straight shot east on 480, but that hadn't been the case. Before ever reaching it, David had seen that the highway was filled with stopped vehicles and pedestrians, and so he'd been forced to weave along the side streets, constantly turning, blowing intersections and scraping against cars and even the sides of buildings as he bulled his way through. Often he'd found the way blocked by an accident, stopped traffic, a car fire or a hungry mob, and he'd been forced to backtrack.

Frequent glances at the gas gauge added to his tension. An armored, full-size Chevy Suburban was not fuel efficient, especially in stop-and-go traffic occasionally punctuated by bursts of acceleration.

Sometimes the dashboard radio crackled with scattered transmissions, but none from a source David trusted, and so he left it alone. As they traveled they saw what was becoming of Cleveland, Ohio; civil breakdown and confusion, unchecked fires and death. At one point they'd driven past a stopped, white church bus with dozens of young, frightened faces pressed against the glass. President Fox had made a noise deep in his throat and touched the passenger window as if reaching out to them, but David drove on without stopping, his stomach in a sick ball.

Abandoned police cruisers and empty ambulances, dropped luggage and overturned strollers, bodies…so many bodies…and running mobs of people, some screaming, some bloody and hunting. Figures thumped against the side of the CAT vehicle, pounding the bulletproof glass and then sliding away. Some went under the tires with a crunch, making David grit his teeth. He kept going, and the President didn't tell him to stop.

It felt like a crawl, moving east through the outer neighborhoods, and the odyssey stretched into the evening and beyond as the sun went down. Even before they were out of the city, the agent briefly thought about heading for Youngstown – there was a military base there that could provide shelter – but it would take them too close to Akron. That would mean more of this, and there was no guarantee the base would be secure. He'd seen soldiers running within those murderous packs, too. No, the order to execute *Bank Vault* had gone out, and that was what he would do. Roughly two hundred miles to the hardened shelter at Feather Mountain – an extraction that would normally have been done by air (accompanied by a heavy team of agents bristling with weapons) – now to be accomplished in a lone SUV soon to run out of gas.

A voice from the passenger seat snapped him out of his thoughts. "Thanks for letting me sleep. Where are we?"

"Just off Route Six," David said, "east toward Chardon. Farm country." Originally he'd planned to head for Interstate 90, go northeast along the lake and into the westernmost tips of New York and then quickly down into Pennsylvania, but that way would take them through Erie, and he wasn't going to intentionally enter a city of any real population if he could avoid it. Cross-country by way of county roads would be slower, but it would mean encountering fewer people, and at this point, everyone but the two men inside the Suburban was a threat.

Garrison yawned and stretched, sat and looked out the windshield for a while and sipped at a bottled water. Then he offered a second bottle to his bodyguard. "How long have you been with the Service?"

"Twenty years tomorrow," said David. "My retirement was supposed to start when we got back from Cleveland."

"I hope you'll stay on for a bit longer," Garrison said with a soft chuckle, nodding toward the world outside.

It made David smile. "Of course, Mr. President." Then, "Are you cold, sir? I can run the heater if you like."

"Aren't we almost out of fuel?" A nod in return, and Garrison shook his head. "Nights in Iraq got a lot colder than this. People don't realize how cold the desert can get." He smiled. "I can take it. I was a Marine a lot longer than I've been a politician."

"For what it's worth," David said, "none of us in the Service have ever thought of you as a politician."

Garrison nodded his appreciation. They were quiet for a while, both of them watching the night. Then Garrison looked at the agent and said, "I'm deeply sorry about your wife."

David was caught off guard, and he stumbled on his words, a sudden knot of emotion in his chest. "Mr. President…thank you…I…how did…?

"The Director told me about it when it happened. I recognized your name when you pulled me out of the limo."

David looked down. "I got your card. I just thought…"

"That one of my staffers wrote it?" Garrison shook his head. "I get it. No, that was me. I wanted to go to the funeral, but they had me in Prague for that peace summit. The least I could do was write a few words. I can't imagine what it was like for you."

"It meant a lot, sir." *Was* like? *Still* was like. David seemed to hear Emily's scream everywhere, and the memory of seeing her falling, falling and hitting like a rag doll, was on a continuous loop in his head. He hadn't shared that with the shrink during his Service-mandated counseling sessions. What would be the purpose? Could the shrink take away those memories? The shrink was surprised that David wasn't angry, but that part was simple. When he was being honest, he knew it was a terrible accident, no one's fault. The lawyers had seen it differently, however. *Manufacturer's defect and improper inspection and maintenance. Gross negligence on all counts.*

The result? A zip line harness that separated from the cable in the center of an open space eight decks high, on a cruise ship in international waters. It was supposed to be a vacation filled with fun and romance, one last attempt to salvage a marriage that was about to end, to choose her over the job. David was hopeful that it would work, *wanted* it to work because he still loved Emily very much. It might have, too. Now he would never know.

The lawsuit settlement had been substantial, permitting David to stop working entirely if he'd wanted. He didn't. It guaranteed that even without his government retirement he would be able to live comfortably for the rest of his life. Again, not what he was looking for. But it had purchased the cabin and property in Alaska outright, giving him a place where he could retreat (*hide*) from the world in quiet and privacy after the conclusion of a long career.

Private. Yes, and again, when he was being honest with himself, that remote cabin ensured that he wouldn't disturb anyone when the void left by the passing of his wife and career became too much to bear. No one would hear the gunshot when he finally put the muzzle in his mouth.

"I couldn't..." David fought the emotion. "I should have done something." He couldn't meet the President's eyes.

"You can't protect everyone, David," Garrison said. "Sometimes things just happen." The man's voice cracked at that, and David looked up to see the president turn away, wiping a palm at his eyes and clearing his throat.

"Sir…"

Garrison looked back. "Your turn to get some sleep."

"Mr. President, I'm fine. I-"

"You've been up since before the sun, I'm sure, and today has been just as hard on you. This is an order from your Commander-in-Chief. You're no good to anyone if you're exhausted, so catch a few hours. I'll wake you if there's trouble. Now give me a quick tutorial on that SMG."

Before today, the idea of a Secret Service agent handing a loaded weapon to the President of the United States was unthinkable (as if POTUS might suddenly decide to kill himself) and would be an absolute career-ender. But things were different now, and so he followed orders and handed over the weapon. The President was no stranger to firearms, so instruction didn't take long. The P90 SMG was an odd but elegant bullpup design where the trigger was forward and the magazine and action was to the rear. It was ambidextrous, stubby and curved, with a fifty round magazine of 5.7 x 28mm rounds that loaded horizontally along the top of the stock. The empty casings ejected straight down instead of to the side. The weapon combined a high rate of fire and the punch of an assault rifle into a small, concealable package, something easily hidden beneath a jacket and able to be pulled quickly without fear of snagging. David had found it clipped muzzle-down into a fast-action bracket beside the CAT vehicle's driver's seat, along with four full magazines.

A shadow moved beyond the hood of the Suburban, a mongrel Shepherd mix without a collar. Both men wondered for an instant if animals could be infected too, but quickly dismissed the worry. There had been no sign of that, and infected humans were concern enough.

"Mr. President, promise you'll wake me before you engage anything."

"Get some rest, Agent King."

David folded his arms, leaned into the corner and closed his eyes. He knew there was no way he'd sleep. Within ten minutes however, he was breathing deeply, quickly descending into dreams that would be tormented by fear, loss and failure.

In the seat beside him, the man now keeping watch knew what that was like.

COLLAPSE

-25-

TAPAK'S DARK GIFT

It wasn't a steady spread each day, as would be experienced with a normal virus. It was more like a steep, short Bell curve. To think that the number of infected would double each day was simplistic, ill-conceived math, and completely inaccurate. This wasn't some screenwriter's idea of vampirism, where each infected individual infected another. Over the course of a day, each one infected thousands, who immediately began infecting thousands more.

By the end of the first day of Soo Yim's exposure, helped along by the modern wonder of air travel, millions were carrying a lively strain of Trident. They passed it on through physical contact, the surfaces they touched, the air they expelled from their lungs.

Day two – still a week and a half away from outbreak – was a mathematical nightmare. The millions already infected passed it along, and upwards of a billion people had caught it by the time day three arrived. By the end of *that* twenty-four-hour cycle, the vast majority of the earth's seven billion people had been exposed. Day four saw the rate of new infections drop sharply, simply because there were fewer people who hadn't contracted the virus. By the time Trident went *live* on October twenty-eight, there were less than a hundred thousand people worldwide who hadn't come into contact with it, primarily because they lived in or were visiting remote locations. That too would soon change, as eventually Trident would seek them out in their isolation, often carried on something as simple as a puff of wind.

Using a simple and obvious model, based upon what they knew and what they'd seen, medical professionals across the globe agreed that there was a ten day incubation period – ten days from exposure – before Trident became active in a victim, the aggressive *Phase-Three* stage that Doctor Rusk and others had classified. It was also quickly determined that many of the infected would not have to wait ten days before undergoing the change, because every non-fatal attack, every bite and wound passed along *activated* organisms that seemed to "switch on" still-dormant organisms in the victim, bringing on the transformation. In these cases, the Phase-Two symptoms of disorientation and sickness lasted less than a minute before the victim – assuming they survived the attack – became a Phase-Three; loss of rational thought (it was guessed,) violence, hunting behavior.

A dangerous killer with a driving need to consume flesh.

Humans are especially skilled at deceiving themselves, and even those learned men and women in the medical research profession are not immune to that flaw. They went at Trident with the understanding that it was a virus, because it looked and acted like one, and assumed that it would continue to look and act like one. A biological mystery, certainly, but one which could eventually be understood through reason and adhering to the rules of science. And of course the ridiculous idea that it was *not* a virus, that it was the manifestation of a dark and ancient Indonesian God, never came up.

They were wrong on many levels, such as the assumption of a ten-day incubation.

Dead wrong.

Albion, Nebraska

The sun was up. *Well,* Jim Springer thought, *it would be if it wasn't hidden behind a storm sky.* The rain was coming down steadily, sliding off his plastic poncho and turning the brim of his cowboy hat into a waterfall. Like Jim, the other men and one woman standing in the bed of the dump truck did their best to ignore the weather and keep their eyes on the road leading into town.

There were three main ways into Albion, all two-lane country roads cutting through empty cornfields and into the tiny collection of houses and silos, small town shops, barns and a railyard. The other two were similarly blocked by trucks and manned by local farmers, all of them armed.

To Jim's right, a deputy sheriff sneezed and tipped his hat forward to let the water spill off. The man to his left was motionless and silent. That one hadn't picked up a gun yet, but Jim wondered.

The news had shown them that what had begun as pocket outbreaks on Saturday had, during the overnight, turned into a full-blown crisis as sickness and violence swept the globe. Death tolls were climbing faster than news broadcasters could report, and the government – something for which Jim and his neighbors had little use – was falling apart. It was clear that there would be no help from that direction, which suited Jim just fine. He would take care of his own.

He glanced back over his shoulder toward the rail yard, where a few corn silos and a string of cattle cars sitting on a siding were still visible through a gray curtain. The deputy did the same.

"At least the rain muffles the sound," the deputy said. "I can't hear 'em anymore. You?"

Jim Springer shook his head. "That goddamn laughing is the worst. Excuse me, Reverend." The silent man on his left said nothing, just stared outward.

The deputy nodded in agreement. "I wonder if that was the right thing to do with 'em, though."

Springer gave him a hard look. "What, we should have let them wander around loose and end up like Genoa?"

The deputy just shrugged.

The cattle cars had been Springer's idea, and even after what had happened he was still convinced it had been the right thing to do. Albion hadn't been immune to the infection, of course, but after the first killing (the local barber had *gone over* and slaughtered his own family – Springer shot him down in the street) precautions had been taken. Anyone showing symptoms, that confused and drooling state right before they turned, had been collected and hurried off to one of the unused cattle cars on the rail siding. Maybe two dozen in all, so far. Of course *that* had gone badly, once those locked inside succumbed and turned on the others. Now all of them were raging against the steel slat walls, reaching through and howling, giggling in their madness.

Jim Springer shuddered, told himself it was just the chill of the rain. Two dozen wasn't so bad, as long as you didn't think about who they'd been before they became monsters. Friends, family…

Before communications started to break down, they'd heard that Omaha had turned into such a nightmare, but on a city-wide scale. Thousands had become crazed cannibals, killing thousands more, fattening their ranks and quickly overwhelming the population.

Also during the overnight, surviving refugees from Omaha had been welcomed into Genoa, the next community over from Albion. They'd brought the madness with them, and in no time the small Nebraska town had turned into a slaughterhouse.

The reverend's mother had lived there.

Jim Springer looked at the young man to his left. Until last night, the reverend had been an optimistic and lively young man. Now he was gray, his features stony, as if all the warmth and charity had gone out of him.

"Look," said the deputy, pointing through the rain. "Here they come."

Springer saw the headlights, a string of cars and trucks stretching back along the road and headed this way. More refugees. Around him, the bolts and slides of rifles and shotguns racked live rounds into chambers. Neighbors or not, Albion wasn't going down like Genoa.

"Jim?" the reverend said, extending a hand but not taking his eyes off the approaching cars. "If you please?"

Jim Springer nodded, and handed the reverend a loaded revolver.

Memphis, Tennessee

An obese woman carrying an armload of sequined jackets bustled out through the gates of Graceland, heading for a nearby minivan with a *HEARTBREAK HOTEL* bumper sticker. Others were emerging from the estate behind her and loading cars with clothing, framed photos and gold records, even furniture. Squeezed into a bloody white jumpsuit off to the left, a pudgy, middle-aged Elvis raced down the sidewalk toward the obese woman, slavering and silver-eyed, fingers hooked into claws. The woman froze and screamed, but didn't let go of the sequined jackets.

A thirty-caliber machinegun rattled, the bullets catching Elvis on the run, cutting him down before he could reach his prey. Specialist Stu "Stewie" (he *hated* that nickname) Goldman, standing in the turret of his Humvee, looked over the barrel of his weapon to inspect his work. Yep, Elvis was dead. In fact *had* been for more than thirty years before Stewie was born. The soldier shuffled right, rotating the machinegun as he searched for more targets, maybe even another Elvis. He'd heard about these guys, obsessive impersonators that infested this city like fleas on a stray. Stewie thought it was retarded, didn't see what the big deal was. His musical taste ran more toward Kanye and Jay-Zee, even the old-school stuff by Snoop and Tupac.

No more Elvis's, only looters, and how weird that he and the men in the two Hummers on this patrol should be doing nothing about that. But the rules of engagement had been clearly explained before they rolled out of their garrison; protect life, not property.

The obese woman loaded her jackets into the minivan, then gave a longing look back toward the gates of Graceland. Apparently she thought better of making a second trip, and the young soldier watched her drive away. He laughed. It didn't really matter *where* she chose to die, did it? Here was just as good as someplace else, and he would have bet a considerable portion of his meager paycheck that fatty would be dead by the end of the day.

The two Humvees started rolling, the Tennessee National Guard unit in front and Stewie's regular Army Hummer following.

The city had turned into a complete shit show. Blocks of buildings were on fire, police and military units were collapsing from within as first-responders and soldiers were overwhelmed by aggressors or the infections in their own bodies, quickly turning into inhuman killers and swarming through the streets, hunting down prey. Their numbers grew at an alarming rate, and Stewie had turned his weapon on more than a few of these monsters in uniform. He didn't feel bad about it.

Only this morning he'd been anticipating the recoil of his thirty-caliber, wondering if he could really do it, fire a machinegun at another person. By now he was well past the wonder, and his weapon was getting more and more work as hostiles seemed to appear from everywhere. At least they couldn't shoot back, though they looked like they would scramble right up the side of the Hummer if they got close enough. Stewie didn't let them get close.

Civilians or not, armed or not, it was combat, and although it wasn't how he'd imagined it would be, he loved it all the same. Combat was what he'd signed up for when he enlisted, turning his back on the family deli and breaking his parents' hearts.

"Nice Jewish boys don't join the Army," his mother said, sobbing when he'd showed her the enlistment papers.

"Israeli kids do it all the time," he responded.

"You're not an Israeli!" Her shrill voice was half the reason he'd signed up. "It's just not what our people do!" She'd been inconsolable.

There was no way he was going to spend his entire life living and working on the Chicago North Side, stinking of cheese and pastrami and waiting for his parents to die so he could inherit a deli he'd have to share with his brother and two sisters. Unfortunately, by the time he was old enough and finished infantry school, most of the heavy stuff was over in both Afghanistan and Iraq, and he had never deployed. He did, however, have to eat shit from guys around his age who'd been there, and treated the *un-blooded* members of the unit no better than they had the Hajis.

But *this!* No crazy desert heat, no snipers or IEDs…safe up in his turret with a shitload of belted ammo standing by *and* permission to use it. This was the best combat of all, better than any video game he'd ever played. Now he only needed a cool nickname. His *war* name. Maybe *Elvis.*

Stewie's Humvee coasted to a halt in an intersection on Elvis Presley Boulevard, drifting into the side of an abandoned delivery van and stopping with a soft crunch. He swung his machinegun in a slow circle, searching for the reason they'd stopped, while the Tennessee Guard unit in front kept going.

Nothing. No targets, no looters or refugees. Why were they stopped? He called down through the turret opening, "Corporal, what gives?"

Teeth sank into his legs and hips, arms wrapped around his waist and fingernails dug painfully into his sides. There wasn't even time to scream before Stu "Elvis" Goldman was pulled inside, pulled down to the teeth.

Dallas, Texas

His name was Ibrahim Farhad, but his friends and professors at the university knew him as Jamal Samir, or simply Jimmy, a native of Morocco studying in the U.S. Not that many of them knew where Morocco was, or that it was even an Islamic nation. Most American students, he had found, couldn't name their own states and had little understanding of their country's history or system of government (though they all knew who the Kardashians were dating.) Soft and lazy in his eyes, they accepted "Jimmy" as, if not actually one of their own, then very similar; a laid-back twenty-year-old interested in girls, beer and partying. And although these things were forbidden by his culture, Ibrahim publicly partook of them all.

"Meet their expectations and you will become invisible," his handler had said. Ibrahim did, and he was. With no trace remaining of his Iranian accent, he was just one of the guys. Some of his classmates even thought he was Mexican.

The charade ended today.

Today he was no longer Jimmy Samir, or even Ibrahim Farhad. Today he was simply the Sword of Allah, about to cut down the enemies of Islam. How fitting that it should be Sunday, the supposed holy day of this land.

He walked from the apartment. It had been selected intentionally because it wasn't far from his destination, and now he had only a few blocks to travel before he reached the walkways and vast parking lots around the target, a mighty white structure with a dome arching into the blue, midday sky. The *real* temple of these godless people. The thought made him smile.

Ibrahim was dressed in an untucked, long-sleeve plaid button-up, skinny jeans and work boots, and a knit cap to complete the hipster image. Beneath the cap his head was freshly shaven, and his skin smelled of the flower-scented oils in which he'd bathed, all part of the rituals of a morning spent in prayer.

The blue nylon pack on his back carried the stuff of bad dreams.

How many years had his people endeavored to obtain such a device, and how careful had they needed to be to smuggle it into this country and into Ibrahim's destiny? His handler said it had been a lifetime of work to come to this point in history. The wires ran from the interior of his backpack through a hole in his shirt and inside down the sleeve to his right hand. The trigger, a cylinder the same approximate shape and size as a roll of mints with a button at one end, was concealed in the palm of a fingerless knit glove, yet another affectation of the hipster.

It was armed. A simple movement of his thumb (possible even if he was shot many times, his handler said) followed by a millisecond of white heat, and he would be standing before his god, a blessed martyr in the Jihad. It made him tremble in anticipation to know that today he would meet Allah. In his wake he would leave their temple in ruins, a gravesite for 70,000 incinerated infidels.

Something was wrong, and he noticed it even as he made his way to the wide, concrete walkway. The vast parking lots…they were empty. Not just a little, like being very early, but empty. Where were the cars, the swarming crowds of people in their jerseys, the fools who painted their faces blue and silver? As if for the first time, it occurred to him that the streets along his approach had been empty as well. Was he so intent upon his mission that it hadn't registered?

The plague...of course. Allah's wrath was already sweeping the city of unbelievers. Ibrahim and his fellows had been so involved in their preparations however, that no one had bothered to turn on a local news station.

Wait. Not completely empty. Two policemen stood a ways ahead of him along the walkway next to a large flashing sign, the kind used along highways, this one bearing a single message. The sudden fear that he might not be allowed to complete his mission caused Ibrahim to stumble a step.

In addition to the handler, there had been three of them in the apartment, the other two young men Ibrahim's age, both attending university as he was, with similar cover stories. Because of their race it was assumed they would come together, and their association raised no alarms. None were on watch lists, and none did anything to draw unwanted attention.

They'd left the apartment one at a time, Ibrahim going last because he had the shortest distance to travel. The first was headed for a pre-positioned car bomb left in a parking lot. He would drive it into the center of a crowded restaurant and shopping district. The second wore a multi-pocket vest beneath a light jacket, each pouch filled with rectangular blocks of C4 studded with steel ball-bearings. This one was headed for the food court of a busy mall.

But it was Ibrahim who had the honor of carrying the most glorious of the three weapons. At a predetermined time, all three would detonate simultaneously.

Now that plan was in jeopardy.

GAME CANCELED, flashed the sign. Ibrahim came to a halt and stared at it, even as one of the policemen started moving slowly toward him. The other stayed back, holding the leash of an all-black Shepherd that stood very still, staring intently at the young man.

Was this the kind of dog that could detect explosives? Or just an attack animal?

The two policemen looked like soldiers to Ibrahim, dressed all in black with their trousers tucked into boots, fearsome with their helmets, body armor and MP-5 submachineguns. Fearsome *aliens,* he thought, as they watched him from behind the round lenses of their gas masks. There was no one here but them, no relief from their boredom except perhaps the boy with the backpack. He needed to disengage, but not so quickly that it would appear suspicious.

The first policeman approached and stopped about four feet away, gesturing at the big, blinking sign. "Not clear enough for you?" he said, his voice muffled behind the mask.

Arrogant and superior. Just like policemen back in his homeland. Ibrahim shrugged. "I have tickets. I was hoping."

The cop shook his head at yet another dumb college kid. "That's too bad," the cop said. "You shouldn't be outside. The city's in a state of emergency." The dog barked behind him, and Ibrahim forced himself not to flinch. "Where are you from?" the cop asked.

Ibrahim's training had taught him not to be overly friendly with American police, but not to be belligerent either. "Here," he said. "I go to school at UT. My apartment isn't far." If asked, he was prepared to show both a university ID and a Texas driver's license with an address only slightly off from the actual location.

The cop looked at him for a moment, an endless moment in Ibrahim's mind, then said, "Get off the street and go home. It's dangerous out here."

Ibrahim gave a nod as the cop turned away, his eyes flicking longingly toward the big stadium. He wouldn't even have needed to get inside (and couldn't, since bags were inspected at the outer gates, and *that* certainly couldn't be allowed) only detonate in the crowds gathering outside. Even from there, the force of the blast would take care of the massive structure and everyone inside. Well, he had a secondary target, and didn't turn in its direction until he had gone back the way he'd come and was out of the policeman's sight.

It took about an hour to walk there. On his way he saw a few cars and hurrying pedestrians, but the streets were essentially empty, lacking the buzz of a major American city. The absence of traffic wasn't the only thing out of place. There were unattended bodies lying on sidewalks, drawing flies. How bad had this plague become? Ibrahim ached to watch the news, check the internet to see how much damage it was causing to his enemies, but he had to focus on the mission. He didn't even dare pull something up on his phone (had in fact left it behind) because he had been warned about what a stray electrical signal might do to the thing on his back. A very thin chance, but not worth risking, not after the operation had come this far. Besides, bodies lying in the streets of Dallas told him what he needed to know.

And it made him worry about his secondary target before he ever arrived.

He needed crowds for maximum shock value, and his new destination – the city's passenger rail station – should have provided that. From more than a block away however, he realized this wouldn't work either. Like the stadium it was closed, and here there were not only police but some soldiers as well. Ibrahim didn't even attempt an approach. He moved on.

There was no third target. The idea that both the stadium *and* the train station would be unviable just hadn't been considered. Ibrahim's backpack weighed heavy on him, an opportunity that might now never come. For a moment he thought about returning to the apartment for guidance, but quickly dismissed the idea. That would be shameful, an admission of failure and a reason for those controlling the operation to select a more worthy martyr for the delivery. Besides, when he left the handler had been sitting in a chair, staring glassy-eyed at a wall, a thin trickle of drool escaping his lips. Lost in religious fervor, no doubt. He would not be pleased to see Ibrahim anywhere outside paradise.

No, he would complete his mission. He knew where to go, a place sure to be both crowded and with easy access. He changed directions.

Another hour of walking empty streets saw the time for the simultaneous detonations come and go. Certainly his brothers were with Allah already, but the thought caused him to frown. He heard the sound of sirens seeming to float from every direction, but they were scattered, lonely sounds, not the concentrated frenzy of first-responders converging on a major blast in a population center. And he would have seen pillars of black smoke from one or both of the others. The skies above Dallas were blue and peaceful. Could they *all* have failed? No. Ibrahim would not fail.

A few more moving cars loaded with people fleeing the city, and he smelled a fire somewhere but saw no flames or smoke. There were signs of looting, more dead bodies in the street, and at one point his journey was almost cut brutally short. In front of an apartment building Ibrahim stumbled upon a young woman in a bloody dress, her blond hair clotted against her face. She'd been handcuffed by one wrist to a wrought iron sidewalk planter and was standing over the corpse of a Dallas police officer. The woman, eyes bright and silvery, snarled and lunged, almost caught hold of Ibrahim's plaid shirt but was jerked back short by the handcuff.

Ibrahim ran away from her, and a throaty chuckling followed him.

Part of the young man's training had required that he study and memorize the geography of the city, and so without a map or GPS he unerringly reached the new target location. A determined smile crossed his face as he saw the parking lots surrounding the large building clogged with people and ambulances. The hospital was clearly filled beyond capacity, because medical staff was conducting triage and examinations out in the lot as hundreds lined up, hoping to get inside. They wore painter's masks and held their children close, many of them watching images on their cell phones, a general horror on their faces. There were policemen here too, but they appeared to have given up any attempt to organize the crowd and simply stood to the side, watching.

No one challenged or delayed him as he and his backpack moved slowly into the parking lot and into the thick of the crowd. *High profile, big crowds, wide open access... The perfect target.*

Ibrahim realized that he was sweating, and a wave of nausea brought him to a halt, stomach cramps suddenly doubling him over. He squeezed his eyes shut for a moment, waiting for the sensation to pass.

Nerves? Excitement with a touch of fear? He shook his head, but when he opened his eyes his vision was cloudy, the shapes around him distorted. *What was this place? Hospital, that was it. Had he come here because he was sick? Hard to remember. The mission. The mission, go inside and carry out the mission.*

Ibrahim took a few steps in the direction of the entrance and stopped again as he was hit by withering nausea once more. He leaned against the trunk of a car.

So hard to focus. Need a doctor. No! You are about to meet God! But for some reason he couldn't remember God's name. After more than half an hour of leaning in that one spot and staring, Ibrahim couldn't remember anything anymore. People moved past and ignored him, and the would-be martyr took no notice. His arms dangled limp at his sides, a grayish drool slipping from his lips. Ibrahim chuckled at nothing in particular.

And then, as was typical of Phase-Twos about to turn, his hands began the reflexive motor activity of clenching and unclenching.

A flash of white that was hotter than the sun. A pressure wave of incomparable heat. Ibrahim, the hospital, everyone and everything in a four block radius vaporized. A black and gray mushroom cloud boiled up into the clear Dallas sky as radioactive particles took to the wind.

Dallas burned.

There was no one to put out the fires.

Long Island, New York

Wagner Davis lay naked in his king-sized bed, the satin sheets in a tangle at his feet from the latest round of violating Amber. He watched the sun come up through a wall of windows down one side of the bedroom. Of course he had to watch it come up *over* the roofs of the seaside houses across the street. His own house, at just over six thousand square feet, was a monument to luxury architecture, tasteful stone and glass with professional landscaping and a five-car garage housing *three* Porches. Impressive. The equal to those houses across the street in every way but one. Where he could *see* the water, they were *on* the water, and that fact left a taste in his mouth so bitter that even the finest sunrise in the Hamptons couldn't wash it away.

"Fuckers," he muttered, reaching for the small mirror on the nightstand and snorting a quick line. It was only a moderate habit, and he could certainly afford it. With a gasp he dropped back into the pillows and looked up at the ceiling.

Amber. Where had the little slut disappeared to? Right, she'd gone to take that annoying little dog of hers for a quick walk. He hated that nasty little dog, but Amber was nastier and in a good way. The thought of her taut, perfect body moving against him, of her willingness to indulge in any perversion made him stiffen.

"Hurry up with that dog," he muttered. She made Viagra unnecessary, but he took it anyway just to make things interesting. On his taxes he had her listed as an *executive assistant* only because *personal freak* wasn't an allowable deduction.

Elsa didn't know about Amber. Well, she probably did, or at least suspected there was an Amber-type, but she didn't care. Elsa had her own money (her family imported diamonds) and her own boy-toys. She was in Tel-Aviv right now, no doubt fucking one of them. Or two. Elsa had a thing for taking on young Israeli soldiers two at a time. She also had a thing for her black American Express card and anorexia. Wagner didn't care either. They had their arrangement, and didn't get in each other's way.

And *his* part of the arrangement had better get her tight little ass back in this bed, he thought, stiffening further. For some reason, the image of his wife with other men was almost as arousing as thinking about Amber. He guessed he was a freak, too.

But his erection quickly softened as he looked out at those houses across the street, the ones *on* the water where *he* should be. Those people had *real* money (Spielberg lived up the block), unlike Wagner, and it made him clench his fists. One of the elite of Wall Street, a premier broker with more than a hundred million in investments and seventeen million liquid, it still wasn't *real* money. He still *worked.*

"Fuckers," he said again, climbing out of bed and pulling on his robe. On his way out of the bedroom he picked up the chrome .45 automatic from where it sat next to his cocaine mirror. Things were fucked out there, and he didn't go anywhere without the pistol, not even in his own home. He was safe enough out here though, he supposed. The grounds were walled with a high gate, the house had a first-class security system, and besides, nothing bad ever really happened out in the Hamptons. But better to carry insurance.

Wagner didn't believe in God, but thank *Him* that this crazy outbreak had exploded over the weekend or he would have been caught in Manhattan when it went down. The thought of being trapped in that madness – millions of people packed together and tearing each other apart – made him shudder.

He padded barefoot down the carpeted stairs and into the foyer, seeing the front door standing wide open. His assistant's stupid little dog stood trembling in a corner, the leash still attached to its collar and a puddle of urine on the floor beneath it.

"Ah, goddammit, Amber," he yelled. "Your fucking dog pissed in the house again and I'm not cleaning it up!"

Wagner's gardener Jesus (or Jose, or fucking Pancho, he couldn't remember) walked through the open front door and came right at the stock broker, teeth bared and a snarl rising from his throat as he reached.

"Jesus!" Wagner cried, calling the Lord's name, not his gardener's, and shot the man in the chest at a range of three feet, right through the heart. A blast of thick, pink snot blew out the man's back and splattered against a wall. The gardener dropped. "Jesus!" Wagner shouted again.

Amber, naked beneath an open silk robe, burst from the adjacent living room and hit Wagner hard, slamming him to the floor and bouncing his head off the marble. He cried out, squeezed the automatic's trigger and blew off half of his own right foot.

Growling, Amber clawed her way up his legs and sank her teeth into his scrotum, ripping it away like she was pulling a weed in the garden.

Wagner screamed, but not for very long.

Jakarta, Indonesia

Rivers of death. That's what it looked like from the air; masses of bodies streaming through the streets below, hunting and killing while many of the buildings they flowed between burned, sending pillars of black smoke into the sky. The government had decided that fire was the best way to deal with this, and dispatched Army flamethrower units into the streets. It had only succeeded in accelerating the inevitable. Smoke curled back through the helicopter's rotors as bodies plummeted from the broken windows of skyscrapers, while still more clustered on rooftops praying for an airborne rescue that would never come.

Indonesia's capital city was lost.

The helicopter was a British-made Sea King with civilian markings, once military like the men riding inside. Most had been Australian Special Forces, former SAS operators who now worked as private contractors. They preferred that label over *mercenaries.* Having streaked in from the sea, the chopper slowed now as it flew over the infested city, the pilot adjusting course as he angled toward the destination coordinates.

Bags, the team leader and Ocker, his second, looked down through the open side door at the carnage below. They wore sand-colored fatigues and combat gear, automatic weapons slung across their chests, and spoke to each other through headsets so as to be heard above the roar of wind and rotors.

"It's a dog's breakfast down there," said Ocker.

"Yeah," said Bags, nodding. "Little brownies tearing the place up proper."

The same was true back in Sydney, of course, they'd all seen it. But they weren't going back to Sydney. A remote medical research lab in New Zealand was their final destination, at least until the next contract. By the look of things, that wouldn't take long. Men with their skill-set would be much in demand.

Ocker looked back at the other five men in the troop compartment, all similarly dressed and armed. His eyes settled on the newest member of the team, a kid from Perth who was former Army, but never part of an SAS team. It was something that didn't sit well with the men. Operators didn't do the hiring, but if the kid didn't carry his weight, they had their own ways of getting him out of the team. The kid's eyes met Ocker's, then darted away and came back. It was his first time out with this group. Ocker gave him a toothy smile and turned back to his friend.

"The grommet looks about to piss himself, mate."

Bags smirked. "Reckon that makes him the smartest one of the bunch."

"We need to be smart for this? That wasn't in the brochure."

The helicopter closed on an eight story building ahead, and the pilot called over the radio headset. "Two minutes."

Bags nodded and held up two fingers to his men, who began tightening their gear and inspecting their weapons one last time.

"He's supposed to be on the roof, right?" said Ocker.

A laugh from the team leader. "Right. And there's a fair go that he listened."

Ocker made a face. "Beauty."

The Sea King slowed, flared and swung its tail to the left, then landed with a bump on the rooftop helipad. A rooftop that was empty of people. The contractors leaped from the chopper and gathered into what looked like a rugby huddle.

"You know where we are," Bags shouted. "Probably the most dangerous place in any city right now. Keep sharp, mates."

They nodded and dispersed. Bags grabbed one of the men by the shoulder, a man who had caught the nickname "Dunny" after an incident in a Taiwanese strip club involving a prostitute, a baby alligator and a men's room.

"You're on rooftop security," Bags shouted over the rapid *WHUP-WHUP-WHUP* of the rotors. He pointed at a door that would lead to a stairwell. "Anyone who comes out of there who isn't us, you cut 'em down, no questions, no waiting to see if they're infected."

Dunny nodded, knelt at the edge of the helipad and trained an automatic weapon on the rooftop door of Pondak Indah Hospital, the biggest medical facility in the city.

"Coms up?" Bags said into his throat mic. He received a "copy" from each team member. Then they were moving, passing through the door and down a narrow concrete stairwell lit by the occasional emergency light. Bags took the lead, the muzzle of his MP-5 moving everywhere his head turned. They descended single-file, rubber-soled boots soft on the concrete steps.

"Seventh floor," he whispered.

As quiet as they were, the stairwell was not silent. A metallic banging followed by a chorus of howls echoed up from below. Small flashlights attached to gun barrels switched on as they continued their descent, the team leader checking each turn in the stairway before moving. A big, blue 7 on the wall beside an open door made them pause. "Ocker," Bags said, and his friend moved past him, down to the mid-floor landing between six and seven. "In position," he called a moment later.

Bags led them through the seventh floor door and into a carpeted hallway. According to his briefing and the schematics he'd reviewed before mission launch, this floor was made up only of labs and offices, no patient areas. It was a small comfort, knowing that right under their feet was a massive building absolutely packed with former sick people, now wild-eyed cannibals. He pointed to the new kid, said "Grommet" and pointed at the floor by the door. The kid took his position. Bags led the other two men of his group to the left, and soon heard voices speaking low and fast in another language, saw shadows moving across the floor of a larger area as someone passed in front of an emergency light.

There were seven Indonesians, a mix of men and women in white lab coats, gathered in a wide hallway with a bank of elevator doors behind them. They jumped at the appearance of the three armed men.

"Doctor Wulandari?" Bags said. One of them, a man in eyeglasses with close-cropped black hair shot with gray, raised a tentative hand. He wore a laptop bag and a soft-sided red cooler on straps that crossed his chest, and carried a doctor's satchel in the other hand. "I am Wulandari," he said.

"You were supposed to be on the roof," said Bags. "Alone." His two men split to cover the wide hallway in both directions.

"We…we heard noises in the stairwell." He shook his head.

"No shit. This bloody place is crawling with laughers. Time to go, Doctor." Bags motioned to the hallway behind him, but when the entire group started to move he held up a hand. "Just you, mate."

Wulandari stopped. "No. My team must go with me."

"Sorry, not part of the package. The helicopter's chockers anyway."

"No," Wulandari repeated. "The World Health Organ-"

"The WHO contracted for *you,* mate," Bags said. "No one else. Now tick-tock, time to leave."

Wulandari set down his satchel and crossed his arms. "This is unacceptable."

Bags blinked. "Don't get stroppy with me, ya little brownie. That's the arrangement." He took a step closer to the doctor and lowered his voice. "Your delay is putting my men at risk every minute we're here. If you think I won't shove you in a fucking bag and carry you out myself, think again."

Ocker's voice came over the headset. "Bags, we're about to get some blow-ins. They're coming up the stairwell. What's the fucking delay?"

"The doc doesn't want to come along."

"Does the contract say we have to bring him back alive? Pop a round in his head and we'll haul the body."

Bags glared at the doctor, then to the mic said, "I'm handling it. How long?"

"Well," said Ocker, "if we leave right bloody now she'll be apples." Then there was a burst of automatic weapons fire that the team leader didn't need a radio to hear, followed by Ocker's tense voice saying, "Action stairwell."

Bags bared his teeth and grabbed Doctor Wulandari by the collar of his lab coat, propelling him past his two men and back down the hallway. The two mercs collapsed back behind their leader, and when the other Indonesians tried to follow, one of them put a burst of nine-millimeter into the ceiling above them, exploding acoustic tiles and darkened fluorescent bars, making them scatter.

"My team!" Wulandari shrieked.

"They'll have to catch the next chopper, mate."

The Indonesian looked at him. "Another helicopter?"

Bags laughed and shoved him out onto the stairwell landing. "Sure, doc."

More gunfire, followed by the *CRUMP* of a fragmentation grenade down the stairs, a blast loud and close enough to make the team leader's ears ring. The new kid followed them onto the landing, then everyone headed up with the package, except for Bags. "You still with me, Ocky?" he asked his throat mic.

Ocker bolted up the stairs two at a time, slapping in a fresh magazine. "They're one floor down."

Bags could hear the horde shrieking and giggling as it poured up the fire stairwell. He pounded his friend on the shoulder to send him up, dropped his own frag grenade down the stairs and ran for the roof.

When Bags came through the rooftop door, his men were loading Wulandari onto the bird, all of them climbing aboard behind him except for Ocker, who stood at the edge of the helipad looking down at Dunny. The man was sitting on the cement, his weapon lying forgotten beside him, head down with his palms pressed to the temples. Drool spilled down the front of his body armor and magazine pouches.

"He's finished," Bags said, tugging on Ocker's combat harness, pulling him toward the chopper. "We gotta leave him."

The rooftop door banged open, and one of the men in the open side of the helicopter sent a string of tracer fire in that direction, cutting down a trio of crazed Indonesians in pale blue hospital gowns. Ocker and Bags boarded, and in seconds the Sea King was airborne, banking away from the hospital and heading back toward the sea. There was no lingering over the fallen city. They'd seen enough.

The troop compartment was quiet, except for Wulandari who was nearly hysterical. “You left them!” he screamed, spittle flying from his lips. “You left them to die!”

“I don’t write the contracts, mate,” said Bags.

The doctor’s face was streaked with tears as he looked out at a shattered city, his home. No one spoke until the green earth below had been replaced with blue.

“Oy,” Ocker said, nudging his friend and gesturing. Bags looked over and saw he was indicating the Grommet, the new kid. He sat slack-jawed, his eyes glassy and the skin purpling around them steadily. Bags nodded, and Ocker unholstered his pistol, firing once, blasting the Grommet in the temple and spraying pink and gray across the bulkhead. Bags leaned across a horrified Dr. Wulandari and shoved the lifeless body out the helicopter door.

The WHO contract to extract Wulandari was worth half a million quid, and Bags wasn’t going to let anyone compromise that.

Besides, he’d been the new kid.

Camp David, Maryland

“Mr. Vice President, we can’t debate this anymore. We have to move forward.”

Collin Hughes, the man being addressed, sat on a sofa in the main lodge with his tie loosened, holding a copy of the Constitution in both hands. He was a man in his middle-fifties who looked as if he’d aged ten years overnight. He shook his head slowly. “I’m not convinced.”

The Vice President’s Chief of Staff sighed and dropped into an armchair beside his boss. The main room of the rustic lodge felt crowded, though it wasn’t really, and could easily accommodate three times the number of people currently in here, far more than the dozen who were either sitting or standing. Most of them were in suits, and a Navy steward quietly serving coffee was the only one in uniform. Two of the suits – Secret Service agents – stood to one side of the room while two others – FBI agents who had arrived with the AG – stood on the opposite side of the room. Both pairs watched the other; the Secret Service agents because they didn't like armed outsiders near the VP, and the FBI because no one was feeling too warm and fuzzy about the Service after what had happened in Cleveland.

The Attorney General, a narrow woman in her late forties, faced VPOTUS as she sat on another couch next to the Secretaries of Commerce and Energy. The Speaker of the House stood near a fireplace next to the oldest and apparently only surviving Supreme Court Justice. President Fox's Deputy Chief of Staff – some would say *the* Chief of Staff since Tommy Barrow had been killed in Cleveland, sat in a hard-backed chair looking pissed-off. If he *was* now the White House chief, that would make him the second-highest ranking person in the room after the VP, but the way the conversation was going – passing over him most of the time – he felt like the lowest. One more thing to add to the night's confusion.

"Sir, *Bank Vault* has been activated," said the AG. She didn't care much for Hughes, but kept her expression neutral. "We can sort this all out when we get to Feather Mountain." There were three choppers out on the lawns below the main lodge, two of them containing fortunate though lower-ranking department deputies, along with VPOTUS's family. A detachment of hand-picked Marines guarded not only the helicopters but also the wooded expanse of Camp David, but that didn't necessarily make anyone feel more secure. Some of these men had gone missing, and there had already been one explosive outbreak in the Marine barracks that left several men dead. People were on edge. Anyone could be a ticking bomb.

"No," said the Speaker, "this needs to be decided now. We can't afford this long a gap in continuity."

The AG wanted to know what the hurry was, her voice sharp. The Speaker gave her a sly look and a dismissive wave. Other voices rose, until the Vice President raised *his* voice to demand quiet.

"Garrison Fox is a friend," Hughes said, "and I'm not going to do this lightly. But we *will* make a decision before we leave." He looked over at the President's Deputy (maybe not) Chief of Staff. "Tell me about the airport in Cleveland again."

The deputy cleared his throat. "A surviving Secret Service agent and an Ohio state trooper made it out there. Both aircraft were still on the ground, and a pair of burned rescue helicopters was on the tarmac. The President's limousine was completely burned with some doors standing open. Burnt bodies and shell casings everywhere. The bodies were too charred to make an identification."

"So he's presumed dead," the Vice President's Chief of Staff told the room.

"That's not what I said," Fox's deputy snapped. "I said they couldn't tell."

"But he might be," Hughes said, holding up a hand. "At the very least missing in hostile territory. Is that fair to say?"

Most heads nodded, but not all.

"We need clear leadership." He waved the Constitution he was holding. "And this isn't nearly as clear as we'd like it."

"Agreed, Mr. Vice President," said the Attorney General. "Which is why we need to make these decisions at the bunker."

"Oh, it's plenty clear," said the Speaker in his easy Georgia drawl, the one that thickened when he was lecturing or bullying other House members. "The Twenty-Fifth Amendment *makes* it clear." He knew it by heart. It was the amendment dealing with presidential succession, and he was next in line if anything happened to VPOTUS.

"One more time, if you please," the VP said.

The Speaker smiled. "Of course, sir. It *clearly* (he nodded at the AG when he said it) states that should the President become disabled, or otherwise unable to discharge his duties, then you, Mr. Vice President, can be easily placed in the role of acting President."

"It's *not* easy," snapped the AG.

Another smile from the Speaker. "Quite the contrary, Madam Secretary. All that is required is for the Vice President and a majority of Cabinet members to submit a letter to the Speaker of the House," he placed a hand on his own chest, "and to the Senate Pro-Tem. Once we sign it, Mr. Hughes becomes acting President of the United States."

"But Congress…" started the elderly Justice.

"Must decide on the matter of disability at a later time," the Speaker finished for him.

"The Senate Pro-Tem is dead," the VP's Chief of Staff said.

The Speaker nodded. "Then only I would need to sign it."

"Wait a minute," said the AG, "you need a majority of the Cabinet." She gestured to herself and the two men seated on the sofa with her. "This isn't the cabinet."

The VP's Chief of Staff leaned forward. "It may be." He ticked off the line of succession on his fingers. "After the VP there's the Speaker, then President Pro-Tem. Alive or dead, none are Cabinet members. State, Treasury and Defense are known dead. Then there's you, Madam Secretary, and that's one. Interior is missing, Agriculture is dead, and Commerce is here. That's two. Labor is dead."

The weight of it all seemed to descend with the roll call of casualties, people they all knew personally.

"Health and Human Services," he continued, "was at CDC Atlanta, but we've lost contact and Dr. Rusk is presumed dead. Housing and Transportation are *known* dead, and energy is on the couch beside you. That's three. Education, Veterans Affairs and Homeland Security, all dead."

"Three Cabinet members," Commerce said, his voice almost a whisper.

"So only the Vice President and two of you would have to agree," said the Speaker.

All eyes turned to the eighty-eight-year-old Supreme Court Justice, the only one who hadn't been torn apart (live on CNN as it turned out) by a mob of cannibals in Washington. The old man frowned, a move that turned his wrinkles into canyons and jowls into saddlebags. "Constitutionally," he said slowly, "the Speaker is correct."

Eyes went back to VPOTUS, who tapped the Constitution softly in one palm. "*Acting* only. Not sworn in, not yet."

"There will be time for that later," said his Chief of Staff. "Only if necessary, of course."

The AG folded her arms. "I'm not convinced. We don't have enough information."

"Acting on the best information available," drawled the Speaker, "we have to conclude that he's gone. I know it's a bitter pill to swallow." He looked at Commerce and Energy. "The country needs leadership, and time is precious. Do you concur?"

Both men nodded. The AG didn't need to shake her head. She was out-voted.

"Then we have a majority," said the Speaker. "Mr. Vice President, if you and the others will quickly draft a short letter, I'll add my signature and we'll be official."

"And then we head to Feather Mountain and start putting this country back together," the VP's chief said.

Fox's deputy stood abruptly and went outside without a word, slamming the door behind him.

"I won't argue with the Justice," the AG said, looking at the old man. "It's his ruling to make. But when Garrison Fox shows up and wants to know why someone else is sitting in his chair, he's going to know that I wasn't a part of this."

"Duly noted," drawled the Speaker.

While the Navy steward went to gather writing supplies, Hughes and his Chief of Staff moved close together and discussed their next moves in low voices. Outside, the first rays of a new dawn's sunrise were glowing through the pine trees.

A rattle of distant rifle fire came from out there.

There was a tremendous crash of metal trays and broken glass in the kitchen, followed by heavy thumping noises. Everyone froze. The FBI agents drew their weapons, and so did one of the Secret Service agents. The other clasped a palm to his forehead and staggered a few steps, his other hand clenching and unclenching.

"Oh, shit," said FBI, aiming at Secret Service.

"Don't you do it!" yelled Service, aiming at FBI.

More rifle fire outside, close to the lodge now, and something banged hard against the front door. A giggle came from the stumbling Secret Service agent. One of the FBI men yelled, “He’s turning!” and aimed.

Secret Service number two shot FBI one. His partner shot both Service agents. Bodies hit the floor as Navy kitchen staff in bloody cook’s whites came spilling through an open doorway, howling and gibbering as they tore into the people gathered in the main room. There was screaming, the sounds of more bodies hitting the floor. The front door to the lodge burst open, swinging back hard and almost knocking down the elderly Justice. A wide-eyed young Marine in blood-soaked camo came through, and several more like him followed. They fell upon the nation’s leadership.

An FBI pistol went off twice more and was silent.

The Vice President died at the teeth of a cook, the Speaker was disemboweled by a Marine and the others died soon after.

Slipping around the open front door and then outside, the eighty-eight-year-old Justice hopped down the porch steps, then headed down the lawns toward helicopters he hoped were still there. The old man hadn’t run this fast in forty years.

-26-

LABCOAT

CDC Atlanta – October 29

Dr. Rusk switched on the high-intensity lights over the table, bathing the naked body in white, making it appear even paler than it already was in its dead, blood-depleted state. The stainless steel instruments and surfaces in the room gleamed.

The physician clipped a wireless, digital microphone to the pale green, rubber apron she wore over blue scrubs. She was also wearing elbow-length gloves, a surgical mask and cap, and clear plastic glasses. She turned on the microphone (it was synced to a look-down digital camera above the autopsy table to make a complete record of the examination) and began.

"Post-mortem procedure, CDC Atlanta. The date is October twenty-nine, the time is two-oh-five AM. Doctor Moira Rusk attending." She looked up at a flat-screen monitor suspended amid the table lights. A CDC employee photograph was imaged beside the biographical and medical history of her patient.

And *patient* seemed hardly applicable.

"Subject is Terry Butters," she told the audio recording, "twenty-seven-year-old Caucasian male." She gave his height and weight. "Time of death was at eleven PM, three hours ago. Initial assessment of cause of death is puncture trauma to the right side of the neck, followed by severing of the right carotid artery." She used a long pair of forceps to pull the broken test tube from the corpse's neck, then plucked out the fragments she could find, placing it all in a plastic container.

Moira hadn't performed an autopsy in decades, and she could immediately tell that she'd lost much of her precision. In her youth she'd had regular opportunity to do the cutting, both as a medical researcher and during her time in Africa serving on a *Doctors without Borders* team, hunting that little bastard Ebola. That was a long time ago though, and now she was both unsteady and going through a process that was certain to be out of order compared to standardized post-mortem procedures. As an administrator at the apex of her career, Moira hadn't expected to ever *need* to perform an autopsy again. Certainly not on one of her own team members. But it was coming back quickly – *like riding a bike, as they say* – and if she made the odd mistake, her patient wasn't in a position to complain.

She returned to her examination; a head-to-toe inspection of the body. Moira looked closely at the skin, rolled the corpse from side-to-side and manipulated the joints.

"Rigor is consistent with time of death," she said, "and lividity looks normal." After death, gravity pulled the remaining blood downward until it pooled and began to congeal in the lowermost areas of the body, darkening and appearing as purple bruising. It Mr. Butters' case, it had collected in his back, buttock, thighs calves and arms, except where the flesh was pressed against the stainless steel table. There, the skin appeared as stark, white circles and ovals, pressure forcing the thickening blood away from the points of contact.

"No unusual marks or wounds, other than a hypodermic puncture inside the left elbow for a mandatory CDC blood draw." She glanced up at the monitor. "Toxicology shows the mandated antivirals, but is clear of illicit substances. Subject tests positive for heavy concentrations of the Trident organism and for the as-yet unclassified parasitic infestation."

Moira selected a scalpel from the tray and moved to the head of the table. "Making my incision to expose the skull." She made a circular cut around Terry Butters' head, cutting through hair, leaving the skin of his forehead untouched. Then with both hands she peeled the scalp up and forward, exposing the curve of the skull and leaving the inverted scalp as a grisly red mask resting on the dead man's face.

"Making cranial incision," she told the mic, triggering the bone saw and running it around the top of the skull. Ivory-colored dust and larger fragments made a small cloud around her hands as she worked. When she was done she used both hands again (and more than the expected exertion) to pull the skull cap off with a sticky, sucking sound.

The corpse's left eyelid twitched.

Moira saw it and dismissed it. Post-mortem muscle reflex was normal, and this was especially minor. The tiny muscles around the eyes were especially subject to contraction. She'd heard of cases where a corpse *sat up* on an autopsy table. Something like that would certainly be enough to frighten the inexperienced, but not Moira. The dead couldn't hurt you. What they carried in their fluids and tissue could, however. That was the only scary thing about them.

What she saw inside Terry Butters' head was still startling, though. The brain was encased in a clear, gelatin-like sac of fluid, the gray matter visible beneath it. Moira hesitated for a moment, then spoke. "Subject's meninges are absent." Those were the filmy coverings that in a normal brain protected the gray matter from the inner surface of the skull as well as outside material. "They have apparently dissolved and been replaced with an unclassified sac of fluid or mucous." This was something new medically, and Moira was fascinated. She'd been briefed on this sac, seen images, but this was her first true contact. The fluid beneath the covering was in direct contact with the brain.

Moira used a hypodermic to draw 10 mL of the fluid into a glass tube, labeled it and set it aside. Normal autopsy procedures required her to sever the spinal stem and remove the brain, weighing it and setting it aside for biopsy. She didn't want to, though. She feared handling it would rupture this strange, new fluid sac (though it had seemed tough enough when she'd put the needle through it a few minutes ago) and she didn't want to risk that just yet. Instead she left the head and moved to the torso, selecting her scalpel again to make the classic *Y* incision.

"Moira Rusk's guide to half-assed autopsy," she muttered into the microphone, then explained what she was doing and why. Fifteen minutes later, after employing the bone cutter, rib spreaders and a liberal number of clamps, the deceased lab tech's chest cavity lay peeled back, the inner workings exposed like an amphibian dissection project in a high school biology class.

"Subject's heart is encased in a similar-but-probably identical sac as the brain."

The heart wasn't beating, of course, but the sac surrounding it experienced a little ripple across its surface. Terry Butters' left eye twitched again, but Moira didn't see it this time. She was preparing another hypodermic and test tube to draw fluid from the heart sac when the door between the autopsy room and the lab opened.

"Dr. Rusk?"

Moira looked up, annoyed at the interruption. "What?" she said. It was a young, female lab tech, and she'd been crying. Moira softened her tone at once. "What is it?"

"It's Dr. Fisher," the girl said, sniffling. "Please, you have to come."

Dr. Rusk put down her instruments at once and followed.

They were standing in the office adjacent to the lab, the room full of cubicles with a door to the outer hallway. A handful of lab workers stood and stared, rubbing their eyes, awoken from where they'd been sleeping on the carpeted floor.

"She just…just left," the girl said, her voice hitching with a sob. She pointed to a desk near the door. "She left that right before they went out."

Moira picked up the plastic access card. "What did she say?"

The girl shook her head. "Just that it was safer this way, and for us to take care of ourselves." Another sob.

Moira moved to the small window set in the door and looked out. The hallway was empty. Annabelle, the lab tech who had killed Terry Butters in self-defense, had been at Infection-plus-ten, and Karen Fisher, at I-Plus-Nine herself, had taken them both out of the lab suites rather than risk endangering the others. Moira's throat tightened as she thought about her friend, and she took a deep breath. The others were watching her.

"Try to get a little more sleep," she told them, surprised at the steadiness in her voice. "We have a lot of work to do, and you need to be rested." Then she pocketed Dr. Fisher's access card and went back into the lab, where two more techs were perched on stools, resting their heads on folded arms at counters as they slept. They'd missed the whole thing.

The thought of her friend unprotected out in those hallways, and the woman's act of compassion by not making Annabelle face a death sentence alone made Moira want to hug herself and cry. She needed distraction, needed to lose herself in work. Getting back to the autopsy would accomplish this. But she needed her laptop, wanted to be able to refer to the notes Dr. Wulandari had sent her from Indonesia, so instead of the post-mortem room she key-carded her way into the patient ward with a soft, electronic chirp.

Snarls greeted her, along with cries of fear.

Three of the test patients had fully turned, and were now raging beasts that hurled themselves against their restraints, thrashing hard enough to make the beds move. They locked onto Moira with hateful, hungry eyes. Four others had slipped into Phase-Two and lay there semi-catatonic, twitching fitfully. They would probably be like the other three within the hour. The remaining patients, still showing no symptoms, screamed every time one of the savage ones did, begging to be released from their own restraints.

Three turned. Four more are about to. Moira looked at them, not moving. *Only one of them was an I-Plus-Ten, and several of the others weren't even close.* It didn't make sense, and she bit her lower lip.

She looked to the other end of the room, about to order the ward nurse to sedate the three who had not yet turned. But the woman was still seated at her desk, head down on folded arms and turned away.

How the hell could she sleep when-

A high-pitched scream from the lab behind her made Moira spin and look through the window in the intervening door. She let out a cry of her own.

The young lab tech who had first summoned her from the autopsy room was standing in the doorway between the lab and the outer office, hands to her mouth as if to hold back her screams. It wasn't working. Ten feet away, Terry Butters stood facing her, his chest cavity pinned open with clamps, skull cap off and the gelatinous sac covering his exposed brain giving off soft ripples. His scalp hung down to cover his face, raw and red on the outside, a thatch of dark hair on the inside.

With a quick movement, Butters grabbed the scalp and tore it from his face, ripping away a new ribbon of flesh down to the bridge of his nose as it came free.

Paralyzed, the girl didn't move, only screamed.

Terry Butters attacked, slamming her into a wall, pinning her so he could tear her throat out with his teeth. The two other techs who'd been sleeping in the lab were awake now, and they started yelling. Terry looked up from his kill to the source of the noise, lunged after them and after a brief race around a pair of lab tables, took them down and bit the life out of them. When the rest of the staff rushed in from the office, Terry killed them too. Their attempts to fight him off with their hands didn't slow him in the least.

Moira stood at the door, one hand on the handle and whimpering as she watched the slaughter. She wanted to run in to help, knew it would mean her death, wanted to open the door so the staff could escape the monster, but none were close enough, and none survived long enough to cross the short distance.

She thought the screams and guttural howls would drive her mad.

It was over quickly, and Moira watched in horrified fascination – unable to look away - as Terry knelt and fed on his victims, a bloody-faced glutton. And then he looked up, noticing her at the small window, and walked over. His face was a scarlet mask, as if he'd been dipped head-first in red ink, and a surgical clip slipped loose from his exposed chest to *ping-ping-ping* across the tiled floor.

He tried the door handle, couldn't move it, then pressed his face against the glass. Even through the thick door she could hear Terry Butters utter a thick chuckle.

Moira backed away, staring at the thing on the other side.

Terry Butters stared back with eyes that no longer looked like cataracts, but small, mercury-colored discs.

-27-

DANCER and DESIGN

Eastern United States – October 29

It turned out that the road they'd been hoping to find wasn't all that far from the crash site. At the edge of the field was a narrow strip of woods and brush, followed by a shallow ditch and then a two-lane stretch of asphalt, empty in both directions. Kylie helped her mom through the trees and up the embankment, cringing every time she heard her mother hiss from the pain of her broken arm.

Trees lined the road on each side, and there were no signs to tell them where they were or which way to go, no lights to guide the way. Above, the sky was changing from dark blue to sea colors as the night receded, but down here along the road it was as dark as a canyon floor. Even the flames of the burning jet behind them made little more than a flickering orange glow through the trees.

"Are you okay?" Kylie asked her mom.

Patricia gave her a smile. "I survived a plane crash. Every day from now on is a bonus."

Kylie nodded without smiling back. It was the kind of thing her father said every time he returned from war.

They looked up and down the road. Which way? Kylie flipped a mental coin. "Come one," she said, and her mother followed. She kept their pace easy, knowing that each step jarred her mother's fracture. Patricia kept up, uncomplaining.

After fifteen minutes they came upon a mailbox beside a packed dirt lane leading off through the trees and into the darkness. The name *Oost* was painted on the side of the box, and the lane was rutted by thin buggy wheels instead of car tires. More Amish. They'd find no phone in that direction, and Kylie didn't think she was brave enough to walk down that road, despite the Sig-Saur in her back waistband. They kept walking.

Although morning was slowly approaching, it was still in the low forties and the First Lady was visibly trembling. Kylie removed her short leather jacket and draped it around her mother's shoulders without a word.

Patricia looked at her daughter for a moment, searching her expression. "I'm sure he's fine."

"Who?"

"Terrence. He'll be okay. And I'm sorry I was so cruel about him. I know you're worried."

Kylie walked and said nothing. It was the first time she'd thought about her so-called boyfriend Terrence

Weaver since they'd been arguing before the crash. Funny, now that she *was* thinking about him, everything felt changed. What a difference a few hours of perspective made.

"I just…" Kylie started. "I don't know. I wonder if I was with him because he was just so different from everyone I knew, not all wrapped up in staying in line and getting along. Maybe I picked him to get back at Daddy."

Patricia said nothing, but noticed that her daughter was referring to Terrence in the past tense.

"He wasn't a good person, not good to me, angry all the time. Abusive. It's not like he ever hit me, but…"

The First Lady looked sharply at her first-born. "If he'd done that, he would have *needed* the Secret Service to protect him from your father and me."

Kylie grinned. "You wouldn't have gotten the chance. My Detail didn't like him either. They nicknamed him *The Puke,* and thought I didn't know they called him that." She shook her head. "Maybe I didn't want to see him for what he really was because you and Daddy already knew what he was about, and I was like a dumb kid who needed to have the obvious pointed out. It's embarrassing."

"Your father and I shouldn't have…"

"No, you were right. He was an asshole."

"Asshole," Patricia agreed, nodding, then stopped herself. "Sorry."

Kylie laughed. "It's okay, Mom. I've heard you say worse."

"That kind of trash talk wouldn't go over too well on CNN though, would it?" Patricia said.

"Is there a CNN anymore?" Kylie said, and the thought quieted them both. They walked in silence then, but Kylie reached out and clasped her mother's good hand.

They couldn't say how far they'd gone, certainly not as far as it felt considering their pace, and the vacant, dark country road made judging distance difficult. The only sign they passed was a yellow deer crossing marker with a pair of rusty bullet holes in it. The cool, early morning air was soon joined by a late October wind that made dry leaves tumble across the pavement. The decaying scent of fall rode the breeze. *Season of death,* Patricia Fox had always called this time of year, her least favorite season. They were both shivering now.

Kylie broke the silence. "Daddy and Devon are going to be okay, right?"

For Patricia at that moment, Kylie was a little girl again, worried about her father overseas and asking questions that Patricia couldn't truthfully answer. As President of the United States, her husband was arguably the best-protected man on the planet, and even at that, as both a Marine and in his current role, he knew the risks and accepted the grim possibilities. Devon was another matter, a boy caught in circumstances not of his choosing.

"I don't know," the First Lady said, deciding that being truthful was best. "We have to put our trust in the people who protect them, and worry about ourselves right now." Easily said. The very thought of them made her want to cry. "Both our boys are smart, Kylie." It was all she had, and of little comfort to either of them.

They started around a long curve, keeping to the shoulder even though they'd see the lights of a car long before it reached them and have plenty of time to get out of the way. Kylie noticed it first, the soft flash of red and blue lights reflected off the trees ahead.

They started to hurry.

The lights against the trees grew brighter, and now flashed across the pavement, the source just around the curve. At last the two women reached the point where the scene came into view; a dark blue, New York State Police car – a Dodge Charger – at an angle in the road, crunched against the side of a Honda CRV. The rooftop light bar and one working headlight on the police car illuminated a scene of broken glass and twisted metal. The police car appeared to have broadsided the Honda on an angle, the SUV catching the worst of the impact, and a body was slumped out through its broken driver's window. The trooper's driver's door stood open. Both women slowed as they approached, smelling the sharp tang of the Honda's ruptured radiator. Spreading fluids made the pavement shimmer in the flashing lights.

They looked inside the Charger – it was empty and the airbags had not deployed, despite the impact – then went to the CRV. The driver, a woman in her thirties, hung out the window with her head sagging on a broken neck, her face bloody. Starred glass and a circle of blood marked the spot on the windshield where her head had originally impacted. *Not wearing a seatbelt*, Kylie thought. An empty booster seat was buckled in the rear but there were no other occupants. Both passenger doors on the right side stood open.

"Where are they?" Patricia whispered, feeling her chest tighten at the sight of the booster seat. Both her kids had used one until they were about eight.

"Where's the cop?" Kylie wanted to know, matching her mother's tone. The whispering was a primal response, as if the dead woman in the driver's seat and the tragedy of the scene demanded reverence. Or caution.

There were no immediate answers. Together they moved back to the trooper car – it wasn't nearly as damaged as the Honda – and looked inside. Kylie recoiled. There was blood on the seat, dashboard and windshield, rivulets of crimson starting to congeal on the glass. Worst of all was the steering wheel. An adult incisor was buried in it where the trooper must have hit, the enamel roots sticky with blood.

Patricia gripped her daughter's arm. "He had *that* happen and still got out?"

Kylie spotted a big, five-cell Maglite clipped to the inside of the door and switched it on, panning it across the trees on both sides of the highway. The lightening of the sky above seemed to only deepen the shadows down here. "Maybe he's in shock and wandered off."

A steady hiss of soft static came from the dash-mounted radio.

"What the hell…?" Kylie said softly to herself, turning in a slow circle with her flashlight.

Headlights appeared further up the road, hi-beams on, drawing steadily closer.

"His back-up?" Patricia said.

Kylie shook her head. "No lights or siren."

The brightness intensified, and they could tell it was more than headlights. As the vehicle reached them, the two women had to shield their eyes with their arms. A full-sized pick-up of some sort, with not only headlights but additional spotlights close together on the grille, further supplemented by a roll-bar lined with high-intensity spots. It was blinding, and turned the scene a stark white. A big engine rumbled to a stop, a door opened and heavy boots hit the pavement.

"You ladies alright? Shit, can't *believe* you walked away from that." The voice had a twang that Kylie had always unfairly associated with the word *redneck.* But this redneck had a vehicle and had stopped to help, both good things.

Patricia squinted into the light. "We weren't in the car. We were in a plane."

A short laugh. "A plane! Goddamn, don't *you* have a story!" A large silhouette moved briefly across the lights. "Where's the trooper?"

"We haven't found him," Patricia said, not noticing that her daughter, who was also trying to look into the light, had placed a hand on her shoulder.

A pause, and then a voice from inside the white blaze. "So you're alone?"

Before Patricia could answer, Kylie gave her mother a squeeze and said, "No, we're-"

"Goddamn!" the truck driver yelled. "There's your trooper right behind you!"

Kylie spun, and in the stark light saw a female state police trooper in her early fifties, the color of her short haircut a near-perfect match to her gray uniform, scrambling up over the embankment at the side of the road. Her eyes were locked on the two women, eyes like bright silver discs, and when the woman snarled she revealed an empty socket where one of her front teeth had been.

Like the ones on the plane, Kylie's brain flashed. She snatched the Sig-Saur from her waistband, thumb snapping off the safety without thought, working on muscle memory from so much time at the range with her father. She fired twice at the horror rushing toward her.

Both bullets struck center mass, rocking the troopers sideways and making her stagger. The infected cop recovered quickly and raced in, arms reaching.

Vest. Kylie shot the trooper in the face instead, and that put her down.

And then there was an explosion of pain in the back of her head, a burst of white behind her eyes brighter than the truck's spotlights, and suddenly she was face-down on the pavement, the fall splitting open her chin. Blood thundered in her ears, and then the white was replaced with grayish-red, a spinning scene of a car accident and a dead state trooper lying not far away. She fought the urge to vomit and failed. Retching on the pavement, the world swimming in and out of focus, Kylie heard her mother screaming as if from a great distance. She felt the Sig-Saur plucked from a hand that no longer had any strength, then had the impression of a titanic man in brown camouflage stooping over the fallen trooper to retrieve her service weapon from its holster.

Kylie tried to rise but couldn't. Her mother wouldn't stop screaming – *it's hurting my ears, please stop*, Kylie thought – and then the growl of the pick-up's engine, the stink of diesel exhaust and the squeal of its tires as it rumbled back the way she and her mother had come.

"Mom?" she said thickly, then slipped into darkness.

Kylie swam up out of deep, black waters and into the light of a cold, windy morning on a stretch of rural New York road. She was bloody, her face feeling tight with it and her hair stiff with dried vomit. Her chin hurt, and she rubbed bits of asphalt from the wound, wincing at the simple movement. When she rose to her hands and knees she almost passed out.

Where was she? There was a car accident around her...no, not her accident. Something else had happened.

The stiff corpse of a female state trooper lying almost close enough to touch brought it back in an instant; the pick-up and its driver, the bark of the handgun, being hit by something. Her mother screaming.

Kylie bared her teeth and forced herself to stand. The pick-up was gone and so was her mother. "You fucker," she gasped, then stumbled to the side of the police car and used it for support. Her head felt like it was about to explode, and she was afraid to reach back and touch the knot that must be at the base of her skull. She side-stepped a bit and collapsed into the front seat, feeling for the key. It was in the ignition, and the engine was still running, as it must have been since the crash. *So far, so good.* But could the car still be driven?

Dropping the transmission into reverse, she backed away from the Honda with a creak and squeal of metal, cutting the wheel. The working headlight briefly illuminated a man in his thirties and a seven-year-old boy coming out of the woods on the other side of the crippled SUV. They were running, teeth bared.

Kylie ignored them, cranking the wheel to the left as her vision swam in and out of focus. She stomped the gas and the big police interceptor under the hood responded with a high-performance growl. The Charger roared away in the direction the pick-up had taken, into the morning and into a countryside much different from the one only twenty-four hours ago.

-28-

DARK HORSE

Upstate New York – October 29

For the first hundred miles or so there wasn't much conversation. At first Devon was lost in the horrors they'd escaped at the boarding school, while Marcus Handelman was quiet with worry, running through contingency plans, none of which seemed to have fallen into place or appeared viable anymore. They were alone on the road, and the agent had said he intended to keep it that way until they either reached Feather Mountain or came in contact with a military or law enforcement unit Marcus could trust. Whatever that might look like.

When they'd started out, the valleys and forested hillsides of Upstate New York had rolled by, dressed in red and gold fall colors and dotted with farms. Now they were traveling through the State Wilderness areas along Route 8, continuing to angle southwest whenever they could. Walls of tall pines would suddenly give way to tiny clusters of homes or side roads that led toward hunting and fishing camps, then quickly return as green walls flanking the road. It was all so peaceful, and the absence of other vehicles traveling the two-lane (Marcus was avoiding major highways, where there would be more people – more *infected* people) gave the impression that this was nothing more than a quiet Sunday morning.

But the monsters ruined the illusion.

They ran at the campus work truck from houses and yards close to the road, chasing after it down the asphalt even as the truck drove out of view. They crouched over dead people (never animals) as they ripped and fed on human flesh. They prowled around traffic accidents or loped out of the smoke of a burning building, drawn by the sound of the passing truck, an indicator of prey. They were human in appearance, but human no longer. Most had smooth, silver eyes – completely without pupils – that seemed to shimmer even in daylight.

Agent Handelman avoided them when he could, knocked them out of the way with the front of the truck when he couldn't, and ran them over when he had to. Streaks of gore painted the hood and spattered the windshield, and they soon ran out of washer fluid trying to keep the glass clear. Devon cringed at every thump and crunch.

"I'm sorry, Dev," the agent said at last, worried about the boy's silence and pale complexion. "About the school…everything that happened. They're a threat, and when they get between us and safety I have to deal with it."

"They're sick," Devon said.

"That doesn't make them any less deadly. You can't think of them as people at this point."

The boy was quiet for a bit, then, "I'm trying."

"I know you are, man." He gave Devon's arm a squeeze. Handelman knew that as a Secret Service agent he was way over the line in terms of how familiar he was with the President's son, the casual nature of their conversations, the way he scolded and lectured. But Devon was more than just a body he had to protect. The concept of dying to save the boy was so imprinted within him that he never even thought about it, but dying didn't protect your principal from the *next* threat, and that he *did* think about.

They saw tractor-trailers that had pulled to the shoulder, maneuvered around cars abandoned in the center of the two-lane and drove past side roads that had been blocked off with yellow police sawhorses, although there was no sign of police. At one point they came upon a sign for the town of Hoffmeister. Across it in black spray-paint someone had written the word *DEAD.*

Marcus kept them moving. He explained that he didn't exactly know their final destination – knew *of* it but had never been there – and although he understood the general location they would have to find a map.

"What is this place exactly?" Devon wanted to know.

"It's a continuity bunker," Marcus told him, "a place for government officials to find safety and still be able to run the country. There's a few of them, but if your dad was in the Midwest or on the east coast then Feather Mountain would be the closest. That's where his Detail will take him. Your mom and sister, same place.

"And it's safe?"

Handelman laughed. "Makes Camp David look like a public park." Then he glanced at the fuel gauge and stopped smiling. The needle was hovering just above the red *E.* "We need to gas up or switch vehicles."

Devon decided that from what he'd seen it wouldn't be hard to find a car no one was using anymore.

Instead, fifteen minutes later they spotted a gas station ahead on the right. It wasn't one of those clean, bright national chain stations Devon was used to, with an endless selection of drinks and snacks (*crap,* his mother called it). It was a little independent place nestled in a notch in the pines on the right, sort of shabby, with a pair of garage bays where a mechanic in greasy coveralls would charge you too much to work on your car. But as run-down as it was, the pumps looked new. A dented Ford Fusion and a tow truck were parked beside a Dumpster next to the building, but there were no other cars.

The Secret Service agent pulled in slowly and stopped, looking it over. A red neon *OPEN* sign glowed in a window. "Power's still on," he said, then eased the work truck up to the pumps.

"Hope they have a restroom," Devon said.

"Not happening," said Marcus. "We'll piss beside the truck, then you'll get back inside and lock the doors.

They did, Devon feeling weird about urinating in public, but he did as he was told. Handelman did the same, ever watching. Devon thought about pissing in the Rose Garden, right in front of the media, and suppressed a laugh. When he was locked inside once more, Devon watched his bodyguard use a personal credit card to activate the pump, and they gave each other a big grin when it worked and Marcus could start fueling.

"I'll be back in a minute," the agent said after he was done, replacing the nozzle. "Stay in the truck." Then he headed for the door to the service station, pistol raised and pointed ahead of him. He disappeared inside.

For what felt like a very long time, Devon sat and watched the front of the building. He wondered if-

Something slammed into the driver's door and Devon jumped, his head whipping in that direction. A kid about his age wearing a high school letterman's jacket was pressed against the glass, smearing the window with grayish drool. He gnashed his teeth and tugged on the door handle, and when it didn't open he started beating the glass with his fists.

"Marcus!" Devon yelled, pressing back against his own door and away from the thing outside the other.

The infected kid snarled and bashed his head into the window, creating a spider-web of cracks. Devon let out a cry, reached for his own door handle, then stopped. He clenched his teeth, leaned *toward* the monster and leaned on the truck's horn.

The kid in the letterman's jacket struck the glass again with his head, expanding the fracture and making the whole driver's window sag inward. This time he left blood on the glass from his lacerated forehead, a wound which he didn't seem to notice. Devon stayed on the horn, watching the kid rear back for another strike, knowing that the next one would surely-

A shape blurred past the front of the truck, and was followed by the double bark of a pistol. Letterman jacket dropped instantly from view. Marcus put a third round into his head as he lay on the ground, then banged a fist against the door until Devon unlocked it.

"You okay?" the agent demanded, breathing hard.

"Yeah." Devon let out a nervous laugh. "He didn't get in."

The agent climbed into the front seat, knocking the sagging glass out with an elbow, clearing the frame of it. "That was smart with the horn," he said, starting the engine and pulling back out onto the road. "This will help us." He tossed Devon a folded, paper road map of New York State.

The young man held it, waiting for words of apology for leaving him alone, for further queries about whether he was alright. Nothing more came from the agent, and after a moment, Devon decided that was okay. The way it should be. Even though he had a bodyguard, the fifteen-year-old knew that he was on the edge of manhood and needed to start thinking about taking care of himself. He couldn't go to pieces at the first sign of trouble. Marcus worried about him, of course, protected him savagely, but the man didn't treat him like some delicate flower. Yeah, that was cool.

As he unfolded the cumbersome and utterly alien thing, he realized he had never actually held or even seen a real paper road map. The look of bewilderment must have shown up on his face, because Marcus laughed. "Millennial kid, lost without his iPhone. Okay, we're looking for the town of Custer. It should be at the western edge of New York, just over the border in Pennsylvania, close enough to be on this map. You think you can handle navigation?"

Devon's eyes crawled over the colored lines, numbers and names. He was already figuring it out. "No problem."

"Good. Then if we get lost and killed, it's your fault."

The President's son grinned and looked over at his bodyguard. Then he froze. Marcus Handelman was pale, sweating, and his hands trembled ever so slightly on the steering wheel.

-29-

DEVIL DOG

Eastern Ohio – October 29

President Fox relieved himself in a dark, oily corner of the open-air garage where they'd parked the CAT vehicle. It wasn't very dignified for a head of state, but the former Marine had pissed under more primitive conditions, and was long past such embarrassment. Besides, there was no one around other than his bodyguard. Garrison joined Agent King a moment later, the two of them standing in the lot behind the mom & pop gas station in rural Ohio. The sun was coming up, but the air was still chilly.

Garrison shoved his hands in the pockets of his fleece. "So what do you think our chances are, David?"

The agent didn't look at him, his eyes constantly sweeping the area. He'd retaken possession of the P90 submachinegun from his boss. "We'll get you to your destination, Mr. President."

"I like your optimism. Shall we?"

Agent King checked the rear door of the gas station, found it locked and kicked it open. The place was what they'd expected; a business barely hanging on, with no money to update from its seventies-era interior, and apparently a failing ambition to even keep it clean. It smelled like stale cigarettes, and the windows were so grimy that they muted the morning light. The place was empty, with a *CLOSED* sign hanging in the front door. They tried the light switches. Nothing. The master switch for the pumps was off, and when they tried it, got the same result.

"Power's probably out for the whole county," David said.

Then they saw movement out front, heard a woman calling a man's name. King unlocked the door, placed a hand on the President's chest and went outside, weapon raised. Garrison ignored the subtle order to stay put and followed.

"Tom? Tom, I need you. Tom!" The woman came into view from behind one of the pumps, a credit card in one hand. She appeared to be in her thirties, with a bob haircut and wearing jeans and boots, a short-sleeve top and a down vest. Small, vicious bite wounds ran up both slender arms, her skin stained red from the elbows down. In the hand not holding the credit card she clutched a carpenter's hammer that dripped with fresh blood.

The woman saw the two men and stopped. "I'm out of gas. The pump isn't working and I need gas. Have you seen Tom?"

The muzzle of Agent King's weapon tracked up slowly to center of her chest.

"I need Tom to help." She puffed at a lock of hair hanging in her face and frowned. "I mean, I know where he is but he's not helping." She gestured toward a patch of weeds that separated the gas station lot from Route 6 running in front of it. The body of a man was face-down in the weeds.

"He tried to help," she said, puffing and frowning at the persistent lock of hair. "He tried to help Tommy Jr. But he was hurting him, hurting my boy." Blood from the head of the hammer dripped onto the toe of her left boot, and she cocked her head. "Can you make the pumps work?"

President Fox and Agent King saw a very old Taurus wagon sitting at the pumps behind her, its bumpers covered in *PETA* and dog rescue stickers. Inside, a metal grid separated the rear cargo area from the back seat, a set-up common among people who traveled with large dogs. Except it wasn't a dog that was bloody and raging back there, throwing itself against the windows and metal partition. It was a silver-eyed, three-year-old boy. His screeching was barely muffled by the glass.

The woman turned. "Honey, mommy's talking. We'll get going in a minute. Mommy will get you some candy." She looked back at the two men. "Have you seen Tom?"

There was traffic on the road behind the woman, a scattering of cars among groups of people walking, many wearing backpacks or pulling luggage, a few on bicycles and many pushing strollers. All heading east. They looked at the scene playing out at the gas station, but no one approached. They all passed quietly.

The Secret Service agent had seen the foot and vehicle traffic as soon as they came outside, but his immediate focus was on the woman with the hammer. Garrison, however, noticed them for the first time and could only stare. *An exodus from Cleveland. Refugees in America.*

Because I failed to act.

Someone on the road must have seen the bright yellow lettering on David's gear, taken a look at the man in the fleece and the ball cap, and made the connection. How could anyone who *looked* like Garrison Fox, who was in the company of Secret Service, not *be* Garrison Fox?

"Hey that's the President!" An arm came up, a finger pointing. Heads turned. "That *is* the President!" another voice shouted. A curse then, more fingers pointing, and suddenly the crowd on the county road was no longer moving east, but edging toward the gas station pavement. "You fucked us good, buddy!" came a shout. "Why aren't you helping us?" a woman demanded.

David King moved close to Garrison, positioning himself between the man and the crowd, trying to watch the woman with the hammer while he scanned the refugees for weapons. This was Ohio. There were sure to be firearms. "Mr. President…" he said in a low growl.

The deep sound of a truck horn cut over the shouts as a sand-colored Humvee bullied through the crowd. People scrambled out of the way as it turned into the gas station, bypassed the pumps and drove straight into a metal air dispenser at the edge of the lot, knocking it loose with an explosion of hissing and coming to a stop.

"We're backing inside, sir," David ordered, his weapon sweeping the crowd now as his other hand reached back and caught a fistful of the President's fleece, pushing him backward.

Before they could take a full step, the woman with the hammer called, "Tommy Jr., you need to go potty? Mommy's coming." She moved to the back of the station wagon. The Humvee, stenciled with Military Police and Ohio National Guard markings, didn't try to back away from where it had wrecked the air dispenser. The agent and the President saw that the front passenger window was splashed red on the inside and pocked with a pair of bullet holes, a uniformed body slumped against the glass. They heard the driver's door creak open, and a moment later a young, female MP in uniform staggered around the back end of the vehicle, one hand clutching a pistol, the other holding her forehead. She squinted at the two men.

"Move! Now!" barked Agent King, and Garrison backed up to the gas station door.

"Potty time," sang the young mother with the bitten arms, popping the rear hatch of the Taurus wagon. Tommy Jr. was on her in a second, snarls and screams mixing as the two of them went to the pavement in a savage tangle.

The people on the road stopped moving and stared.

The female MP staggered toward King, peering at him with glassy eyes, shaking her head and raising the handgun.

"Stand down, soldier!" David shouted.

The MP took another step, aimed the pistol…

David King cut her down with a short burst from the P90. Out on the road, refugees ran at the sudden gunfire, dropping possessions and scattering into the far field or running up the road. Cars that had been creeping among the foot traffic suddenly accelerated, dodging the running people (not completely successfully) and putting distance between themselves and the gas station.

In the doorway behind his bodyguard, Garrison Fox watched in anguish as a bloody three-year-old finished disemboweling his mother, then ran on little sneakers toward the lone Secret Service agent. A short burst of automatic weapon fire ended it, and only then could Garrison look away, knowing he'd be forever haunted by the image of that rabid little thing being hurled to the ground by high-velocity bullets. Haunted by *everything* he'd just seen.

Agent King came to him. "Mr. President, we have to move."

It made sense to switch to the Hummer. It was fully fueled, the CAT vehicle was not, and the fuel wasn't compatible; diesel in the Humvee, unleaded in the Suburban. Agent King wasn't happy about it. The CAT was armored and had comms that could reach out to USSS in Washington…although there had been complete radio silence since they left the airport, despite repeated calls. And there was the small matter of the turret-mounted mini-gun. David admitted that he couldn't drive and shoot (the incident at the airport had been a unique situation) and he'd be damned if he'd have his President standing and gunning away in the turret as the perfect target while he chauffeured in safety.

As a concession, the Secret Service agent removed the firing bolt from the mini-gun and threw it into the weeds as far as he could, then dumped the weapon's belted ammunition in a barrel half-filled with recycled motor oil behind the garage. No matter what was happening, it just wasn't okay to leave a fully functioning, full-auto mini-gun sitting around where anyone could find it.

David transferred a black nylon bag of gear and weapons from the Suburban to the Hummer, as well as an identical bag containing flash-bang grenades, a trauma kit and a small cooler containing two liters of O-negative blood, the President's type. Garrison removed the head-shot body (the dead female MP's partner) from the vehicle's passenger seat himself and set him on the pavement, handling the fallen soldier as gracefully as he could.

The CAT vehicle had a spare bullet-proof vest, and David insisted the President put it on over his fleece (it was too bulky to fit under), however he lost the argument when it came to weapons. Garrison Fox now wore a dead MP's pistol belt, and rode in the passenger seat with a loaded, Ohio National Guard M4 assault rifle standing up between his knees.

"Don't worry, Agent King," he said, tapping the rifle, "we're old friends. And if I do any shooting it will be because you can't."

Difficult logic to argue with, and David admitted to himself that it was better to have two shooters than one, especially if the other guy was combat-tested. "Copy that, Colonel," the agent said, acknowledging his Commander-in-Chief's former job, making the President smile and point at the road.

They got back onto the eastbound county road, but soon came upon the tail end of the refugees that had run at the sound of gunfire. Slow moving vehicles and people stretched out before them across a long flat space and up over the next hill, and at a few points along the road, fights appeared to be breaking out, joined by the distant pop of gunfire. Both men knew what that meant; the infected were turning, and then turning on their fellow refugees. Route 6 was no longer a safe option.

David put the all-terrain capabilities of the wide, military vehicle to good use and took them overland, bouncing across recently harvested fields. The GPS in his cell phone was still working – they were still many hours from Feather Mountain – and they soon found a deserted country road headed in the general direction they wanted to go.

The radio in the Hummer, which should have at the very least connected them with a National Guard company headquarters, was silent except for and occasional faint and garbled transmission. Ghosts in the machine.

Riding shotgun and watching the hills of Eastern Ohio roll by, President Fox allowed himself to sink into his thoughts. He wasn't pondering his own situation or even the safety of his family (for the moment, at least) but brooding on the condition of his country, a responsibility that had superseded personal concerns from the moment he took the oath of office. The image of a road choked with refugees, here in the American heartland, was impossible to shake. He knew it was a scene that would be playing out across the nation, his own citizens forced to flee their homes and go…where? They were hoping for, and had every right to expect, at least some kind of organized, intelligent response to the crisis from their government. Given the frenzy and speed of the pandemic however, it was clear that their government had failed them.

I *failed them.*

No, even POTUS had no control over viral infection.

You could have mitigated the damage, slowed it down, been better prepared.

The logical side of him pointed out that closing schools and the stock market, imposing travel bans and declaring martial law would have had little to no effect. But his heart, the source of his powerful sense of personal responsibility, refused logic's argument.

Your fault. It's your fault.

But the best-made contingency plans and even medical science couldn't have predicted this. Viral cannibalism. Garrison didn't realize he was slowly shaking his head as he watched farm country slide past the crimson, bullet-pocked window.

He thought about Dr. Rusk at CDC, about the researchers at USAMARIID, the Army's counterpart to Atlanta, about the scientists at the Pasteur Institute and other facilities across the globe. Were they finding any answers? Any hope? Were any of those people still alive? He needed information, and nearly shook in his frustration at the lack of it.

He thought about his government. With the President missing or dead, who had stepped up to lead? The presidential succession plan was *relatively* clear, though never actually put to the test. Who was acting President? Someone had to be, they couldn't *all* be dead or out of position, could they? Garrison ran down his mental list of positions and people in order from top to bottom. He knew who he'd *want* to be in charge, but the thought of some of the others as POTUS – even on a temporary basis – made him cringe inwardly. They were people selected for their political muscle or job proficiency, but never even considered for the ridiculously unlikely event their number would be called. Not for the top spot in national leadership.

Again, he needed information, and it didn't appear to be coming anytime soon. There was no shortage of horror, though. He was presented with that at every turn.

Feather Mountain, a secure facility supposedly safe from chemical or biological threat…a place where he would find information and professionals to help him begin trying to get hold of a country spinning out of control. They had to get there if he were to have any chance of saving his fellow citizens…or the world.

When the Hummer passed a silver-eyed farmer on his hands and knees at the gravel shoulder, face buried in the open belly of a woman in a flower-print dress, President Fox closed his eyes and thought about his family.

-30-

FEATHER MOUNTAIN

Western Pennsylvania – October 29

Joshua Rowe awoke to darkness, disoriented until he saw the soft blue glow of a digital clock over the doorway. It read 08:05. Two hours later than his normal time to rise, but then it had been close to four-thirty in the morning before he'd finally allowed himself to go to bed. Less than four hours of sleep, but it would have to do. He hadn't wanted to sleep at all, to leave the mountain's nerve center of communication and information, but even generals in a crisis needed rest. Exhausted leaders made poor decisions, and in the military that translated to people getting killed. The *wrong* people.

He turned on the lights, illuminating a small, spare room that served as quarters for a senior officer. At least it had its own adjacent latrine and shower. Rowe wasn't a man who needed luxury. He'd slept in his fatigues so he pulled on a fresh undershirt and an olive-green wool sweater, splashed water in his face and laced up his combat boots. The pistol belt went on last, and he checked the weapon to ensure he had a round in the chamber.

People had gone missing within this maze of rock and steel, and after what happened around 1:00AM, he could no longer consider Feather Mountain to be a secure facility.

All through the previous evening and well past midnight, General Rowe and his team had watched the nation and the world come apart through satellite imagery. Cities were burning at home and abroad, aircraft were falling from the sky, the power grid was starting to fail, leaving entire states blacked-out. Communication was failing too, and with it went any kind of coordinated response to the crisis.

Communication, Rowe thought, leaving the relative warmth of his small quarters for the chill of the subterranean corridor bored through the rock outside.

It had come down to communication, and not necessarily the systems themselves, but the people who ran them, who were responsible for carrying out the strategies developed pre-crisis that would protect life and provide the essentials; shelter, food and medical care. FEMA was attempting a massive response, with thousands of moving parts, but couldn't get off the ground because the people tasked with moving supplies and setting up shelter points were often unresponsive; missing, dead or preying on their fellow man. It was a dynamic being repeated across the country, as emergency plans at both state and local levels failed as well. Only a few shelter points had been successfully established in different states, but these were at risk of being overwhelmed by too many refugees or collapsing from within as the infected inside their perimeter suddenly turned.

The views from the satellites cruising high above the U.S. showed people streaming away from population centers in every direction, like ants evacuating a hill that had been kicked open by a cruel child. There was no way to calculate the death toll at this point. The only certainty was that it was staggering, and still on the rise. The internet, where it was still working, carried the same messages being repeated over and over; fear, despair, horror.

Rowe checked the corridor in both directions, one hand resting on the butt of his pistol. Hooded, overhead lights created pools of white and shadow that marched down the length of the passage. The general watched and listened.

The American military was faring only slightly better than the civilian population. Their ranks were no less susceptible to outbreaks of madness than any other group of people, although the ready presence of weapons made it somewhat easier to put down sudden, violent eruptions of turning soldiers. Not in every instance, though. And gunning down their comrades was taking its own psychological toll on the surviving troops. Many of those lost were members of the officer corps, leaving men leaderless and without orders. Regardless of the exact nature of the collapse, the end result was that with each passing hour the availability of combat-effective troops was plunging, with some units – in one case an entire battalion – evaporating altogether.

The Navy was suffering from what could only be classified as infection-fueled mutinies, with entire ships being lost or disabled at sea. The only untouched part of this branch was that small group of submarines that had been submerged since before the outbreak, something that had prevented Trident from entering their sealed, little worlds. Hearing what was happening above the waves, those sub commanders had no intention of surfacing any time soon.

Even harder hit was the Air Force, its bases quickly becoming non-operational due to losses in ground personnel and pilots. Aircraft that were flying suddenly weren't, as their pilots turned and were no longer capable of (or had the desire for) the concentrated thought required for the complexities of flight. Fighter pilots who did manage to land were often met by ground crews whose only desire was to pull them screaming from their cockpits.

And of course, Rowe thought, *there's the small matter that the President is missing and we have no government.*

The general made his way to the left, boot heels echoing in the silence. He could have called for an escort, but he was armed, unafraid to use his weapon, and frankly he didn't think the comm center could spare the personnel. Joshua Rowe had been a warrior for a long time, and he could take care of himself. He was more worried about the safety of those under his command and the nation as a whole than he was about his own mortality.

He stepped into one of the large, domed chambers where many passageways came together in a hub, stopping before a bank of elevators set in one wall. The distant hum of machinery answered when he pressed the button, and as he waited he turned in a slow circle, watching the corridor openings.

A high-pitched giggle floated from one of them, though he couldn't tell which, or how far away. The handgun came out of his holster. Another giggle echoed through the open space, possibly from a different direction this time.

Members of the general's team had gone missing. It looked like he'd found some of them.

Or they had found him.

A shadow darted in one of the openings, off to the right in his peripheral vision, accompanied by a quick scuffle of boots on polished stone. The general spun and raised his pistol, but there was nothing there. Another shuffling sound, this time to his rear, but when he turned, ready to fire, the passageways – at least as far into them as he could see depending on the angle – were all empty.

What about inside the shadows? Something could easily be crouched in one of the dark patches, unmoving and unseen.

A low growl bounced off the rock walls, impossible to pinpoint, and another blur of movement caught the corner of his eye.

I'm being hunted.

Rowe heard the elevator doors slide open behind him, then felt a hand grip his shoulder. He whirled and brought up the pistol, hesitating just a fraction of a second before blowing the head off his very startled Army surgeon.

"Oh, Christ!" the doctor gasped. "I was coming to wake you, sir, I-"

Rowe pushed the man back into the elevator. "We'll talk inside, Colonel," he growled, turning and keeping his sidearm trained on the domed room until the doors were finally closed and the car began to move.

It had begun last night, just before midnight. A member of Rowe's team, one of the IT people, had gone into a room adjacent to the comm center to get something or other. Engrossed in what was happening on the video screens, no one had noticed his hour-long absence. When he returned, racing into the big room like a raving beast, he'd attacked one of the female biohazard specialists, biting her arms, neck and face as she'd tried to fight him off. Rowe had ended the attack personally with a single nine-millimeter bullet to the side of the IT tech's head. The girl was now in medical, loaded up with antibiotics and a strong sedative.

The doctor Rowe brought with him had pulled the general aside and spoken softly. "This is only going to be the first," he said. "The mountain was probably free of Trident until we brought it inside. By now we'll have passed it on to everyone."

"What about the decontamination process when we arrived?" Rowe demanded.

The doctor shook his head. "That can't clean off what's inside us."

Both Rowe and the Army physician knew the infection status of their own team, the data compiled before they jumped off. The general, his surviving IT tech and the girl who'd been attacked were immune. The doctor and a communications specialist were in remission, and the rest showed complete contagion. That was the at-risk group, and the IT tech that'd attacked was part of that group. They'd all known the risk, but couldn't have predicted how soon, or how suddenly the infected would succumb.

The general found the captain in charge of the facility and told him to take three men to the armory. Everyone was to have a rifle as well as a sidearm. The captain acknowledged, took one of his men and Rowe's two security specialists, and left the comm center.

They never came back, and hadn't been heard from since they went out the door.

The captain's team had taken all the rifles, and Rowe wasn't going to risk more staff to go look for them armed only with pistols.

Until fatigue forced him back to his quarters, General Rowe had stayed in the communication center, listening as more and more units failed to report in, or watching on screen as the country and the world slipped into anarchy.

Now, after that chilling encounter outside the elevator, he was back in the big, circular chamber with walls of screens and rows of consoles, his XO catching him up on the events of the last four hours. The man had dark circles under his eyes, and looked so tired his hands trembled.

"General, the PROC fleet in the Formosa Straits crossed the center line last night, headed for Taiwan. The Taiwanese already had fighters on combat air patrol, monitoring their movements, and when the ships crossed over without responding to radio calls, the patrol started lighting them up with ship-killers."

Rowe massaged the bridge of his nose with a thumb and forefinger, making a grunting noise. "How hard did the Reds hit back?"

"Not at all, sir," said the XO, getting his commander's full attention. "Four ships were sunk, and the rest of the fleet broke formation. Not evasive maneuvering, sir, more like wandering, no sense of order."

"Like our own ships," Rowe growled.

"Yes, sir. The PROC didn't launch so much as a single SAM against the attacking Taiwanese. When the fleet formation drifted apart, the Taiwanese jets headed home, but half a dozen went down anyway."

"The pilots turned," Rowe said, nodding. At least the U.S. wasn't the only country with that problem.

The Major tried to stifle a yawn and rubbed his eyes. "Pakistan and India are shooting at each other. It's conventional right now, nothing nuclear yet. Each side is blaming the other for unleashing the plague as part of a bio-warfare campaign."

"Of course," said Rowe.

"The European nations have closed their borders," the major continued, "and Russia isn't talking to anyone. Here at home…" he gestured to the screens, "…complete chaos."

"What about the President?" Rowe wanted to know.

The major shook his head. "We had brief comms with Camp David. POTUS is missing and presumed dead. VPOTUS was supposed to be heading for Feather Mountain, but we lost contact with Camp David shortly after we got them. We did make contact with a Marine helicopter pilot who says he's inbound from Camp David with high profile passengers, but that VPOTUS is *not* aboard. He's a few minutes out by now, sir."

Rowe rubbed his own eyes and wished for coffee. "Okay, let's get-"

"Sir!" A communications man at one of the front consoles yelled and pointed up at one of the screens. "We have a thermal bloom inside the continental United States, consistent with a low yield nuclear detonation."

"Where?" Rowe demanded.

It took a moment for the tech to bring the satellite image in closer. "It looks like Texas, sir. Best guess is Dallas."

Dallas? Rowe thought. *There wasn't anything nuclear in Dallas, nothing that could cause an accident like that.* "No missile tracking?"

"Negative, sir, the skies are clear."

That leaves terror. Rowe clenched his teeth. As if things aren't bad enough.

"General," a mountain staffer called, "that Marine chopper is on the approach, and we're getting radio traffic from some more small aircraft requesting permission to land. Their codes are legitimate." The female sergeant had a binder of laminated pages clearly identifying what aircraft were authorized to land here for *Bank Vault* (the *only* time planes were permitted on the airfield) and what authorized clearance codes they were to use. "We have a larger contact calling in sir, but it's not cleared."

Rowe pointed at the tech who had reported the detonation. "Get me more on Dallas. XO, go assist with air traffic control for those inbounds."

The major responded with a giggle.

"XO?" Rowe looked to see his second-in-command staring at the floor, clenching and unclenching his fists, drooling onto his combat boots.

It had been a long night of fitful sleeping and rotating watches. Donny Knapp, the three men from his unit and Corporal Woods, the female quartermaster they'd discovered on base, had spent the small hours of the overnight either watching out the windows of the tiny cinderblock building beside the airstrip or trying to rest propped up in corners.

There wasn't much to this place; a table and chairs, a base radio set and an electrical panel to control the field lights, a closet with some cleaning supplies and a deck of cards. They were all grateful for the small latrine just off the single, main room. On a back wall was a large map of the Feather Mountain installation depicting roads, structures and fence-lines. Most of it was covered in pine forest, and

Second Lieutenant Knapp had spent a lot of time looking at it. He was surprised to see just how close the main gates were to his current position.

When they'd gotten here, there was no sign of the two men who'd originally been assigned to the blockhouse, the two they'd seen when the general's helicopter arrived. They'd just wandered away…or something.

Everyone was tense. They'd expected an attack all night, but it hadn't come. There had been sightings though, distant silhouettes running across the airstrip, dark, loping shapes in the moonlight. And there had been the laughter, the crazed, wavering giggles that floated out of the black forest. Hearing them, knowing the Green Berets and the rest of Knapp's company were out there but having nothing to fire at, frayed the nerves.

Donny turned away from the window where he'd been standing and looked at the newest members of the squad. They had come running out of the forest around four this morning, pounding on the door to the little structure and pleading to be let inside. Donny let them in, but the squad had kept their weapons pointed at the new arrivals until their lieutenant was satisfied that neither one was showing signs of turning.

Both were Green Berets, survivors of the massacre in the woods. They'd managed to hold onto their rifles, so Donny redistributed magazines from his team to replace the blanks the two men had been using. That made seven of them now. Donny wondered if there were more out there, hiding within the trees or running to escape being devoured by their brothers-in-arms.

Specialists Valenti and Quayle were sleeping hard on the concrete floor now, wrapped in rain ponchos with their rifles close at hand. Donny had peppered them with questions about their unit and what happened, but they were as confused as everyone else. They said that every Green Beret they knew was either dead at the hands of their friends or transformed into madmen. The only reason they'd survived, they said, was because they ran. They didn't display any shame at that as they told the story, and instead wore the haunted expressions of people who had witnessed something truly horrific and were still trying to come to terms with it.

Donny turned back to his window. Full daylight now. They'd see what the morning would bring. He doubted it would bring the arrival of a more senior officer to take over and relieve the young second lieutenant of his burden. His thoughts were interrupted by a *click* and a voice from the base radio set.

"Mountain-Six to Airfield-One."

That must mean us. Donny grabbed the mic. "Go, Mountain-Six. Second Lieutenant Knapp here."

"Roger, Airfield. Be advised you have aircraft inbound to your position."

"Air Force One?" Donny asked.

"Negative, Lieutenant," said the voice. "Three small fixed wing and one rotary. They're all squawking proper codes and are authorized to land. We'll handle traffic control from here. I need you to switch on the field lights."

Donny nodded at the radio, then looked at a well-labeled wall console almost identical to the circuit breaker panel in a private home. He flipped any switch marked FIELD, and instantly the massive airstrip was flanked by rows of blue and white lights, brilliant even in daylight.

"The field is lit, Mountain-Six," he reported.

"Roger. We have the inbounds stacked at ten minute intervals, with the rotary wing coming in last. The fixed wing pilots have been directed to immediately taxi to the ramp upon landing."

Donny had boarded and exited enough military troop aircraft to know that the *ramp* was a term for the large, concrete pad just off the runway where planes could turn around or park.

"Lieutenant," Said Mountain-Six, "your objective is to keep the area clear of hostiles and obstructions in order to facilitate the safe landing of these aircraft."

Donny looked out the window. *Obstructions like that.* A uniformed man was running across the ramp, heading for the airstrip and the little cinderblock house. The blood on his uniform indicated that he might just be wounded, but the fact that he had been disemboweled and his entrails were now dangling out of the wound and flopping against his knees as he ran told a different story.

"Copy that," Donny told the radio, then snapped his fingers at the squad. "Akins, Corporal Woods." He pointed out the window. "Deal with that and then get it off the runway." *I just called it an* it.

Akins just stared, but the black, female quartermaster punched him hard in the arm, then grabbed his combat harness and hauled him outside. Donny watched as they ran toward the thing now running at them. He swallowed hard. He hoped the man's condition meant that he'd turned…

"Air Field-One," said the voice on the radio, "you are to collect all arriving personnel and secure them at your position."

Donny started shaking his head slowly, watching as Woods and Akins stopped fifty feet from the running soldier and cut him down with long bursts of automatic fire. Then they grabbed him by his boots and hauled him to the grass at the edge of the pavement, leaving a red smear on the concrete.

"Mountain-Six, be advised that I can't spare any men to escort them to the bunker."

"You're not listening, Lieutenant." The voice had an edge to it. "That is a negative on the escort. The mountain is compromised. Secure the arrivals at *your* location until further orders."

Great, Donny thought. Plane-loads of high-ranking officials exposed and in the open, protected by seven tired soldiers. He acknowledged the command, just as Woods and Akins were returning to the cinderblock house, both of them breathing hard.

"Was he…?" Donny started.

The corporal shook her head. "Infected and turned, sir."

Behind them, Private Akins grumbled to his buddies that *he* hadn't killed the soldier, *he* had missed on purpose. *She* had been the one to shoot him down. The killing was on *her*.

Donny was getting sick of Akins and his bullshit, but there wasn't time to deal with it now. He looked at his corporal. "Wake up our Green Berets, then get the squad outside. Defensive perimeter around the blockhouse. Company's coming."

The lights descending from the sky were stacked too close together, certainly too close for the ten minute landing intervals Mountain-Six had described. Donny was no pilot, but to him there looked to be less than a minute's worth of space between each.

The first to come in, a white business jet, was wobbling and didn't have its landing gear down. At a speed much too fast to attempt landing, it swept the length of the airstrip as low as a crop-duster, engines screaming. It nudged up at the far end, avoiding the tops of the pines, but then tipped in a hard bank to the left and plunged nose-first into the forest. The resulting fireball boiled into the sky amid a confetti storm of burning October leaves. The soldiers around the blockhouse felt the heat and pressure wave even at this distance.

The second jet – just one minute behind – landed perfectly, rolled off the runway and onto the ramp, then just sat there with its engines idling. The side door didn't open to let out passengers.

Donny tapped one of the Green Berets – Quayle, he thought - on the shoulder and pointed at the business jet. "That's your field of responsibility, nothing else."

"Roger that." The young man knelt and trained his assault rifle on the motionless plane.

Aircraft number three, another identical small jet, suddenly banked right, climbed and disappeared, leaving the area altogether. Donny suspected he'd never know why, and would never see the plane again. He was right.

Almost at the same moment, an olive-green helicopter with MARINES stenciled along its tail boom appeared over the trees to their right, coming in with its nose aimed at the blockhouse. The pilot got as close as he dared, pivoted the chopper and landed, the wind of his rotors making Donny's squad shield their eyes from the dust and grit blowing around. A handful of figures emerged from the Marine helicopter, hunched over and running toward the soldiers. Once they were clear of the rotors, the aircraft lifted off and headed back in the direction from which it had come.

The new arrivals moved immediately to the only officer they saw. There was a woman with two kids, a boy and a girl, both pre-teen. A man in a suit immediately moved in front of them, identifying himself to Donny as Secret Service. Another man in a suit said he was the White House Deputy Chief of Staff, and he identified the last passenger, an elderly man in rumpled clothes, as a Justice of the Supreme Court.

Donny recognized the Vice President's wife from seeing her on TV. He looked at the White House man. "POTUS and VPOTUS?"

"No to both," the deputy said, "but neither is confirmed." His eyes cut away when he said that. "Let's get this group inside *Bank Vault.*"

"I'm sorry, sir," Donny said, "I have orders to hold you here for the time being. Security reasons."

"My God," the Vice President's wife said, "We can't stay out here." She pulled her children close.

"We'll protect you, ma'am." Donny realized it was probably a lie even as he said it. He was about to show them into the blockhouse when his corporal caught his arm and pointed at the sky above and beyond the opposite end of the runway.

"That wasn't on the list," she said.

It was huge, a four-engine prop that dwarfed the business jets, painted in a camouflage pattern, making it military. Donny didn't need the camo to tell him what it was, for he'd flown on planes like that many times. It was a C-130 cargo plane, the workhorse of the skies. Now everyone was looking, and there was a collective gasp as a cluster of tiny silhouettes – pin-wheeling bodies – dropped from the rear of the plane to fall helplessly into the forest.

Its cargo ramp was down.

And it was landing anyway.

-31-

BUFFALO TWO-EIGHT

Western Pennsylvania – October 29

The word *HARVARD* was stenciled across her flight helmet, the combination nickname/call-sign she'd picked up at the Air Force Academy for the not-so-original reason that her home town was Boston. Of course her sharp, nasally accent, combined with an academic scoring that put her at the top of her class, assured anyone who knew it that the call-sign was more than appropriate. She was fit and petite, physically a good fit for the tight confines of a fighter cockpit, and she certainly had the brains and reflexes for it. Being a jet jockey held no interest for her, though. She liked the control of commanding large aircraft, the bigger the better. A spray of freckles across her nose made her look younger than her thirty-one years.

Major Erin Boyle was alone in the cockpit of her C-130 Hercules. Well, not exactly alone if she counted the two dead men in here with her; the co-pilot still buckled into his seat and the flight engineer lying on the steel decking just behind her. She didn't need to see the bullet holes in their flight helmets or the blood and brains on the seats and control panel to know they were gone. She'd done the job herself.

Something was pounding on the steel door that separated the cockpit from the cargo area. Several somethings.

Under optimum conditions, the C-130 was a cumbersome aircraft; almost a hundred feet long, thirty-six tons empty with a wingspan of one hundred thirty two feet. Now it was handling like a busted freight train, its flight characteristics completely out of whack. For whatever reason, perhaps out of panic, the loadmaster who traveled in back had performed one final, stupid act before he died. And there was little doubt that he was indeed dead. A small video monitor over the pilot's seat gave the major a view of what was happening in the cargo area. *Nope, no doubt.* The loadmaster had lowered the cargo ramp in-flight, at altitude.

The Hercules was in fact designed for this, for making slow, low-altitude runs where palletized equipment with parachutes was pushed out the back, or more often gear on heavy skids (also with parachutes) pushed out only feet above a runway to slide to a stop on the pavement. But that was for *low* and *level* flight, and the ramp was closed soon after delivery. The aircraft wasn't meant to fly in this state for long periods of time. The ramp had been down for more than an hour now, and the airflow drag was rapidly exhausting her fuel.

Maybe he opened it hoping they'd fall out. Erin shrugged. *Didn't matter at this point.*

She was orbiting now, looking out through the cockpit's side window at a very long, very sexy, empty runway out in the sticks of western Pennsylvania. It was active, as several approaching business jets proved, as well as the chatter between the planes and a controller called Mountain-Six. Her laminated maps showed the runway and the surrounding area, labeling it *FEATHER MOUNTAIN MILITARY RESERVATION – RESTRICTED.*

Surely not for her, though.

"Mountain-Six," she called over the radio, "this is Buffalo-Two-Eight, alpha-foxtrot cee-one-thirty out of Pope. I'm at two-seven-zero, range ten miles from yah field." She listened to the thumping, a sound that even the hum of the four big turbo-props couldn't drown out. The thumping was made worse because she knew what was on the other side of that door.

Major Boyle continued her orbit. "Mountain-Six, I am bingo fuel and declaring an emergency. Request permission to land."

She saw the first of three, white executive jets scream over the runway and vector into a fireball amid the trees. A second jet was coming in close behind, but he looked to be approaching and descending in good order. Before she could call in the crash, a voice responded to her call.

"Buffalo-Two-Eight, Mountain-Six. That's a negative on your request. This is a restricted field. Suggest you divert north to Custer."

"Mountain-Six, I am a *military* flight and need emergency landing clearance."

"Copy that, Buffalo-Two-Eight, but you are not authorized to land at this field. Custer is close, and their field is long enough to handle your aircraft."

Major Boyle mouthed an obscenity, then opened her mic. "Custer is off the air, (it came out as *Custah*) Mountain-Six, and I already did a fly-over for a visual. Their field is obstructed by other aircraft and ground personnel, so they're a no-go. You're the one, Mountain-Six."

The voice came back immediately, and with a sharp tone to it. *"Negative,* Buffalo-Two-Eight. You are *not* cleared to land at this location." After a brief pause, the controller added in a more level voice, "Sorry, but that's how it has to be."

The second jet had made it in and taxied to the ramp, but Erin watched as the third banked away and cruised out of sight. She'd heard no radio traffic between them and Mountain-Six, and wondered why they were leaving. Then she saw a military helicopter cruising at treetop –level, angling toward a small structure on the field.

"Military reservation," Erin muttered to no one but the dead. "Goddamn secret squirrel base, probably goddamn CIA." Squirrels came out as something close to *squells.* An instructor in Colorado Springs once told her to 'Speak goddamn English, because the Air Force isn't going to issue you subtitles,' then announced that he was taking her to the *yahd, fah* some P.T. The memory made her smile, despite the flashing warning lights above her fuel gauge.

The pounding at the cockpit door was non-stop. She wondered if it was the navigator, the loadmaster or some of her passengers. Major Boyle's mission had been to ferry sixty-four combat troops from North Carolina to Pittsburgh, but after she had almost reached her destination the mission had been canceled without explanation, no new orders presented as an alternative, and then there had been no further contact with her command.

And oh, yeah, she thought, *every goddamn one of those sixty-four soldiers turned into a goddamn cannibal during the flight.* Erin had been transporting a cargo of monsters for more than an hour.

But not for long.

"Ah, roger that Mountain-Six," she said in her cheerful pilot's voice, "I'm coming around fah my final approach."

"Negative, Buffalo-Two-Eight, that is a neg-!"

"Yah breaking up, Mountain-Six." She made a scratchy, whistling sound into the mic.

Erin swung wide and then lined up with the airstrip nestled amid the pines, eyes sweeping across her instrument panel and frequently coming back to the blinking fuel gauge. She'd have to do this on the first try, no touch and go because there wasn't enough gas to take this pig back up and around for a second attempt.

And she'd have to land with the ramp down. She couldn't close it from the cockpit.

That should be fun.

As she lined up, she glanced at the small, side-view mirror outside her window and saw several bodies tumbling out the back and into freefall. She nodded. *A few less to worry about.* The air controller was still demanding that she wave off, but she ignored him. *No time to chat.* Erin Boyle had been flying since she was sixteen, and being paid by the Air Force to do it since she was twenty-two. She'd taken the C-130 all around the world, had flown, landed and taken off in every conceivable type of weather, had even come in steep and fast to set down on desert airfields being peppered by mortars. This was an empty, flat airstrip on a cool, still

October day. *Yeah...sexy.* But she'd never set one of these down with a deployed cargo ramp.

Sparks and heated avgas. Oh, yeah, lots *of fun.*

Despite the possibility of completing this landing as a tumbling fireball, and the incessant banging of raving cannibals at the cockpit door, Major Boyle's hands worked with the smooth precision of a machine, lowering the landing gear and control surfaces, reducing power and easing the yoke forward as she lined up on the field. The tarmac rushed up at her, blue and white lights flashing by on each side in a blur, and then a *TH-THUMP* followed by the *CHIRP-CHIRP* of rubber on asphalt. Normal landing noises. The sound coming from the tail was not; a terrible screeching of metal being twisted and dragged, causing the massive aircraft to shudder and forcing her to tighten her grip on the yoke, even as she cut her engines back. A glance out the side-view mirror revealed a rooster tail of white sparks flying back from the cargo plane as it landed.

Her heart rate remained constant, never elevating.

A dull whump, *a flash, maybe an instant of pain. When we ignite that's what...*

Before she could complete the morbid thought, the C-130 was rolling into a taxi, the spark shower gone and her hands maintaining enough power in the turbo-props to get her onto the ramp, quite some distance further down than where the white business jet was parked. Erin shut down her engines and her systems as routinely as if this were the end of any other flight.

"Buffalo-Two-Eight!" her radio screeched. "You are-"

"I know, I'm not cleared to land." She switched off the radio. After a moment of sitting and waiting to see if she would blow up after all, she unsnapped her helmet and tossed it into the lap of the corpse in the other seat. Scotty had been a close friend, but when he went cannibal he'd given up all claims to a decent treatment. She didn't regret shooting him.

Erin glanced out at her mirror again, seeing a stream of soldiers in full battle gear exiting the open rear of the aircraft, running across the tarmac like a mob. She looked over her shoulder and out the window, seeing that her unholy delivery was heading for a small structure and a tiny knot of people gathered outside it.

I'm sorry, she thought, and she truly was.

The pounding at the cockpit door continued – *they* hadn't run off with the others – and the newly arrived Air Force major wondered how *she* was going to exit the aircraft.

Donny Knapp stared in horror as scores of infected soldiers spilled down the now-mangled ramp of the C-130 (and what a show *that* landing had been) and immediately began charging toward his little group. Only about two hundred feet separated them, and the soldiers howled their madness and hunger.

The young lieutenant thought fast, pointing at the Secret Service agent. "Get them inside," he ordered. The man responded at once, moving the Supreme Court Justice, the President's deputy and the VP's family into the cinderblock house, leading with his pistol drawn.

"Jones," he barked, turning. "Watch our six. Everyone else on line and firing." He snapped his fingers at the Green Beret watching the executive jet. "Except you. Stay on it." Then hell broke loose as assault rifles and a squad automatic weapon fired at once, ripping into the wave of snarling, silver-eyed troops.

Specialist Hancock had made it through Green Beret training, had served in Afghanistan and seen his share of live trigger time against targets that wanted to destroy him. His marksmanship and added firepower could be a deciding factor if added to those who were already blasting away, but he hadn't fired a shot. The wet-nose butter bar had him watching a plane, as if the devil himself might emerge at any moment.

As a Special Forces operator however, he was first and foremost disciplined. Regardless of Hancock's opinion about the qualifications of the younger man, a U.S. Army officer had assigned him an area of responsibility with clear orders. He would carry out his assignment, trusting in men he didn't know to handle their responsibility and put down the monsters racing toward them across the airfield.

Because of this discipline, he was in position and paying attention when the side door of the business jet popped open and dropped into a set of short stairs. Flailing bodies tumbled out through the opening and ended in a tangle on the concrete at the bottom. All of them were in business suits, all but one, a pilot in a white uniform shirt spattered red, his arms and face covered in ragged bite wounds and claw marks. He fought free of the tangle, jerking his legs free from clinging hands. For a moment it looked like he might make it, but then they pulled him down. Hancock was glad he couldn't hear the man's death screams over the gunfire.

One of them was crouched and feeding, but the rest scrambled up out of their tangle and started running, heading for the blockhouse. Hancock sighted on them through his combat optics. A dozen in all, hands curled into claws, grayish drool slinging back from snapping mouths, eyes radiant as bumper chrome. In addition to being a Green

Beret, Specialist Hancock was also close to finishing his bachelor's degree in Political Science (he had plans for after the military) and as such, he was a news junkie. He recognized the two men at the head of the pack from their frequent appearances on TV. One was the Director of the Central Intelligence Agency. The other was the senior senator from Illinois, the man challenging President Fox for election to the White House.

Hancock put them both down with three-round bursts, one for each chest.

Looks like the election's over, he thought, then went to work clearing out the others who had spilled from the jet before shifting to add his firepower to the squad.

Private Jones knelt beside the cinderblock wall, his rifle trained on the not-so-distant row of pines that marked the tree-line. He didn't like having his back to what was coming out of that cargo plane – in fact it scared him so badly that he was shaking. At least being able to shoot at something would be better than this. But someone had to watch the rear, and as usual, he got the shittiest detail.

He wanted to go home. He wanted to curl up in a ball in the back of his closet as he'd done when he was a child. Jones blinked back tears, listening to the howls climbing above the gunfire. He forced himself to keep watching, not to run, not to hide. He didn't move, and wondered if somehow he had become paralyzed because *all* he wanted to do was move.

Shadows shifting within the pines.

No, it's my imagination. I'm just...

Definitely movement; rapid, darting shapes.

It's wind, it's deer, not...

A lone soldier emerged from the tree-line, a bloody Green Beret with pine needles matted to his uniform, a man with eyes like bright coins. His lips peeled back and he started running right at the young private.

Then a hundred more like him burst from the trees and charged.

Private Jones felt his bladder let go as he screamed, *"Action rear!"* and started firing.

Bang...bang-bang...bang. The metal door rattled in its frame. *Nope, not going away.* Harvard was out of her seat now and staring at the oval-shaped door, fists planted on her hips. She could unbolt it and go out cowboy style, blazing away with her nine-millimeter, but there was no telling how many were out there. Besides, she might be a cowboy in the air, but she was no gunfighter. Pilots weren't selected for their skill with handguns.

It had to be plan-B, almost as risky. A twenty foot fall to the unforgiving concrete could finish her just as surely as hands and teeth. She stepped onto the pilot's seat, reaching up to grip a pair of yellow handles set in a two-foot-square hatch directly above. Stenciled in yellow letters was the word *ESCAPE* (*how appropriate*) and a warning about depressurization (*of no consequence here on the ground.)* She pulled both levers at the same time and pushed upward.

Nothing. The hatch didn't budge.

She pushed again, much harder this time, remembering the voice of some instructor telling her that sometimes excessive heat (like in Iraq) could cause the rubber seals of the opening and the hatch itself to fuse together. *That would be bad.* She grunted and heaved.

The emergency hatch popped with a sticky, ripping sound, and she moved it to the side, letting go of the handles. It slid across the smooth, curving skin of the aircraft and plunged to the pavement. Then she pulled herself up and out through the small opening, grateful that she worked out and watched her diet. She wasn't sure how many of her bigger, male colleagues could actually have fit through the small space. A moment later she was in the open and crouched on the upward curve above the cockpit.

The roar of gunfire made her look right. The odds of infected soldiers versus the tiny group of defenders was overwhelming, and Erin felt a sharp twist of guilt in her chest, knowing that she had just delivered at least half of those monstrosities. She wanted to get down there, to join the fight, but the cooler side of her made it clear that Erin and her sidearm would not tip the balance of that battle.

She rose and walked carefully up the centerline of the aircraft's spine until she reached the wings, then chose the starboard side, the one opposite the battle. Another sixty feet brought her to the extreme end, where she sat and dangled her legs off the tip of the wing. It was still going to be a considerable drop to the concrete. She checked the area below for infected soldiers, but they seemed to be occupied elsewhere.

Her remorse over delivering monsters to the remote airstrip and her desire to somehow make amends by joining the fight were emotionally based, and emotions had no place in a military flier's world. The Air Force had taught her that a skilled pilot was a highly valuable resource, one to be protected and recovered for future use. Anyone could pull a trigger, they'd said, but few could handle complex aircraft. Evade and escape, those were the words she'd been conditioned to live by should she ever have to ditch in combat. That she was now operating under wartime conditions was painfully obvious.

Major Boyle gripped the edge of the wing and swung over, hung fully extended (now she wished she was taller) and let go. She tried to bend her knees to absorb the impact, but it was a long drop and although she stayed on her feet, landing in a crouch, she felt a sharp jarring all the way up her back, as well as a soft pop in her left knee. She winced. Then she was jogging and favoring that leg, moving away from the C-130, away from the continuing sounds of battle on the other side of her aircraft. Pistol in hand, the pilot disappeared into the pine trees.

Bodies were falling, but not fast enough, and not enough of them. Soldiers in packs, helmets and slung weapons continued to close the distance, with more leaping out the back of the stopped cargo plane.

It's the body armor! Donny suddenly thought. He was about to order his squad to slow their fire and aim for the heads, but before he could, Jones screamed "Action Rear!" He pivoted and saw a wave of *things* – men of his company mixed with Green Berets – swarming out of the pines.

They're too close, too close, no chance...

"Vaughn," he shouted, "shift fire to our rear!"

The PFC swung his SAW around to try to suppress the oncoming wave, firing from the shoulder, expended brass flying through the air and tinkling against the side of the blockhouse. Lt. Knapp, his nostrils burning from the expended gunpowder, added his own assault rifle to the mix, chopping into targets that had no fear of gunfire.

Donny heard Vaughn yell, "Gonna have to load another belt!" and saw that Private Jones had already dropped an empty magazine and was fumbling to insert a fresh one. All of a sudden the fire to protect their rear had dropped off to only Donny's aimed three-round bursts.

Too close! Never reload in time!

And then both waves of snarling cannibals slammed into the defenders, front and back.

Donny heard screaming, and decided it must be him.

-32-

DANCER and DESIGN

Western New York – October 29

The First Lady sat unmoving in the passenger seat of the big, jacked-up Ford F-250, listening to the hum of oversized tires on asphalt and to the madness coming out of her captor's mouth.

"No more rules now," he said, grinning.

He talked so much and so fast that Patricia had the idea that he frequently had no one to talk to, or at least anyone who would listen. Smart or at least perceptive people, she decided, would move away from this man as quickly as possible.

"No more TV news telling me what to believe," he said. "No more government telling me what guns I can and can't have. No more rules!" He banged the horn with each word, but then frowned. "I'm gonna miss that ancient alien astronaut guy, though. The one with the nutty hair." A wink. "Now *there's* a man who knows what's what. I'm surprised the CIA hasn't shut him up already."

Shortly after he'd taken her and hit Kylie in the head with a tire iron (*Is she dead? Is my daughter dead?*) he had pulled over long enough to retrieve a short piece of chain and a couple of padlocks from a rusting tool chest installed in the truck bed behind the cab. He had tapped the rear window with the muzzle of one of the pistols frequently, staring at her, just in case she got any ideas while he was outside. She did, of course, but none that made any sense, and then he was back in the cab. He locked one end of the links to an empty gun rack mounted in the rear window, then looped the other end around her neck and padlocked it tight. When she'd tried to fight against it, he grabbed her broken arm and gave it a shake, making her scream and causing her vision to gray at the edges.

It was full morning now, and the road was empty. She couldn't tell what time it was exactly, or how long they'd been driving; the dashboard clock was broken. A passing highway marker said *219* in a shield symbol, but couldn't tell her what state they were in. The New York State Trooper car made it a good bet, but *where* in New York, and were they even still in the state? She had also finally remembered what *Bank Vault* was, and where it was located. Not that she would ever see it.

Over on the passenger side her feet were lost in trash; McDonalds wrappers, empty Mountain Dew bottles, potato chip bags and dog-eared porn magazines about naughty nuns. Both the truck and the owner smelled like a damp, blackened onion. He was still talking.

"…and I said, 'I did not grope that customer,' and he said, 'Yes you did, it's right there on camera,' and I said, 'Show me,' and he said, 'No.'"

Patricia didn't want to look at him, was trying not to, but he was loud and animated and she was afraid he would hurt her again. She wanted to at least see it coming. Not that she would be able to stop him. He was over six feet and easily three hundred pounds, with arms that were soft-looking but strong underneath the flab. His face was flushed and patchy with a beard coming in unevenly, and his dark, collar-length hair hung like oily curtains around a stained trucker hat advertising Winchester Firearms.

He'd introduced himself as Billy.

He'd informed her that her new name was Cunt.

"…so I said, 'That don't prove nothing,' and he said, 'You're fired,' so of course I said, 'Fuck you, Mr. Hermes,' and he said, 'Get out,' and I said, 'Make me,' and he said 'I'll call the police,' so I left cause I don't need trouble with *them* again and they got it in for me anyway."

Billy pounded the horn with a fleshy hand. "Stupid grocery store. That job sucked anyway." He looked at her and grinned. "They're lucky the world died when it did. I was gonna go back and put their active-shooter training to the test, go all Columbine on them, starting with Mr. Hermes."

Spittle flew from his lips as he spoke, and then his eyes grew glassy and distant. Patricia thought he was probably imagining the carnage he would visit on a store full of grocery employees and shoppers. She shuddered. Then his eyes cleared and he corrected the truck as it started to drift across the center line.

"But the world died." He laughed. "Caught me off guard. The end of the world, I mean. I was out looking for work, but of course no one's hiring 'cause the economy is for shit 'cause of that cock-knocker in the White House." His lips sagged into a pout. "Didn't have my guns with me cause the police took them away after I…that *thing* happened…and said I couldn't have guns no more but of course I got a lot stashed here and there, even at the house and they're hidden so good no one found them." The pout turned into a smile. "Lucky I found these." He patted the butt of one of the automatics shoved in his waistband, barely visible beneath the roll of his belly. Patricia wished it would go off and blow a hole through his crotch.

"Nope, no work to be found, but don't need it now." He looked at her from the corner of his eye and gave her a sly grin. "Got a new mission now."

Patricia looked away and closed her eyes, the chain cold and tight against her slender throat. She wanted to cry but fought back the tears. Kylie's image tried to surface but she forced it away. Thinking of her daughter now would cause her to lose it, and she didn't think Billy would take to a crying woman very well. Or he might enjoy it, and that was a sobering thought.

"I'm lucky I found you out there," he said cheerfully, but then frowned and shook his head. "Nah, *you're* lucky I found you. Otherwise you'd of gotten eaten by those things. Lucky, right?" When Patricia didn't answer immediately Billy raised his voice. "*Right,* Cunt?" He reached over and gripped her arm at the break, squeezing.

Patricia screamed and cried that yes, she was lucky Billy found her.

He smiled and nodded. "Almost home. Got a place up in the woods outside of town. Real private. Can't hear a damn thing from up there."

Patricia's stomach twisted and she closed her eyes again. "What are you going to do?" she asked, her voice as steady as she could make it, but the words still coming out as a whisper.

"Repopulate the earth, of course," he said, then brayed laughter, spittle hitting the windshield. "Isn't that what they do in all those end-of-the-world stories?" He laughed again, more like a bark, then gripped her left thigh and gave it a painful squeeze. "Course you're too old and dried up to do any breeding. So we'll just practice."

Patricia opened her eyes and looked out the side window, watching woods and pavement blur past. If the chain wasn't holding her in place she would open the door and throw herself out, hoping for a broken neck and a quick end.

He chuckled. "Nah, I hate kids. Besides, if it was about making babies I would have grabbed that young one you was with. Wasn't she a hot little piece of candy?" Billy wiped the back of his hand across his lips, his eyes taking on that glassy, faraway look for a moment. "Yummy candy," he whispered.

Billy shook his head, grinning and loud once more. "But she looked like trouble, more than I could handle, blasting away with that pistol and all. You looked easier. You're my first. Better to start slow, don't you think? No more rules, so practice, practice!"

Patricia didn't want him to hurt her again, so she nodded and gave him a soft, "Yes."

His grin broadened, showing off crooked teeth stained by chewing tobacco, and gaps where others had been but were no longer. There were more gaps than teeth. His voice grew serious. "You're the first woman I took, but you're also my first woman. You understand me?"

Patricia nodded, staring straight ahead at the road.

"Hey Cunt," he said quietly, and Patricia looked over to see that he had produced a big Buck knife from somewhere. He thumbed open the large blade with a *click.* "If you laugh at me 'cause I never been with a woman, I'll start cutting tender pieces off you."

Patricia whispered that she wouldn't laugh.

She'd always thought of herself as tough, and believed that if she was ever placed in a life-or-death situation she would be courageous and act. But something as seemingly simple as a broken arm had changed all that. Every move of the bone was excruciating, and Patricia learned that in real life, blinding pain trumped heroism. It was an unpleasant shock to find that she was no longer the woman she might have been, or thought she would be. She had heard that many middle-aged men who survived heart attacks, experiencing recovery weakness and hit by the realization of their own mortality, were struck a near-mortal blow to their masculinity and sense of self. Patricia thought she understood some of what they went through, now.

Billy tucked the knife away and brightened. "Almost there. Need to fill up first, though." A mile later they passed a green sign that read *LIMESTONE,* and shortly after that Billy pulled the jacked-up Ford into an empty Exxon station.

When he heaved his bulk out of the driver's seat he took both handguns with him; the Secret Service agent's Sig-Saur and the dead trooper's Glock 37. "You want anything from inside? A snack or a pop?"

She shook her head.

Billy shrugged. “You be good now while I’m gone.” Then he told her specifically which tender piece he would slice off first if she was not. He slammed the door and lumbered toward the front of the little gas mart.

Now the tears did flow, and Patricia blinked at them. Her chest hitched with sobs as she thought about the family she would never see again.

The sun was a ball of agony, threatening to make Kylie’s head explode. She was certain that would happen long before it crept above the windshield. With one hand on the wheel of the speeding police cruiser, she fumbled along the visor.

Please…oh, please…

Her hand closed on a pair of mirrored, aviator sunglasses, and she put them on with a sigh. That and keeping the visor lowered helped, but only a little. And there was nothing *little* about the pain in her head, centered on the egg-sized knot at the back of her skull and radiating outward. Her hair back there was stiff with dried blood, and the one time she’d dared to touch the knot she had screamed and almost passed out.

Kylie was nauseated and wanted to close her eyes, just for a moment. But that was Death trying to seduce her and she fought against it, biting the inside of her cheek hard enough to draw blood. It kept her eyelids from drooping. *A concussion for sure.* In the rearview mirror was a character from a Hollywood slasher movie; hair tangled, lines of dried blood curling down her face and neck, chin scraped raw and eyes dazed and slightly drooping.

Biting her cheek didn’t do much to ward off the double vision that made the road ahead swim in and out of focus.

And it did nothing to push back the growing despair and pointlessness rising in her with each passing mile.

She suddenly realized that this pursuit was nothing more than rage-fueled action without logic or focus, as if her quarry would conveniently keep driving along this road at a leisurely pace so she could catch up to him. Stupid. The man who took her mother could be anywhere by now, could have turned off on any one of a dozen side roads or a hundred dirt driveways. Now she wasn't certain the truck had even gone in this direction.

The pain made it hard to think, and that was what she needed to do more than anything. Kylie hit the brakes and stopped the Charger in the middle of the road, not bothering to pull over. The reflection of flashing emergency lights on the hood reminded her that the rooftop light bar was still on (and that light made her squint, too) so she hunted across the dashboard panel until she found the proper, labeled switch and shut them off.

Kylie sat and stared at the empty road for a while, listening to the rumbling engine and the drumbeat in her head. She noticed that the dead trooper's front tooth was still embedded in the steering wheel, and she flicked it away in disgust.

Think.

Who was he? Where did he go? How long has it been?

Her mom was hurt, and a violent stranger had taken her, someone who would… Kylie fought back a sob and wiped fiercely at the tears welling up in her eyes. That feeling of hopelessness was pressing down hard.

No. This isn't over. Think.

Her eyes drifted across the patrol car's dashboard, silent radio, passenger seat pouch of clipboards and pens, settling on the computer terminal and keyboard mounted at an angle between the front seats. The screen was black except for a blinking yellow cursor. She noticed that the glass was smudged with fingerprints. Touch screen.

Think. Think. Yes, maybe...

She tapped the screen and a menu appeared. One of the options was *Dashcam,* and she tapped that. More choices appeared. She tapped *playback,* and that brought up options such as date and time parameters, as well as the symbols for VCR controls common to TV remotes. She frowned. The dashboard clock said that it was ten o'clock, but what time had it been when she and her mother came upon the crash? Much earlier. The date was fuzzy in her head, too. Instead of typing in a range, she simply hit the *rewind* symbol, and a moment later the playback filled the screen, with the control symbols still visible at the bottom. The image was a windshield viewpoint of the stopped patrol car, the same view she could see when she looked up. Kylie tapped rewind again, and a *2x* symbol appeared, the playback moving faster, passing back through when she'd stopped the car, and then when she'd been driving, the empty road unwinding before her as the car seemed to run backward. It made her a little woozy, but she forced herself to watch. Another tap to *3x* really got it moving, and she saw the morning sun quickly dropping and fading back into the pre-dawn.

There!

A scramble of movement and light, people walking backward fast. Kylie hit the *stop* button and pressed the *play* arrow, revealing a close view of the trooper car sitting still, crunched against the side of the minivan, where a dead woman hung from a driver's window. The night sky was only just starting to pale, and the scene was lit by the police car's single headlight and flashing emergency bar. She saw a flashlight beam swinging about, and then was momentarily startled to see herself enter the frame, followed a moment later by her mom as they inspected the minivan. Then they both moved off camera.

Weren't these things supposed to have sound? She remembered audio when she'd watched police chases on YouTube, but this one was silent. Maybe the crash had damaged the microphone.

A few minutes later, steadily brightening headlights approached from the right and Kylie clenched her teeth, the pain in her head replaced by a simmering fury. *Here he comes.* The jacked-up pickup truck appeared, lights blazing, and stopped at an angle close to the wreck. The silhouette of a big man stepped down to the road, but the glare of the truck's spotlights was too great for her to make out any detail. She could see that he was carrying a tire iron, though. He moved off camera too, but not for long.

Fast, white muzzle flashes came from the left. Then Kylie made a sound that was half sob, half scream as the big man reappeared, dragging her mother who was struggling against him. The man slapped her in the head three times, making Kylie shriek at the video and grip the sides of the monitor. The man shoved her mother into the cab of the truck and climbed in behind her. The screen went white as the truck backed up and turned, its spotlights shining right into the camera.

This isn't going to work. It's too bright.

Then the image returned to normal as the truck maneuvered around the wreck, showing its tail end to the patrol car.

There!

Kylie jabbed the *pause* button, freezing the playback on the rear of the abductor's truck. The lone headlight of the police car illuminated a bumper with two stickers; one for the NRA and the other reading *God Bless America.* It also gave her a clear shot of an orange New York State license plate. She grabbed a pen and pad from the passenger seat pouch and scribbled it down.

She tapped the stop symbol and the dashcam video was replaced by the menu screen. The monitor swam out of focus and she closed her eyes briefly, placing her palms on the seat for balance. When she opened them she looked down the list of options;

VIN SEARCH

ADDRESS/GPS

DL SEARCH

TAG SEARCH

She tapped the last option, then typed in the digits and state of the plate she'd written down. The computer showed a series of moving bars, indicating that it was thinking. It occurred to Kylie that although there might not be a dispatcher at the other end of the silent radio, a database didn't depend upon an operator.

If it was still working.

She waited for a NO SERVICE message of some type to appear.

Instead, the image changed to a screen displaying the information linked to that plate; vehicle type and VIN number, pending criminal wants (none), registered address (a place in Limestone, New York) and registered owner.

William Peebles.

A message in white letters asked, DL LINK? She touched it, and a window appeared in the upper right corner with a digital image of Mr. William Peebles' driver's license. Six-foot-four, three hundred ten pounds. A blinking message next to the license read, FELONY CONVICTIONS, and beneath this was a list of weapons charges and sex offenses.

Kylie looked at the round face of a man in his mid-twenties, trying to grow a beard and smirking with stained teeth. He stared back at the camera with small, piggish eyes.

"Got you, fucker," Kylie growled.

On the tag registration screen another message asked, ADDRESS/GPS LINK? She tapped it, and after a moment the screen changed to a GPS format similar to the apps on phones. The position of her trooper car was a blue arrow, and the route she would need to take was highlighted in purple. Information at the bottom displayed distance and projected time of arrival.

Bank Vault. Feather Mountain, Pennsylvania. Like her mother, memories of a security briefing suddenly came back to her. Kylie looked at the map as a whole and her eyes widened. She wasn't just close to Limestone, but to the military facility where they were supposed to find refuge.

We're almost there!

First a quick stop at the home of Mr. William Peebles.

If that's where he is, and not in a million other possible places.

She shook her head (*bad idea, that hurt*) and looked out the windshield. She wouldn't allow herself to think he was anywhere other than the address showing on the GPS. She couldn't. Then she dropped the transmission into gear, squealing the tires as she accelerated. Kylie didn't know what she would do about William Peebles when she caught up to him.

But she knew he'd be sorry she had found him.

-33-

DARK HORSE

Upstate New York – October 29

It started with the sweats, then moved into nausea and shaking that made his entire body tremble. Before long, Marcus Handelman, AKA *Captain America* to the kids at Devon's prep school, grew delirious. The maintenance truck they were driving began to weave across both lanes as the Secret Service agent fought to keep his focus, muttering nonsense and talking to people who weren't there. Devon shouted at him, demanding he stop, and thankfully Marcus pulled over.

They were still in New York (Devon had never really appreciated how big the state was) and the truck they'd taken from the Harrison School was alone on the road. Over the past few hours, that hadn't always been the case. Always angling southwest and keeping to secondary roads, they had come out of the high forests and into rolling country, then shot through Utica. There were lots of infected there, and some that had run at and bounced off the truck. There were fires and traffic accidents too, some fleeing cars and trucks, and people walking along the side of the road that Marcus ignored. They'd passed through Cortland, Ithaca, Horseheads and Corning, drawing closer and closer to the Pennsylvania border. Around them now were rolling hills and harvested fields, a distant cluster of red and white farm buildings and little else. According to Devon's paper road map they were nine inches away from their destination of Custer City, Pennsylvania. Ninety to a hundred miles.

After stopping, Devon had convinced his bodyguard to switch to the passenger seat where he could recline a little and be more comfortable. Marcus agreed, saying, "Only…for a…few minutes…get going." His speech was slurred. Now he slept there, face beaded with perspiration, occasionally muttering things Devon couldn't make out, but sometimes screaming like he was in combat. "Cover! RPG left, two hundred meters! Willie's hit!" The outbursts never lasted long, but they always startled the young man. Devon assumed he was reliving some kind of overseas action during his time with Special Operations Group, but he decided he would never bring it up with Marcus about them, assuming he lived. It felt private, and if Marcus wanted Devon to know the details of his life before the Secret Service, he would tell him. Probably he would not, or wasn't allowed to.

The fifteen-year-old sat behind the wheel, looking at the agent, wondering if he was going to have to kill Marcus Handelman. He gripped the Sig-Saur he'd taken from the agent's shoulder holster – Marcus hadn't noticed – and now the pistol rested in his lap, the muzzle pointed at the sleeping man.

There were tears in Devon's eyes, and he didn't bother to wipe them away. Marcus had said he was in remission, not fully immune like Devon and the First Family, but that his body was successfully fighting the Trident infection and that he would be fine. Had he lied? Was his body now losing that fight? Or was what Devon was seeing just part of the battle? And was it like this for everyone supposedly in remission? He didn't know, and wondered if anyone did.

Would Marcus turn, and then turn on him? The agent's pistol was heavy in his hand. *Protector. Friend. Big brother.* Could he do it, shoot the man who had saved his life numerous times?

You're holding his gun. The answer must be yes.

He didn't want the answer to be yes, didn't want to hurt his friend. A tear fell from his cheek, landing on the black steel of the automatic. Out here on this country road, with a magnificent, late fall sky above, Devon had never felt so alone.

Pull him out of the truck and leave him on the side of the road.

Devon shook his head in disgust at even having had the thought.

That's what Marcus would tell you to do. Avoid the risk that he might turn, and spare yourself the grief of having to kill him.

The boy looked at himself in the rearview. That was the coward's way out, and he was no coward. If Marcus

Handelman turned into a monster and he had to shoot him, then he would do it. But he'd be damned if he'd just abandon the man. Devon wanted to be a Marine, and they didn't leave their people behind.

A hundred miles. I can do this.

Devon was too young for a driver's license, hadn't even started Driver's Education yet, but that didn't mean he was helpless. He'd driven go-carts, and at Camp David his dad had allowed him to drive the golf carts everyone used to get around. The prep school maintenance truck was bigger, heavier and could go much faster, but the principles of driving were the same; gas, brakes, steering. And besides, it wasn't like he had to worry about other traffic.

From the roadmap it was clear where he needed to go, and Devon was sure there would be a doctor once they got there. Of course there would be; they would have the best available because that was where his father would go. He put the pistol on the bench seat beside him, started the engine and pulled back onto the road, going slow until he got a feel for it. It was easy, and he smiled as he headed west.

In less than an hour, Devon would be fighting for his life.

One was a small town banker, a wide, fleshy man with thinning hair and wearing a short-sleeve Yankees jersey that revealed thick, hairy forearms. The other was a soccer mom in her late thirties dressed in a blood-splattered sweater. A woman who'd never had so much as a parking ticket, was now a cop-killer. Both were covered in scratches from their run through the woods. The banker's face bloomed like a cherry from the effort, and the soccer mom had dead leaves in her hair.

They had just emerged from the trees and stepped onto the asphalt. Not far away, an eighteen-wheeler had jackknifed and tipped over, but not before it had slammed into a red Hyundai Santa Fe, wrapping the economy SUV around a tree and killing everyone inside. The air smelled of oil, spilled gas and radiator coolant. A sign off to one side of the road, covered in the seals of the Kiwanis, Lions and Chamber of Commerce, welcomed travelers to the town of Wellsville.

"He deserved it," the soccer mom said. It was the only thing she had said since they ran from the soccer field, and she had already repeated it a dozen times.

The banker's eyes were glazed with shock. "Should have canceled practice. Coaches should have canceled." His voice was dreamy and distant, and he wasn't talking to the soccer mom.

"He deserved it," the woman replied as they stood staring at the fatal traffic accident that completely blocked the road.

"Mary…" the banker whispered. It wasn't the soccer mom's name, but she wasn't listening anyway. Her head was full of screaming.

The craziness occurring around the country was something happening in other places, not here in sleepy Wellsville. Weekend girl's soccer practice for the ten-to-twelve-year-olds had gone on as usual, the only exception being that a sheriff's deputy had parked his patrol car on the grass next to the white sideline, and stood leaning against a fender watching the girls play. Also, about a quarter of the families had kept their daughters home. But not the banker, and not the soccer mom.

"He deserved it," soccer mom said, staring at the overturned tractor-trailer and still gripping the bloody, short-handled landscaping shovel she'd used not long ago.

"Mary," the banker sobbed, tears rolling down his round cheeks.

It had been fast and confusing. A few girls sitting on the sidelines because they weren't feeling well suddenly ran onto the field, bearing several of their teammates to the ground before beginning to claw and bite. Some parents had done the same, attacking kids and startled adults alike. Then a pack of snarling, silver-eyed Wellsville residents charged in from across the street, running between the parked minivans and SUVs and immediately joining in the slaughter. There was screaming and snarling. Blood. Cries of the dying.

Soccer mom's daughter Mackenzie was taken down and savaged, but soccer mom had lost sight of her in the madness and hadn't seen her go down. When she did see Mackenzie again, the girl was back on her feet, teeth bared, growling as she clawed the eyes out of a cowering girl in a soccer uniform before biting out her throat. Now standing only ten feet away and too stunned to scream or even move, soccer mom had been frozen in place, then roughly shoved aside. The sheriff's deputy was there, firing his gun.

Firing at Mackenzie.

Killing Mackenzie.

Some municipal worker had left his spade planted in the mulch of a sapling over the weekend, and without conscious thought soccer mom seized it and hit the deputy in the side of the head with the blade-like edge. There had been a red explosion and the man fell with a grunt, but soccer mom kept hitting, straddling the fallen deputy and swinging again and again, screaming her daughter's name, turning the thing beneath her into something that looked like a man's body with a big lump of raw, ground beef sticking out of a uniform shirt.

Then the others had come, adults and children with bloody hands and faces, many of them with bright, luminescent eyes. Soccer mom ran, fled for the nearby trees and was quickly joined by the stout, wheezing banker, both of them driven by primal fear, their daughters forgotten for the moment.

The others had chased them, but lost contact in the trees.

The banker sagged to his knees on the asphalt now, and buried his face in his hands, his big body wracked with sobs. Soccer mom didn't notice.

"He deserved it," she muttered, brushing a clump of bloody hair out of her eyes. She left a crimson smear across her forehead.

From the other side of the overturned truck came a loud, *SCREEE...SCREE-SCREEE*, and soccer mom's head snapped up at the familiar noise. Behind her, a handful of children burst from the trees, howling as soon as they saw the two people on the road, rushing toward them.

Soccer mom ran, leaving the kneeling, sobbing banker behind as she headed for the other side of the jackknifed tractor-trailer.

Devon decided he liked driving, as he'd known he would. It was fun, especially on an empty road, the maintenance truck climbing up and down the rolling terrain without the worry of traffic. He kept it at a steady fifty-miles-per-hour, aching to go faster but smart enough to recognize that he was too inexperienced a driver to handle a sudden obstacle or situation at speeds any higher than that. The only other vehicle he'd seen was a silver four-door headed the other way at nearly twice his speed. As it passed, he caught a glimpse of a frightened-looking grandfather at the wheel and kids in the back with their faces pressed against the side window, looking at him.

In the passenger seat of the truck, Marcus slept. He didn't seem to be sweating as much, or at least not tossing and turning as he had been a short while ago, and Devon decided he'd take that as a good sign. He didn't want to think about the alternatives.

His pleasure at driving his first real vehicle abruptly evaporated when he came over a hill and saw what was in the field off to his right. A commercial airliner had gone down, its wreckage strewn for hundreds of yards across scorched earth, but some of the fuselage still recognizable, as well as a high tail bearing the American Airlines logo. People stumbled around the crash site, but whether they were shell-shocked survivors or cannibals looking to feed on the dead Devon couldn't say, and wasn't sticking around to find out. He went a little faster, and was glad when he could no longer see the crash in his rearview mirrors. Seeing it in his head however, was something the speed of the truck couldn't put behind.

Open farmland passed into wooded areas, where the hills were steeper and the road curvier. A sign read, *30 MPH AHEAD – REDUCE SPEED*. He did, dropping to thirty, and that was what saved him from dying on impact. The maintenance truck came around a sharp curve to find an overturned tractor-trailer blocking the road, its wheels and dark chassis like a mouth about to swallow Devon as he rushed toward it.

He let out a cry, straight-armed the steering wheel and stomped the brakes. The tires made a *SCREEE...SCREE-*

SCREEE sound as the rubber slid across the asphalt, coming to a stop a mere five feet from the jackknifed truck.

"Holy shit," Devon whispered, gripping the wheel hard enough to make his knuckles turn white. And then he saw her, a woman who appeared to be wearing a fright wig of dried leaves and blood, coming around the cab of the eighteen-wheeler, a short, bloody shovel in one hand. Her eyes locked on Devon and she shouted "Get-out-get-out-GET-*OUT!*" as she ran.

In the space of a half-second, Devon told himself that the eyes of the infected he'd seen had either been dark and malignant or silvery and utterly alien, just what he would expect from monsters. What he was seeing in this woman's glare was different. It was pure, human crazy.

He froze, and she reached the truck, grabbing his school sport jacket through the broken side window. She pulled with surprising strength, as if she intended to drag him out through the opening.

"*Get out!*" she shrieked.

Devon jerked back. "Go away!" he shouted, too frightened to come up with anything else.

The soccer mom made a growl deep in her throat, let go of his jacket and swung the shovel. Devon flinched away, the blade barely missing his face but slamming into his left shoulder. The pain was explosive, and bright little starbursts erupted before his eyes. They both screamed.

"Get out!" She gripped the shovel handle with both hands, raising it and pointing the blade right at his face like it was a spear. Devon's right hand found the Sig-Saur on the seat beside him, his thumb flicking the safety off with a reflex ingrained in him by his father, the weapon coming up even as she thrust.

The pistol roared, ten inches from her breastbone, close enough for the muzzle flash to set a circle of her sweater on fire. The soccer mom staggered back, the shovel clattering to the pavement, and then she dropped as if her legs had suddenly been cut from beneath her. Devon heard her head smack the asphalt with a sickening *thud.*

Devon's heart was racing as he shoved the hot muzzle of the pistol into the split between the bench seat and the back, dropping the transmission into reverse and hitting the gas. The tires squealed, the truck swayed violently and for an instant he thought he was going to lose control. Then he hit the brakes, jerked the transmission lever and accelerated, avoiding the body in the road and moving forward around the nose of the tractor-trailer. He scraped the right fender and clipped off the passenger mirror, but then he was clear.

On the other side, a dozen girls in some kind of uniform were crouched and kneeling around a big, red lump in the road, cramming meat and organs into their mouths. A few looked up. Devon looked away and gunned it, ignoring the thirty-mile-per-hour limit and leaving the horrible feeding behind.

A few minutes later, Marcus stirred in the passenger side. "You okay?" he asked, his eyes still closed and his voice weak.

Devon, tears running down his face, said nothing and kept driving.

-34-

DEVIL DOG

Eastern Ohio – October 29

Garrison Fox wasn't as lucky as his son. On a back road approaching the Pennsylvania border, the Hummer Agent King was driving came over a rise at just under sixty-five and there it was; a jam of stopped, eastbound traffic filling both lanes, a beige Tioga motorhome right in front of them. King jammed the brakes and tried to swerve as Garrison braced himself. The vehicle's big tires left black marks on the road as it slid forward, and then there was a tremendous *CRUNCH.*

Both men were thrown forward, but they'd been smart enough to wear their shoulder belts and it saved them.

"You okay," Garrison asked, massaging his neck and wincing.

King nodded, unsnapping his seatbelt. "Are you hurt, sir?"

"No." Garrison unbuckled and got out, bringing his rifle with him as he moved off to the right to get a wider view of the traffic jam. Agent King grabbed a handful of red flare sticks from a box behind the driver's seat, lighting and tossing them onto the road and out over the crest of the hill from where they'd come. He didn't want someone else doing the same thing and ramming into *them.* Then he went forward to inspect the damage.

Out on the gravel shoulder, the President stood and stared. A quarter mile-long, double row of vehicles was backed up from a point where a short, concrete bridge crossed a stream. It formed a natural choke-point for the road, and blocking the bridge was a cluster of trucks and Humvees in Army camouflage patterns. Hundreds of people were gathered at this end of the bridge and milling among the stopped vehicles along the length of the back-up.

More refugees, Garrison thought. *Why aren't they being allowed through?*

He looked again at the roadblock. The men moving around the vehicles there, and in particular one man standing behind a thirty-caliber machinegun mounted atop a Humvee, were in civilian clothing, not military uniforms. A sudden chill ran through him.

"What's our status, Mr. King?" he called.

A curse came from the front of their own Hummer. "No real front-end damage that I can see," David said, "and the engine still sounds good. Our bumper is locked up with the RV, though. Lots of twisted steel."

Up near the bridge, Garrison saw what looked like a fight breaking out among the refugees. A moment later, a little farther back, he saw several more civilians rush from between the stopped cars and plunge into a knot of people who had been standing just off the shoulder, watching and waiting. Bodies went to the ground, and the *pop-pop* of pistol fire came from somewhere within the traffic jam.

"We're about to run out of time," The President said, bringing his M4 to his shoulder and resting his index finger along the trigger guard.

David barely heard him. He was already back in the driver's seat, putting the Hummer in reverse and trying to back it out of its entanglement with the motor home. The engine revved, the tires spun and smoked and both vehicles rocked, but the Hummer remained stuck.

From where he stood, Garrison could see more and more attacks breaking out up the line. *It's spreading.* Then quick motion in his left peripheral made him turn. A middle-aged man and a boy with outstretched arms and grayish drool spilling from their lips were rushing at the Humvee, almost to the open driver's door where David King was still wrestling with the stuck vehicle.

Garrison had no time for thoughts of innocent, sick civilians or the American people he'd sworn to protect. A combat Marine's instinct kicked in and the M4 stuttered twice, a pair of three-round bursts hitting center mass. Man and boy collapsed only a yard from the Hummer.

"Thank you!" David shouted over the sound of the gunning engine.

"Isn't this *your* job?" Garrison shouted back. Movement on his right made him turn again. A trio of the infected was running toward him up the right shoulder. He dropped to one knee, braced his forward elbow against it in a compact shooting position drilled into him first during boot camp and AIT, advanced infantry training, then throughout his career as an infantry officer, and fired again, five quick squeezes, the muzzle ticking left and right. Three raving cannibals went down.

About half a magazine left. "Reloading," he yelled, not to inform any particular teammates that his firing was temporarily down as he switched to a full magazine, but again out of deeply ingrained habit. A moment later he was looking for targets again.

From up at the bridge he heard the long chatter of the thirty-caliber, and saw the gunner in civilian clothes sweeping his deadly machine back and forth across the crowd of refugees gathered in front of the roadblock. *Dear God!* Garrison's stomach twisted with nausea as he saw bodies falling, those not killed in the initial sweep scattering in all directions, parents picking up small children and running. The gunner began hunting their fleeing backs with bursts of automatic fire.

President Fox's lips peeled back from his teeth in a bestial snarl. He put the combat optics to his eye and thumbed the assault rifle's selector switch to single-shot. *Son-of-a-bitch living out some sick fantasy...*

The M4 kicked.

A wet, pink puff appeared behind the gunner's head and he dropped from sight, his murderous weapon falling silent.

"You good?" Agent King called, climbing out of the Humvee.

"Five-by-five," the President responded.

"Good, because I need you over here, sir. I'm going to stand on the bumper and bounce it. I need you gunning it in reverse every time I do, okay?"

Garrison swept the area again with his weapon. The only people close to them were refugees running into the fields and away from the slaughter. The screaming was louder now, more constant, and the gunfire from motorists was down to a few random pops. That told him all he needed to know about which way this battle was going.

Sudden movement in the big, rear window of the motor home above them made the President stop and swing his rifle up. A teenage girl had just hurled herself against the glass, palms slapping at in in panic and her face contorted into a terrified, muffled scream. A moment later a shadowy figure appeared behind her, and Garrison saw hands reach around her head, fingers hooking into her mouth and eyes and dragging her back out of sight.

"Mr. President!" David shouted, snapping Garrison out of his horror. For the briefest instant he'd thought about charging into the motor home to rescue the girl, but he knew it was already too late, and even if he tried it, Agent King would probably shoot him personally. Instead he forced himself to run around the Humvee and jump into the driver's seat.

King gripped the hood and jumped up and down on the bumper, while Garrison gunned the engine each time he came down. Tires continued to smoke and both vehicles shuddered. There was movement to the right and left now, but Garrison couldn't tell if it was fleeing refugees or attacking cannibals, and didn't dare take his focus off his job.

Come on! Come on you son-of-a-

With a squeal of metal and a violent lurch that made the Secret Service agent leap clear, the Humvee tore itself free of the RV. Garrison had barely hit the brakes to stop his reverse when Agent King had his slung P90 to his shoulder, firing bursts first to the left, then pivoting to fire on the left.

"Get in, King!" the President shouted. "We're leaving!"

A few more bursts from the P90 hurled running bodies to the ground, and then David King was climbing in, slamming the door and thrusting his SMG out the passenger window, still firing. "Go! Go!"

Garrison cranked the wheel hard left and stomped the accelerator. The heavy utility vehicle shot off the road, bounced through a shallow drainage ditch and tore out into a field to the north. He accelerated across the October ground, the plow furrows making it feel as if they were driving across a washboard at high speed. Moving at a forty-five-degree angle forward and away from the traffic back-up, they were able to get a broad view of what was happening.

People were still running between the parked cars, a few were crouched and hiding, while others fled across the fields. Many were pursued by others, no longer refugees but nightmares in human form. The two men watched as they saw frightened civilians go down under flailing arms and snapping teeth.

At the same time they noticed that someone else had climbed up to the gunner's position of the Humvee on the bridge, and this man abruptly swung the ring-mounted machinegun out toward Garrison and David's field. Crackles of white announced the muzzle flashes just as gouts of dirt started kicking up around their bouncing Hummer.

King pounded a fist against his door. "What is that crazy-?"

The ding of bullets punching through the sheet metal of their soft-skinned vehicle was followed by shattering glass in the rear, and a grunt from Agent King. He sagged against his door. Garrison saw the blood and shouted, "No!"

He pushed the Hummer as fast as it would go, swerving dangerously in an attempt to evade the distant machinegun. More dirt kicked up around them, and one bullet punched through the hood. The President waited for the burst of steam and hot oil, but it had missed the engine's vitals. A few more bullets clattered off the rear, and then they were at the edge of the field, angling left to put their tail to the gunner and racing directly away alongside a line of Cottonwood trees growing beside the narrow waterway. A bend in the stream suddenly put the trees between them and the madman on the bridge. The bullets were no longer coming their way, but Garrison didn't slow down, the Humvee still thudding across the field. Agent King flopped in the passenger seat, his eyes closed. Garrison kept going until he found a break in the foliage and what looked like a wide, shallow point in the stream. He crossed the ford, gunned it up the opposite embankment and kept following the stream, now on the other side.

The GPS showed their little blue arrow in the center of a green space with no road in sight. All Garrison could do was keep driving.

He did find a road, though it was another half hour of cross-country driving before he came upon the narrow dirt track cutting through farmland; tractor ruts more than anything else. The GPS recalculated and kept him going in the right direction. He crossed into Pennsylvania and eventually found his way to paved roads, still heading east and pulling off to conceal the Hummer behind trees or buildings when he saw other vehicles. Those he couldn't avoid paid him no attention. Shooting across Interstate 79 and passing between Edinboro and Meadville, he found his way to US 6. The GPS showed him that the Alleghenies were ahead, and he was about two hours from *Bank Vault,* the military installation at Feather Mountain.

Garrison had stopped shortly after crossing the border and pulled David into the rear seats. Thirty minutes of effort left the floorboards covered in bloody gauze and packaging. Now the Secret Service agent reclined against the far door, shirtless and with his torso wrapped in bandages and a trauma pad. It had taken all the supplies from the first aid kit to get to this point.

"I think we've stopped the bleeding," Garrison had said.

David was gray, his eyelids half open. Occasionally he sipped at a bottle of water, and the slight movement was obviously painful. "Thank you, sir," he said, his voice soft. He added, "I'm sorry I let you down."

Garrison wanted to yell at him for saying something so stupid, but held back. He knew the emotion in his voice would crack into a sob. He'd been here before, gripping the hand of a man – one of *his* men - critically wounded in combat and clinging to life, trying to keep them talking as they waited for a medevac helicopter. But there would be no such chopper today.

Instead, the President shook his head and gave the man's hand a squeeze. "Bullshit. You took a bullet that would have hit me. You have *more* than fulfilled your duty, Mr. King."

The agent sighed and closed his eyes, the hint of a smile at the corner of his mouth. "That's what every Secret Service agent imagines, right? Taking that bullet?" He coughed, and a few drops of blood appeared on his lips. Garrison wiped them away. Another sigh, but more like a wheeze. "It was going to happen anyway," the man said. "Here or Alaska. This is better."

Garrison didn't understand, but didn't press.

Agent King opened his eyes and looked at the President. "You have to get there, sir. You have to keep going, and don't you hesitate to put me out the second I jeopardize that mission." He took a deep breath and winced. "Do you hear me?"

"No one's getting put out anywhere."

The Secret Service sniper suddenly reached out and gripped Garrison's wrist tightly. "A lot of good men and women went down to get you this far. I..." He coughed. "Honor that sacrifice, Mr. President. Acknowledge."

Garrison looked at his agent, and at the fresh patch of red seeping through the trauma patch taped to his side. "Copy that, Agent King. But you're still going with me."

David nodded weakly and closed his eyes.

Now, less than two hours from their destination and driving through increasingly mountainous terrain, King slept in the rear seat, belted in so he wouldn't slip off the seat. President Fox drove with his eyes looking eastward and his assault rifle ready on the passenger seat beside him.

Almost there.

-35-

LABCOAT

CDC Atlanta – October 29

The Laughing Dead.

Because of her complete immersion in work, pop culture only existed on the distant fringe of Moira Rusk's life, and so she didn't connect the similarity between the title of the sensational TV series and what she was hearing from the lab. All but two of her staff (those bodies were destroyed and hardly recognizable, but mercifully mostly out of view behind a work table) were back on their feet now, crowding against the door to the patient ward despite the fatal wounds inflicted on them by Terry Butters. Severed arteries, ragged throat wounds and disembowelment hadn't kept them down. Bloody and silver-eyed, they bumped against one another as they pounded at the door, smearing the glass with their gore and making horrible chuckling sounds.

They *were* dead, at least clinically, but something was keeping them up and functioning, fueling their movement as well as their need to kill and devour. Moira had her suspicions about what that might be, but to confirm she would have to perform more autopsies, and she needed the lab. Needed *them* out.

She'd already secured the door between the post-mortem room and the lab, the door through which the late Terry Butters had made his dramatic and deadly entrance. And they couldn't get into the patient ward. Now she needed to clear them from the rest of the suite. She thought she knew of a way, but wondered if she had the courage to do it.

Moira considered the patients raving in the ward behind her; they had all turned now. At the first reports of outbreak violence, she and Dr. Fisher had decided to place them all in restraints, and thank God for that. But even now, as they thrashed against the Velcro straps, howling with rage and hunger and long past resembling anything human, the thought of what she had planned for them made Moira close her eyes and take a deep, shaky breath. She'd taken an oath to *heal,* to do no harm. But it couldn't be helped. She needed answers.

Before any of that though, she'd have to deal with the ward nurse.

The woman was in Phase-Two, that dazed and lethargic period where symptoms were presenting – staring, drooling, reflexive clenching and unclenching of the hands – the time right before she would turn into a violent Phase-Three. She was still slumped at her desk at the far end of the room, perched on a simple swivel chair on rollers, with her head on the desk and turned away. A puddle of urine had collected beneath the chair.

Time was short. Moira didn't know how long she'd been like this, and it was dangerous to assume that Phase-two always lasted an hour, just because Mr. Butters had before making his first attack in the lab. The nurse could turn at any minute, and Moira had no way to defend herself if that happened. She supposed she could try to fight her off with a scalpel, but that was laughable. A scalpel hadn't kept Butters on the table, and he'd been cut wide open.

After a quick trip to the supply closet, Moira began wrapping the ward nurse in white fabric surgical tape. Round and round she went, lashing the woman's arms to her body and body to the back of the chair. She wanted to tape her mouth shut too, but that would require lifting her head and Moira was afraid the movement would bring her out of her daze. It felt like she would never be finished, but after using up twelve rolls of tape she decided it would have to do. She'd have preferred the Velcro restraints, but there were none to spare.

Moira got behind the restrained nurse, pushing the woman and her rolling chair to the oversized door that opened from the ward into the hallway outside. She took the plastic access key card from the pocket of her scrubs and clenched it between her teeth, feeling her heart accelerate.

A cautious peek out the window set in the door. Nothing there. Then she blinked. A while back she'd looked out this window and seen the arm of a dead person lying on the floor, the rest of the body out of view. Now the arm was gone. In its place was a red handprint on the white paint, the kind of mark someone might leave if they were using the wall to lever themselves off the floor.

Of course you got up. Just like Terry Butters.

She caught a sudden chill, the implications of it all becoming quite clear. *Eighty percent turn rate*. She thought about the world's population, about the vastly outnumbered few who'd been lucky enough to have immunity. Then she thought about the considerably reduced number of those who'd survived the initial killing during the outbreak, an even lesser number surviving the subsequent hunting. She didn't realize she was quietly doing math in her head until the calculations abruptly went sideways at the thought that those infected who *were* killed didn't *stay* dead, or at least didn't stay down. That element essentially *doubled* their numbers, giving them a second chance to kill.

Then a single word cut through her thoughts. *Extinction.*

Even as it hung there before her, another thought came to Moira Rusk, something clearer than anything she'd ever considered. Her mission was no longer about understanding or even curing this plague. She knew she wouldn't live long enough to do that. No, it was finding a way to destroy them irreversibly, to save a thin slice of humanity by eradicating the rest.

And she would do it, destroy them all if she could.

Moira took a deep breath, one hand resting on the back of the nurse's chair. She held her key card to the proximity reader and quickly put it back between her teeth. The indicator light turned green and the unit made a soft beep before the door popped open several inches, the vacuum letting off a hiss. Then she was moving, shoving the wheeled chair ahead of her as she went out into the tiled hall.

The woman in the chair suddenly growled and snapped her head to the right, biting at the air and struggling against the tape. She let out an animal scream that carried down the empty corridor, and Moira gave her a tremendous push to the left. The chair rolled about six feet, and then the nurse's thrashing tipped it over. She went down about where the red handprint stained the wall, slamming into the tile face-first with a crunch. She immediately twisted her head to snarl at Moira, still struggling, her nose broken and her face a bloody smear. There was no reaction to the pain.

Moira left the door to the patient ward open and ran right, down to the lab's outer door, the one that opened into the room filled with cubicles. The nurse's howls chased after her, making the doctor's skin ripple with goose flesh at the thought of what those sounds might summon from the depths of the CDC.

A quick look through the window in this door showed the cubicle room to be empty, although something could be hiding within one of the mini-offices and she wouldn't know it. The partitions were blood-splattered and the carpet soaked brown in places from the earlier slaughter. At the far end, the door to the lab stood open. That's where they would be (she hoped,) crowded against the door to the patient ward.

Before she could lose her nerve, Moira took the card from between her teeth and held it to the reader. A beep, a hiss and the door popped open. She pulled it wide, stepping inside. Her hands were shaking.

Hey you? Come and eat me you bastards? She settled on, "Terry Butters!" and wondered if the thing would understand its name. The shout worked, regardless, for a chorus of howls answered and a moment later the dead boiled out of the lab and into the office. Silver eyes locked on the fifty-eight-year-old physician.

Moira ran.

It was ninety feet to the ward door, and Moira sprinted toward it. She heard them spilling out of the office behind her, giggling and chuckling their madness, a flesh and bone chainsaw of teeth and nails.

The door. I have to make it to-

Moira gasped and stumbled. Doctor Karen Fisher was standing in the hallway beyond, her hair in tangles and clotted with gore. Her lab coat looked more like a butcher's smock now, and she was hunched slightly forward, arms dangling like an ape. She twitched her head up just the slightest, and the fluorescents caught her eyes, causing them to give off a metallic shimmer.

Moira's friend let out a piercing shriek and raced toward her as the pack from the lab closed from behind. The older woman let out a small, strangled cry and started running again, legs pumping and heart hammering, knowing that Karen would get there before she did, that she would be torn apart from in front and behind.

But it was Moira who got there first, only a couple yards ahead of Karen Fisher and the pack. She grabbed the door's inner handle and flung herself inside, pulling as hard as she could. Bodies hit the door from the other side like football tacklers and slammed it the last few inches closed. The vacuum hissed as it sealed.

Crazed faces pressed against the small window, hands beating at the door. Moira looked into the face of a creature that had once been her friend and sobbed, but she quickly wiped her eyes. There was no time for heartache. She wasn't done.

Moira hurried through the door to the lab, praying they had all followed her into the hallway, that a few weren't lingering, and knowing she was dead if they had. The lab was empty. She shot through it, almost went down when her shoe hit a blood puddle on the floor, throwing her against a wall with a grunt, then she recovered and headed through the cubicles. She tensed as she ran the last few yards, waiting to be jumped by something lurking behind a partition, and then she was pulling this door closed, gripping the handle tightly. She didn't realize she'd been holding her breath until she let it out in time with the door's sealing hiss.

She closed her eyes and leaned her forehead against the coolness of the small window. When faces appeared there and the pounding commenced once more, she paid it no mind. The medical suite was hers now.

The doctor let out a deep sigh and walked back to the lab. Her hands had stopped shaking. It was time to get to work.

By definition, the Latin term *Post Mortem* meant *after death,* the only time that such invasive and destructive processes could be performed on a human being. Any one of the procedures would kill a living patient almost immediately, which was why – under normal circumstances – there were so many safeguards to ensure that the body on the slab was *truly* dead and not simply paralyzed or in a coma. Moira would have no need of those safeguards in these circumstances.

Although they were on wheels, the patient beds wouldn't fit through the post-mortem door, and there was no way she was going to remove the Velcro restraints on any one of these ten raging things in order to shift them to a gurney, so she decided to bring the autopsy to them. Relocating instruments, carts and what lights she could from the other room, she pulled patient number ten's bed into the center of the ward and set up around it. She couldn't bring in the small video camera wired into the lighting system above the stainless steel table, so there would be no visual record. She'd have to go slow and be careful to verbalize and describe everything she did and saw. The wireless microphone clipped to her rubberized apron had enough range for the receiver in post-mortem to pick it up.

Number ten raged and strained against its bonds, snapping at the air. A man in his forties, the subject's eyes appeared normal, not silver, though she couldn't remember ever seeing that level of intensity or hatred in a *normal* person. She wondered if the change appeared after clinical death, and said as much aloud so the mic would record it. Using a pair of surgical scissors, she cut away the man's hospital gown, leaving him naked.

I'm about to perform a live autopsy, she thought, shaking her head. *It's the kind of thing Hannibal might do in a Thomas Harris novel.*

She selected a scalpel and for the microphone said, "This is Doctor Moira Rusk…"

EXTINCTION

-36-

DANCER and DESIGN

Near Limestone, New York – October 29

Chained by the neck with an impromptu leash, Patricia sat in the cab of Billy's big, redneck pickup truck, palming away her tears. She knew they wouldn't do her any good, but they came anyway. Her large, foul-smelling abductor had plans for her at a house he said wasn't far away, and Patricia felt a hollow terror knowing that her remaining hours would be filled with brutality and pain.

She wanted to be strong, to fight for her life, but knew it would be a brief and pointless struggle. The tears fell harder, and she was no longer thinking of her family. The thought of what he was going to do to her was about to make her fall apart.

Billy emerged from the gas mart with a bottle of Mountain Dew in one hand, a bag of Doritos clenched in his teeth and what appeared to be a hand pump attached to a long hose gripped in his other, meaty paw. He climbed into the cab, setting the Mountain Dew in a cup holder and tossing the chips into her lap. "Sure you don't want any?" he asked. "You're going to need your energy."

When Patricia shook her head he pulled the big Ford around to the side of the station, parking next to a collection of circular metal covers set in the concrete. Billy got out and fumbled with one of the covers, the pump and the hose, his face turning red from the exertion of squatting and struggling. Patricia wished a stroke on him.

"I've never done this," he shouted to the cab. "But I'll figure it out." And he did, though it took more than an hour for him to manage it and transfer enough fuel from the underground tanks to top off the Ford. He took a break in the middle to cram Doritos into his mouth and chug the Mountain Dew. He also asked her how she thought she'd look in black rubber, crunching and looking out the window and not seeming to be actually interested in the response. She didn't give one.

"Do you think I should fill some extra containers?" he asked. "I'm already pumping, might as well. I saw some inside."

Patricia said he should. Anything to delay what was coming.

Billy finished his little break, leaving the pump hose in the underground tank. "I'll be back," he said, throwing a wave over his shoulder as he lumbered toward the gas mart. "Gotta make a poop."

Patricia shut her eyes and put her head down, the links of the chain pressing deeply against her throat, but unfortunately not enough to strangle her. The cold steel on her skin had a sense of finality to it, and she wished she could have told Garrison once last time that she loved him.

Billy sat on the toilet, grunting in a small bathroom at the back of the store, the door open so he'd have some light. "Gotta eat more fruit," he groaned, straining until he felt pressure in his temples and forced himself to relax, breathing deeply. It wouldn't do to kill himself taking a crap, not with a freshly dead world out there filled with every conceivable delight.

Outside the bathroom he could see shelves filed with chips and bottles of cheese and salsa. He'd stock up on provisions before he left for the house.

No power here meant no power at home, since it was just over a mile away. He had a generator though, so it wouldn't matter. The house was a pile of shit and he knew it; the property was covered in junked cars, rusting oil barrels, broken appliances and trash. He just threw his house garbage out into the rest of the shit, and didn't the bears love that? The inside of the house was as much a trash heap as the outside, but Billy didn't care. Landscaping and interior decorating wasn't what drew his interest.

The cellar, though…that was his passion.

Sitting on the bowl and trying to move his bowels, Billy smiled at the thought of it. The cellar might have started out as a damp, dirt-floored space filled with dark corners and spiders, but now it was a clean, bright, fully equipped dungeon, exactly what he'd been fantasizing about since he was nine or ten-years-old and first started drawing pictures of what he thought naked women would look like after they'd had their body parts sawed off. And wasn't it amazing what you could buy online and have delivered in just days, the purchases arriving in nice, discrete unlabeled boxes. Billy planned to use every toy he'd ordered, or at least as many as he could before the old cunt wore out and the life drained away from her.

After twenty minutes he felt movement at last and let out a deep sigh. The bathroom filled with the rich odor of his waste.

Billy had lied to Cunt, and that made him smile, too. She wasn't the first woman he had taken, was actually the second but the first one hadn't really counted. A housewife snatched from the darkness of a big discount store's parking lot. She died of asphyxiation in his dungeon before he could even get going. Oh, he'd had some fun with the body afterward, but that didn't really count either.

The real problem had been with disposal. He could have buried her in the woods – God knew it was isolated enough – but the bears would have simply dug her up. Then he'd had a spark of brilliance and tucked her into an old refrigerator, chaining it shut and leaving it in plain sight in the trash field in front of his house.

When the cops came to take away his guns (it wasn't an *incident,* really, more of an *indiscretion,* he decided) they hadn't even glanced at the fridge, and the stink seeping out from within was lost in all the other filth. But now there were no more cops, no more rules, and no more worries about how to dispose of corpses. He could toss them outside or even prop them up in a lawn chair on his porch if he wanted to. The bears could have them. Or maybe even the hungry things that used to be people.

This time would be different. Cunt (he'd called the other one that, too) wouldn't be allowed to die before he'd had his fun. Billy had learned, and knew how to be more careful this time. Practice, practice.

Billy finished up and headed through the store, selecting a pair of empty, red gasoline containers from a high shelf and putting another bag of Doritos between his teeth. When he went outside, the door gave a happy little jingle that made him smile around the bag of chips. Off to the right, Cunt sat in his truck staring at him through the passenger window. He started toward her but then stopped.

Parked at the pumps was a New York State Police Charger with a crumpled fender and a broken headlight.

Uh-oh.

The trunk was open.

"Hey," a voice said from behind him. Billy dropped the gas cans (not the chips) and spun, reaching for one of the handguns stuck in his waistband. As he turned he came face-to-face with the muzzle opening of a shotgun only inches from his nose. The piece of yummy candy from earlier was holding a twelve-gauge Remington 870, a sweet model with a pistol grip and a smooth, black finish. He had one just like it at-

Kylie pulled the trigger, and Billy's head above the lower jaw exploded in a storm of red and gray, bone, teeth and hair. The body collapsed with a heavy thump.

She'd spotted the jacked-up Ford from the road, saw her mother chained by the neck in the front seat, and then rage took over. Now she spat on the corpse, then went through its pockets until she found the padlock keys.

Patricia flinched when the shotgun went off. The result was horrifying – she'd never seen anything so awful, not even in horror movies – and instantly knew she would never erase the moment from her memory. But another part of her nodded with an unfamiliar, dark satisfaction.

Several minutes later her daughter was there, unlocking the chain and helping her down from the truck. They hugged and cried for a long time.

"Are you okay?" Kylie asked at last, looking her mother over for injuries beyond the broken arm.

Patricia nodded. "Are *you* okay…with *that?"* She nodded toward Billy's headless corpse.

A flinty look appeared in her daughter's eyes. "Very okay. In fact once doesn't feel like enough."

"I know what *Bank Vault* is," her mother said, and Kylie said she had figured it out too. Patricia shook her head. "How did you find me?"

Kylie guided her toward the Charger. "I'll explain when we're on the road. The GPS says Feather Mountain isn't far. We're almost there."

-37-

LABCOAT

CDC Atlanta – October 29

Dr. Rusk sat back from the microscope and rubbed her eyes. She was perched on a stool in the lab, the work table before her covered with test samples, glass slides, reference materials and a spiral notebook where she was recording her findings, thoughts and theories, crazy though they might be. Her gore-spattered autopsy apron hung on a hook by the door to the patient ward, and she had changed into fresh, pale blue scrubs.

She yawned and glanced at a wall clock. The afternoon was quickly running out. How long since she'd last slept? She was too tired to do the math.

Three autopsies since she'd retaken the lab suite, the grisliest, most unimaginable time of her life. Cutting into three patients that continued to shriek and bite and thrash even as she spread open chest cavities, even as she removed organs. The last one had bucked so hard in its restraints that her hand had slipped, and the scalpel she was holding sliced a deep cut through the index knuckle of her left hand. Now it was clean and wrapped in gauze, uncomfortable and awkward. She'd taken only ibuprofen for the pain, though she could have gotten something much stronger from the supply closet. She wanted to stay clear-headed.

The patients had fought – long after they should have been dead – right up until one of three things happened; infliction of trauma to the alien, gelatinous sacs that encased their brains, hearts or spinal cords. A simple needle stick didn't do it, because the sac immediately closed around the puncture much like a muscle. But an incision of any real size caused a quivering, mucous-like substance to spill out into the rest of the body until the sac was essentially deflated. The gelatin stopped wriggling within seconds, the patient stiffened and went silent, and the luminescence went out of their eyes at once, leaving them as lifeless as dull pewter.

Spinal trauma. Heart or brain trauma. It killed them, *really* killed them. Would that knowledge be useful to anyone? That same trauma killed healthy human beings, so what was the difference? The difference was that any *other* trauma, such as fatal wounds to the body's organs other than those three, had no effect at all. To test her theory Moira had taken a bone saw to one patient's big toe and took it completely off. Other than bleeding, the patient didn't react except to keep raging. She decided that sawing off all four limbs wouldn't change them. They would be just as aggressive, only more restricted.

She said as much in her scribblings in the notepad, then tapped the pen against her chin.

No change. That wasn't entirely true. All her subjects had been alive – infected but still alive – when she began the procedure. Their eyes had been dark and hungry-looking, but biologically appeared normal. It was only after clinical death (excessive blood loss, the massive trauma caused by spreading the chest and removing organs) that the eyes changed to that glimmering, solid-silver surface without pupil or iris. She scribbled some ideas about what the change in the eyes might mean…possibly altered vision to aid in hunting…but also noted that she was merely speculating.

The change from Phase-Three to Phase-Four, from violent predator to *dead* violent predator, was what frustrated her the most. The intervening time period was inconsistent. Terry Butters had taken more than an hour. His victims had turned in less than ten minutes. Her three autopsy patients had been still during the metamorphosis for six, twenty-two and fifty minutes respectively before their *rebirth.*

All of them were just as vicious as they'd been before death, but continued to exhibit motor function that, quite frankly, was impossible for a corpse. She had no equipment to get an EEG reading (looking at brainwaves and post-mortem rooms didn't go together), so she was speculating again, although her lab work seemed to have confirmed what she was thinking.

At its heart, Trident was parasitic.

It was alive.

Moira yawned again and pulled her laptop toward her through the debris, enabling the voice-to-text function, a blinking red light above the screen indicating that the microphone was live. She looked at her handwritten notes and continued, dictating what she had scribbled down and including her own conjectures as well as conclusions she'd drawn from news broadcasts before those had gone off the air completely. There was no particular organization to what she said, she just talked. She was too fatigued, and this wasn't prep for an on-stage presentation to the AMA. Time was running out and she had to get it all on the record.

"Moira Rusk," she said, "continuation of notes. I'm not sure if I said this before…maybe I just thought I did…so just to be safe. Phase-One is asymptomatic. The theory that Trident incubated for ten days was only partially correct, and was more of a false flag, because it seems to have been true only in early contact cases. It accelerates somehow, and I now believe that Trident is running on its own, internal clock, with a maximum of thirteen days from its first contact with the index patient – whoever that was – until what I've been calling the *turning.* That's regardless of when a victim contracted the virus."

She looked at her notes and stifled another yawn, wishing for coffee. There was none to be had here in the lab suite. Then she blinked, realizing she would never drink another cup of coffee in her life.

"I'm fatigued," she told the recording, "so this will probably come out scattered. In simple terms, first exposure cases went a full ten days before turning. Those who contracted the virus even *three* days after the zero-point, who should have had a week and a half before outbreak, are prematurely turning at the same rate as the others. That's why I'm suggesting acceleration. So even if you caught it yesterday, you'll have turned by Virus-Exposure-Day thirteen, and that's tomorrow. I have no idea why that would be. I'm babbling."

Moira recapped the rough numbers for resistance/remission and outright immunity. "By my calculations, anyone who *can* turn *will* have turned by end of day tomorrow."

She turned a few pages in the spiral notebook. "Phase-Two is the brief, symptomatic period we've all seen; lethargy, distraction, excessive salivation and reflexive motor activity, sometimes loss of control over bodily functions. An hour of this seemed the norm at first, but like everything else that has become inconsistent too." She thought about the ward nurse and how she'd been able to subdue the dazed woman. "However long it lasts, this is when they're most vulnerable." It sounded like an odd thing to add to a clinical evaluation, but necessary considering her species was facing eradication from the aggression of another.

"Phase-Three is the savagery we've seen, with predatory behavior and loss of reason, or at least how we understand it, and I don't think that part is always accurate. Some of them behave like single-purpose killing machines, attacking head-on without regard for risk. Others exhibit varying degrees of problem-solving ability and cleverness. All of them are without fear and completely resistant to pain. And it should be noted that Phase-Threes are still alive in the clinical sense, and can be incapacitated or killed by most forms of violence."

The howls of the seven remaining patients in the adjacent ward floated through the intervening door. "Be right with you," Moira murmured, then looked at her notes again.

"I've seen evidence that a Phase-One, asymptomatic infection victim bitten but not killed by a Phase-Three, will undergo an almost immediate change – minutes only – and turn, becoming a Phase-Three themselves and bypassing the Phase-Two symptomatic period." She tapped the pen against her chin. Was this even making sense? "My theory is that the turned strain, passed via fluid transfer, somehow activates the dormant strain. There are initial indicators, but someone else will have to figure out those details."

Moira took a deep breath. "Trident is definitely parasitic. The parasites hatching from the early virus structure attach themselves to everything; muscle, organs, nervous system, and they quickly manufacture the gelatinous sac growths in a manner similar to the way insects create cocoons or egg sacs. The growths house a large concentration of the parasites, and protect both them and the key organs." A glance at her notes. "I also believe that the parasites have developed a *hive mind,* communicating and taking orders given by the organisms within the sacs, allowing them to continue controlling the host's brain and body even after death."

"And Phase-Fours *are* dead, in every sense that we understand, but the parasites keep them going." She talked about the sacs around the brain, heart and spinal column, convinced she was repeating herself but pushing forward anyway. "It appears that Phase-Fours can only be truly destroyed by rupturing one of these sacs, their three most vulnerable points. This makes them considerably more resilient than human beings. Admittedly, I have no idea if they are effected by other elemental conditions; fire, toxins, oxygen deprivation. I haven't seen lung function in Phase-Fours. An earlier report suggested high doses of radiation could destroy them, but right now I can't remember where I heard that or if it came from a credible source."

Moira huffed in frustration. There was so much she didn't know, and never would.

"Not that I think it will matter in the larger scope," she continued, speaking to the microphone, "but I have a simple theory on the cannibalism. This is pure speculation, but in a normal parasitic paradigm, the host is steadily consumed until it is no longer of use to the intruding organism. Perhaps, in order to keep the host functioning, the proteins and potassium inherent in human flesh are being consumed to provide the parasites with a food source other than the host, creating a symbiotic relationship."

She shook her head and muttered, "Or they might just be goddamn monsters."

Moira made a disgusted face and hit the recorder's stop button. She was a physician, a scientist, and she owed a better effort than this to anyone who would see her work. She had no illusions about living long enough to ever be questioned about her research quality though, especially now.

A headache had begun, accompanied by chills and nausea.

Her time was almost at an end.

"So make it count," she said to the empty lab, then rose and put her autopsy gear back on. She wanted to do as many more as possible while she still could, add her findings to the growing record of audio, typed notes and attachments, then upload the file to the cloud. Virologists worldwide who subscribed to the service – and that was most of them since it was a relatively small community – would be able to review Moira's work and maybe pull something useful from it. That meant she had to get her ass in gear, she thought, palming sweat off her forehead.

Twenty minutes later she had prepped the next subject and pulled them and their bed into the now-gory center of the ward. She'd dragged away the bodies of the three previous subjects and left them in the office cubicles. This one, a young woman from Atlanta who had volunteered as a research subject when the dormant virus was first discovered, raged and bucked against the Velcro restraints, eyes filled with hate as she tried to bite at her tormentor.

The knuckle Moira had accidentally cut with the scalpel was throbbing, and she remembered that she wanted to try sedation with the next one in an attempt to make the procedure go more smoothly. She filled a syringe with 6 mg of morphine (there was no way an IV would stay in place, so a drip was out of the question) and pinned the patient's right arm to the bed, putting her weight behind it to hold her down. Then she punched the syringe in just below the elbow and injected the amber fluid.

That amount of opiates, administered that quickly, should have put the patient into a relaxed state almost immediately.

Instead, it yielded a very different effect.

With the injection site as a central point, a black necrosis erupted around the puncture and began radiating outward rapidly, corrupting the flesh and engulfing the arm down to the fingers and up to the shoulder in seconds. Veins turned black and raced ahead of the necrosis, spreading out across the girl's chest and neck.

Staring in horrified fascination *(it's so fast!)* Moira thought about watching mold grow and spread through high-speed, time-lapse photography. The girl suddenly went rigid and silent, her mouth frozen in the open position, eyes fixed on the ceiling. In an instant they clouded over silver.

The eyes had no luminescence however, and as the flesh blackened across the patient's entire body, they turned that same, dull pewter color as those patients she'd destroyed by cutting open the protective sacs full of parasites. The entire process took less than sixty seconds, and now patient number seven was motionless on the bed, looking as if she'd been placed in an incinerator.

Dead. Moira let out a gasp. *Truly dead.*

She stared at the empty hypodermic she was still holding.

Morphine.

-38-

FEATHER MOUNTAIN

Western Pennsylvania – October 29

Donny heard growling and opened his eyes, feeling a weight on his chest that made it difficult to breathe. He saw that he was nose-to-nose with an infected soldier, mere inches away from a pair of dull, steel-gray eyes and a mouth frozen in mid-shriek. The soldier wasn't wearing a helmet, had a bullet wound in the side of his head and smelled like sweat and human shit. Donny's face hurt (*rifle butt, someone swinging it like a bat, caught it on the cheek*) and he tried to lift a hand to touch the swelling. He couldn't. His arm was pinned between him and the dead soldier. The growling was closer now, thick and rattling as if the maker of the noise had a throat full of mucous.

It came back to Danny in a rush. Two waves of infected soldiers had hit them, from the airfield and from behind, pouring out of the trees like the human wave attacks of the Korean War he'd studied in ROTC. There had been so much firing, and suddenly it was hand-to-hand, rifle butts and combat knives and bayonets. His entire body was sore, especially his shoulders and arms, and he remembered grabbing soldiers by their combat harnesses, plunging his knife up under their jaws, flinging bodies aside before doing it again with the next attacker. He'd caught a glance of Vaugh his SAW gunner crouched and loading a belt of ammunition, hit and disappearing under a pile of infected troops, of Private Jones being pinned against the wall of the cinderblock house and being ripped apart as he screamed and beat at his killers with his fists. The air had been filled with the sharp odors of blood and gunpowder, and the hungry cries of maniacs.

The growling was coming up on his left. *Stay hidden beneath a corpse and hope it goes by? Wiggle out from under and take it on? Lie here and wait until it eats you?*

Donny had lost his pistol at some point, and he wasn't holding his knife anymore. *Action is better than waiting. Soldier up.* He heaved upward and rolled the body to one side, freeing his trapped arm as he scrambled to his feet. A silver-eyed infantryman *(is that Captain Dunham?)* lunged at him from ten feet away, and Donny realized it was too close, too late. He threw his arms up reflexively.

A single pistol shot blew out the side of the captain's head, and the body crumpled. The Secret Service agent who had come in on the Marine chopper took a few steps closer on Donny's right and fired again. Another headshot, this one a North Carolina National Guardsman who was riddled with bullets but was nonetheless rising to his hands and knees.

"They're getting back up," the agent said through clenched teeth, turning and firing again at something else. "They're coming back!"

Donny looked around at a sea of carnage. Bodies were crumpled on the ground in every direction, and it reminded him of one of those medieval movies where they showed the aftermath of a great battle, the dead and dying carpeting the field, entwined with one another. The air stank of human waste, and he realized that the *wounded* he saw stirring were infected soldiers with uniforms soaked red, shot through the necks and thighs and arms, wounds that should have kept them down.

Their eyes were radiant and inhuman.

The Secret Service agent's pistol cracked again, and Donny saw another guardsman take the hit to the side of his head. A snotty mass of gray and pink blew out the other side of his skull and he fell.

A hand gripped his boot and he looked down to see an infected soldier using it as leverage to pull himself out from under a pile of bodies. He kicked the soldier in the face and stumbled away. *Losing it...how can I...?*

"Lieutenant!"

Donny turned to the voice, seeing Woods, his female quartermaster-turned-infantryman not far away. She had fixed her bayonet to the tip of her assault rifle, and the blade was slippery with gore. So was one side of her dark brown face. The woman reached him and grabbed the collar of his uniform. "We need to go, sir!"

Donny blinked at her. The woman's uniform was soaked crimson and he could see bite marks on her forearms. She swam out of focus, and he slowly touched his face where he'd been hit by the rifle butt. *Really rang my bell,* he thought dreamily.

Woods shook her head and picked an assault rifle up off the ground – there were plenty, the guardsmen had all been fully equipped – shoving it into her lieutenant's hands. "They're getting up, sir. We have to move." She snapped her fingers in front of his face, then shouted, "Snap out of it, butter-bar!"

It got his attention and he squeezed his eyes tightly, then looked at the weapon he was holding and back up at her. "What…?"

The corporal started pulling him toward the cinderblock house where the agent now stood with his back to the door, pistol extended at arm's length and sweeping back and forth. "Vaughn and Jones are dead," Woods said. "I saw them go down. I don't know what happened to our two Green Berets, probably dead too. Out under *that.*" She waved at the ground hidden by fallen uniforms, then stopped to thrust her bayonet, pinning a growling head to the ground, making it silent.

Donny saw Akins, the malcontent and would-be deserter standing at one corner of the blockhouse. He had obviously been collecting magazine bandoliers from the fallen and now had at least a dozen of them hanging around his neck, looking comically overloaded. He shouted something and fired several bursts at a target Donny couldn't see on the other side of the blockhouse.

Then more clearly Akins yelled, "Is he fried or functional?"

"He's good," the corporal shouted back.

How many hit us? Donny eyes swept over the aftermath. *A hundred? More?* Bodies were moving out there, some rising to their feet. Others were kneeling in clusters, feeding. Feeding on *his* people.

Were more coming?

Donny forced himself to think, demanded that his head clear so he could lead instead of being a liability to his men. There weren't many options, and he reached a decision quickly, pointing at the Secret Service agent. "Get your people out of the blockhouse and take them up the hill to the bunker." He pointed at the sloping road, then looked at Woods. "You and Akins go with them to provide cover." He jabbed her in the chest of her body armor. "Make sure they get inside."

The agent went in to collect his charges as Akins moved to join them. "What about you, El-Tee?" Woods asked. Akins fired a few bursts to the left, and Donny waited so he would be heard.

"I'll try to hold them here," he said.

A blue business jet with Air Force markings did a fly-by over the field, and Donny watched it go. "We still need to hold the airstrip. He looked at the bodies, at the rising shapes. "I'll clean this up."

Woods shook her head and started to say something, but Donny gave her a hard look. "You have your orders, Corporal." Then he started taking bandoliers of magazines from Akins' neck and slung them around his own. When Akins started to complain, Donny simply said, "Find more."

The agent emerged from the blockhouse with his collection of civilians, all of them looking frightened and somewhat amazed that they had come through the deafening sounds of battle outside their shelter intact. The President's Deputy Chief of Staff seemed to have it together a little more than the others. "I tried the radio," he said, "but the mountain isn't answering. Are you sure-?"

"Yes," said Donny. He wasn't in the mood for a debate. "You're going. My people will escort you."

The deputy nodded. "A plane is asking for permission to land, and we heard calls that might be another aircraft."

"I'll handle it," Donny said.

A minute later Woods had them organized and moving at a good pace toward the road, Private Akins leading and collecting magazines from the fallen as he went. "Watch your ass, Lieutenant," the corporal said.

Donny snapped his own bayonet into his rifle as a response. While the corporal hustled after her departing group, Donny checked to make sure that he had a full magazine inserted in his M4. He went inside to the radio and broadcast, "All aircraft inbound to Feather Mountain. You are cleared to land at your own discretion. Be advised we have no air traffic controller, so you'll have to talk to each other and sort it out. Do *not* crash into my airstrip or obstruct it with parked planes." Then he added, "the LZ is hot."

He went back outside, shouldered his rifle and went to work.

There was a dark humor to the situation. General Rowe knew more about what was happening in the world and country – courtesy of satellite imagery and spotty communication – than he did about what was happening inside the complex he was supposed to be securing. *Less humor*, he thought, *more dark irony.*

The major who served as his XO, the one who'd slipped into the dazed, pre-violence stage of the infection, had been relieved of his pistol and locked up in an office just off the comm center. Rowe didn't know what else to do with him, and neither did the Army surgeon.

The general stood in the back of the room, away from the staff still manning the terminals, joined by the surgeon (a Lt. Colonel) and a sergeant named Stipling who was part of the original Feather Mountain team. The sergeant was visibly uncomfortable. It wasn't normal for an enlisted man to be invited into private discussions with generals and colonels.

"I'm not sure I'll be able to carry out your orders, General," the surgeon said.

"Explain."

"We know the infection status of our people, and you wanted the Feather Mountain team tested. First," he ticked off a finger, "they're not all in this room." He looked to the sergeant.

"That's correct, sir," the man said. "The captain and three others left for the armory and never came back. Beside the three of us, five are in comms, but the rest are out in the complex; two engineers, a quartermaster, your combat medic and ours, one of our female sergeants and your remaining biohazard specialist."

"And they're not answering when you called their sections, and not responding to loudspeaker announcements," Rowe said. It wasn't a question.

"That's correct, sir," the sergeant replied.

"Then we have to consider them hostiles until proven otherwise."

The Army doctor nodded slowly, clearly not liking the general's ruling. He ticked off another finger. "In order to perform the tests, I'll have to take those people to medical." He looked at the door. "Out there."

"Then it's a good thing you're armed, Colonel," Rowe snapped.

The surgeon frowned and straightened. "I'm not a combat soldier General, but I'm no coward."

His remark had been sharper than he'd intended, and Rowe put a hand on the surgeon's shoulder. "I'm sorry, Doctor. That wasn't what I was suggesting."

The lieutenant colonel nodded and looked across the room, lowering his voice. "Sir, we have to make a decision about what we're going to do with the Feather Mountain people who test positive, as well as our own infected comm tech."

The statement hung there in a pregnant silence. The people the colonel was talking about would turn, maybe not right away, but it would happen. When it did they would become a danger to everyone and an added threat to what remained of the bunker's integrity. And that was the only thing that mattered, at least from the point of carrying out their mission. The tactical solution was simple; eliminate them before they became a threat. The reality was far from simple. These were United States soldiers, not enemy combatants. They were co-workers, people with families. Rowe couldn't – and wouldn't – simply execute them.

Isn't that exactly what I'll have to do when they turn? When they're truly dangerous?

They would all have to be isolated and secured. But even as he made that decision, the general realized that since not everyone turned at the same time, undoubtedly he would be trapping people in rooms with others who would become remorseless killing machines. And in the end, how was that different from shooting each one in the head?

Over the course of a thirty year military career, the dictates of combat had forced Joshua Rowe to sacrifice troops, with the understanding that it was for the greater good. Instead of becoming easier, those decisions grew more and more difficult, putting a weight on his soul he knew he'd carry until his final day.

Don't you dare feel sorry for yourself, you son of a bitch. Your burden *is nothing compared to what you have planned for your troops, each of whom carries a terminal strain of the virus through no fault of their own.*

Rowe cleared his throat. "Colonel, you're going to take Sergeant Stipling, our infected comm tech and the rest of the Feather mountain group down to medical. Anyone who is positive will be secured. Tell them it's temporary, and per my orders." He looked at Stipling. The man was Feather Mountain staff and his infection status was unknown. "You understand where we're at in this, don't you, Sergeant?"

Stipling nodded. "I do, sir. I'll make it happen for the colonel, even if it includes me."

Rowe sent up a quick, silent thanks for the man's devotion to duty, along with a prayer that he would test in the clear.

"After that's done," the general said to the surgeon, "bring the rest back to comms and secure it. We have one uninfected comm tech. He stays here alone until you get back." Then he nodded toward his remaining IT man, wishing for an infantryman. "The specialist and I are going to make a second try for the armory, and then we're going hunting."

Both the colonel and the sergeant started to protest, but the general held up a hand.

"The President may be missing or dead, but there may be others inbound to our location; Cabinet members, senators, Joint Chiefs and others. Some have already landed as you know. Our mission is unchanged. We are to provide a secure facility so they can reestablish a working government." He scowled. "That can't happen while the infected are out stalking the tunnels, and we can't clear them out with a couple of side-arms. We need firepower."

"Sir," said Stipling, "after they land, how are we going to get the passengers of those aircraft safely up to the bunker?"

"Lt. Knapp is out there," Rowe said. "That's his problem." *If he's even still alive.* "You have your orders, gentlemen. Good luck."

The doctor looked at Sgt. Stipling, then handed over his side-arm to the more experienced man before gathering those who would join him in medical. The group was gone minutes later. Rowe called the IT tech over, briefly explained their objective and handed over the XO's pistol belt.

The tech looked at it as if it were an alien artifact. "General, I haven't even touched one of these since basic training."

"Son, when the time comes, I suggest you remember how to use it real fast." Rowe checked his own weapon, and the two men headed out into the labyrinth of Feather Mountain.

-39-

DARK HORSE

McKean County, Pennsylvania – October 29

"What was that all about?" Devon asked from the passenger seat. Marcus was driving now, no longer displaying symptoms and, although still weakened, appeared to be getting better with each passing mile.

The agent took a drink of bottled water. "I guess the dying virus made one last grab for me." He shrugged. "Maybe it was part of the remission. A doctor could tell us, but I'm feeling better."

The fifteen-year-old wanted to say how happy that made him, but was afraid it wouldn't be manly. Instead he just smiled.

Handelman's Sig was back in its shoulder holster. When Devon had returned it, the agent immediately smelled that it had been recently fired. "While I was out, was everything okay?"

Devon answered "yes" too quickly.

"It's pretty cool that you were driving while I slept. Anything you want to talk about?"

"No."

Marcus nodded and left it alone. The haunted expression on the boy's face told him the essentials of what he needed to know, and the part of him that cared deeply for the young man wanted to fix it, to make that expression go away. The deeper, male part of him pointed out that the world was now a far more dangerous place than it had been, and fair or not, Devon Fox was going to have to grow up fast.

"Well, whatever happened," Marcus said, "you look like shit and you need a shave."

The fifteen-year-old ran a hand across his face and flushed with pleasure.

Using the map, Devon guided them to 219, the road that crossed into Pennsylvania and would lead them to where they were going. The land here was increasingly hilly and forested, terrain that was quickly rising to form the Alleghenies. They passed farms, tiny communities and the occasional car accident, saw the remains of houses where fire had gone unchecked and reduced them to charred skeletons, but no people.

The infected were out in force though, skulking alongside buildings, rushing toward the road at the approach of the maintenance truck, even loping after it down the center yellow line once it passed. Men and women, children and the elderly, most of them wounded (some badly mangled and torn open) hunting across the landscape and seemingly ignorant of the damage to their bodies. Not all were silver-eyed, but most had that alien, chrome gleam.

The closer they got to Custer City, the more infected they saw in military uniforms.

"Why?" Devon asked as they passed a pair of bloodied soldiers scrambling up out of a drainage ditch and onto the shoulder, grabbing at the truck with fingertips as it shot past.

"There's a base outside Custer," Handelman answered. "A place with an airstrip. My understanding is that it's a depot of some kind, a place where combat and transport vehicles are stored. In the event the equipment is needed, it's flown out to its destination on big, C-5 Galaxies and the troops meet it wherever that might be."

He swerved around an infected boy running into the road. Not because he didn't want to hurt it or that it was a child, but because he couldn't risk damaging the truck unnecessarily.

"We're not going to that base," Marcus said. "But Feather Mountain is close, and it has its own airfield. That's how your dad will fly in."

The look on Devon's face said he wasn't at all sure that was true.

"Part of the *Bank Vault* plan is for mechanized infantry to fly into Custer, get their equipment and mobilize to provide added security for Feather Mountain." Marcus gestured out the windows. "These soldiers are probably part of that. I'm sorry I don't have much more information."

It was a factual statement. As a senior member of a First Family protective detail, his head was *filled* with plans for almost every conceivable contingency, including a hostile alien landing. That one was something the agents chuckled about in private, but there *was* a plan, although it wasn't significantly different from the contingency for invasion of the continental United States by a foreign military power. It was all a lot to know, but no one could know every aspect of every plan. In many cases the broad strokes had to be enough.

Regardless of the plan or the improbability of the circumstances that would set it in motion, the mission was the same; protect the principles at all costs.

"It would be better if they weren't part of it." Devon said as Marcus maneuvered around a troop truck abandoned in the center of the road. "It just brought more of them here."

Marcus agreed. The mobilization intended to provide security had only multiplied the threat level.

Custer City was a backwater burg, Marcus noted, small and struggling to keep its head above the poverty line and not doing a very good job of it. The agent suspected that if not for the jobs the Custer Military Depot provided, as well as the relatively local Walmart (they'd passed signs advertising it) the town would dry up and blow away.

The Secret Service agent slowed and wove around a few armored vehicles in the road, unmanned and unintentional steel roadblocks. The last was an armored personnel carrier with a New York State Police Charger crunched into its tail end, doors hanging open and airbags deployed. There was no one inside. Just down the road from the wreck, the map directed them to an unnamed, two-lane blacktop that split off and disappeared up a slope and into the forest on the right. A large, white sign with black printing stood prominently beside the road.

MILITARY RESERVATION
UNITED STATES ARMY

U.S. Government Property
Trespassers subject to arrest

And then beneath this in bold, red letters,

USE OF DEADLY FORCE AUTHORIZED

They hadn't gone more than a quarter mile up this final stretch of road before Marcus hit the brakes and Devon braced himself against the dashboard. The road was packed with bloody soldiers all heading in the same direction, and more swarming through the trees on the right and left.

The infected were moving up the mountain.

-40-

DANCER and DESIGN

Custer City, Pennsylvania – October 29

It was a relatively short drive down US 219 from New York into Pennsylvania, and the view from the trooper car made what had already been rural, lonely country even more desolate. No one had responded to the car accidents and fires, no government agency had shown up to provide shelter and necessities, and no one had been there to protect travelers walking south from the predations of the infected. Dropped belongings, tattered clothing and wet patches on the pavement were all that was left of refugees who had headed this way on foot.

In the passenger seat, Patricia Fox covered her mouth and shook her head. All these poor people, all the shattered lives…how could the country ever recover from a nightmare of this magnitude?

Kylie was in a hurry, knowing the turn was coming up fast, and her eyes were on the GPS display. Not long, only a look, but enough so that she didn't see the soldier running toward the grille, missing an arm and glaring with eyes like mercury. Kylie caught movement, her head snapped up and the infected soldier *threw* himself into the air at the oncoming police car. Both women screamed and Kylie stomped the brakes as the body hit and caved in the windshield's safety glass.

Out of control, the trooper car slammed nose-first into the tail end of an abandoned armored personnel carrier. The infected soldier was hurled back out of the windshield and hit the armor, the blow crushing his head like a rotten melon.

This time the airbags did deploy. The impact to Kylie's already-broken nose made starbursts explode before her eyes and covered her face with fresh blood, and the aviator sunglasses she was wearing shattered and cut her around both eyes, coming just short of blinding her. Then blackness.

The erupting airbag shoved the bones in Patricia's broken arm violently together, cracking the tibia in a new place. She would have screamed if the air in her lungs hadn't been brutally shoved out of her.

A ticking engine. The hiss of escaping steam and no movement inside the wrecked charger. The scrape of boots approached from outside.

The First Lady gasped like a goldfish taken out of its bowl, trying to push against the airbag, her eyes squeezed tightly against the brilliant pain in her arm. Her head felt like it was filled with a throbbing mass of warm, wet towels, and when the pounding started at the side window, the sound seemed very far away.

This is how we end, she thought, then realized she hadn't been driving. "Kylie?" The front doors on both sides opened at the same time, and Patricia tensed as hands gripped her. Teeth would come next.

"Be careful, she's hurt!" a woman said.

"I will," a man responded, hooking his arms around Patricia's waist and pulling her from the wreck as gently as he could.

"I think she's dead," someone said. "What about the other one?"

A voice called back from the opposite side of the car. "Can't tell."

"This one's not dead," said the man holding Patricia, helping her to stand.

FLOTUS cradled her broken arm with the one that still worked, leaning on her rescuer so she wouldn't fall over, and looked around. There were four adults and a couple of teenagers, and it seemed that everyone was armed with a pistol, shotgun or rifle of some sort. The man keeping her from falling was big with a flowered shirt and a full, red beard. He had an assault rifle slung over one shoulder.

"Can you stand?" the bearded man asked, not letting go.

Patricia nodded and tried, still hanging on and trying to catch her breath. "My daughter…?

"Here she comes," he said. A man in his fifties and a younger woman had Kylie supported between them, and were helping her around the trunk of the totaled squad car. The blood from her broken nose made her injuries look worse, but her eyes were open.

Mother embraced daughter. "Oh, God, honey you're alive!"

Kylie let out a strained laugh. "I'm a mess."

Patricia held her daughter as tightly as she was able.

"We need to get moving," one of the women said, looking nervously in every direction, then led the group toward a pair of vehicles parked on the shoulder up the road near a turn-off; a florist's van and a short, yellow school bus. More people were gathered there, a few looking toward the wreck but most of them watching outward.

The woman leading them suddenly stopped and stared at Patricia. "My God, you're the First Lady."

Patricia smiled and nodded. "Thank you for pulling us out. This is my daughter Kylie."

The woman shook her head in wonder. "Where's your protection? Shouldn't you already be someplace safe?"

"That's where we're going." Patricia pointed to the turn-off where the two vehicles were parked. "Right up there."

"I knew it!" said the bearded man. "Our map said there was a military base up there, and we thought going there made sense. What could be safer? But there's a big sign warning people away. We didn't want to get shot."

"It has to be safer than out here," the First Lady said. "I think we'll be okay. I'm supposed to be there, and you'll come with us." Her rescuers nodded. She didn't know them, where they were from or even if they represented intact or only partial families. But they were among the living and willing to help others. As far as Patricia was concerned, they were heroes.

A shout came from the vehicles. "They're coming!"

"Droolers," said the bearded man, unslinging his assault rifle. When he saw the question on the First Lady's face he said, "The infected, the ones who turned into animals. It's what they do."

Kylie stopped. "Wait, I have to go back. The shotgun is still in the car, and the pistols too."

"No time," the bearded man said, moving up to the lead and putting the butt of the assault rifle to his shoulder. They all hurried to follow.

Everyone climbed into either the van or the school bus, Kylie and her mother into the latter, and they stayed close together as they found a seat near the front. Both women noticed that the bus was packed with children, making up at least half the refugee group. The kids stared at them.

The woman who had recognized Patricia handed Kylie a package of moist baby wipes. "These are for your face," she said, and Kylie accepted them gratefully. "Take this too," the woman said. "It has a full load." She pressed a snub-nosed, .38 caliber revolver with worn checkered grips into Kylie's hands. "It was my dad's," she said, then found her own seat. The vehicles started rolling, the bus in the lead, and turned up the steep forest road to Feather Mountain.

Out the side windows, Patricia saw soldiers – *hundreds of them!* – running toward the two vehicles from every direction. Even as the bus and van pulled away from them, the infected pursued, flowing onto the mountain road behind them.

The main entrance to the grounds of Feather Mountain was simple; a fence-line, a rolling gate and a guardhouse on the other side. Simple only at first glance, though. The guardhouse was a squat structure of reinforced concrete and blue, outward-tipping ballistic glass. The fence, taut and made of heavy gauge steel, rose ten feet to a tight coil of razor wire, the kind used on prison perimeters. It was set in a four-foot-high concrete slab at its base, giving it a total, impressive height of fourteen feet. The wide, movable gate was made of the same steel and hung in a reinforced frame, with a concrete pad beneath it that vehicles would have to cross in order to enter. Most forbidding was the row of retractable bollards; fat, solid steel posts painted bright yellow that protruded up out of the pad, each four feet high. They could hydraulically sink into the concrete in order to allow access, and completely deny it when extended, as they were now. Both Fox women recognized it as the same type of defense that protected the White House. Nothing was going to crash through either the gate or the line of fence.

The bearded man stood before the gate with his hands on his hips, the bus and florist's van stopped behind him. He looked at the massive fence disappearing out into the pines on both sides and whistled. "Man…Jurassic Park."

The smoked glass domes of a CCTV system looked down at the gathering of refugees from atop the fence and the corners of the guardhouse, but it appeared no one was home because no amount of waving or yelling at the cameras had gotten anyone's attention.

"Now what?" Kylie said, watching the shadows deepen within the pine forest as afternoon drew swiftly on. The woods looked hostile, a dark place to shelter monsters.

"No way we can ram it," the bearded man said, slapping the top of a steel bollard. "And the controls for these and the gate will be in there." He pointed at the guardhouse on the other side of the fence.

"Someone could climb it?" Kylie suggested, then was sorry she had. It would be dangerous, and between her wounds and the way her head was making her feel she knew it couldn't be her. It was selfish to volunteer anyone else.

The bearded man gave a humorless laugh and patted his stomach. *"I* sure can't do it." A look around the group and at the shaking heads revealed that no one else thought they could either, or at least didn't want to try it.

"We're going to be stuck out here when the sun goes down," said the woman who had recognized the First Lady. "And you all saw them. They were following us. It won't take them long to get here."

Hearing the quaver of oncoming panic in the woman's voice, one of the other adults quickly gathered the few children standing around and shepherded them back onto the bus.

The bearded man looked at the woods, then back at the gate and scratched his hairy face. "This sucks," he muttered.

It had been bloody, gruesome work, but there'd been no choice. Now the front end of the Harrison School maintenance truck looked like something from a horror movie. Gore covered the hood and windshield; chunks of flesh, tatters of uniform and even an entire, severed hand that had become wedged beneath a wiper blade. The windshield was covered in webs of cracks and the safety glass sagged inward in places. Headlights were broken, the grille was folded in and the metal of the hood was wrinkled and popped ajar. Radiator steam hissed from beneath it and the engine was making a loud knocking that made the truck rock in time with the noise.

The infected had been in the way. Marcus Handelman was forced to use the truck as a battering ram. They'd gotten through – the mob was only thick on the road for the first quarter mile or so – but their transportation had paid the price. The Secret Service agent hoped they would make it to the base, but if so it would be a one-way trip. The truck was finished.

Devon watched the woods out the passenger window, looking for figures running between the trees. He didn't see any. "At least you killed a bunch," Devon offered, trying to sound casual but knowing that their time on wheels was about to come to an end. And once that happened it was over for them too. They wouldn't survive out there on foot.

"Not as many as I would have liked," Marcus said through clenched teeth. He was gripping the wheel too tightly. "We would have needed a steam roller to get them all."

"Yeah," said Devon, "and they would've had to line up in a nice, neat row and waited for you to run them over," then thought, *even that wouldn't have gotten the ones moving through the trees.* Although the moment was behind them now, Devon was sure he could still hear the horrid thuds the bodies of the soldiers made when the truck slammed into them, and the crunch they made beneath the tires. He'd looked back once to see blood and flesh kicking up in an arc behind the truck the way mud or rain might spray out behind tires. He hadn't looked back since.

At last the road emerged from the trees onto a broad, gentle slope where the forest had been cut back some distance from a high fence-line. More signs warned people to slow down and report to the gatehouse, that this was restricted, government property and trespassers would face the most serious of consequences. Up at the gate they could see a small cluster of people standing near a yellow bus and a delivery van.

Marcus stopped a distance away and was about to warn Devon to stay put, but by then the boy had spotted his mother and sister in the crowd and was out and running before the dying truck even stopped moving.

"Mom!" He raced to her and started to cry as he reached her. Kylie started crying too and joined them as Patricia Fox held her children fiercely with one good arm. Agent Handelman parked the truck near the other vehicles and approached. The First Lady looked at him over her son's shoulder, tears filling her eyes.

Thank you, she mouthed to him silently. *Oh, thank you.*

They stayed that way for a while until Patricia reluctantly released them, and then there were the questions about what had happened, what each of them had gone through. Marcus stood close by, hearing the fates of Dancer and Design's protective details. The subject quickly turned to Garrison Fox, and Patricia looked hopefully to the Secret Service agent, but there was nothing he could tell her.

Marcus moved to the bearded man and they stood together surveying the gate. He wasn't happy about all these armed civilians being around his (now) three protectees, but after what he'd seen coming up the mountain he suspected they'd need all the firepower they could get. Devon Fox joined them a moment later.

"Could we cut our way through?" the bearded man asked. "Are there tools in your truck?"

"Maybe," said Marcus. "But that's probably high carbon steel. Bolt cutters might not work. And even if we *could* cut a gap big enough for one of us to slip through and get to the controls, it would leave the fence compromised. They'd figure it out and get through." No one asked which *they* he meant.

"Is that worse than staying out here?"

The agent shook his head and looked back at the road coming out of the forest. "No it isn't."

At the first mention of tools, Devon had gone to the truck and searched through the storage boxes. He found plenty of landscaping and hand tools, but no bolt cutters. He returned with a heavy pair of wire cutters.

Handelman shook his head. "No way they'll get through those links."

Devon looked up. "I was thinking about using it on the razor wire. We can climb the fence, snip it and go over. It would only take one person to do it."

The agent nodded slowly and held out a hand. Devon saw how pale his bodyguard still looked. "I got this," he said, and before the agent or anyone else could stop him, he shoved the wire cutters in a pocket and leaped onto the concrete fence base, hooking his fingers through the links and shoving the toes of his shoes into the openings, moving upward.

"Get down here *now!"* Marcus yelled. His mother, sister and some of the others were yelling too. Devon ignored them. He was young, athletic and the word impossible had yet to enter his life's vocabulary. In less than a minute he was at the top, hanging on by three points and gripping the cutters.

"Watch the tension," Marcus warned, and then Devon snipped the flat steel ribbon of coiled razor wire. There was a metallic *twang* and a hiss as sections of the high-tension wire snapped back in either direction. Devon felt a half-second of pressure on the cheekbone beneath his right eye, followed by sharp pain from the horizontal slash the steel ribbon had cut across his face. He gritted his teeth to hold back a cry – *it really hurt!* – then scrambled through the new gap in the wire, over the top and down the other side, dropping the last five feet.

Marcus glared at him through the links, color darkening his face. "I'm going to kick your ass, kid."

"You can do it later," Devon said, wiping at the blood and wincing. He moved to the guardhouse, opening the door and flinging it wide as he leaped back. A uniformed MP with silver eyes burst through the opening, snarling and looking around, spotting Devon.

Rapid shots from a Sig-Saur and a burst from an assault rifle cut the MP down before it could take a step toward the boy.

Standing beside the Secret Service agent, both their weapons thrust through the chain link, the bearded man muttered to the agent, "I'm gonna help you kick his ass."

Devon Fox peeked into the guardhouse, announced that it was empty and went in. Minutes later there was a hum of hydraulics and electric motors, the steel bollards retracted into the concrete pad and the gate rolled open. Marcus joined his principle in the guardhouse, and within minutes the school bus and the florist's van came through. As soon as they cleared the opening the gate closed and the bollards rose once more to their upright position.

Marcus gave Devon a brief hug and a frustrated sigh. "You did good. I'm still going to kick your ass."

Devon grinned. He had buckled on the dead MP's pistol belt, and Marcus had no objection. They climbed aboard the little bus (where another scolding was waiting for the fifteen-year-old from his mother) and the bearded man climbed behind the wheel. Then they were moving up a steep road they all hoped would lead them to safety at last.

-41-

FEATHER MOUNTAIN

Western Pennsylvania – October 29

There were seven of them; four from the bunker staff, one from Rowe's team, the Army surgeon and Sergeant Stipling. The sergeant was on point, gripping the nine-millimeter pistol. The surgeon had told the others that they were heading to medical for testing, on the general's orders. He was himself a colonel, and good soldiers that they were they came along without question. Now Stipling led them through the cold, echoing passages bored through the mountain.

The group moved wordlessly, instinctively softening their footsteps to reduce noise. They'd all been told what was out there. It was only because of their silence that they were able to hear it, a distant, ghostly laughter reverberating off the rock. It was the sound of madness, and of promised horror.

Sgt. Stipling didn't like the idea of all of them crammed into a single elevator, so when they reached the chamber where the bank of steel doors was set in one wall he chose the stairs instead. He eased open the door and checked the cement stairwell up and down. It was quiet.

"Up to level one," he told the group, motioning them in. "Stop at the door. Don't go through it until I get there."

The soldiers moved past and descended, most of them nervous and wishing they'd been picked to go with the general to the armory. The mountain was no longer a place to walk around unarmed.

The sergeant counted them off as they passed, then looked around sharply. One missing. It was the other comm tech from Rowe's team. She'd been last in line. Stipling peered back up the corridor from which they'd come. It was empty, a long tunnel of light and shadow.

A giggle echoed down the passage. Stipling went into the stairwell and closed the door behind him, wishing it had a lock.

Medical was a short distance from the upper level door, down a wide stone passage, and the group reached it without incident. When they arrived however, they found the outermost door standing open, a red smear on its edge as if grabbed by a bloody hand, and a trail of gore leading from the smooth, stone floor of the passageway across the white tiles of the examination room.

Sgt. Stipling had everyone spread out to check the suite of rooms; patient exam cubicles, a small surgery, radiology, a tiny office next to a supply closet and two rooms of beds for patients, one for standard medical cases and one for quarantine. He had told Rowe's surgeon that the mountain had a full-time medic (one of those missing) but that there was no on-site physician. Military doctors would make scheduled visits to the facility, and anything the medic couldn't handle was driven to the small clinic in Custer City when necessary.

The surgeon had nodded. It had been the Feather Mountain medic he'd left here with their bitten female soldier who had been medicated and left to rest. There had been no answer to the repeated calls to medical, and when Rowe's combat medic went to check on them, he hadn't come back.

The gore trail – Stipling believed it was coming *out,* not in, though he couldn't say why - was streaked across the floor from beyond the open door to the patient ward. Standing behind the sergeant, the Army surgeon suddenly went cold. That was where his patient was. The two men looked in, and the surgeon immediately turned away with a choking sound. The room was destroyed; beds were tipped over, an IV tree was on the floor in the puddle of a popped fluids bag, and then there was the blood. So much of it. It spattered the walls and white sheets like a crime scene, and a wide pool of it was on the floor around the bed where the patient hung halfway off the mattress.

What was left of her.

Stipling blinked. He'd served in Afghanistan, and had seen men die, but he'd forgotten just how much blood a human body could hold. There wasn't much remaining to this body. It had been mostly devoured.

The sergeant closed the door as the rest of the group reported that the medical suite was clear. He handed his pistol to one of them and posted the sentry near the outer door, then went to the doctor who was a few yards away, bent over with his hands on his knees, breathing deeply.

He laughed weakly. "I see blood all the time," he said, his voice barely above a whisper.

"Not like that, Colonel," Stipling said. "It's okay."

The doctor shook his head. "She was my responsibility. My fault. I should have…"

"Colonel," the sergeant said firmly, gripping the surgeon's arm. "We have to get this done."

The doctor nodded, straightened and let out a long, shaky sigh. Then he went to work. Within an hour, which was free of disruption from the hallway, all of the Feather Mountain team members had been tested for the active strain of Trident, and the results were in. During that time, Stipling noted that the door to the quarantine ward was fitted with a lock, and hunted down the keys.

Looking pale, the doctor took the sergeant aside and spoke quietly, listing who was fully infected. Then he looked at the man and said, "As for you…"

Before he could finish, the sergeant retrieved his pistol from the door sentry (that man was one of the infected not yet come to term) and held out the pistol butt-first along with the keys. "I'm not that lucky."

The surgeon looked startled. "No! You're clear."

Stipling's face darkened. "This isn't a fucking game show reveal, Colonel." The other man looked at the floor and shook his head. The NCO looked at his fellow soldiers, thinking it would have been easier to be one of those locked away instead of being the one who had to turn the key. Stipling gestured for Rowe's infected comms tech and three of the four Feather mountain staffers, to move into the quarantine ward. That left only one soldier with the physician.

"We have to place you in a secure area for now," the sergeant told them, gripping the pistol tightly but keeping it low at his side. Would they go?

"For how long?" one of them asked, a computer tech Stipling had known and worked with for two years. A friend.

"As quick as I can make it, John," he lied. "I'll be back for you." And he knew that *wasn't* a lie.

The yet-to-turn soldiers hesitated for only a moment, then filed into the quarantine ward as they'd been ordered. Stipling turned the key with a sharp *click*. "Let's get back to comms," he told the colonel, not looking back at the faces peering through the glass.

As a general officer, he hadn't had cause to fear for his life in a long time, but here in these echoing tunnels he felt the familiar and unwelcome sensation wrapping itself around him once more like the cold blanket of a drowning victim lying in a coroner's van. Joshua Rowe had been in hot spots around the world, had been under fire and even found himself on the run with an armed enemy hunting him. That had been Fallujah. And even then, the enemy would have killed him at a distance if it could. He had never been stalked by something that wanted to get close enough to use its teeth. Until now.

The journey from the communication center to the armory would take them two levels down and about a quarter mile over. Under normal conditions it would be about a fifteen minute journey. But Rowe and his IT tech-turned-infantryman were moving slowly, pistols extended, every shadow and sound a potential threat.

"When they come, they'll come fast," the general had said to the young soldier. "You'll have only a couple of seconds before they're on you, so hit your target."

The tech looked less than confident.

Now he was leading five yards ahead of the general, edging up to the entrance of a domed chamber that contained the central elevator banks, the same one Stipling and his group had encountered not too much earlier. As on the upper level, this room had several bulletin boards on the walls, a pair of golf carts plugged into charging stations and a Plexiglas-covered map of the entire installation. The tech pushed the button to summon an elevator car, then stood watch as the general checked the map to verify their position and the route that remained ahead of them.

Unless something had gone terribly wrong with Sgt. Stipling and the doctor, Rowe knew how many unfriendlies were out there, even if he couldn't say exactly where they were. By his calculations there were ten of the infected unaccounted-for and running loose in the complex, a mix of his team and the Feather Mountain staff. He would have to find them and kill them.

They found him first.

The attack came from the sides, a woman and a man, both in uniform and running from a pair of tunnels on opposite sides of the chamber. Their uniforms were ripped and the woman's face was mauled, her right ear dangling on a flap of skin. The man hit the IT tech before he could bring his pistol to bear, and the woman came in low at the general, screeching and aiming for his waist.

Rowe shot the woman down, three in the chest and one in the forehead, dropping her close enough to touch his boots.

The tech died screaming under the teeth and hands of Feather Mountain's former captain. The infected officer tore a piece of flesh loose and looked up to see the muzzle of Rowe's pistol, just in time to be executed at point blank range.

The general swore, then collected dog tags from all three just as the elevator arrived. Chuckling came from another tunnel and he hurried inside, stabbing the Sub-3 button until the doors closed. As he was hanging the dog tags around his neck he realized he'd left the second pistol on the floor of the upper chamber, and cursed. But a single handgun wouldn't matter. If he didn't make it to the armory, Feather Mountain would be lost. Assuming he was able to clear the complex of the infected and not be killed by the next ones he encountered.

Sub-Level Three looked much like the others, especially the elevator chamber with its bulletin boards, golf carts and parked bicycles. A sign in red letters directed him toward the armory, and he advanced down the corridor with his nine-millimeter extended at arm's length, feeling his heart slamming in his chest. One of the fluorescents up ahead was flickering, deepening the shadows and making them dance.

Rowe suddenly slipped, caught himself from falling and looked down.

He had stepped in blood, a wide pool of it on the polished stone floor, speckled with pieces of flesh and clumps of hair. He stepped to the side, looked around and then froze as he suddenly realized something.

The armory would be secured, just as it would in any military facility.

Rowe didn't have access. The Feather Mountain captain would have a pass-card or know the code, and he was dead on an upper floor, put down by Rowe himself.

Stupid! He made a fist, wanting to hit something. He would have to go back up to check the body. Assuming there was a card to find and not a memorized code he would never obtain. He walked to the next corner and turned right, following another *armory* sign. He would check first to see if it was a keypad or a card reader so he'd know what to look for.

The armory door was standing ajar, prevented from automatically closing by the body of one of the soldiers originally sent down here with the captain. The dead man had been mutilated and partially consumed, the space around him looking like the floor of a stockyard slaughterhouse.

The general went in, reaching blindly through the darkness until he found the lights, tensing as he snapped them on. Nothing came at him in the sudden glare, and Rowe saw racks of combat gear, weapons and ammunition. Five minutes later he was wearing body armor, an ammo vest with pouches full of magazines, a combat knife and several grenades; illumination, concussion and frag. He gripped an M4 assault rifle to which he'd snapped in the bayonet, and a second pistol was shoved in his belt. With a deep breath he headed back into the corridor.

He pulled the dog tags off the dead man at the door and hung them with the three already around his neck. It was time to add more to the collection.

Rowe moved back toward the elevator chamber and disappeared from sight.

Muzzle flashes and the echo of gunfire came from there moments later.

Donny was reminded of mowing a lawn, the methodical pattern of moving up and down in lines. His camo trousers were soaked and his boots glistened with blood as he went, stabbing downward or pulling the trigger, systematically working across a field of bodies. Some were trying to rise, others made it to their feet and came at him. Donny cut them all down, and as he finished he was confident that none would be trying to get up a third time.

But then a burst of movement in the nearby trees, a flash of luminescent eyes in the falling light told him the battle was far from over. He fired a full magazine into the woods, saw nothing go down, and then wondered if he'd really seen anything at all.

He was so very tired, and when he rubbed his eyes he smeared pink and gray across his face.

The executive jet with Air Force markings was now parked on the ramp near the C-130, its passengers and crew trotting toward him. The pilot wore captain's bars on a white shirt speckled with dried blood, and the others were all in civilian clothes, probably diplomats or ranking government officials, Donny couldn't tell and didn't care. He didn't recognize any of them. Then one of the older men introduced himself and waited expectantly as if the young lieutenant should know who he was and react accordingly, but Donny only shrugged. The name meant nothing.

One of the civilians was a woman with two children, ages five and six. She said she was the British Ambassador to the United States, and Donny allowed a small smile. Her accent gave her away. The smile vanished when he saw how the children were clinging to their mother, and how she was trying to put on a brave face.

A fighter jet made a low, screaming pass over the field, and everyone flinched and ducked except for Donny. He didn't have that kind of energy to waste. He watched the aircraft – a new F-35 *Lightning* – bank and circle for an approach.

"Everyone here is cleared for *Bank Vault,*" the older man said. Apparently he was in charge. Or had placed himself there.

Donny nodded and pointed past the cinderblock house, beyond the killing field. "Follow that road until you reach the bunker."

The older man's eyes went wide. "Alone? Where's the security force?"

Now Donny thought he did recognize him, a jackass senior senator from someplace he couldn't remember, a man who spent a lot of time in front of the cameras and always seemed to be tangled up in one scandal or another involving women or misappropriation of funds. Donny was too tired to curl his lip.

"I'm it." Then he added, "sir." He looked at the pilot. "Take a weapon and some magazines, captain. The infected are in the woods, and they move fast."

The pilot gripped the younger officer's shoulder as he went by. "I'll get them there, Lieutenant. Watch your ass."

Then they were heading up the hill, the Air Force captain leading the way with an M4 he'd taken from the dead. Donny turned back to watch the fighter jet land, and once it was parked on the ramp he wandered slowly toward it across the tarmac, eyes constantly sweeping the airfield and trees, never forgetting to check his six. The pilot jumped down from the cockpit and met him in the center of the runway.

Donny was surprised to see it was a woman, shorter than him with a nine-millimeter in a shoulder holster worn over her flight suit and a name tag that said *Forrester.* She was about his age, and strikingly attractive. The call-sign stenciled across her flight helmet said *Bright Eyes,* but although dark and beautiful, they didn't look particularly bright to Donny. They looked tired like his own.

He saw the silver bar of a first lieutenant on her collar and pointed toward the departing group. "The bunker is that way, ma'am."

"You can save the ma'am, soldier," she said. "What bunker?"

Donny didn't understand. "Don't you know where you are?"

Bright Eyes shrugged. "I was out of gas and you had a clear runway. Works for me." Then she stared past him at the field of the dead. "Your work?"

"Some of it."

The female fighter jock looked him up and down, seeing his blood-slicked boots and bayonet, the face in need of a shave. She smiled, and Donny realized she had just checked him out the same way he and other young lieutenants appraised the ladies in the officer's club.

"Combat infantry," Lt. Forrester said, nodding and still smiling. "Just what the doctor ordered."

Donny couldn't tell if she was making fun of him or flirting, but he decided he liked it. "There's a secure bunker in the mountain," he said, "a place for the brass to shelter and run the government. If you follow that group you'll find it."

"Why are you still out here?" she asked.

"I have to keep the airfield secure."

"By yourself? Nice job, tough guy, and thanks. It would have sucked to try to set my bitch down on a runway covered in cannibals."

Donny didn't know what to say, but he knew he liked looking at her eyes. They *did* seem bright, after all.

"I'll hang out here with you," Bright Eyes said. "Keep an eye on my plane and keep away from politicians and senior officers. That okay with you?"

Hell yes! He shrugged like it didn't matter one way or the other.

And then in the distance off to the left they heard the long, rapid blasts of a car horn. "The gate's that way," Donny said. "It's not far, come on."

The two lieutenants took off at a run.

-42-

DEVIL DOG

Custer City, Pennsylvania – October 29

He approached from the south, moving north up Route 219. Since entering Pennsylvania there had been no more roadblocks or encounters with madmen and automatic weapons, but also very few refugees, at least that he could see, and that didn't bode well for the state of his nation. Those he came upon scattered when they saw the Humvee, and Garrison couldn't help but wonder at what terrible experiences they'd had to make them run from a military vehicle and choose to take their chances on foot with the infected. He saw several car accidents and abandoned vehicles, none with living people around, and the overall feeling was that his species had simply been swept away.

The infected ruled now, and they were everywhere. Garrison had crushed more than a few with the grille of the Hummer when they'd been in the road, and he'd felt no remorse. The President no longer thought of them as innocent Americans brought down by sickness. They were now a hostile, occupying force, enemies that were systematically exterminating the citizens he was sworn to protect.

He would have shared his feelings with David King, but the Secret Service agent who had rescued him from a burning limousine and gotten him out of Cleveland had died almost an hour ago. Now he was cold and silent, his body strapped into the rear seat. Garrison didn't have the heart to put him out on the road, where he would be nothing more than meat for the infected. The man deserved better than that, and Garrison had promised they would go to Feather Mountain together.

The Custer Army Depot was off to the right now, located at the south end of the small town, and Garrison was able to get a good look at it from the road. The base was a sprawling area behind a perimeter fence, a maze of warehouses and paved streets that stored two divisions worth of combat equipment; tanks, fighting vehicles, trucks, artillery and the munitions needed to support it all. A long, nearby airstrip had been built to allow the massive C-5 Galaxies to fly in and ferry equipment out to any combat zone in the world, and right now three of the gigantic planes were parked at intervals along the runway, hinged noses raised and rear ramps lowered to either take on cargo or disgorge troops. A fourth C-5 was a blackened, burned-out hulk at the distant end of the runway.

Even from the road Garrison could see people down there, but the way they moved instantly told the President that the base was in enemy hands. The soldiers and airmen loping through the streets and fields around the airstrip were on a different mission now, and some of them either heard or saw Garrison's Hummer because they seemed to instinctively turn and move in his direction, despite the distance.

As he passed the turn-off that lead to the gates of the Army depot, Garrison saw that at least part of a mechanized column had started its roll-out to reinforce Feather Mountain. It hadn't made it very far. Now combat vehicles sat at odd angles on and off the road, and it was clear that there had been fighting. Vehicles had been raked by heavy machinegun fire, a few completely destroyed by tank cannons, and the bodies of uniformed soldiers littered the ground. Black clouds of crows wheeled above them and hopped along the ground, picking at the dead.

But some of those soldiers were up and moving.

Garrison used the shoulder and even drove off-road to get around the shattered column.

There were a few more vehicles to avoid before he reached the mountain road that would take him to *Bank Vault,* and the climb up through the forest didn't take long. A handful of infected soldiers ran at the Humvee, and there was an occasional glimpse of movement out in the trees, but otherwise the road was clear.

As he emerged from the pine forest and onto the slope leading to the perimeter fence and gate, Garrison saw why the road had been so empty.

The infected were already here.

Garrison slowed the Hummer and stared, a sudden hopelessness tightening in his chest. A single look estimated several hundred, probably more. Most were in Army camo and battle gear, but there were civilians mixed in as well. The infected were spread out across the gate and down the fence-line in both directions (even a handful on the inside of the fence) but none were attempting to climb it. That suggested that the virus might have erased that level of intelligence, or possibly eliminated the kind of organized motor skills required for such a task. Most of them were violently shaking the fence, however. Testing for weak points or out of simple frustration? Perhaps more intelligence left than Garrison had presumed.

He stopped fifty yards from the fence, and as the infected noticed the movement and engine noise they started to turn. Then POTUS noticed the lone vehicle abandoned nearby at the edge of the road, a dark green maintenance truck so beaten up and covered with gore that it looked like one of those possessed cars from a horror movie. He saw the emblem on the driver's door.

The Harrison School – Maintenance Department.

It took a moment to process, and Garrison found himself staring at the familiar seal, the approaching mob momentarily forgotten.

Devon.

He made it here.

"Oh, God," he whispered. Had his son managed to make it all the way here from Vermont only to be pulled from the truck and devoured? A choking sob caught in his throat. Was he one of the creatures that were even now running toward the Humvee, all memories of his father replaced by the need to kill and feed?

He'd never answers these questions sitting here like a dumb animal waiting to be slaughtered. He leaned on the horn, giving it several blasts. Someone might still be monitoring the gate. Maybe he could get their attention. Then he grabbed the duffel of Secret Service weapons and ammo, Agent King's P90 and his own assault rifle. After that he scrambled up onto the roof of the vehicle and dropped the duffel at his feet. David King had warned him not to dishonor the sacrifice made by so many to ensure he reached safety, and the infected stood between him and keeping his promise. He'd have to clear them out if he was to have any chance of even entering the Feather Mountain installation.

If nothing else, he would die standing up, and that mattered to a Marine.

As he brought the M4 assault rifle to his shoulder and thumbed the selector switch to single fire, he thought about the horde rushing toward him, specifically about those in civilian clothes. If Devon was among them, could he do it? He didn't think so.

With his feet in a wide stance atop the Humvee, the President of the United States started firing and dropping targets. Targets in body armor drew aimed head shots, and those without such protection caught rounds center mass. He swung left, right and forward, hitting those at the leading edge of the mob. Bodies crumpled on every side, immediately trampled by their uncaring, ravenous brethren running behind. Garrison Fox was an expert marksman in an elevated firing position, but he was a lone rifle, and a turn in any direction allowed those on the opposite side to get closer. Every precious second spent changing magazines allowed them *all* to get closer.

Thirty yards.

Twenty.

Even as he kept up a withering pace of fire, his brain did the math. He would run out of ammo, not be able to reload quickly enough or the infected would reach him too fast on too many sides.

He wasn't going to make it.

Intellectually, Donny Knapp had always understood why, during officer training and infantry school, they had been made to go on seemingly endless runs in full combat gear; body armor, helmet, full pack and a full load of ammunition plus weapon, between forty and sixty pounds depending upon the mercy level of their instructors. It was exhausting and he'd hated it. Now the conditioning was paying off as he pounded down the hillside at a full run, the smaller and less-encumbered female fighter pilot nicknamed Bright Eyes racing to keep up. If his memory of the base drawing was correct, they were headed for the installation's front gate.

The sound of the car horn had been almost immediately followed by constant gunfire.

"I only hear one rifle!" Lt. Forrester shouted from behind him.

In training, Donny had initially found it difficult to run and breathe at the same time, much less speak, but the cadence they had sung helped with both, and the task was much easier now. "Pick up the pace, Lieutenant!" he called back, increasing speed.

It wasn't that far from the airfield, the slope dotted with clumps of pines sweeping down toward a long perimeter fence, a paved road angling from the left toward the gate. Donny figured that would lead back to the base buildings and then the bunker entrance. He saw the concrete and blue glass guardhouse ahead. Another paved road ran parallel to the fence on this side, probably the patrol route for the base MPs. One of their vehicles, a Hummer with military police markings and a red and blue rooftop light bar, was parked behind the guardhouse.

Infected soldiers were shaking the fence from this side, a handful of uniformed men and women, most wearing MP armbands. On the other side, a mob was swarming another Humvee while a man in a Windbreaker stood atop it, firing in all directions.

Lt. Knapp and the F-35 pilot engaged.

They stopped running, getting close behind the MPs at the fence, and opened up with the assault rifle and nine-millimeter pistol. Bodies fell, and those that didn't immediately go down turned to attack the prey that had suddenly appeared at their backs. They didn't make it far, and Donny slapped in a fresh magazine as the pilot finished off the last one with her sidearm.

"Advance," Donny called, moving up to the fence. Bright Eyes took a position to his left, reloading her pistol. She only carried one spare magazine, but she'd seen that all the fallen MPs were armed, and knew how she'd reload next.

Donny attacked the mob around the Humvee from the rear, firing his assault rifle into the crowd, bullets punching through necks and arms and the backs of helmets, blowing out knees and shattering the bases of spines. The pilot's pistol cracked as she engaged her own targets, but even though the crowd was thinning, its progress slowed as bodies had to be stumbled over, the forward edge of the mob had reached and was encircling the Humvee.

Donny cursed and dropped an empty magazine.

Bright Eyes cried out as an MP sat up, grabbed her around the waist and pulled her down.

Donny spun toward her just as a silver-eyed MP rushed around from behind the guardhouse and slammed into the infantry lieutenant from his blind side. They went down in a flurry of clawing hands, thrown blows and snapping teeth as not far away Bright Eyes let out a piercing cry.

The M4 was empty, and so were the pouches of his combat harness. There were more magazines in the duffel bag at his feet, but the infected were climbing onto the Hummer from all sides now, and Garrison knew that in the time it would take to dig out a mag and reload, they would be on him.

Instead he used the empty weapon as a club, smashing it into snarling faces and knocking bodies off the sides. When one of the creatures grabbed the M4 and tore it from his hands, Garrison kicked the thing in the chest, sending it backward into the mob, then gripped Agent King's P90 and swung it up and around on its nylon strap.

BBBUURRRPPP.....BBUURRRP...BBUURRRP...

Garrison cleared the hood of snarling figures, then swept the SMG down the right side of the Humvee and across the rear deck.

BBUURRRP...BBURRP...

Bodies fell away. Something grabbed his right ankle from behind, and then there was a flare of sharp pain as teeth sank into the flesh there. Garrison cried out and pivoted at the hips, ramming the stubby barrel of the P90 into the top of a civilian's head, blowing infected brains across the faces of the horde with a short burst. The hand and teeth released as the limp body slid off the roof and into the crowd.

More were climbing onto the hood, creatures that were once human but now existed as drooling, slavering *things,* and Garrison ran a burst across them, dropping some but not all. Howls and the slap of hands on metal came from behind him.

King said fifty rounds in the P90 mag. How many-?

CLICK

The SMG was empty. Its spare magazines were in the pouches of King's ammo vest, which was lying on the floor of the back seat with the bloody gauze and bandage packaging. They might as well be on the moon. He let the P90 drop on its sling and pulled his handgun, turning in a circle and blasting at faces only a couple of feet away. Despite his constant firing, a crowd still surged around the Hummer, far more than fifteen rounds of nine-millimeter could handle. Hands clutched at him from all sides, and the President spun and fired, punched and kicked. When the slide locked back empty he pistol-whipped a face with silver eyes and reached for the combat knife strapped upside-down to his ammo pouches, tearing the blade free.

"Mother*fuckers!"* Garrison cried, teeth bared as he attacked with the only weapon he had left.

Teeth tore through his uniform and bit deeply into his left bicep. Donny's scream wasn't of pain but of fury. He'd lost his grip on his rifle, and when the MP's mouth came snapping in he tried to hold the creature off bare-handed. Grayish saliva trailed across his cheek as he got his palms on the sides of the MP's head, let out an animal cry and thumbed out both of its silver eyes.

It didn't react or hesitate. Blinded, the head dipped as the bite came in at his throat.

CRACK! A pistol shot only inches from his face made him jump, the sharp report deafening. The infected MP slipped off to the side, half its head gone, and a moment later Donny felt himself being hauled up by his combat harness. "On yah feet, soldah," said a woman's voice. It sounded faint and far away.

Donny shook his head, trying to clear his head of the ringing caused by the handgun his rescuer was still holding. It was a woman in a flight suit, older than the F-35 pilot with her hair in a tight bun. A nametag read *Boyle,* and the gold oak clusters of a major were sewn onto her collar.

She glanced at his bitten arm. "Looks like it fahkin' hats."

Donny blinked. What language was that?

The major slapped the side of his head. "Get yah head cleah and get back in it, soldah."

The infantry lieutenant found his rifle still slung around his neck and reloaded as he stumbled toward the fence. Bright Eyes was on her feet again, having dispatched whatever had pulled her down, but there was blood on her helmet and a fresh bite on one hand.

"Keep up yah fiyah!" the major yelled, and Donny and the two female pilots poured bullets through the fence and into the mob swarming the vehicle on the other side.

Garrison rammed the combat knife up under the chin of a trooper from the 101st Airborne, a young man who had flown from the Carolinas to provide security against the infected and arrived in Pennsylvania as one of them. The body fell away from the knife (not before clawing three raw stripes of flesh from Garrison's face) and almost immediately another soldier made it to the roof of the Hummer and bit deeply into his left shoulder. POTUS rammed the blade through one eye and shoved the soldier away.

Still more were getting on the roof, and Garrison was winded, his arms weakening. He knew he had the strength to fight off one more attack, two at the most, and there were dozens coming at him.

Suddenly he was downrange at a firing line, the crack of semi-automatic gunfire filling the air, making him flinch and crouch, instinctively covering his head. The infected that had climbed the sides of the Humvee were flung back, bullets ripping chunks out of them. On the ground, figures turned toward the source of the fire only to be cut down. Garrison felt more than heard the hiss of bullets zipping past his head and punching into the unarmored vehicle beneath him.

In less than a minute the firing stopped, leaving Garrison crouched atop a bullet-riddled and gore-slicked vehicle parked in a field of the dead. As he straightened, he saw the perimeter gate rolling back, a row of anti-ramming bollards sinking into a concrete pad to open the way. Two women in flight suits were soon joined by a young infantryman who emerged from the guardhouse and moved toward him. Garrison climbed down and met them.

Both women stiffened when they realized who he was and snapped off salutes, which Garrison wearily returned. The infantry lieutenant simply stood there staring, then said, "Where's your plane?"

President Fox laughed and clapped a hand to the back of Donny's neck, pulling their foreheads together and letting out a relieved sigh. "Still in Ohio, son. But here I am anyway."

Minutes later the gates were closing behind them. With all the battle damage, they were afraid that the Humvee wouldn't start, but it turned right over. Then they were rolling up the road with four lives aboard.

Garrison sat in the back seat cradling David King's head in his lap.

-43-

LABCOAT

CDC Atlanta – October 29

Morphine. That's all it had taken.

Moira was back in the lab, perched before her laptop. In the patient ward, the last of the ten subjects was a blackened, motionless corpse like the others lined up in the beds beside it.

After the initial discovery that a dose of morphine killed them, Moira experimented with lesser and lesser amounts, using only half an mL on the second-to-last patient. Even that tiny injection had destroyed the patient just as quickly and efficiently as larger doses with the others. On the final one, Moira decided to try something and dripped a single drop of the amber fluid onto the patient's chest, without injection.

The result was immediate. The body stiffened, the eyes went steely and lifeless, and the spreading necrosis consumed every inch of flesh in less than a minute.

Morphine. Easier to make and distribute than bullets. Certainly it could be weaponized, turned into an aerosol of some sort and perhaps delivered through airborne spraying, the tiny droplets wiping out thousands at a time. But others would have to carry out that part. Her time was done.

Sweat dripped from her brow as she stared at the laptop screen with its blinking recording light. She had added her startling discovery to the file…

Was I talking? I did add it, right? So hard to focus.

…and prepared the entire file for uploading to the cloud…

Did I? Or did I just think *I did it?*

…and now all that remained was for her to click *send* so that others would learn from her gruesome research. Her right hand rested beside the mouse, clenching and unclenching rhythmically. The nausea had passed, and that was good. She wanted to wipe the sweat from her face but it didn't feel worth the effort. Perhaps she should tell it all to the recording again, just in case she hadn't already. But being able to speak was now lost to her. All that came out was a giggle and a string of grayish drool that spilled onto the knee of her scrubs.

Focus! Hit send before it's too late!

The yelling in her head reminded her of her mother's voice, a woman with a short temper and a love of the bottle. She'd frequently told Moira that she was a stupid girl who better find a husband, because she was white trash who would never accomplish anything on her own. Daddy was different. He was kind, a man with hands that never hit who taught her to ride a bike…

Stop! You're slipping away, hit send!

Her right hand twitched on the lab table beside the mouse.

Hit send. Send. That was a funny word. What did it mean? Daddy would know. He'd been smart, he would... Moira sat and stared at a screen that was rapidly losing meaning, her clenching and unclenching hand bumping the mouse.

Send. Need to send. Need to...

Thirty minutes later, Dr. Moira Rusk was a snarling thing kneeling over the body of a dead lab assistant, ripping and pulling and feeding.

-44-

FEATHER MOUNTAIN

Western Pennsylvania – October 29

Dusk was coming on as a pair of headlights climbed the last hundred yards of road to arrive at the bunker's blast doors. They illuminated a small school bus and a delivery van parked off to the side, a small group of people gathered beneath the fluorescent-lit alcove that sheltered the mountain's entrance. Others in uniform were organized into a defensive perimeter facing outward, weapons trained on the approaching Humvee and the coming night.

Garrison Fox immediately picked out his wife in the crowd, and like his son earlier he was out the door and running before the vehicle stopped rolling. Patricia, Kylie and Devon rushed to him, and the family wrapped itself in an embrace of sobs and happy tears. Garrison didn't care who saw him cry. His family was alive, and they were together.

Everyone wanted to talk at once, and Donny's tiny squad stared at him as if he'd just arrived in a spaceship.

"You brought back the *President?"* Corporal Woods said. Akins stared at his lieutenant in awe, then snapped off a salute. "What are your orders, sir?"

Lt. "Bright Eyes" Forrester walked past, nudging his arm. "Badass," she said.

Donny smiled, then looked at his troops, pointing toward the civilians. "Use them to reinforce this perimeter, anyone with a weapon. It's almost dark, and there's more of them out there."

Private Akins hurried to carry out his officer's command.

Donny joined the First Family at the blast doors, along with Handelman and the Secret Service agent who had come in with the Vice President's family. A couple of civilians were there as well, and one shook Donny's hand, thanking him and introducing himself as the White House Deputy Chief of Staff.

"You can drop the deputy part," Garrison said. "You're the man now. Tommy would have wanted it that way. It's how I want it."

"Yes, Mr. President."

Garrison looked at the man-door beside the vehicle entrance, at the built-in camera, optical scanner and proximity reader. "Knock or ring the bell?" he mused, then looked at Donny Knapp and raised an eyebrow.

"I'm sorry, Mr. President. I'm a brand new second lieutenant, and nobody tells us anything. I don't have access."

"Hmm," Garrison said, looking at his nametag. "We'll figure it out. How's our defenses, Knapp? I want my family and the others safe."

Donny's eyes flicked over to a dark hardness that had not existed in him only days before. "Nothing will get through us, sir."

Garrison nodded and started to turn, then pointed at the young officer. "And that's *Captain* Knapp, now."

"But sir, I'm only a second-"

"Don't argue with your Commander-in-Chief, son." Then the President winked.

"Yes, sir."

The major with the Boston accent saluted Donny even though she still outranked him, and the others in uniform followed her lead. Then Captain Knapp was reorganizing the perimeter, augmenting with the armed civilians from the bus, all the pilots and both Secret Service agents. There was no way to alert those inside the mountain – if anyone was even alive and un-turned in there – and pounding on steel doors would accomplish nothing. They would just have to hope someone would notice them out here, so President Fox and Kylie took their places on the line. Devon remained close to his mother like a protective young wolf, pistol in hand.

No one spoke as they watched the sun slide behind the trees, the sky shifting through golds and reds and into a deepening blue, stars beginning to poke through the night. Laughter floated on the cooling October air, coming from the forest and the cluster of base buildings not far away. Donny knew there were probably a couple hundred infected soldiers still within the base perimeter, despite how many they'd killed at the airfield. If they massed again and attacked in a wave like last time, the little group would be trapped against the side of the mountain, overwhelmed and slaughtered.

Knowing they were out there in the darkness and not being able to see them was unsettling, but that lunatic chuckling – as if they were amused by the terror they inflicted – was like a promise of bad things to come.

They waited, staring into the night and waiting for death to arrive.

"We hold the line," Donny said, walking its length, having some brief, quiet words with each of them before speaking to the group. "There is no fallback position. We stand and fight, no matter who falls." He stopped at POTUS. "You set, Mr. President?"

"Good to go, Captain."

Shadows moved in the deepening gloom, but whether it was furtive movement or a trick of the light no one could tell, so no one fired. There was too little ammunition to waste it on phantoms.

A metallic *BOOM* from behind made them all jump, and the group turned to see the giant blast doors split down the middle and retract into the mountain, leaving a widening, vertical seam of darkness. Weapons turned in that direction, ready for whatever monstrosities would come spilling out.

The lone figure that emerged was no monster. He was a fiftyish soldier with a severe, gray crewcut wearing blood-splattered combat gear. He looked tired, and more than a few bites could be seen on his exposed arms and through rips in his uniform. He smelled of gunpowder, and a red-soaked pressure bandage was tied to his neck. It was joined by what looked like a couple dozen, bloody dog tags worn as a grim necklace. Stars were pinned to the man's collar.

Garrison and Donny walked slowly toward him, and Donny saluted the man he recognized as the general who'd ordered him to hold the airfield. Rowe looked at his Commander-in-Chief. "Welcome to Feather Mountain, Mr. President. The facility is secure."

ECHOES

-45-

DEVIL DOG

Feather Mountain Continuity Bunker – November 1

The Army surgeon was happy to have patients he could actually help, and he tended to the wounds of all the new arrivals. As a precaution he tested them all for the active virus, including the President. Everyone was in the clear. That was important not only for the obvious reason; Feather Mountain was a large, complex facility, and everyone needed to be healthy because in time they would all be assigned jobs, from maintenance to food preparation to learning the consoles in the communication center.

Agent David King was laid to rest in a pine grove near the mountain entrance. The laminated, Secret Service ID card bearing David's image went into Garrison Fox's pocket, where he would carry it every day for the rest of his life.

Major Erin "Harvard" Boyle of Boston was told that eventually the President would be flying again, and when he did, any aircraft he was aboard would be designated Air Force One. Harvard would be the commanding officer in the cockpit.

Lt. Forrester, call-sign Bright Eyes, had a different mission in mind, one of her own choosing. One night she cornered the newly promoted Captain Knapp in his quarters and attacked. It was a most welcome engagement.

Garrison heard the entire story of Devon and Agent Handelman's escape from Vermont, mostly from his son. He expressed his gratitude to the agent and gave him a warm handshake, naming him head of the presidential Protective Detail, such as it was. Marcus accepted without hesitation, but Devon Fox would forever remain his favorite protectee.

"Mr. President, you're needed in comms." Sgt. Stipling had found his Commander-in-Chief in the mess hall having a quiet conversation with Kylie. Garrison had heard about his wife's abduction and the steps Kylie had taken to get her back. As a father he anguished for what his daughter had gone through, while at the same time swelling with pride. She was tougher than he'd ever imagined, and he told her so. There were happy tears between them.

Garrison followed the sergeant to the communication center where General Rowe was standing near a console. "Put it on speaker," the general said to a nearby tech.

"Mr. President," Rowe said, "we've been broadcasting in the clear almost continuously since everything started falling apart, hoping to make contact with surviving units." He smiled. "We're starting to get responses."

"All reporting units," the tech broadcast, "National Command Authority is listening. State your composition and location."

There was a pause before the speakers crackled.

"Sergeant Bruce Irving, 82nd Airborne with a force of twenty-five just west of Chicago."

"Lt. Colonel Jessup, Georgia National Guard," drawled the voice of an older man. "I've got two hundred pissed-off troops south of Savannah, Mr. President, and they're ready for some payback."

"Trooper Easton, California Highway Patrol in Death Valley. We have fifty combatants, mostly civilians with a few cops, soldiers and jarheads, along with three times that number of kids and older folks. We're sheltering at the Marine camp at Twenty-Nine Palms, and we have retaken the base."

There were others. A Navy destroyer with a skeleton crew steaming off the coast of Virginia; an airbase in Alaska; several U.S. submarines in international waters; pockets of civilian survivors that had formed themselves into militia units and were scattered across the western states; small National Guard and reserve units everywhere.

"This is Captain Bauer, Pennsylvania National Guard. I've got three truckloads of troops and a pair of fully loaded Bradley fighting vehicles. We're rolling into Custer right now, Mr. President, and we're about to retake the Army Depot and airfield. Should take a couple of days, then we'll head up to Feather Mountain to give your people some support."

More calls were coming in, clusters of uninfected humanity that had survived and come together, each expressing their eagerness to start fighting back. Garrison Fox thanked them all and told them they'd be receiving orders soon.

General Rowe walked away from the console with the President. "Sir, we've been contacted by a Doctor Wulandari, an Indonesian virologist working in New Zealand. He says he received an upload from the Secretary of Health and Human Services."

"Moira," said Garrison. "She was at CDC Atlanta. Is she…?"

"There's been no contact, sir. But Wulandari says she was doing research since before this started and had a breakthrough. She found a way to eradicate the infected, Mr. President. Wulandari is working on that now, and he's going to keep in touch with us."

Garrison shook the general's hand. "We have a chance, Joshua."

Donny Knapp stood in the vast, domed central chamber of the entrance to Feather Mountain, the tarp-covered Humvees and Stryker armored fighting vehicle behind him, Woods, Akins and Sgt. Stipling standing to one side. Donny wore a relaxed expression and half a grin. Bright Eyes had made her nocturnal visits to his quarters a habit.

Twin silver bars were now on his collar tabs. The President had pinned them there himself.

"Attention!" Sgt. Stipling barked, and all four soldiers stiffened and saluted as Joshua Rowe strode into the chamber. "At ease," he replied.

"Good afternoon, General," Donny said.

"Captain." Rowe stopped before him. "I have orders for you."

"Yes, sir."

"You've heard the broadcasts," the general said, "and help is coming to strengthen your force. More aircraft are headed this way, too. Feather Mountain is about to become a very busy place."

Donny nodded.

"I'm making you commander of base defense, and I'm going to need you and your team in the field, out there where you can clean up the remaining resistance inside the perimeter and make the base clear for arrivals. You up for that, Captain?"

Donny looked to his troops. Sgt. Stipling and Cpl. Woods nodded, and Private Akins gave him a thumbs-up and a smirk.

"We'll get it done," Donny said.

Rowe smiled and nodded. "I have no doubt of that."

"General, one thing." Donny jerked a thumb over his shoulder. "With your permission, I'd like to put that into service. Might make things go a little more quickly." He was gesturing toward the big Stryker with its lethal, thirty-millimeter Bushmaster.

Rowe's grin broadened. "Go kick ass, Captain."

Garrison Fox stood with his wife to one side of the fully equipped studio here in the mountain. Patricia's arm had been properly set and was in a cast slung across her chest. The Army surgeon believed she would regain most of not all of her movement once it healed. Their children sat at the back of the room.

The President was in a clean and pressed suit and he was freshly shaven, but his face still bore the cuts and bruises of his ordeal. He would allow no attempt to conceal them, and besides, no amount of makeup would ever hide the deep sadness in his eyes. But that sadness was tempered by determination.

Patricia plucked a piece of lint from his jacket and smoothed his lapels. "You're very handsome."

Garrison looked into her eyes and whispered, "I love you. I thought I'd lost you."

"It would take more than the end of the world to get rid of me, Garrison Fox. I love you too."

He kissed her, then held her at arm's length. "Time to start putting this country back together," he said.

"And you're the man to do it." She stood on her toes and gave him another kiss, this time a soft one at the corner of his mouth that never failed to make him smile. And then the smile faded, his eyes taking on a resolve with which she was both familiar and proud.

"Mr. President?" An Army tech with a clipboard was standing a polite distance away. "We're ready for you, sir."

Garrison nodded and followed the man to a podium in front of a blue curtain and flanked by American flags, waiting as the tech clipped a small, black mic to his jacket and tested a bristle of larger microphones. Set in the face of the podium was the Seal of the President of the United States.

The tech moved to a professional-sized, studio television camera and put on a headset. "Sir, we'll be broadcasting on all available radio and television frequencies, as well as streaming live."

Garrison cleared his throat. There were no teleprompters, no paper speeches or notes atop the lectern, only his freshly scarred hands. This would be straight Garrison Fox. The red light atop the camera turned on, and the tech gave him a cue.

"My fellow Americans..."

-END-

Photo © Linda Campbell

John L. Campbell was born in Chicago, but has lived all over the U.S., and attended university in both North Carolina and New York. His novels include the *Omega Days* series, *Cannibal Kingdom,* two collections of short horror and suspense, and a horror novella based on actual events. Under the pen name Atticus Wulf, Mr. Campbell released the supernatural/historical thriller *A Judge From Salem* and his apocalyptic novella, *A Cruel and Bitter Nothing.* His short story *Courageous Little Philomena's Wondrous Bait* was nominated for a Pushcart Prize. A member of both the International Thriller Writers and the Horror Writers Association, Mr. Campbell is active on the horror and comic convention circuits, and resides with his family in New York where he is continuing his work on the *Omega Days* series, as well as other projects.

Visit him online at johnlcampbell.com,
Facebook.com/JohnLCampbellAuthor,
and twitter.com/OmegaDays

Made in the USA
Las Vegas, NV
14 May 2021

22921795R00267